BARBARY COAST

Also by Peter Smalley

HMS Expedient
Port Royal

For Clytie, my constant companion on the voyage

The Holy War is eternal between
the followers of the two faiths.

Rais Hamidou
(the last and fiercest
of the Islamic corsairs)

CONTENTS

PART ONE: THE ERRAND

May, 1789

Lieutenant James Hayter RN stood at a window in Birch Cottage, his house at Winterborne in Dorsetshire, his back to the room. 'I must go away, my dear.' He held out a letter briefly behind him, without turning round. The letter bore an Admiralty seal, newly broken. His wife, Catherine, gave a little sigh, then contrived to be cheerful and to smile.

'I knew that it must come, this summons. You are commissioned again in *Expedient*?'

'No.' Reading, holding up a hand.

'Then you are commissioned in another ship? Oh, James, they have given you your own command!'

'No.' Reading on, shaking his head. At last he turned, holding the several unfolded sheets. 'No, I am sent on an errand—upon the shore.'

'Ashore?' Her heart lifting. 'Then perhaps you will not have to go away after all.'

'Oh, I must certainly go.' He allowed the letter to fall on the table, and made a face. 'It ain't a duty I relish, though.'

Catherine glanced into the cradle in the corner, lifting the fold of the fabric draped above.

'I must go into the west,' continued James, 'to Dartmoor, and bring him back. In least, I must make the attempt. I must try.'

'Bring him back?' Looking up from the cradle, and the infant within, that stared up at her in rapt half-comprehension. 'Has someone run away there? One of your seamen? Why must you go? Could not a sergeant of marines——'

The infant, her son, recalled her to her duty in a sudden cry of complaint, of unmistakable complaint.

'I must ask Tabitha if she has warmed his gruel. His gruel must be warmed to an exactitude, else he will refuse it. He would not even take milk from the nurse when her person was not warm.'

'Mm?' James, distractedly, turning again to the window. Catherine had gone out of the room, and he heard her voice in the kitchen, and the further cries of his son in the cradle. James stared out at the rise of the hill behind the house, at the clouds slowly tumbling and unravelling there over the brow. A puff of wind shook the window pane. 'Rain,' he murmured to himself. 'Christ's blood, I must ride all the way there in the rain.'

'Who must you find, and bring back?' Catherine, returning with the warmed gruel.

'Eh? Why, Captain Rennie, in course. He has gone into Dartmoor, and has never been heard of for months together. If I do not find him, and cause him to return, well . . .'

'But why does not he return on his own, James?' At the cradle. 'Oh, oh, you are too eager.' Cooing, and making other fond noises.

James picked up the letter, and let it fall again on the table. 'I expect that had they known the answer to that, my darling, they would not have wrote to me.' A sigh. 'But they have wrote, they have made their request, and I must depart upon my errand.'

'Then you are not newly commissioned, as yet? I can see that you are vexed.'

'Oh, I am not vexed, you know.' A brief smile. But he was vexed. He had been expecting—daily expecting—a letter from their Lordships, informing him that he had been made post and given his own ship—or, if not that, then at the very least his own sloop, with the rank of master and commander. He had earned such elevation, he had shown well his last two commissions in HM *Expedient* frigate thirty-six, had done all that had been asked of him, and considerably more; had faced great hardship and peril, and done his duty with a will. Had he not? Well, he had—and now this letter. Not the letter he had expected, not at all. A damned vexing and discommoding task, in pursuit of his elusive erstwhile commanding officer, Captain Rennie. Captain Rennie, that had gone deep into Devonshire, had apparently married a wife there—glancing at the letter—a widow named Susan Hendlesham, and had given his address to the Admiralty as Belveer Crag Farm, Catling Tor near Widestone-upon-Moor, Devonshire. Missives had been sent there by their Lordships, requiring Captain Rennie to attend at the Admiralty in Whitehall, there to be apprised of his duty in a new commission—a third commission for himself and *Expedient*.

No answer to these letters had been received. Three had been sent, and now their Lordships' patience was at an end. Accordingly his second-in-command—his erstwhile second-in-command—must by the desire of their Lordships go into Devonshire and discover Captain Rennie, discover him and bring him from that place to London, without the loss of a moment.

'What if he don't want to come, though?' James, to himself. Rain had begun to fall, and cold drops dashed and speckled on the quartered panes of the window. 'Supposing this widow of his is a rich woman, and he don't want or need anything of new duties and commissions, hey? What then? I have never met his bride. I did not know that he had took a wife, even. I have heard nothing from him, nothing at all, since we paid off. I thought we was firm friends, but evidently——'

'I cannot quite hear you, James.' Catherine. 'Come by me, and look at your darling boy.'

James threw down the letter and went to stand at the cradle

with his wife. 'He is getting bigger.' Peering down. 'Good heaven, I declare that since Sunday last he has grown nearly an whole foot.'

'James, you are such a fool.' Laughing. 'That is the blanket cover, folded over his little legs.'

'Ah, is it? I was teasing, you see.'

'You were not, you were not.' Laughing again. 'You thought he was becoming a giant.'

'Did I? Ah well, if you say so.' Glancing at the rain on the window, and frowning.

'He will soon need his stick of coral, I think.'

'Coral?'

'For his teeth.'

'The child has no teeth. I must take a boat cloak in this weather. Tabitha had better come from the kitchen and help me pack a travelling valise. Now, if you please.'

'James—you are not vexed with me . . . ?

Turning to her: 'Never think that.' Taking her in his arms. 'Oh, my darling, never think it. You are my life, my heart and soul.' And he kissed her.

———◆———

James had thought of riding all the way to Dartmoor, stopping at inns; his horse Jaunter—his father had long since made him the gift of the horse—was a fine strong animal and would have borne him there with ease, and this had been his immediate and original intention when the letter came. Steady incessant rain had dissuaded him, and instead he rode into Weymouth with the object of taking ship from that port and sailing west to Plymouth. No ship was available there to take him in that direction; the few small ships in the harbour were all bound east from Weymouth, as the tide served. A cutter was expected on the morrow, or the day following, bound for Plymouth, if he cared to wait. Very probably passage might be arranged in her for a lieutenant RN.

He spent the night at the Harbour Inn, the same pleasant small bow-fronted hotel in which he and Catherine had spent their honeymoon. By luck—and in fond memory—he was able to engage the same room, but when he was shown in there his heart did not lift as he had thought it would. Through the window dusk crept across the harbour in the falling rain, and the glimmer of lights on the far side, beyond the harbour wall, lent the room a chill, melancholy air. His heart sank low in his breast, he felt the absence of his beloved Catherine, keenly felt it, and was touched by desolation. He turned on his heel, nearly knocked over the boy that carried his valise, and abruptly descended the stairs.

'But that room has a very fine view of the harbour, sir.' The innkeeper's wife, ruffled. 'The finest in all the house.'

'Yes, well, I—I don't want that view, d'y'see.'

'But you asked for it particular, sir, when you came in just now. What is the matter?'

'Nothing, nothing, I assure you, madam. It's just—well, I want a smaller room, with no view at all. If you please.' Producing his purse.

'Yes, sir, very well. Just as you like.' Puzzled, smiling, nodding. 'Will you be wanting to eat your dinner here?'

'In my room, if you please.'

And he did eat his dinner in the new room—cramped and stuffy, overlooking the stable yard—ate it without great relish, drank a glass of wine, and reflected on his departure from Birch Cottage.

'What do you suppose Captain Rennie's wife to be like?' Catherine had asked as Tabitha brought his valise out into the paved court at the front of the house. 'Pretty, d'you think? Or handsome? Or neither?'

'I have no idea, my love. Perhaps she is a demi-rep, that has stole his fortune and left him destitute upon the moor.' Taking Jaunter's bridle as the boy led him from the yard at the rear.

'Has he a fortune?'

'Not a very great one.'

'Is not it then more probable that the lady herself is possessed of the fortune, and not the other way round?'

'Yes, more than probable. I had thought the same thing myself.' He kissed his wife fondly once more, and swung up into the saddle. 'At any rate, I must solve the mystery. Why does a post captain with his name on the Navy List not jump at a new commission? Is he too rich—or is he dead? Hey?'

'Surely dear Captain Rennie cannot be dead?'

'I do not think so for a moment. Goodbye, my darling. I shall come back to you absolutely as soon as I am able.'

As James undressed and lay down to sleep the momentary desolation he had felt earlier came in on him again, and he tossed and turned on his pillow, unable to settle, unable to shake off his sense of gloom and sink into relieving slumber. Rain pelted at the window, and wind sighed in the chimney. At length he sat up, lit his candle, and found a book in his valise—Fielding's *Joseph Andrews*, a favourite since his days as a midshipman. He lay back and prepared to be entertained by the absurdly endearing Parson Adams.

He woke to grey light over the stable yard, the angry shouts of a stableman and the clop of hooves. The candle guttered in its holder by his bed, and his book lay open face-down on the floor. He rose, glanced out and down and saw his horse Jaunter being roughly handled. Furiously he fumbled with the window, flung it open, and in his fiercest quarterdeck:

'You there! Belay that! Now stand where you are until I come down to you!'

And furiously he pulled on shirt, breeches, stockings and shoes, and thudded down the narrow stair.

'Sir?' A startled maidservant, spilling a ewer of hot water.

'Where is the door to the yard?'

Wordlessly she nodded there. James strode down a passage, turned through a scullery, and banged out into the yard. The stableman was nowhere to be seen. Jaunter stood quiet on the damp cobbles, twitching a little, and his eye turned on James. A gentle whicker, and the beast came to his master, and James stroked the horse's nose and neck, and murmured:

'Yes, old fellow, I am here. Never fear the wretch, that I shall find presently. You are quite safe.'

His plan had been to send Jaunter back with that very stableman to Winterborne. Well, that would not do now. He must stable the horse elsewhere in Winterborne—at Mayhew's Yard. Briefly he considered shipping the beast to Plymouth, instead of hiring a horse there and riding on up into the moor. But how in heaven's name could a great horse like Jaunter be hoisted into a cutter? And to what end? There was no manger in a cutter, even if a horse could be got below, which it could not.

'No, I must leave you at Mayhew's, old fellow.'

Twenty minutes after, shaved and properly dressed, he came down to the parlour to the smell of bacon, and coffee. Word had come from the harbour mouth that the cutter was in sight. Activity had diminished James's melancholy mood of the night before, and a hearty breakfast banished it altogether. He made arrangements about his horse, forgot all about the offending stableman, and busied himself in packing, and paying his bill. He gave a shilling to the maidservant who had spilled his hot water and sixpence to the boy who carried down his firmly strapped valise. Rain had again begun to fall, and the wind was blowing steady and strong from the west. He sniffed that wind as he strode to the harbour wall, pulling on his cloak. The boy came behind him.

'Have you ever thought of a life at sea?' James, settling his hat firmly on his head, and turning to take his valise.

'Oh, no, sir. I likes the solid ground under my feet.'

'Aye, then perhaps you are wise, on a day like today.' And

as he waited for the cutter's boat to ride in across the dark reflecting water, he felt a sudden return of melancholy, as if it had been blown in over him by the damp, saline wind, and he shivered.

***

The cutter was the *Curlew*, ten guns, sixty-eight feet in length, 110 tons burthen, with a complement of forty-two officers and men. Her commanding officer was Lieutenant Dutton Bradshaw, a square-faced, square-standing young man of five-and-twenty, without an ounce of spare flesh anywhere on him, and a penetrating grey gaze that James mistook at first for harshness of character and an unforgiving nature. Lieutenant Bradshaw's welcome, however, was altogether less astringent, his voice pleasant, and his manners gentlemanlike. He agreed at once to take James to Plymouth, when he had stepped up the side ladder from the returning boat, and presented himself, hat off, upon the deck.

'But how did ye know we was coming, though?' enquired Bradshaw. 'Where is your dunnage?'

'I carry everything I need in this one bag, thankee.' Indicating his valise. 'And I did not know *Curlew* was touching here until yesternight. I had thought to take passage in a small merchant ship, but none was going my way.'

'Pure luck, then. I was to have picked up a lieutenant of marines from the fort, but he ain't here after all, so my senior middy tells me. No hanging cot?'

'No.' Shaking his head.

'Hammock, then. You won't mind that?'

'Not at all. Wherever you can fit me in. Am very much obliged t'you.'

'Very good. I shall stand to the south, a little, stand off and then beat into this westerly, that is strengthening by the glass. I do not care to be driven in on a lee shore should it decide to veer south, out of spite.'

'No, indeed.' Ducking as spray flew across the deck in beads of liquid glass.

'What is your business at Plymouth, Mr Hayter? D'you join your ship there?'

'No, at present I am not in fact commissioned—well, except by letter, to undertake a certain task.'

'Ah. Mm.—Mr Quentin!' To a midshipman, as *Curlew* came rolling and pitching on to her new heading. 'Shake out the reef in the forestays'l, if y'please, and let us crack on, now.'

'Aye, sir.'

Lieutenant Bradshaw led the way to the companion. 'Let us go below, and get you berthed, hey?'

'I did not mean to be mysterious, just now,' said James as they crouched their way into the cramped little great cabin. 'To say the truth I was embarrassed, a little.'

'Eh? Embarrassed?'

'Well, yes. You see, I am sent on a particular errand, to find and bring back my commanding officer, Captain Rennie, who has——'

'Rennie? Captain William Rennie?'

'Yes. He——'

Of the *Expedient* frigate?'

'Yes. He——'

'So you are *that* Hayter? Then I will like to shake your hand, by God.' And he did so, warmly. 'I know your exploits ain't strictly supposed to be famous, Hayter, but nearly everyone in the Service does know about them, in fact. You have done some wonderful fine things in that ship, stupendous things.'

'I would not say stupendous, you know.' Discomforted, but pleased.

'Oh, but they was stupendous, there can be no question. Not that you are able to say anything about those cruises, in course, and I will not press you. But we had all thought—that is, it was generally thought in the Service that you should have got your own command, afterward.'

'Yes, well, I am not privy to their Lordships' delib-
erations——'

'No, no, and I ought not to have spoke of it.' Embarrassed
in turn. 'No doubt you are again commissioned on some
mighty stratagem, and unable—forbidden—to speak of it.'

'No, I assure you, it is just as I've——'

'You shall hear no further word from me, sir. Hence-
forward I am silent as the grave. *Hendle! Hendle!* Where the
devil is the fell—— Ah, there you are.' To the steward who
now stood at the door. 'Have we any wine?'

'Only what is hid away in your locker, sir.'

'Then fetch along a bottle, man, so that I may honour my
guest.'

'Aye, sir. If you would be so kind as to shift your person to
one side, sir, so that I might reach the locker . . .'

'Yes, yes, very well.' As Lieutenant Bradshaw moved away
from the locker *Curlew* lost her footing, and dipped her head,
and her commanding officer thrust out an unavailing hand,
teetered and measured his length on the decking. James and
the steward anxiously helped him up.

'I am all right, I am all right.' Feeling his head. 'I think that
I may have just struck my noddle a glancing blow on the
corner of the——' His hand, when he took it away from his
temple, was red with blood. To James's great surprise and
relief the lieutenant seemed to think this a capital joke; he
laughed heartily at himself, his fall, his blood-dripping scalp.
'What a damn' fool I am, taking a tumble in my own cabin,
ha-ha-ha. Hendle, a cloth and a basin, as quick as you like.
Hayter, my dear fellow, will you be so good as to open our
wine?'

James thought it rather too early in the day to be thinking
of wine, leave alone drinking it, but as a guest in the ship he
wished to be amiable, and he took a bottle from the locker
and did as he was asked.

As they were drinking their wine—Lieutenant Bradshaw
with a bandage wrapped round his head—there were shouts

on deck, and Midshipman Quentin appeared at the door.

'We have sighted a cutter, sir, wearing strange colours, and she is running away to the south.'

'Running, Mr Quentin?'

'She is that smuggler, sir, I think. The *Swift*.'

'The *Swift*! You are certain?'

'Very nearly certain, sir. Black-painted, and her mast raked, and a heavy press of canvas.'

'Very good, I shall come on deck directly. Will you join me, Hayter? We may have some sport this day, I reckon.'

'Aye, gladly.' And as they went up the companion: 'I have not heard of *Swift*. Is she a very notorious vessel in these waters?'

Swift was notorious, said Lieutenant Bradshaw. Excise cutters had been attempting her capture many months, and she had always eluded them; she was faster, more weatherly, better handled than most vessels the Excise Board could send to sea.

'What does she carry, that the Excise Board is so anxious to intercept?' James stood with the bandaged Bradshaw on the quarterdeck as the latter focused his long glass on the fleeing shape away to larboard. The sea was rolling rough, the wavetops whipped back in a white blur by the wind, and *Curlew*, beating to windward, was dipping her flat-steeved bowsprit deep, her headsails streaming at the leech and foot.

Lieutenant Bradshaw lowered his glass, and raising his voice against the wind: 'We will let her captain run away a little longer, then come about and run with the wind on our quarter, fly down on him at an angle and halve the distance between us before he is quite aware of the danger. On his present heading—west-sou'west, and a point west—he will aid us, and we shall have the wind gage.'

'Surely he must see your change of course, and go about himself, to run south-east?'

'Ah, but he don't want to sail sou'east, d'y'see. There is a 'cise cutter waiting there for him, two cutters probably, and he dare not risk his precious cargo. He must continue on his present heading, try to outrun us, and double back in darkness—or run away altogether back to France.'

'What does he carry?' James asked again.

'Cognac and tobacco, the finest of both. His plan was to run up into Lyme Bay and wait for dusk, standing off, then run west into Branscombe, or Salcombe. He was not expecting another cutter, having evaded the excisemen. But he has been too bloody bold, the rogue, in broad daylight. Hey?'

'Indeed, so it would seem. May I venture to ask: what is your own plan?'

'To run him down and make him strike, the villain. I can outgun him with my smashers, and he won't risk an action.' Nodding at the squat eighteen-pound carronades in two batteries of five, larboard and starboard. 'Mr Quentin! Stand by to go about! As soon as it is done, we will beat to quarters! Lively, now!'

As they began to run with the wind on their starboard quarter, Lieutenant Bradshaw employed a heavier press of canvas than ever James would have risked: topsail and t'gan'sail, weather stunsail, fore and aft mainsail, unreefed— a vast belly of number six—and three headsails. Every rope was taut, shrouds and stays hummed and whined, and the clean-lined, deep-draughted little ship sliced through the water with an urgent seething of foam along her wales. High at the gaff her ensign snapped and rippled broad on the halyard, and her pennant curled and streamed from the mast trucktop. The mast creaked, the braced yards creaked, the tiller creaked under the helmsman's hands, and James thought that it was no surprise nor wonder that such a vessel was called a cutter, because by God she did cut, sweet and true. Guncrews crouched in readiness by the carronades, shot boxes and cartridges to hand, and half-pounder swivels had been slotted along the rails. James stood away at the rail, anxious not to hinder the working of the ship. Lieutenant Bradshaw, peering through his glass, asked over his shoulder:

'Would you like a pair of pistols, Hayter?'

'Eh? D'y'mean to board her?'

'Oh, yes, certainly I will board her. Whether or no we shall have to fight our way into her I cannot say just at present. You had better have a brace of pistols, anyway, in case we are obliged to. Mr Alderton!' Another midshipman.

'Sir?' The boy was green-faced with nausea, but endeavoured to be eager.

'Go below to the cabin and fetch my pistol case, if y'please, and bring a pair of sea pistols from the chest for Mr Hayter.'

'Aye, sir.' Hurrying to the companion, suppressing a retch.

'I hope to God that boy don't puke in my cabin,' muttered Mr Bradshaw. 'It is a stench very hard to eradicate at sea, once it has seeped into the decking timbers in so confined a space.'

'Vinegar,' said James. He had brought his own glass on deck—a long Dolland—and now raised it to peer at the raked mast and black hull of the cutter they pursued. Her colours were unlike any James would in usual recognize—not British, not French, nor Netherlander, nor Spanish.

'What are her colours?' he mused aloud.

'Blackguard's colours. Villain's. Anybody's and nobody's. What was that you said just now about vinegar?'

'Oh, I should simply wash out your cabin with vinegar—if young Mr Alderton should spill his rations.'

'Ah. Mm. Let us hope we do not spill something else, today. In least, not our own, hey?' Again over his shoulder as he peered through his glass.

'I had not bargained for this in getting a lift to Plymouth,' said James, but not aloud. Aloud, he did say: 'Are we gaining, d'y'think?'

'We are.' With certainty, lowering his glass. 'We are gaining, by God.' And he took a great breath, sucking it fiercely through his teeth, and stared aloft. 'I love a chase!'

'What are his guns?'

Lieutenant Bradshaw continued his critical appraisal of his mainsail a moment, stepped and said something to the helmsman, then came to stand with James.

'Not above twelve guns, I think. Four-pounders, or perhaps sixes. Each broadside of his, therefore, can be at most thirty-six pound by weight of metal. We are ninety pound.'

'Indeed. However, should he manage to fire first, thirty-six pound of roundshot will do very considerable damage to a cutter.'

'Mm, possibly—*if* he fired first. Only think what ninety pound would do to him, though, should he choose to defy me. Matchwood, Hayter. Splinters and matchwood. Nay, he will not risk that. He will strike, and save himself.'

'D'you know who commands her?'

'Eh?' Again glancing aloft.

'Who is *Swift*'s captain? Is he an Englishman, or a Frenchman?'

'Don't know that he's neither. He is wily, at any rate, whoever he is. Not quite wily enough for Dutton Bradshaw, however, as he will discover right soon.' Another fierce, fuelling breath.

James raised his glass, and saw at once that the chase was altering course, swinging to head directly south towards the Channel Isles and France. Lowering his glass: 'He is standing away to the south, I fear.'

Lieutenant Bradshaw stiffened, whipped up his glass, and in a moment muttered: 'God damn the fellow. I meant to take his ship a prize.'

'A prize? We are not at war. Surely the Excise would have first claim on him, or in least on his cargo.'

'These things may be managed.' Darkly. 'It is a question of—— Well, I had better say no more.'

Midshipman Alderton reappeared, still very green, carrying a pistol case and two extra pistols awkwardly balanced in his arms. Seeing him Lieutenant Bradshaw gave him a curt nod. 'Thank you, Mr Alderton, we shan't need those, now—y'may take 'em below. Mr Quentin! We will stand down, and resume our course for Plymouth!'

A last glance at the dark shape and raked mast of his ertswhile quarry, and quietly: 'Yes, I will see you another day, sir, y'may count on it.'

And he turned away aft, whipping his glass up under his arm, and pinning it there a prisoner.

—•—◦—•—

At Plymouth on the morrow James debated whether or no to present himself to Admiral Liston, the port admiral, and decided that since he was not in fact commissioned, and had no business at Plymouth except to hire himself a horse, he would not trouble the admiral. James went into *Curlew*'s boat with Lieutenant Bradshaw, when that officer took his despatches ashore, and they shook hands at the dockyard gate and made their farewells.

'Do you spend the night here at Plymouth, Hayter?'

'No, I must take to the road at once.'

'Ah. Then good day to you.' Very correct in his dress coat, the sewn canvas despatch packet under his arm.

James sensed at their parting—had sensed in the boat—that Lieutenant Bradshaw did not quite look at him in the same light as when he had first learned of James's association with HM *Expedient* frigate. Lieutenant Bradshaw had not said so, but James felt that he was in some way blamed because they had not come to an action with the elusive *Swift*. It had not been James's failure—nor indeed anyone's in *Curlew*—that they had not brought the smuggler to an account of himself—but it was James's distinct impression that he was silently accused, and silently blamed, all the same.

Lieutenant Bradshaw had made no gesture of disaffection or disapprobation; he had been perfectly polite and courteous, had in all particulars behaved gentlemanlike—and yet James did feel his displeasure.

'Did I ask too many questions of him on his deck?' wondered James. 'Did I appear too cautious about those pistols? Did I express myself poorly in the matter of prizes? How have I offended the fellow?' That he could not find an answer to these questions began to make him feel low. He drew a deep breath—and now the answer did come to him: 'He was *discomfited*, in course. I was present when he failed— thought he had failed—and he felt himself belittled before a fellow sea officer.' James shook his head, smiled wryly, gripped his valise and dismissed the thing from his mind with relief.

He did not go into the dockyard, nor visit any other naval establishment. He did not pass the night, nor even the whole of the day, in this most naval of England's ports, but ate a quick luncheon at an inn, hired a sturdy chestnut hack, and in newly falling drizzle donned his cloak, strapped up his valise and rode away out of the confines of the town on the road to Exeter. The slopes of the moor rose high and misty away to the north. He hoped to ride this first day so far as Buckfastleigh, and there stable his nag and lay his head over-night. He was thankful for his cloak, and an old uncockaded hat, as the drizzle turned to rain and the air grew chill. Although he was not officially commissioned, he was on naval business as an emissary of their Lordships, and so had felt obliged to wear his undress uniform coat, waistcoat and breeches. As he rode on he wished that he had worn the ordinary working clothes he customarily donned at sea, and smiled at the memory of Rennie's frowning reproach.

'Must you wear that damned piratical rig, James?'

'It is my working clothes, sir. For going aloft, examining the rigging, the tops, and the like—and for going below, into the hold.'

'Hm. Ymm. It don't look quite right to me. Y'might be took for one of the people, dressed like that.' A sniff. 'That kerchief round your head, good God.'

'If you wish it, sir, in course I shall shift into a frock coat . . . ?'

'No no, it's of no consequence—it just don't look altogether—— Well well, never mind.'

He arrived at the Cockerel Inn at Buckfastleigh late in the evening, very wet and tired, having twice strayed off the road in the gathering gloom of dusk and rain and lost his way. He wished to revive himself by means of a hot bath, and brandy and hot water, but neither was available at that hour. The cook had gone to bed, there were only cold cuts to eat, and cold pie; he might eat hearty at breakfast, if he pleased. He saw his horse stabled, and was shown up to a chilly little room. A hastily laid fire smoked in the cold chimney, and the wind off the moor blew that smoke back into the room, and half-blinded, half-choked, James lay miserably down on his bed and made himself think of cheerful things to ward off gloom, and melancholy. He thought of Catherine, and the infant James in his cradle, and the dog Sparker, of Birch Cottage lying warm and pleasant in the lee of the hill—and instead of cheering him these thoughts and pictures brought him near to tears, and he took up his book and plunged with a will into the world of make-believe—and this at last relieved him and brought him to slumber.

In the early morning he found that his wet cloak, and his coat and breeches, had been returned to him dried and pressed, and that his boots had been brushed clean of mud, dried and polished. He shaved, his spirits rising, and went down to a hearty breakfast—very necessary to him—in the fire-bright parlour. Afterward, he asked for directions. The landlord's wife:

'Mr Cuthbert! Mr Cuth—— Now, Cuthbert my dear, the gen'man wishes to find Widestone-upon-Moor. Ain't that right, sir?'

'If you please.' Drinking off his third cup of coffee, and wiping his lips.

'That is a fair distance from here, sir, by moor reckoning.' The landlord rubbed his whiskers.

'Moor reckoning . . . ?'

'Yes, sir. There is really always an addition to the actuality of distance. You might say, now, ten mile. But that would not mean ten mile, no. That would be more like fifteen, or even twenty.'

'Ah. In short, the road is not adequately marked, nor sign-posted, hey?'

'Oh, well, there is signs, sir. But they may take you round and about. Many will point in four differing directions, and all point to the same place.'

'Yes, I see—Widestone-upon-Moor?'

'That is a fair distance from here, sir, northward, and west a little into the moor. Howsomever, you will never reach it by going north. You must skirt the moor, up by Ashburton, and Caton, and Coldeast, and *then* go into the moor, making west.'

'Making west, very good. From Coldeast, you say?'

'Oh, no, sir.' Mrs Cuthbert. 'No, you must take the road from Bovey Tracey, up into the moor to the Hay Tor, winding up. That is the only safe way, in this weather.'

James glanced out of the window, peering at a bright, clear, sunny morning. 'Surely the weather is fine today, Mrs Cuthbert?' Turning to her. 'The day is ideal for travelling.'

Mrs Cuthbert shook her head, and smiled in apology for the moor. 'The mornings is very deceiving, sir. At noon, well, it might still be fine—but by *afternoon* there will be weather.'

'Then I had best make a start,' said James cheerfully. 'The Exeter road to Bovey Stacey, and then west into the moor, have I got it aright?'

'Bovey Tracey, sir. About nine mile. I should pause there, and look to the weather again.'

James rode briskly through the morning on the undulating Exeter road, through vales, and stretches of open country bordered by trees, and up through steeper gradients with spreading views, and was always aware of the great rolling rise of the moor away to larboard.

He came to Bovey Tracey at noon, crossed the racing mill-stream by the narrow bridge and went into the low stone inn at the bottom of the hill to ask for further directions. Again he was cautioned—in the cloudless brightness of a near perfect day—as to the ferocity of the weather, and again he was inclined to be dismissive.

'I have seen worse than this at sea,' he smiled, and stood a round of drinks in the taproom to show that he was an amiable fellow.

'This is your first time upon the moor, then?' A gentleman's voice, behind him. James turned round, glass in hand. In the shadow made by the shafting sun at the window, and a haze of pipe smoke on the air, he could not see the face above the form. The form came forward, and James saw a dark brown coat, well cut, dark waistcoat and breeches, and buckled shoes, and above them the pleasant clean-shaven face of a man in middle life, and a not quite stern grey gaze.

'Aye, it is.' James, politely. 'May I offer you a splash of something, sir?'

'That is kind in you. Do you go through?'

'Through?'

'To the dining room. I am about to do so. In turn, may I ask you to join me?'

The brown-clad gentleman introduced himself. He was Dr Symonds, the local physician. He intended that afternoon—weather permitting—to ride up into the moor and call upon an elderly spinster who lived alone at Orrington. She had not been altogether hale of late. No, she had not sent word. She had asked for no assistance. But he felt himself obliged to call upon her, all the same. It was an instinct in the country physician, to know when all was not as it should be with his patients, and his duty therefore to act upon that instinct.

They went through to the dining room—a wide, low, but

well-appointed room, with a fire and fresh table linen, and
encouraging smells from beyond. They sat at a table near to
the fire, for in here the air was chill, and ate their very
substantial meal, which Dr Symonds referred to as dinner.

'In this part of the country we prefer to eat our large meal
at this time, rather than at five o'clock, which some few
people like to call dinner. I myself do not. Anything in the
late afternoon, or the evening, is certainly supper.'

'Then that is very like the Royal Navy, Doctor.'

They drank small beer, then claret, and ate four courses:
two of meat—one cold—one of fish, and the last a syllabub.
The doctor was all for including a fifth course of cheese, and
calling for port wine, but James politely declined, saying that
he must really make some progress into the moor. He spoke
of wishing to locate Captain Rennie.

'Perhaps you have heard of him?'

'Rennie . . . ? No, I do not know that gentleman.'

'At Widestone-upon-Moor?'

'Ah, well, no. No, another physician attends those people
that live farther out upon the moor. I go in usual only so far
as Orrington, short of the Hay Tor on the road across.'

They settled the bill between them, went out into the
stable yard, and presently set off, riding up between the deep
hedgerows on the narrow winding road into the moor,
climbing higher and higher above the little town, their
horses' hooves clattering and echoing on the stony surface.
Soon they came to a fork in the road, and the doctor declared
that here he must turn left for Orrington, and that James
must go to the right.

'Proceed on this road so far as the Hay Tor, that great
outcrop yonder'—pointing—'and you will find a signpost for
Widestone-upon-Moor. It is about five mile from there,
across the top of the moor.'

'I am obliged to you, Dr Symonds. I have much enjoyed
your company.'

'May I suggest—nay, indeed insist—that should the

weather begin to close in you turn back, and come down off the moor at once?'

'Oh, I assure you——'

'It is folly to remain on the height of the moor in rain and mist, Mr Hayter.' Earnestly. 'More than folly, in fact—it is dangerous outright.'

'Doctor, I have heard a great deal today about the weather on the moor. But I am a sea officer, you know, with large experience of the worst conditions and fiercest climates the world may produce. With respect, I do not think I will allow myself to be overcome by a patch or two of clammy mist upon a bit of open heath in England.'

'Bit of open *heath*? My dear sir, Hay Tor is near fifteen hundred foot high, and other parts of the moor stand higher than two thousand——' The doctor broke off, looked hard at James, and at last shook his head. 'I can only urge you to consider what I have said.' A sigh. 'You are your own man, in course, and I must not presume to detain you. Good day to you—and good luck.'

And he turned his horse's head, clicked his tongue, and set off at a brisk trot for Orrington.

Half an hour later as James rode up past the jutting scar of the Hay Tor, and came to the wide, wild height of the spreading moor, he found his breath quite taken away. It was the sheer scale of it, the far-stretching expanses of heather and bracken, clumped with gorse, the distant crags and rolling slopes, and the immense silence, broken only by the half-lost cries of birds, and the sighing wind. Although the sun still shone full upon him, he saw now in the west a smudge of grey on the horizon, and a stand of cloud tumbling tall and slow in the sky there. Sinuous tracks spread away north and west, glistening in the sun. Across the slopes tiny shapes moved, black against the land, and James saw in his glass that they were ponies, ambling and cropping at the sparse growth. In the far distance a flock of black-faced sheep lay under the lee of a crag. On the broader slopes were high gleaming smears of moisture, and silver streams slipped and meandered down into deep shadowed clefts. The horse twitched under him, and James became aware that he had come to a complete stop, caught up in childlike awe at the spectacle before him.

'This will not do,' he admonished himself, and he urged the horse forward to the signpost that stood against the sky a quarter of a mile ahead. In a few moments he read:

WIDESTONE-UPON-MOOR 4½

and rode on in the direction indicated.

The moor rolled broad and green before him, marched across by low stone fences, with clumps of yellow gorse; in the distance rocks and crags reared at the crests, and darkling brown heather rode like patches of kelp upon a great petrified ocean. Aside from those ancient stone fences James could see no sign of human intervention in this strange, eternal place. There was no hint of habitation, no sign of human life. And yet Widestone must lie there ahead, its church spire hidden in a fold or hollow, down by a stream or a village pond. He began to be glad that he would soon find Widestone, for however spectacular the moor it was not very welcoming, somehow.

His horse now grew reluctant under him, and James was obliged to dig in his heels to encourage the animal.

'You are not to be compared with Jaunter, eh?' Heels. 'I must start you to compliance, every yard of the way.' Heels. 'What is the matter?'

The horse shied a little, gave a fretful snort and rolled its eye. A puff of cold wind tugged at James's hat, and he settled it firmer on his head, sawed at the bit and dug in his heels again, firmly, to remind his mount of its duty to take him where he wished to go.

'Walk on, you brute.'

A sharper, colder breath of wind—another, and another.

The sky was darker, all at once. James looked west, and found to his astonishment that the far distant, tumbling pile of clouds had descended upon the moor, and was now rolling toward him in a tidal wall of mist and rain.

'It cannot be,' he declared, gripping with his knees as the horse skittered and crabbed. 'Good God, it cannot be the same clouds, that was twenty mile distant only a few moments since.'

But these same clouds now rushed all about him in a whirl of misty rain, closed over him, and he was cut off from landscape, sky, sun, the wide day, and enveloped in the gloom of twilight. At the same instant the weather closed in, his horse reared back in alarm, plunged madly forward, stopped sudden, and threw him from the saddle. He fell clinging to the rein, was twisted and dragged, and struck his head with a sickening thud. In a last dim flutter of consciousness James saw the horse plunge away down the slope and lose itself in the mist.

⊰◈⊱

He woke to the delicate sound of teacups clinking in saucers, the murmur of conversation, and the woodsmoke smell of a newly lit fire. He was lying in the corner of a pleasant green room, on a green upholstered, buttoned sofa, his head resting on a pillow on one of the low, scrolled arms. A needleworked rug of a subdued red and yellow pattern covered the floor, and newly lit candles burned in reflection in their holders at two wall mirrors. Flames flickered half-hidden by a worked firescreen at the grate. Green curtains had been drawn at the windows. In the far corner two fine side chairs stood at a mahogany table; on the table were a tall silver kettle, a tea caddy and a porcelain teapot. On one of the chairs sat a straight-backed gentlewoman with a basket of embroidery in her lap, and a teacup raised to her lips. On the other chair sat Dr Symonds. James took in all these details in a fascinated daze, a daze interrupted as he began to raise his head, a blanket falling from his shoulders:

'Ah, he is awake.' Dr Symonds rose and came to him. 'My dear young sir, you gave us a fright, you know. When you was carried in, we thought that all was lost.' But his tone of voice suggested that he did not mean it. He took up James's left hand, and with a light, firm touch felt for the pulse at his wrist. 'Yes, it has steadied—excellent, excellent. I think it may be time for you to take some light refreshment—that is, if you feel able.'

'I am—I am able.' James's voice was very subdued, and a little hoarse. He sat up, aided by the doctor, and saw the doctor's wife looking at him. She smiled, and rang a silver table bell.

'Some gruel, I think,' said the doctor.

'I should prefer brandy.' His head swam a little as he made the request.

'Brandy, sir? No, I think not. You have struck your head a severe blow, and brandy will not aid your recovery.' Nodding, a grimacing little medical smile. 'Gruel, Mr Hayter, if y'please.'

'I struck my head . . . ?'

'Aye, on the moor. Your horse took fright, and you was thrown.'

'I do not—quite recall . . .'

'No? That is quite usual, in such a case. Your brains took a buffeting, and your memory has been knocked out of 'em with your senses. You will recover both, I am in no doubt.'

A maidservant brought in a bowl of gruel, with morsels of bread soaking in it.

'Shall I come and help you?' inquired the doctor's wife, peering kindly at James.

James attempted to rise and bow in her direction, fell side-wise down on the sofa, and was mortified by his clumsiness. 'I beg your pardon, madam . . . I am not quite myself.'

'You must not exert yourself, you know,' said the doctor,

and nodded to his wife, who came and took the bowl of gruel and sat by James on the sofa. 'My wife will be pleased to aid you with the spoon.'

'You are kind, madam. I am a poor guest, I fear.' Turning to the doctor. 'How did I come here? Did I faint at the inn? I remember . . . I recall that we dined together . . . and then I recall nothing.'

'You was thrown by your horse,' repeated Dr Symonds, who was entirely used to amnesia in the local hunt; many a horseman fell at a fence, and addled his senses a day or two, during the season. He gave his odd little grimacing smile, meant to be reassuring, and felt James's forehead. 'There is no fever, and that is very well. Your pulse is steady. You will mend, sir.'

'Are we at the inn? Is my horse at the inn?'

'No, you are presently in my house, and your horse is safe in my stable.'

'Our house,' chided his wife gently, and she spooned gruel to James's mouth. 'Dr Symonds is forever forgetting that he does not live here alone, and has never done so these twenty years.'

As dutifully as a child James allowed himself to be fed his gruel. It was nearly untasting, but warm, and warming. He felt himself a little strengthened, and presently:

'Madam, you are very kind. I am at fault in not having introduced myself. I am Lieutenant James Hayter.' Bowing his head, which made it swim.

'In the circumstances, Mr Hayter, I think there is no need of formalities. My husband has told me all about you.'

'Have I come from Winterborne today? Or was it yesterday? Am I at Weymouth?'

'No, you are at Bovey Tracey.' A smile. 'Please to open your mouth—there, that is the last spoonful.'

James swallowed that spoonful, smiled hesitantly in turn; looked at Mrs Symonds, at her husband, then slowly round the room. His smile became a puzzled frown.

'I rode here? To this house?'

'No, sir, you did not.' The doctor, cheerfully and patiently. 'You was carried down from the moor by a carter returning from Widestone, that found you lying on the ground, and your horse wandering under the Hay Tor. He lifted you into his cart, and brought you here.'

'Ahh . . . Tell me, is Captain Rennie here? I have come a long way to see him.'

'He is not, Mr Hayter, no,' said Mrs Symonds. 'We understand that you have come to Dartmoor to seek out Captain Rennie, but we do not know him, he is not one of Doctor Symonds's patients.'

'I see.' He nodded, frowned again, and was caught up by a sudden, deep yawn. 'Forgive me, I must just close my eyes a moment, I am rather tired. You are very kind . . .' And he fell at once into a heavy doze, and Mrs Symonds covered him with the blanket.

'Should he not be put to bed, my dear?'

'Later, we will move him later. Let him sleep there on the sofa for the moment.'

James remained at the doctor's house four days, put to bed there in a small room downstairs where Mrs Symonds could nurse him. On the second day he suffered a slight chill, that the doctor at first feared might become a fever. The chill passed, and on the morning of the fourth day James was quite recovered; his head was clear, and his memory had returned. He dressed, breakfasted with the doctor and Mrs Symonds, thanked them warmly, opened his purse and was rebuked, and left the house and Bovey Tracey behind him, with the doctor's admonition echoing in his head:

'Treat the moor with respect, and it will not harm you— will you remember that?'

At Widestone James asked directions at the inn, a low granite building with a thatched roof, opposite the tall-spired church.

He mentioned Rennie's name, thinking that here deep on the moor such a man as an innkeeper might know it. The innkeeper did not, but he knew the name Hendlesham.

'Aye, she is a widow woman, that lives at Belveer. That is far out on the moor, mind. You must never go down into the Dart Valley, you must go nor'west into the higher moor. The paths is very winding and deep-cut.'

'Paths? Ain't there a road?'

In the firelight of the parlour, the innkeeper's creased face, peering at him. 'What you might call a road, sir, don't exist far out on the moor. There is paths, or ways, but no roads at all.'

'And are these paths signposted?'

'There is marked stones, sometimes. But I would not trust them entire, less you knows definite wheer you is going.'

'I see. Is there somebody here, in the village, that I might pay to guide me?'

'The boy will show you the way out of the valley, and point you nor'west, but then he must return—I has work for him in the yard.'

'Very good, thank you.' James drank off his mug of ale and placed a coin on the table. As he came out into the bright day a brief dizziness assailed him, and his head felt tender as he put on his hat. With it came an attendant oppression, as if the light itself had had a darkening effect on his courage and temper. He took a deep breath, and made his back straight. The boy came from the yard, leading James's horse.

'If you will mount, sir, I will lead the horse.'

The way wound out of the valley into rolling green country divided by crumbling stone fences. Trees stood along the streams, but they were not the towering, stately trees of cultivated country parklands. These trees were low, twisted, hunched over as if in a perpetual wind, and the shelter beneath them was mossy, dark and damp. The boy led the horse out on the moor, pointed to a steep-sided quarry with a dark pool at the bottom, and said:

'Pass by the workings, yonder. Keep to the way acrost the top, and you will find Catling Tor directly, you cannot mistake it—it will be the largest tor you may see ahead, very savage against the sky.'

'Very savage against the sky.' James, taken with this phrase. 'I will look for it with that in mind.' He gave the boy a coin. 'Thank you kindly. You have been of the greatest assistance.'

The boy touched his forehead, muttered something about having to be on his way, then stood staring a moment out over the moor. James peered in that direction.

'Is the weather turning again?'

'No, I were looking at the buzzard.' Pointing. 'It has found its prey there, and it hangs on the wind, waiting to fall.'

James unshipped his glass, focused, and saw the bird, high over a copse on the far side of the quarry. It circled slow, hanging as the boy had said. Its cry came faintly on the air: 'Meee-yew—eee-yew——'

'What has he found, I wonder?'

'That is a she bird, sir, bigger than a him. There!'

And they both watched in fascination as the brown-plumed bird dropped with ferocious speed straight down, and was lost to view behind the trees.

'A rabbit, I expect. Or a mouse.' James nodded in admiration, lowering his glass. 'Or perhaps a fledgling, eh?' A moment of silence, and he turned and found that his companion had disappeared, as if swallowed up by the folding moor. James put away his glass, nodded again and repeated:

'Savage against the sky . . . an excellent description.'

And he urged the horse on gently with his heels. Today he was more careful of the animal, and spoke to it in a kindlier tone:

'Walk on, now, my beauty. You will find me good-natured, and we shall traverse the moor amiably together, hey?'

*

The path James followed led him by the steep-sided, flooded quarry, and when he reached the higher level beyond he saw a large settlement of stone dwellings. At first he took them for a village, but as he rode nearer they were revealed as crumbled to ruin—clear evidence of ancient habitation. West of the village plinths of rock had been arranged in a circle—for what purpose? The worship of primitive gods? He paused to make a quick sketch.

A little farther on the ground again dipped away in a long, rolling slope. At the bottom were the disused remains of a mine, with ruined buildings, a long sluice channel, and excavations. Trees stood along a narrow stream that wound past the workings. James, following the path, rode down there. He made sketches of the largest ruin, which he took to be a tin-smelting house; he dismounted and walked round it, sketchbook and pencil in hand. His sea officer's habit of observation—accurate observation, accurately recorded—had been sharpened by his foray into the moor, as if he had stepped ashore in a strange remote land whose natives had long ago become extinct.

When he remounted and rode on he found that the path, again deep-cut and bordered by thick thorny hedges, wound away up the opposite slope not west—but to the north.

'But I do not wish to go north,' muttered James in consternation. 'I wish to go west—west.'

He approached the summit of that slope, up out of the deep path and through a grey crumbling spill of granite, and at once caught sight of a tor some few miles distant, rising out of the moor to the west. It stood against the sky like the broken jaw of a giant warrior felled in battle, half his skull smashed and his jutting, broken teeth exposed to the elements. The rest of him lay mouldering in a long grey hump to the south.

'That is the Catling Tor, unless I am much mistook. What a place. How can people live at such a dismal place, I wonder?'

James examined the sky, and saw no cloud there, no looming mist, but the grim appearance of the tor made him shiver. He looked at his watch, and was surprised to find that it was nearly four o'clock.

'Eight bells? Nay, where has the time gone to?' He peered at the watch, shook it slightly, and brought it to his ear. Was there something amiss? The mechanism rewarded him with its comforting, regular, subdued ticking. 'Where has the time flown to, my beauty?' To the horse, and the animal pricked its ears. 'And how the devil are we to tack west for that tor when the path will not permit it, hey? When the path veers north, and north?' He stood in the stirrups, and came to a decision. He would follow the path northward to the top of the next rise, the tor away to larboard. When he reached the height of the slope he would jump the hedge and make a run west across the open moor.

Half an hour later he peered from the saddle into the depths of a horribly steep gorge. The horse shied away from the drop, and James dismounted to stand right at the edge. Stones rattled and cracked into the drop as his boots disturbed the earth, and echoed hollowly down as he strained to perceive the bottom. Faintly, deep in deep shadow, the rush of water.

'Damnation, we cannot cross here. I must find a vantage point, and discover how to make my way from there.' Another glance at his watch, an anxious glance.

An hour passed, and another, hours of fruitless movement back and forth across the moor, through patches of heather and gorse, through the granite-strewn rubble of ruins, up sudden little rises to long, wide views of open ground, scattering black-faced sheep—only to find the same damned impeding gorge to the west of him, between him and that elusive tor riding the sky. Darkness now loomed behind him, and declared its implacable intention ahead in the dying orange glow of the sun. Pale stars glimmered high above. His horse was tired, and increasingly unsure of its footing on the rough ground. James himself was tired, and beginning to be fearful. He took a deep, resolving breath.

'I will make for that rise again, to the north, one last time— and hope to God we may find our way before night.'

He turned the horse's head and dug in his heels, Dr Symond's parting admonition sounding like a shoal bell in his ear:

'Treat the moor with respect . . . will you remember that?'

***

Rain, and the last of twilight. Ahead on the dim path, rearing up, a great dead tree, its gnarled and withered branches spread like the fingers of a mad witch, casting a spell upon the air. Behind this apparition a looming house, tall chimneys and the darkness of trees away to the left. Was this Belveer? Was this Captain Rennie's house, Belveer Crag Farm?

A stare of glass, of windows in the fading light. Was that the glimmer of a candle in one of them? James, on foot this past half-hour and longer, led his horse along the path, beneath the clawed branches of the tree, and came to the front of the house. It was stone-built, solid-built to withstand the rigorous climate of the moor, with two tall chimneys, six windows in two storeys, and a low door. James approached, peered in at a window—there was no candlelight here. The house had the look, the drear sullen quiet, of a house empty of life. Night falling.

James tied the horse's reins loosely to a bush. 'Well, my beauty, what must I do?' He stood back a little, peering along the front of the house in the rain and gloom. 'I must make the attempt, at least, hey?' He strode to the door, and knocked loudly. '*Captain Rennie! Captain Rennie, sir! It is James Hayter, and I am come on an errand!*'

Silence. He knocked again—and again. Without result.

'*Captain Rennie! Are you here, sir!*'

Again, silence. James hesitated a moment, was sluiced by an icy deluge of rain from the roof guttering overhead, and now he seized the heavy iron knob of the door and shook it. At once the door gave inward, creaking on its hinges and releasing a waft of stale air. Stone flags and—was that a staircase? Another drenching splash of rain, and he stepped inside. There was a staircase.

'*Captain Rennie!*'

Feeling his way he found the banister, and the first step and riser, and began to climb.

'*Are you here? Is anyone here?*'

At the top of the stair a light, and a dim figure. James saw the barrel of a pistol, and heard the flintlock clicked open.

'*Do not shoot! I mean no harm!*'

'Who are you?' The familiar voice, a little frail perhaps, and tremulous, but familiar all the same.

'Captain Rennie, sir? Thank God it is you! Thank God I have found you!'

'Who are you? What d'y'want in the dead of night?' The light held up, the familiar face caught in its glow.

'I am Lieutenant Hayter, sir. James Hayter.'

'Don't know anyone of that name. Who let you in? How came you to this place? Answer me, else I will pistol you where you stand.' The weapon waved menacingly, but the voice behind it more than frail now—diminished and quavering, belying the ferocity of the words it spoke.

'Surely you will not shoot an old friend, sir, will you? That has come to seek you out?'

Recognition crept across the candlelit face above, knowledge came into the eyes, and now the barrel of the pistol was lowered. Rennie stared down, his mouth a little open, and at last gave a pitiful cry—half sob, half groan—and sank down on the highest stair. James ran up there. In the next hour, downstairs in the slowly warming kitchen as a fire took hold in the grate, James heard everything. Captain Rennie, his sparse hair unkempt and greying, his face haggard and lined, his spare frame reduced, his shirt and breeches hanging on him, poured out his bitter heart. His breath was stale and foul, his skin was ashen, his eyes sunk deep in his head. His hand trembled and quivered as he raised a glass of brandy to his lips and sucked the spirit down.

His wife, Susan, was dead. She had died two months ago, of a fever. The doctor at Chagford had been sent for when she fell ill, but had not come to Belveer until the following afternoon. By that time Susan had fallen into a deathly faint, from which she never wakened. Rennie's voice neither strengthened nor weakened as he spoke, except when sometimes he broke off, effortfully swallowed and held in a breath—and then continued. He did not weep. He was past weeping, he said. And so James heard the story.

When *Expedient* paid off at the end of her last commission, at Portsmouth, Rennie and James had by a quirk of fortune each found himself in possession—that they did not declare to the Admiralty—of some few thousands of money, in gold. It was not prize money, exact, since England was not at war, and no sea officer might claim prizes—and yet it had been won at sea.

James had husbanded his money, had used it wisely and moderately in the paying of some few debts and bills, in carrying out small repairs to his house, in providing his dearest Catherine with dresses and bonnets, &c., &c. He had put a thousand pound aside for his newborn son. James, in little, had done nothing to draw attention to himself.

Nor had Captain Rennie, who had employed his modest fortune in finding himself a wife.

'We met at Portsmouth, where I had took rooms at the Marine Hotel. Susan was a——' He bit his lip a moment, swallowed fiercely, and then continued. 'My future wife was a widow. Her husband Captain Hendlesham had died in a hunting accident—the place is not above two mile from this house—and she had come to Portsmouth to recover from her loss with his family, his widowed mother and her sisters.

They are a maritime family, you know, her husband had been master of an Indiaman for the Company. He had done well in the East, and had retired to Dartmoor to farm, and hunt, and take his ease.'

'So this was his property? Captain Hendlesham's?'

'Aye, Hendlesham's. It had been in his family years ago, and he bought it back. I knew nothing of this at first. Susan was a—a handsome woman, in mourning, that I had met by chance at a social occasion, a dance.'

'A dance?' Surprised. Rennie almost never danced— avoided dancing at all cost, if he could.

'Indeed. I had thought that I must attend to the social graces, you know. To find a wife a man must make himself presentable in society, and agreeable—and he must dance.'

'Indeed, and I did not mean to suggest——'

'At first the family was hard on me. She was in mourning, she had not long resumed going into society, following her bereavement, and they did not look kindly upon my paying attention to her.' Draining the last of the brandy in his glass, and reaching for the bottle. 'They thought I was an adventurer, trying to steal Susan's property away from her. A blackguard.'

'That was hard.' Gently.

'Just so, it was. Hard, and unjust. But I—I loved her, d'y'see. I loved her from the moment I first saw her, James. And I was determined to win her.'

'When was you married?'

'We was wed after the passage of only six weeks.'

'Six weeks? Then you won her right quick, sir.'

'Well well—we did not wait on the approval of her late husband's family, that might never have been given. We eloped, d'y'see. I was not altogether proud of it, James, but we wished to be together as man and wife.'

'You loved each other.' Simply.

'Aye, we did.' A pause, a breath. 'We did, and we wed, and came here to this fine house.'

'I am sure the house is very fine, seen in daylight. I have only seen it in darkness.'

'Belveer is old, and sound, and fine. Susan and I were happy here, very happy and content——' Another breath, effortfully held in, and at last released. 'I will never know such things again.'

'I am very sorry for your distress——'

'Oh, I am not distressed. I am past distress, James. Past anything of emotion, or belief.'

'Sir, you are very thin. You do not look well. Perhaps if you ate something——'

'You disapprove of this, eh?' Holding up his glass.

'No, sir, in course I do not. I am a sea officer, after all.'

'Yes, we are all drunkards. How else may we survive?' He drank off the glass, and refilled it. 'Will you tell me why you have come here, James?'

'I think perhaps tomorrow, when you are rested. I am very tired, sir. May I find a bed with you here, tonight? Then in the morning——'

'You may tell me now.' A hint of the old tone of command.

'Under the circumstances, I——'

'What circumstances?' Sharply, holding the brandy bottle and peering at James.

'Your very great loss, sir.'

'I tell you I am past it. Past it. There is nothing the world may hurl at my head, now, or send baleful to me in my dreams, that I will notice at all. I am indifferent.' Sucking down a mouthful of spirit. 'I am immune.'

James knew that this was untrue, but did not say it. Instead: 'Very good, sir, as you wish.'

'Well?'

'I wonder, have you received any letters of late?'

'Letters of condolence, you mean?'

'No, sir, not exact. I meant—I meant letters from their Lordships.'

'From the Admiralty? Why should they write in

condolence? What do they know of my *circumstances*? Hey? They are cold men, far away in London.'

'I must get to my business, sir, and speak plain. Not letters of condolence, but letters concerning your new commission.'

'Eh?' Putting the nearly empty bottle clumsily on the table, so that it tipped and leaked. 'What say?'

'Your new commission in *Expedient*.'

Rennie looked at James a moment, then away into a distant place. At length: 'Yes, well, I know nothing of such things. I am immune to such things, James. I look into the past, and all there is gone, and lost. What is there ahead? Very little, I think. I see very little there, neither, and I am indifferent and immune.' He focused again on James's face. 'You apprehend me?'

'Sir, I am commanded to——'

The light went out of Rennie's eyes, and he slumped in his chair. The glass fell from his hand and smashed in fragments on the stone floor. He began to tip thwartwise from his chair, and James jumped up and caught him before he fell.

James slung him across his shoulder and got him up to his bed—the captain was not heavy—and covered him over. Then James descended, found and lit a lantern, and went outside in the rain and chill. He led his horse to the rear and found a stable. He rubbed the animal down, fed and watered it, and returned to the house, exhausted. And exhausted he lay down in a narrow bed in an empty room, without undressing, and fell at once into deep slumber.

He woke to bright sunlight, and the sound of knocking.

'Sir?' Shaking Rennie's shoulder. 'Sir? You must wake up, now, if you please.'

Rennie gave a great snort, rolled violently out of bed, and stumbled to his feet. 'What? What?'

'Tea, sir.' Indicating the tray on the table. 'I have brought you tea—and this.' Holding up a sealed letter. 'The bearer was most insistent that it should be answered without delay. Today, in fact.'

'Bearer? What bearer?'

'He waits downstairs.'

'Does he, indeed.' Scratching his head, scowling. 'Then he may go away, until I send for him.'

'He has been paid to wait, sir.' Patiently. 'And to take your reply.'

'Is that tea, James?'

'Aye, sir. It is.'

'Thank God. Hm. Will you—will you be so kind as to pour me a cup, hey? My hand ain't quite steady when I wake sudden.'

James poured tea, and handed him the cup. Rennie sucked it down greedily. 'Hm, yes, again.' Nodding. James poured a second cup, and then a third. Colour returned to Rennie's ashen cheeks. James stood back a little, avoiding wafts of stale breath. Rennie drained his third cup of tea, fumbled for and found his chamber pot, relieved himself in a copious stream, thrust the pot away under the bed, and sniffed deep.

'Now, James. What is the despatch?'

James handed him the letter. Rennie broke the seal, and opened the letter. A moment, another moment, and he cursed under his breath, then aloud:

'The bloody wretches! The villains!' He strode to the window and glared down at the young man waiting with his horse.

'The bearer himself is not one of them, sir.' James.

'What?'

'He is not responsible for what is in the letter, certainly.'

Turning away from the window. 'No no, in course he is not.'

'It cannot be from the Admiralty, else they would have entrusted it to me.'

'Admiralty! No no, it is infinitely worse. The worst possible news, James.' He flung the letter down next to the teapot.

'I am sorry to hear it.'

'Not so damned sorry as I am. They intend to dispossess me of this house. To throw me out.'

'D'y'mean——'

'The blackguardly wretches. I have scarce buried my beloved wife, and they surround me like a pack of wolves, baying for my blood. God damn them.'

'Will I send the young man away, sir?' James, walking to the window, glancing down.

'Hm?' Rennie looked at him. 'Hm?'

'Do you wish to send a reply by the messenger, or——'

'It is not her own family, James. It is her late husband's family. You see, they have never accepted me, never at all. I was like a common thief, to them. A footpad, that had crept into her heart in the night with only one purpose—to steal her fortune.'

'I had better send the messenger away, don't you think so?'

'No no, no no no. I must attempt a reply. I must write a reply.' Puffing out his cheeks. 'I am sorry there is no servant in the house, James. I am all alone here, quite alone. Will you be so kind as to go down and give the young man a glass of something, and ask him to wait? I will compose a reply, directly. I must shave myself, and find my pen.'

'There is hot water in the kitchen, sir.'

'Ah. Hah. Very good.'

'And I have found a bowl of eggs, if you will like to eat a breakfast.'

———— ≡◆≡ ————

James and Captain Rennie rode away from Dartmoor on the road to Plymouth, in bright sunlight. Captain Rennie had decided, in his reply yesterday to the cruel letter from the Hendlesham family lawyers, that he would not contest the family's claim on Belveer Crag Farm. He and James had spent a further night at Belveer, and Rennie had gathered his papers, packed up his few possessions, and put his affairs in order so far as he was able in the short time available. His dunnage would be sent on to the Marine Hotel at Portsmouth, where he was known, and where he intended again to take rooms. For now, he and James would make their way to Plymouth, and take ship there for Chatham, and proceed by ferry upriver from Chatham to London and the Admiralty.

'Might not we go to Portsmouth, sir?' James had suggested. 'Take ship for Portsmouth, and you could look at *Expedient* there? And then go on to London by turnpike coach. She lies there, if I am not mistook, at Portsmouth.'

'No no, it will be faster altogether to go by sea all the way, James. Have not their Lordships instructed me to come to them without the loss of a moment? In any event, it will cost us nothing if we go direct by naval cutter, or packet. There is always cutters and packets, and coaches cost money, hey? *Expedient* may wait a week or two longer.'

'Very good, sir.' James had abandoned any notion, now, of returning to Winterborne before going on to London. Their Lordships had been most particular in their instruction to him: he must not only find Captain Rennie, but accompany him to London. This suited Rennie absolutely, and he said so—among other things—more than once.

Taking James's arm before they left Belveer: 'I may probably have said certain things, James, when you came here. When you first came in I was in my cups, you know. Be so good as to disregard what I may have said. Will you?'

'Certainly, it is already forgot——'

'About all of life being lost to me, and the like? I was in my cups.'

'Indeed, sir.'

'Good, very good. I am a post captain, with my name on the list, and I am called to duty.'

'You are, sir.' Nodding.

'My duty is to my King, and to my ship—to *Expedient*.'

'Yes, sir.'

'*Our* ship, hey?'

'Ah, well . . .' He did not like to say that he had not again been commissioned in *Expedient* himself; nor that he would—having delivered up Captain Rennie—in all probability, according with his fervent hope and wish, be offered his own command. 'She is certainly yours, sir.'

'*Our* ship, James. And I must thank you warmly for agreeing to accompany me to London.'

'Well, sir—that is my very specific duty, by their Lordships' command. And in course, may I say, my very great pleasure,' he added.

'Thankee, James. It is my very great pleasure, likewise.'

Later, on the road, he said: 'To say the truth, was you not to've come when you did, James—well well, I might have—I might have done a foolish thing.'

'I am sure you would not, sir.'

'But ye did come, thank God.' A breath, sucked in and held, and his head turned away a little. In a moment he had gathered himself, and they rode on down through a wooded vale, the rolling moor hidden from them away to starboard, and slowly retreating in their thoughts.

At Plymouth—they rode briskly through the day, and arrived at nightfall—they found a naval brig sloop that would take them to Chatham on the morrow. James was greatly encouraged that his friend—although he still looked gaunt, and thin—had apparently recovered all of his old vigour, and his sense of himself as a serving sea officer.

This conviction was to be short-lived.

⊷ ⊰◊⊱ ⊶

Rennie had failed to join the captain of the brig, Commander Dobell, twice at his table in the small great cabin, and James made it his business to discover the trouble. He found Rennie lying in his hanging cot in his tiny cabin—temporarily given over to him by the sailing master—in a state of trembling discomfort; his face was very pallid and moist.

'I am a little fatigued,' he replied to James's anxious questions. 'It is only a slight fatigue.' He lay back in the narrow cot, then at once heaved himself up, and James saw that he was clutching his piss-pot, into which he vomited with wracking utterness.

At first James assumed that it was simple seasickness, an affliction many sea officers suffered after a period on the beach; James had endured it himself in the past. Rennie's condition did not improve. It deteriorated, until he was ghastly blue-white in the face, and lay in a demi-faint. There was no surgeon in the brig, and James prevailed upon Dobell to put Rennie ashore at Weymouth. James accompanied him ashore in the boat.

Ashore, Rennie was carried on a litter to the Harbour Inn, and under James's supervision put to bed. A doctor was summoned. By now Rennie was in a delirium, fitful and babbling one moment, sweating and groaning the next. The doctor gave Rennie a drug to calm him.

'He has suffered a spasm,' said the doctor outside the ground-floor room James had engaged for Rennie.

'D'y'mean a stroke?'

'I do not. He has suffered a spasm, that may very probably have been brought on by something he ate, or drank, but not by that alone——'

'He is poisoned, then?' A glance at the closed door of the room.

'Nay, not poisoned, neither. A crisis has been caused—precipitated—by an event.'

'Seasickness?'

'I think not. It is something more.'

'Yes . . . ?'

'Yes. And now, sir, since neither the good captain nor yourself is a local man, I must ask—with respect—I must ask for my fee.'

James paid him. 'But what is your diagnosis? That is—what is the treatment?'

'Those are two distinct things, sir. The first is spasm. The second is rest—bed rest, and a reduced diet. Broth.'

'For how long?'

'Just so long as it may take, sir.' A judicious pursing of the lips, a glance at the door. 'I will look in again in a day or two.'

And he went away, leaving James to fret and puzzle, and decide. The decision did not take him long to reach: Rennie must be kept in his bed here in Weymouth until he was wholly well—until he was hale. James wrote a quick letter to their Lordships, explaining the delay, regretting it, and giving his assurance that Captain Rennie would come to London as soon as he was recovered and able. He sent the letter back in the boat to the brig, with instructions to the midshipman to deliver it into the captain's hand.

James then engaged a room for himself—the large upper room, with a view of the harbour—and sent a message to Catherine at Winterborne, explaining that he was detained at Weymouth, and why, and asking her to join him. The infant James might safely be left in Tabitha's care a day or two, might he not? Would Catherine come to him alone?

Catherine came the day following, at a little after four o'clock. She was alone, and James's heart lifted for the first time since he had ridden away in the rain from Birch Cottage.

＊＋＝＊＝＋＊

Catherine had travelled to Weymouth in their neighbour's carriage. Mr Brimley, that James and his wife had come to know well, was a slightly eccentric country gentleman who had spent time at sea as a boy and was well disposed to the Royal Navy. He had not come to Weymouth himself on this occasion, for which both James and Catherine were glad. Brimley was an admirable fellow in his way, he was inclined to be gallant with Catherine, and was invariably kind—but his notions of conversation were ebullient and declarative, and best suited to a more jovial circumstance than the present one.

'Where is Captain Rennie?' Catherine had asked at once. 'Does he require to be nursed?'

'The doctor has seen him, and will come again.'

'Yes, James—but who is at his bedside, who tends him hourly?'

'Hourly? I don't know. There is maids in the hotel, that——'

'Oh, James, certainly he cannot be left to scullery girls, with mops. He must be nursed.'

'Surely—you do not mean that you will nurse him?'

'In course I must try, James. Poor Captain Rennie.'

'Is that altogether necessary, my darling, d'y'think? I had hoped to give you some respite from your nursing duties at home, by suggesting you leave your child in Tabitha's care——'

'Our child, is he not?'

'Our child. I had hoped that we might be alone together——'

'Yes, I know.' Fondly, smiling at him. 'And in due course we shall. But first I must be assured that Captain Rennie is quite comfortable, and has all that he needs.'

And James had shown her into the sickroom, where Rennie lay palely asleep. Catherine was dismayed by his gaunt condition, and at once began making arrangements. She summoned the landlord's wife. She gave her instruction about foodstuffs and their preparation; she gave instruction about the fire and how it must be kept burning bright; the window and fresh air; the changing of bedlinen; the need for hot water at any given hour; for the curtains to be changed at once to muslin; for basins, ewers, jugs, spoons, water glasses. James observed her in part astonishment, part consternation.

'What has become of the bewitching creature I married?' he wondered. 'That I wished to come here to me, and spend a few stolen days of bliss? I am married to an housekeeper, that has the beginnings of a scold in her, in her voice and manner. This ain't what I planned, nor wished for. Not at all.' And he found himself put quite out of temper by the whole business, and did not care any more that Rennie was gravely ill. Were not his own needs more important? 'In due course!' he muttered savagely to himself.

And in due course he came to his senses, saw that Catherine was not a scold, nor anything like, that she was simply doing what was right, and that he had been wrong. He had determined, when Catherine should arrive, to retrieve his horse Jaunter from Mayhew's Yard, to hire another horse for Catherine, and to ride with her in the neighbouring country. They would, he thought, be alone together, romantically alone, in a way impossible since the earliest days of their marriage. He abandoned these plans, and sent Jaunter home to Winterborne with a hand from Mayhew's.

'It was foolish to've kept the animal here at Weymouth at all. I should have sent him home before I went to Dartmoor. All I have done is spend money on stabling for nothing.' And having thus grumbled his way back to moderate good humour, he contented himself with looking over the fort, walking about the town, and waiting for Rennie to recover his health.

Catherine saw to it that her evenings were free of nursing duties, so that she might dine with her husband, alone in their room—as they had in those first few days of their honey-moon—and recover something of the early joys of their union.

Captain Rennie did recover. It took the better part of a week, since for many weeks before this he had neglected his diet and his health, abandoned regular habits of life, and had drunk to excess, in an effort to assuage his grief, and misery, and despair. Had in truth so neglected himself that the attending physician was of the firm opinion that an early return to full health was an impossibility.

'Do not you think, perhaps, that the doctor wishes simply to extend the period of his visits, and thus increase his fee?' Catherine had asked James privately. 'Captain Rennie is already much restored.'

'You are very astute, my darling. The doctor is a grasping fellow, that wants his payment daily—insists upon it.'

'He does not quite approve of me, I think.'

'Don't approve of you!' Indignantly.

'He thinks I am too much in the sickroom, too attentive there. I am an usurper of his medical opinion and position— his gravitas.'

'He thinks that, does he, the impudent fellow? Then we don't want him any more, I think. I shall pay him off, and he may go to the devil.'

And he did pay the doctor off, on the morrow. Rennie improved steadily under Catherine's care, and at the end of a week he was strong enough to rise, dress and walk along the harbour wall a little way, and take the air in James's company. Presently:

'We must really take ourselves out of this and away to London, James. It is all very fine your beautiful wife tending to me—and never think I am ungrateful—but we cannot linger here. We must not.'

'I am ready whenever you are ready, sir. I am at your disposal.'

'Very good, very good.' Turning his head seaward, sniffing the breeze. 'Yes, James, we will go to Portsmouth after all, I think. I don't mean to stop there, however. I wish merely to look fleeting at our ship, and make sure of her, as it were, and then go on at once by coach to London. Hm. Look fleeting, hey? Hhhh. A capital joke, that. Fleeting? At a ship? Hhhh.'

And James saw that Rennie really was recovered. But was he recovered quite enough to take a further heavy blow, a blow that James himself must soon deliver?

*

Roman Tangible, boatswain of HMS *Expedient*, a Perseverance class frigate of thirty-six guns, was—as one of her standing officers—never far away from her. In usual he lived aboard, but at present she was refitting and he was living out of the ship, lodged in the town. *Expedient* lay moored in the second channel, below the ships in Ordinary, immediately outside the great basin of Portsmouth Dockyard. Roman Tangible was supervising her re-rigging; he had reached an accommodation with the foreman rigger, through the good offices of the master shipwright: Mr Tangible gave the instructions, the foreman rigger relayed them as if they were his own, and the rigger artificers did the work. Mr Tangible would tolerate no fault of workmanship, no delay, no excuse. He was very rigorous.

This morning he concerned himself with the foremast futtock shrouds, the staves, and catharpins, and made known his displeasure in the question of burton pendants.

'Served?' he demanded of the foreman rigger. 'You call them pendants served?'

'I do say served.'

'Tuh. Mff. We will see about it when I have my own people—that is all I will say, today.'

'I am glad I ain't *serving* wiv 'im, at sea,' the foreman muttered to his mate, as Mr Tangible descended from the top, his hands taking nearly all of his weight on the shrouds, and his feet dancing nimbly down the ratlines. 'A right bastard, 'im,' said the foreman.

'Ain't all boatswains bastards, though? Rope's-end bastards?'

They watched him go ashore in the boat.

At about that same time, James Hayter came to the dockyard gate with Captain Rennie. They had been put ashore in the packet boat—the packet having brought them from Weymouth—at the Hard, and now Rennie was intent on that quick look at *Expedient*.

'We will not go aboard her,' Rennie had decided. 'We will

look at her, and see the progress of the refitting, and then come away. After all, James, we are not yet commissioned official, hey? We have not been given our papers, nor our instructions. This little visit is strictly *un*official, in truth.'

'Yes, sir. As you say: unofficial. There is something I think I must tell you——'

'In a moment, James. I think I see Mr Trent, our purser.' Pointing. 'Through the gate, there. D'y'see him? Mr Trent!' Advancing toward the gate.

James followed him. 'Is that Mr Trent, sir? Are you sure? I think it cannot be him—unless he has halved his tonnage.'

The marine on the gate nodded them through; both officers were known to the yard.

It was Mr Trent. He had indeed discarded a great deal of his former weight, and his colouring was markedly changed. Formerly he had been rubicund; now he was merely pink.

'Mr Trent!' Rennie, making for him purposefully, his hand raised.

'Captain Rennie, sir!' Pleased, his hat off and on. 'I am very delighted to see you again, sir. You are—' peering at his still gaunt face '— you are quite well?'

'Indeed, indeed. But are you quite well, Mr Trent? You are thin.'

'It is due to our doctor, entire.'

'Doctor Wing?'

'Aye, sir. Thomas Wing has had a remarkable effect upon me, upon my whole life. He has transformed me. I had what might be called an episode, a peculiar episode, following on an heavy meal, and Doctor Wing took me under his—he advised me, most particular.'

'Hah, did he? Well well.'

The image of Dr Wing, who stood not above four foot six inches in his shoes, taking the large Mr Trent under his arm, protectively, made both Rennie and James smile. But both of them had cause to know how valuable a medical man Dr Wing was, and how fiercely determined he could be in pursuit of his principles, and their smiles were sympathetic rather than sardonic.

'I am glad Wing is at Portsmouth,' said Rennie. 'I would like to——'

'Not at Portsmouth itself.' Mr Trent shook his head. 'He is at the Haslar presently, at Gosport, assisting Dr Stroud.'

'Ah. Well. At another time then, when we return from London, where we go this afternoon. Do you go to *Expedient* now, Mr Trent?'

'I was about to take the wherry across to the Weevil, sir, but I could just as easy accompany you aboard *Expedient*, if you wish it. She ain't stored as yet, in course.' Hastily added.

'No no, Mr Trent. You go across to the victualling yard, and we will look at the ship. Glimpse her, you know, just glimpse her, and be on our way.'

'In that case, sir, I shall bid you farewell for the present.' His hat off and on again, and he went about his business.

'Sir, if you please . . .' James, earnestly. 'I must ask for a moment of your time.'

'What?' Rennie turned and looked at him. 'Hm?'

'There is something I must say to you, sir. I do not think it can be delayed any longer.'

'Very well.'

James began to speak, but now the din of the dockyard was all around them. Through the rasping of saws and the shouts of artificers, through the wafting stink of tar and sawdust and dung, through the reflected dazzle of the great mast pond, a dray trundled past the two sea officers, its wheels grinding dully on the cobbles, and the horses' hooves clopping loud.

'So you see, sir, I am——'

'Didn't hear a word y'said, James.' His hand cupped to his ear. 'Come, say it all again as we walk.'

James took a deep breath. 'I do regret it very much, you know—but I fear that I will not be joining you again in *Expedient*.'

'Not be joining me . . . ?' Staring at him. 'What on earth d'y'mean, James?'

'I mean, sir, that in all probability, in all likelihood—I shall be offered my own command. And so, you see . . .'

Rennie stared into the distance, toward the great block of the rope house, his mouth a little ajar. At last, an intake of breath, and:

'Yes—yes, I do see.' Looking at James again. 'I had made an assumption. I had no business to make it. In course, you *deserve* your own command.' Nodding. 'Well well, that being so, I need not detain you, James. You will not wish to look at a ship with which you are no longer concerned. We will meet at the Marine Hotel at noon, as arranged? To take the afternoon coach? That is, if you was still intent upon going up to London . . . ?'

'I am very sorry to have offended you, sir, but I——'

'No no no, James. You have not offended me, good heaven. I must not think always and exclusive of my own career. You have yours. You wish to move up. I will not detain you, now.' And he lifted his head, squared his shoulders, and strode away across the yard.

'He has took it hard,' muttered James to himself, and sighed as he turned and made for the twin pillars of the gate.

The noon gun found James waiting at the Marine Hotel. He could not have avoided travelling in the coach with Rennie; even if Rennie had implied that it was a matter of choice for James, it was not; he must accompany Rennie to London and the Admiralty. Their luggage—the term dunnage did not quite fit their simple impedimenta—had been taken from the packet's boat to the hotel, and now lay there under the care of a porter. The coach would depart in thirty minutes, at half past noon sharp, from the crowded High Street outside the hotel. James peered along the street, then returned to make sure of the bags—a large valise of his own, brought by Catherine to Weymouth in Mr Brimley's carriage, and two bags of Rennie's.

James nodded to the porter. 'I am just going down to the coffee house, I shall be a few minutes. If Captain Rennie should come back here before I do, will you say to him——'

'Yes, sir, you has already told me. I am to detain him, until you return.'

'Not detain, good heaven. With my compliments, say to him that I will not be long.'

'Yes, sir, cert'nly. You go on to the coffee 'ouse. I shall be 'ere.'

James nodded again, irked that the man should find him a nuisance, and made his way out into the street, and along to the coffee house. All manner of horse-drawn traffic filled the street, and the miasma of chaff, dust and stale dung hanging in the air caused James to lift his vinegar-sprinkled handkerchief to his face as he hurried down. The day was warm, and the stench of the Point drifted up the thorough-fare, adding to the already noisome atmosphere. James ducked inside the coffee house with relief, and sat alone at a small table.

He ordered chocolate, and settled to wait. After a few minutes, when the pot of chocolate had been brought to him, he called for paper, pen and ink, and dashed off a quick letter to Catherine. Coins to a boy, who brought wax and then took the sealed letter away. The chocolate lay forgotten at his elbow as he glanced at his watch—and saw that the half-hour was nearly gone. Further coins, dropped hastily on the table, and he hurried out again into the street. James did not see the dark-clad man that followed him out, nor notice him following as he made his way back to the Marine Hotel. The man was unremarkable in appearance, in clothing, face, manner—all but invisible in the crowd.

Rennie was not at the hotel.

'Surely you have seen him?' James, vexedly to the porter. 'I described him to you. Spare, middling height, in a naval coat and hat.'

'And I would of seed him, sir, most cert'nly—was he come here. But he is not come. He has not arrived.' Firmly, closing his eyes in certitude, shaking his head.

'But that is quite absurd.' James walked again into public rooms of the hotel, stared about him, in a doorway bumped against a large gentleman in a plum coat—who frowned in indignation—and nearly fell over two young ladies who were hurrying to meet two lieutenants of marines. James sighed, struggled back through the press of people, looked all round a last time, and stepped out into the street. The coach was filling up. His and Rennie's valises had already been taken out by the porter and stowed. If Rennie did not come at once they would be obliged to travel on the outside. James had secured inside seats—at a pound apiece—but almost certainly all of the seats inside were twice sold, and it would be a matter——

'James! James!'

He turned, and saw Rennie, very flushed, waving to him from across the street. Rennie plunged into the traffic. Twice he was nearly knocked down—by a dray, and a cart—and then he was at James's side.

'Decided to pay my respects—whhh—a little out of breath, James—pay my respects to the port admiral. You remember him, certainly, Admiral Bamphlett. Alas, he was not there——'

'We must get aboard, sir, without the loss of a moment.'

The bellow of an ostler, and the answering bellow of the coachman, grand in his caped coat and tricorne, his whip poised. Horns sounding. Six horses shuffling and snorting in the traces.

'You have secured inside seats, James? Then there is no need of undue haste. I am wanting breath as it is—whhh . . .'

'I have secured seats, sir, yes, but I——' Pushing Rennie without ceremony toward the coach. 'I think we may be very lucky to *secure* them, in truth.'

They did secure them—just—and the coach, with much cracking of whips, and blowing of horns, and bellowing from ostlers clearing the way, lurched into the traffic, and began the long journey to London. At one side, opposite to the hotel, the dark-clad man watched their progress, until the coach moved out of sight, then he slipped away up the street to another inn, the George, and hired a horse in the yard at the rear.

━ ⚓ ━

London, on the following day. James and Rennie, having spent the night at Mrs Peebles's private hotel in Bedford Street, where they were made comfortable after their long journey from Portsmouth, had decided upon a walk in St James's Park, to take the air and stretch their legs before going to the Admiralty. They strolled through the avenues of trees and along the canal, then went through from Birdcage Walk to Great George Street and on to the foot of Whitehall.

As they came into Whitehall:

'Did you see that, James, just now?' Rennie, in a disapproving tone, glancing back over his shoulder.

'See it, sir?' James tucked fingers in his stock, and adjusted his hat, and brushed a little dust from his coat. He wished to look smartly turned out when they arrived. 'See what?'

'That woman, back there.'

'I did not see her, no. Have a care for your feet, sir, there is much dung.'

'Yes, it is a damned disgrace. Where are their crossing sweepers, I wonder? But did not you notice that woman, pissing in a crouch by the wall? A most shocking thing, in broad daylight.'

'I did not notice. But this is London, after all—anything may happen in London. You will recall what Dr Johnson has said.'

'Johnson?' Again glancing back.

'Aye, he said: "London is a city famous for wealth and commerce and plenty, and for every kind of civility and politeness, yet it abounds with such heaps of filth as a savage would look on in amazement."'

'He said that, did he? Then he is a wise fellow.' A sniff.

'Should we engage chairs, then, d'y'think? And avoid the filth?'

'Chairs! Certainly not, James, when we have the use of our legs.' And he strode up Whitehall toward Horse Guards and the Admiralty. From away to the right, and the direction of Westminster Bridge, came the wafting stink of the river on the east wind. James stamped something off his buckled shoe, scraped the shoe on the cobbles, and followed, catching Rennie up as he crossed at King Charles Street and lifted his hat to a lady and a gentleman that crossed in the opposite direction. This couple in turn passed by a nondescript man in a dark coat, who had paused apparently to consult his watch. He quickly put away the watch, and walked on up Whitehall at a discreet distance behind the two sea officers in their dress coats, and tasselled dress swords.

He watched them go in at the Admiralty, made a note on a slip of paper, tucked it in his sleeve, and walked on without haste toward Charing Cross, and a building there, hidden in a lane off the Strand.

Inside the Admiralty building Rennie and James—having made their presence and their business known to a minor official, one of the dozens of clerks employed in their Lordships' service—were taken into a side room, an ante-room, and asked to wait. There was no window, but there were four chairs and a diminutive table. The bare floorboards gleamed.

Here at the centre of things naval standards of cleanliness clearly prevailed. Rennie found this reassuring; James found the atmosphere austere, and rather bleak. But soon his duty would be done. Rennie had made no further mention of their discussion at Portsmouth, it was as if James had not spoken of their imminent official divergence. Was that a good thing?

Presently, after some twenty minutes had passed, they were asked by the clerk to go into the adjoining office. Here there was a window, but it looked out on a wall, and the light was not greatly better than in the anteroom. A desk, books, a cabinet, chairs. The same gleaming floor. A figure rose from the desk.

'Ah, Captain Rennie, good day to you.'

'Good God.' Rennie, peering, then recovering: 'That is, you are Mr Soames, are you not?'

'I am.' Bowing. 'Soames, Third Secretary.'

Rennie nodded. 'Yes, hm. I had understood . . .' glancing at James '. . . from their Lordships' letter, that we was to interview Lord Hood, that Lord Hood would——'

'I fear you are mistaken, Captain Rennie.' Smoothly, touching a fine lace handkerchief to his nose, and tucking it in his coat. 'With respect, Lord Hood is not even in London. He is at Chatham. Today and tomorrow both, at Chatham. His Lordship has many important matters on hand, above your ship, sir.' A faint, unbending smile.

'Ah. Ah. Then who are we——'

The nearly noiseless opening of an inner door, by the cabinet on the far wall, the slightest creak of hinges, and:

'You are to interview me, Captain Rennie.'

'You, sir!' Rennie could not keep the dismay from his voice. James stood perfectly still, perfectly correct, his hat under his arm. Sir Robert Greer walked in, glanced briefly at Mr Soames—who left the room at once—and laid his silver-topped ebony cane on the table at the side.

'Me, sir.' The same not quite booming voice, vibrant and deep, the same utterness of self-possession, the same black coat and silver-buckled shoes. The penetrating eyes, black as coal, turned on James.

'Mr Hayter, you have done your duty, and I thank you.'

James bowed. 'Very good, Sir Robert. If I may I will wait outside—with your permission.'

'Wait outside? Why?'

'I have—I have accompanied Captain Rennie to London, sir, to the Admiralty, as I was required to do, and now I think that my duty is complete, is it not?'

'It is not even begun, sir. Gentlemen, let us sit down. Soames!' Taking a document from his pocket, and laying it on the desk.

'Yes, Sir Robert?' Soames, appearing at the inner door.

'We will like a decanter of sherry, and some biscuits, as soon as it may be arranged. And then we are not to be disturbed before half an hour.' He sat down at the desk. 'Now, gentlemen.' A pinch of snuff, from a small silver box. 'Now, then—your new commission.'

Rennie had sat down, but James remained standing. Sir Robert looked at him—an impatient, peremptory look, but James:

'I do not quite understand you, Sir Robert, with respect. I do not know quite why you include me in this new commission. It has been made clear to me by their Lordships that I was not to rejoin *Expedient*, and that I would very probably be given my own——'

'Sit down, sir.' Not harshly, but firmly. 'Allow me to apprise you of your future duty, if y'please.'

'Very good, sir.' A glance at Rennie, and James did sit down. 'However, if I may iterate——'

'Y'may not, Mr Hayter, just at present. Ah, yes, on the desk.' To the servant who brought in the tray of sherry and biscuits. Sir Robert waited until the servant had withdrawn, closing the door behind him with a click, then:

'I am instructed and authorized to say to you both that their Lordships, in considering your previous service to the nation, have decided that to separate you would be an imperfect disposition of your abilities as captain and lieutenant of one of His Majesty's most valued and important vessels. Accordingly, it has been decided that the abilities adduced will again be of best use to the King in a new commission in that vessel, HM *Expedient*.'

James exchanged another glance with Rennie, a glance that said silently he wished whole-heartedly to be glad, but could not be glad—under the circumstances.

'I know that you had looked to be moved up—is that the expression, Mr Hayter?' Sir Robert poured sherry.

'Yes, sir, it is.' Stiffly.

'Had looked to be moved up, and that you are therefore perhaps aggrieved because you find your rank unimproved.'

James was silent. Sir Robert pushed a glass of sherry toward him. James ignored it.

'In course, you will not refuse the commission?' Sir Robert poured another glass of sherry. 'A new commission to a ship officer, any new commission, is better than lying upon the shore, ain't it?'

'No sea officer would wish to be left on the beach, sir.' Again stiffly. 'However——'

'Indeed, sea officer. A very lamentable fate, that you would wish to avoid, yourself?' Pushing a glass toward Rennie, who took it up.

'I would, sir.' James, a breath. 'However, that don't mean——'

'What is our new commission, Sir Robert?' Rennie interrupted him. 'D'you hold our instructions, written out?'

'I do hold them, Captain Rennie. In a moment I shall refer to them in detail. But first I will like to propose a toast to your further success.' Holding up his own glass. 'To you, gentlemen, and to your ship.'

Rennie raised his glass. James glanced at him, at Sir Robert, at the glass on the table—then reached for it, and held it up. Stiffly held it up, and stiffly said, in concert with the other two: 'To *Expedient*.' And drank off the contents in one furious swallow.

Sir Robert began to inform them as to their new duties. Rennie listened with full attention, and took in every word, but James—while he made himself look attentive, leaning forward a little and inclining his head—scarcely heard anything Sir Robert said. When he had finished speaking Sir Robert gave the document to Rennie, gravely put it in his hand, nodded and leaned back. Rennie glanced through the pages, and looked up in surprise.

'But where is my commission?'

'Your commission? You have it in your hand.'

'No, Sir Robert, I do not have it in my hand. My name is not mentioned in these pages. All that is said is . . .' glancing down again '. . . yes, it says only "The officers of the ship" and . . . and . . . yes: "The duties of these officers, in the said ship", and so forth. I am not mentioned, neither is Mr Hayter.'

'It is simply the form in which the document was wrote out, Captain Rennie.' Sir Robert's bloodless lids closed over his eyes, and he shook his head in reassurance. 'Nothing more, nor less.'

'Do not think me impertinent, Sir Robert—but "form" will not do, you know, in the Royal Navy. I must have my warrant of commission before I may assume command of my ship, my named ship. So must Mr Hayter have his warrant, also. Again, do not think me impertinent, but in usual these warrants are granted by their Lordships—wrote out and their signatures and seal attached, in this very building.'

'Then no doubt the warrants will come to you, Captain Rennie.' Entirely unruffled, rising. 'And now I must take my leave of you.' Grasping his cane. 'Soames!'

'Sir Robert?' Soames, at the inner door, the sleeve of his dark coat shining a little at the elbow.

'Is my carriage . . . ?'

'Your carriage is waiting, sir, indeed.'

'Thankee, Soames.' Walking to the door. 'Excellent sherry.' A last backward glance at Rennie and James. 'Gentlemen.' And he was gone.

Rennie took a deep breath, drank off his sherry and poured half a glass more. 'Well well, it is a most demanding task he sets us, James, hey? Demanding, but we are ready for it.'

'Ah, yes.' Nodding, a half-smile.

'I had rather we had got our warrants today, but never mind. I am in no doubt they will come to us at Portsmouth.'

'Yes, mm.'

'We must have our papers. We cannot go aboard her, official, until we are both properly commissioned to do so.' Swallowing his sherry, and putting down the glass with a self-busying sigh.

'No. No.' Nodding.

'On second thought, we had better secure the warrants today. They are here, in the hands of one of those furtive clerks that lurk about the upper floors, hid beneath unpowdered wigs, hm?' Rennie was enjoying himself. He slapped the instructions purposefully against his palm.

'Yes, sir. No doubt you are right.' Distractedly, staring at the wall, at nothing.

Rennie straightened his back, and let the document fall to his side in his hand. 'Come come, James.' Gently. 'You must not permit vexing sentiments to get the better of you. You must not allow y'self to think that ye've missed your best chance, and so forth. Your chance of command will come, in due time.' A breath. 'For the present you are a sea officer, with a commission, with duties—and a fine ship in which to carry them through. Yes?'

'Yes, *Expedient* is a fine ship, sir.' Turning, putting down his sherry glass.

'Well, then . . .' Peering at James, a slight frown.

Mr Soames now came back into the room, swinging the inner door open in a way that suggested—clearly suggested—he was a man determined to resume possession of his own quarters without further delay:

'If you are quite ready, Captain Rennie? If you are quite finished?'

'Yes, yes, Mr Soames. Yes, we are ready, thank you. James?' Rennie held out a hand, nodding toward the outer door.

'Very good, sir.'

Outside, in the passage, Rennie said to the clerk who had brought them to Soames:

'Is Commodore Maxwell here, today?'

'I believe he is, sir, yes.'

'Good, very good. Will you say to him that Captain William Rennie is here, and would take it as a kindness if the commodore would permit me a moment of his time.' When the clerk had gone: 'He is an old friend, James, lost a leg in '82, and now husbands the Admiralty charts. He will like that touch, I think. "Permit me a moment of his time." Hey? He will think that a neat touch. And then he will open a door and say a word, and get us those damned warrants, and we may make a start for Portsmouth.'

'I do not wish it.' Suddenly coming to a decision, and facing Rennie.

'Eh?'

'I do not want my warrant of commission, sir. I mean to resign it, and return to Dorset.'

*

James was at Vauxhall Gardens, by himself, rather drunk. He had gone there in order to indulge himself. Had paid his half-crown, then a pound for a box, deliberately to indulge himself and become inebriated, before returning to Dorset. There he would have to explain to Catherine what he had done, and tell her that he meant to go into the merchant service, to sign John Company's papers, and make his fortune in command of an Indiaman. That was preferable, was it not, to allowing himself to be ill-used by the Admiralty? Preferable to further years of impotence on the long list of lieutenants RN? In course it was. But he needed to purge himself of all his frustration and anger before he went home, to rid himself of the sense of betrayal and bitterness he had felt when Sir Robert Greer made clear the official position. He would purge himself in pleasure, then go home and write the necessary letters—in addition to his letter of resignation, already delivered—that would set his life upon a new course.

And now Mr Soames found James, sitting alone in his box, amid many boxes crowded with merry-makers; alone and morosely drinking a bottle of champagne, and staring out at the bright-dressed throng beneath the coloured lanterns and the spreading trees.

'Mr Hayter, I am right glad I have been able to discover you. I had thought to have very grave difficulty in the press, but here you are.'

'Soames!' Looking at him morosely. 'What d'y'want of me?'

'Well, now, Lieutenant, it ain't what I want, exact.' With mild asperity. 'It is what I am instructed to do. Asked to do. I am asked to show you something, Mr Hayter.'

'Show me what?' Irritably, draining his glass.

'Something of singular interest, to persuade you to give up your——'

'There is nothing you could show me would make me change my mind. I have resigned. The letter was left at the Admiralty today, as you are well aware, I think. Please to leave me alone, will you, Mr Soames? I am at my leisure now.' Refilling his glass.

'Ah, well, I wish that I could leave you alone, sir. I do. But I cannot. I may not.' His peculiarly astringent cologne wafting from the lace kerchief he brought from his sleeve to his nose.

'Damnation, Soames.' A glare, then: 'Oh, very well, you had better sit down. I did not mean to bite off your head, nor behave ungentlemanlike. Will you join me in a glass of wine?'

'Thank you, I will.' Soames sat down. 'A little refreshment will be welcome—before our journey.'

'Journey . . . ? You there, I say!' Waving to a girl with a tray of glasses. He ordered another bottle of champagne, and took an extra glass for Soames. 'Journey? I may tell you, Mr Soames, that I intend to remain here, all the evening.'

Waving vaguely about him. 'It is very gay here, no? I shall remain here, and drink my fill.'

'I will happily help you to drink another bottle of wine, but then we must be on our way.'

'Your way, Soames, not mine.' A pull of wine. 'Where do you go?'

'To Chelsea, Lieutenant—to Chelsea, where there is a man who wishes to say something to you.'

'What man? Don't want to see him. Don't propose to go to Chelsea, neither—not now, nor at any other time.' Turning to look Soames in the eye. 'Nothing he could say to me would make me change my mind, d'y'apprehend me? You waste your time, you know, if y'think otherwise. Hey?' Nodding. Another pull of wine. 'Very good.'

'Drink up, Mr Hayter. It will aid you in what you are going to see, and hear.'

By the time Soames had persuaded him to get into the carriage that he had ordered, James had arrived at a condition of reckless amiability, blithe adventurousness, and vague hope of amorous encounter. In little, he was very drunk. At the back of his mind as he stepped into the carriage had been the increasing certainty that if he did what Soames asked of him, he would end the evening in the arms of a courtesan. Soames had given him broad hints. Soames would arrange it, had arranged it, and all would come delightfully right. He fell asleep.

When he woke as the carriage arrived at Chelsea, James was blearily aware that they had come to a great building. A building that stretched away into the distance, tall windows lighted from within.

'What is this place?'

'It is our destination, Mr Hayter. Pray follow me.' A sharp glance in the lantern glow. 'Are you able? You are not ill of wine?'

'I am entirely able, thankee.' And blearily he stepped out of the carriage, missed his footing on the down-folded step, and nearly fell on the gravelled ground. His balance recovered, James found himself at Mr Soames's heels. Soames, who was entirely sober, and brisk, having allowed James to drink all but a glass of the second bottle of wine, skirted the great façade of the building, crossed a courtyard, and entered by a side door—a door that was open. The smell of beeswax, cold stone, and lamp smoke.

A staircase of stone, with a metal banister, Mr Soames ignored. Now he took James's arm at the elbow, opened a second door—they had turned down a panelled corridor— and led him through. A second, narrower, wooden stair— again ignored, and yet another door. Soames turned the knob, ushered James through, and stood back. James was aware of dim light, not unlike the glimmering light 'tween decks in a man-of-war, at night. The room was long, and low, and windowless—and the air was uncomfortably stale.

'Nay, foul . . .' he muttered to himself. His eyes smarted with lamp smoke in the gloom.

'Are you hhhere . . .?' The intimate whispering voice startled James. Intimate, yet oddly emphatic, as if it had whispered in an echoing cave.

James advanced a little, stumbled over something, felt himself clumsy—peered. Was there a fire there, in a grate, at the far end? A glint of metal in the coal-red glow. A figure.

'Sso pleassed you hhhave come . . .'

'I have come,' said James loudly. 'Don't know why I am here, though. Who are you, sir?'

'I am the prisoner . . .' The sibilant whisper grated on James's nerves. The fumes of wine had turned to iron filings in his mouth, and his head ached. The insistent voice: 'I am to tell you the truth . . .' Again the glint of metal, and to his amazement James saw that the figure addressed him through a silver speaking trumpet, a quarterdeck trumpet.

'Why d'y'whisper at me?' demanded James. 'Who are you?'

'Captain Dance-in-the-Dark, I am. Captain Firefly-in-the-Dusk-hhhh . . .' The trumpet shaken in the air, and a drop of spittle hissed in the grate.

James stood still a moment. 'Mr Soames!' he called. 'Mr Soames, are y'there?' Silence. 'Why have you brought me here?' Silence. And now James felt the hairs prickle at the back of his neck, and a cold hand clasping at his entrails. He hesitated a moment, and then drew his sword. Took a breath of the foul air, and advanced toward the glow of the grate. In a warning tone:

'I am brought here I know not why, and I don't like it. Any sudden jump, any sudden movement at all, will result in two foot of steel in your guts. D'y'hear me?'

'Run me throughh, I beg you . . . Aye, run me throughh . . .'

The smell of a long-unwashed body, and a glimpse in the smoky, dim glow of a filthy dress coat, a naval coat, and of bare feet in the coal dust at the stone hearth.

'Good God, who are you?' James advanced a step closer. 'Are you a sea officer, sir?'

'Ain't ye going to run me throughh? Ohh, what a shhame, what a shhame and a pity . . .' The silver trumpet lowered. Then as quickly raised, and the husking voice, now more earnest: 'Hobgoblin I am not. I am not even quite mad, not yet. Almosst, though. Driven near to it. I am ruined, you ssee. Brought low in dissgrace. Reduced to thisss . . . ssickness and ruin, bankruptcy and disshonour . . . by the actions of a *monsster* . . .'

'I am not one for riddles, sir. Speak plain, else I shall walk away from this.' Still holding his sword ready, glancing all about him, then looking again at the slumped figure. 'D'y'hear me, now!'

The figure appeared to recognize this tone of voice, its ring of authority, and responded—in a more confiding tone, softly in the trumpet's throat:

'Ssir Robert Greer-hhhh . . . is a name you know . . . ain't it?'

'I know him.'

'Ahh, do you? Do you? I am glad-hhhh . . .' A waft of stale faecal odours, and unrinsed breath.

'Well?' Impatiently.

'Thiss . . . iss hiss doing.'

'What is? That you are living here like this, in filth?'

One bare foot stirred against a chamber pot, and the contents of the pot slopped and settled, sending forth a stench that made James turn his face aside with a wince of disgust. And now he saw something that chilled him, that caused the cold hand to clench within him, banishing the last numbing effects of wine. A great iron bolt and ring were fixed to the wall, and from that ring fell a heavy chain, lost in shadow behind the figure slumped by the fire. James leaned, peered, and saw that the chain wound in under the figure, and was fixed to a leg.

'Christ's blood, you are shackled.'

'I am.'

'And—and Sir Robert Greer has caused this to be done? You are confined by his order?'

'I am.'

'In God's name, why?'

The hapless officer began to snuffle, and sob, and bowed his head. James bent down to him, steeling himself against the stench, and repeated the question. And now the prisoner gripped his wrist, and held it fiercely. Bringing up the trumpet to James's ear, the prisoner whispered:

'Ymusst do as Ssir Robert suggests, you know, Mr Hayter . . .'

'You know my name?' Attempting to pull free, and finding his wrist held tighter than ever.

'Elsse you will suffer ruin. Ruin like mine-hhh. A life imprissoned . . . becausse of the gold you never declared . . .'

'Gold!'

'Aye-hhh gold. That y'took off a French frigate far away-hhh, and divided among you-hhh. That you never mentioned in letters, nor journals, nor any papers-hhh.

Thoussands in French gold, Mr Hayter . . . I am correct-hhh?'

'Go to the devil!' Jerking his wrist, unable to free it. Feeling his head begin to spin.

'Ohh, I am with the devil-hhh. I am already ssupping with him. As you will . . . iff you do not do as you are told-hhh.'

'Who *are* you, damn your blood!' And now James gave a tremendous jerk, pulled free his arm, staggered back and pointed his sword. And felt a hand on his shoulder.

'No! No, Mr Hayter, I beg you. No swordplay, now.' And James turned to find Mr Soames, his kerchief held to his nose. 'There is no need of violence. The poor man is chained.'

'I know he is chained! Who is he? Who are you?' Turning again on the hunched figure by the fire.

'He will not hear you any more.' Mr Soames, a little shake of his head. 'He has lapsed into his quotidian stupefaction. We must come away.'

'Come away! Why in the name of Christ did you bring me here? Answer me!'

'I have done only as I was asked, Lieutenant. All that you have seen and heard here, you have seen and heard by another's instruction.' Mildly, tucking away the kerchief.

'Aye, Sir Rob——'

'A personage that will in course deny everything, if he should be accused. As will I. I have not brought you here. You was drunk, at Vauxhall, and invented the whole out of confusion.'

'What the devil d'y'mean?'

'I mean, Lieutenant, that you have been timely warned, timely warned and required to come to your senses and accompany your commanding officer, Captain Rennie, to Portsmouth, and there make your ship ready for the sea.' A smile of the mouth, never reaching the eyes. 'Please to follow me, will you? We will make our way to the carriage, and find your lodging, at the Strand. Mrs Peebles's hotel, ain't it? An excellent house, with quiet rooms and a good table, at very reasonable cost.'

'What of this poor wretch? Are we to leave him here, like this?'

'Unless you wish to join him, Mr Hayter . . . ?'

'I will come with you now, Mr Soames. But you have not heard the last of this, d'y'hear? I am not without connection, I am not without influence—and I will *not* be so used.'

'Indeed, indeed. This way, Lieutenant.' And he opened the door. James gave a last glance at the figure in the glow of the grate, then with a furious sigh quit the room in Soames's wake.

In the morning when he woke, James did wonder if he had not dreamed the whole disquieting episode. Had not invented it whole, involuntarily invented it in his addled head, in drunken disturbed imagining, from self-disapprobation. He had turned his back on the King's service, out of pique and petulance and resentment, because he had not been favoured with his own command, and this had made him— beneath the surface—miserably confused.

'My own mind has turned upon me, in sleep, and thrust my ingratitude and folly back at me in a lunatic nightmare,' he said to himself. 'A lunatic dream of whisperings, and chains, and dark accusation.'

Then as he lifted his razor to shave, he saw in the looking glass the mark of a bruise at his wrist, where the madman had gripped him, and the stink of the fellow came back into his nostrils. He knew that he had dreamed nothing, that everything had been real, and his dismay and anger returned. He stared out of the window unseeing a moment, then strode from his bedroom along the passage and banged on the door of Rennie's room.

'Nnnhh?' A sleep-muffled grunt from within. James took this as permission to enter, and he banged into the room. Rennie roused himself from his pillow and sat up, his sparse hair spiked on his head. 'What? Who is it, good God?'

'Was you aware, sir, of the gentleman held at Chelsea?'

'Oh, it is you, James.' Rubbing his eyes, a gaping yawn. 'What o'clock is it?'

A church clock answered, nearby. Eight tolling strikes. Rennie reached to the table by the bed, and fumbled open his watch.

'Sir, I must ask you again. Was you aware of the officer held there, at the hospital?'

'Eh? At the hospital?'

'So—you do know of him?'

'I do not. What officer? D'y'mean at Greenwich?' Scratching his head, a brief shiver.

'No, sir. The officer that is held by order of Sir Robert Greer at the Royal Hospital at Chelsea, chained up there. That knows all about our gold. That gentleman.'

'You have gone mad.' Getting out of bed. 'Belay that. You had already gone mad, yesterday, and resigned your commission.' A frowning look. 'You have spent the night in drink, no doubt.'

'In fact I drank champagne last evening, but I am entirely sober today, sir. If the officer chained up at the hospital knows about our gold, then so does Sir Robert Greer. You see?'

Rennie closed his watch-case, sat very quiet a moment, then: 'Begin again, if you please, James, and tell me everything. You was at Chelsea, and you saw an officer there, that knew Sir Robert?'

'Aye, he did. He described to me the circumstances of our acquiring the French gold at sea on our last commission—thousands of money. He threatened me, in truth, with a fate similar to his, if I did not do as Sir Robert asked. Said that I would be imprisoned, chained up in rags and so forth.'

'But—how has Sir Robert discovered——'

'We shared the gold, sir, you remember. Every man aboard was given his share. One of them has let it slip ashore, and Sir

Robert—that has spies everywhere in home ports—has heard of it, and now——'

'But, good heaven, why does Sir Robert behave in this fanciful way? Why did not he confront you himself, hey? Unless in course he——'

'He did not know of my intention to resign my commission when he left us yesterday. I did not know it myself until afterward. It was only then, when Sir Robert had already gone away, that I came to my decision and informed you, sir, and wrote my letter. I was at the pleasure garden later, and Mr Soames found me there, and took me to Chelsea in his carriage.'

'Ahh, Soames—yes, I see. He was the intermediary, that led you to this unfortunate officer—what was his name?'

'I do not know.'

'Don't *know*? Surely you was introduced to him by Soames?'

'No, not exact.' And James described the circumstances of the encounter in detail. Rennie listened in careful silence, then:

'Yes—yes.' An intake of breath, a nod. 'Plainly, it is a threat to us both. We are both to do as we are told in our new commission. You are required by Sir Robert to withdraw your letter of resignation, and I am cautioned not to think of resigning in turn, if I could not have you as my first.'

'Oh, well, the officer at Chelsea did not say your name, sir—did not once mention it.'

'He did not need to, James. His task was to mention the gold, in the guise of a madman, through that absurd speaking trumpet.' Smiling grimly.

'*Guise?* Oh, no, sir. This man was certainly——'

'Yes, he was certainly—Sir Robert himself.'

'That ain't possible! The fellow was a stinking, babbling, barefoot wretch, chained up!'

'You saw his face?'

'Well, I—I saw the shape of his face. The light was very dim, and he lifted the trumpet when he spoke——'

'Exact! Exact! You never did see his face distinct, and his

voice was disguised by whispers, and by that damned trumpet! I tell you, James, the man you saw was Sir Robert Greer, I will stake my warrant of commission on it.'

'But *why*? Why would he go to such lengths?'

'Because there is more to our new commission than he has told us, much more. We should know him by this—know that he will never say all of the truth if he can say half of it, or less. He is a man wedded to disguises and subterfuge and intrigue, to gain an advantage. He is as honourable as a bilge-dwelling rat, or a sea worm burrowing under copper, the fellow. We know that he——'

'Had you noticed a man in a dark coat across the street, yesterday?' James, at the window, peering down.

'Eh?' Striding to the window. 'Have you found another madman, James? Is it Sir Robert again, hm?' Laughing. 'I can see no particular man, only people walking down to the Strand from Long Acre . . .'

James stood beside Rennie, and looked again. 'He has gone. But he was there, near to that barrow, not half a minute since. I could swear I saw him there, yesterday . . .'

Rennie turned away from the window, and presently, his tone altered:

'Listen, James, I said "our commission" just now, and I hope that it may be so. Unless you mean to defy Sir Robert and quit His Majesty's service, after all? I leave for Portsmouth this morning . . .' taking up his watch again '. . . at nine o'clock. I urge and entreat you to come with me, with all my heart. Withdraw your letter, and come. Will you do it?'

James stood very quiet a moment, his head bowed. At last he made his back straight, and:

'I had better order a quart of tea, don't you think so, sir? When we have a long journey ahead?'

And he rang the bell.

PART TWO: THE DUTY

Six Cleveland bays drew the coach at a brisk six miles an hour through the leafy countryside south of London. Rennie and James, having again secured inside seats—Rennie had paid this time—were dozing, seated opposite each other at windows. On Rennie's side—the forward-facing side—were two gentlewomen, perhaps mother and daughter, or aunt and niece. On James's side were a portly gentleman in a coat of elaborate cut and decoration, a silk-and-foil-woven waist-coat, a powdered wig, and buttoned gloves, who carried with him an air of deep self-approval; and his diminutive and nearly silent wife, in her lace bonnet. Their journey would take all of twelve hours, and they would arrive at Portsmouth, at the Marine Hotel in the High, in darkness.

At Martyr's Ground, a mile or two south of the village of Cobham, the coach was waylaid. All of the inside passengers were now more or less somnolent, and brought into full awareness only when the coach abruptly slowed, then came to an abrupt, skidding halt, amid shouts, whinnyings of alarm from the horses, and much upset of luggage. The stout man, seated at the other window on James's side, pulled down the glass and thrust out his head.

'What has happened?'

A man on a black horse now rode forward to the window. His head was covered by a broad black tricorne, and his face by a black cloth mask. He struck the stout gentleman a blow to the head with the butt of a horse pistol.

'That has happened!' he said in a fierce, muffled voice. 'And worse to follow if you pushes out your head again!'

'Good God,' said Rennie as the stout gentleman staggered back and fell in his lap. His wig had come off, showing him to be entirely bald, with a nasty blood-leaking gash on his scalp. His wife came at once to his aid, with a little cry, and tried to staunch the flow of blood with her handkerchief. The two other ladies sat as if frozen, handkerchiefs clutched to their faces, eyes staring in terror.

The door opposite to the opened window was now wrenched open by a black gloved hand, the hand of a second horseman.

'The two officers will please to step down!' he instructed.

'Two officers?' Rennie looked at James. 'Can he mean——'

'Yes, sir.' James, in urgent *sotto voce*. 'I think he does mean—ourselves.'

'The damned scoundrel, the damned villainous——'

'Step down now, gentlemen, if you please!' A horse pistol was now aimed at Rennie through the open door, and there came the nervous snort and stamping of its owner's mount, as if the animal itself were urging Rennie to comply.

'We must do as he says, sir,' murmured James. 'We cannot risk the lives of these ladies.' He smiled reassuringly at the ladies, nodded and smiled. The ladies looked at him as if he were quite mad, and shrank back further into the seat. Rennie extricated himself from the slumped form of the stout, wounded gentleman, stood with his back bent, and descended by the down-folded step from the coach. The pistol was withdrawn as he came out, and the horseman urged his animal back. As he did so James—behind Rennie—thrust his captain heavily to the ground, drew a pocket pistol from his coat and shot the horseman full in the neck. The horseman lost his hat, gave a terrible throttled gasp, and sagged in the saddle. The horse pistol tumbled away from his hand into a clump of grass by the roadside, and James leapt out of the coach, keeping his head well down, and drew the second of his pair of pocket pistols.

'Damnation, James!' Rennie, on the ground, in anger and alarm. He attempted to rise, and James pushed him flat with his foot.

'Stay where ye are, sir, for Christ's sake.' And he turned, his back to the side of the coach as the other horseman rode round from the rear. Turned and aimed—and fired. The flinted lock snapped, there was a spark in the pan and a puff of smoke, and nothing more. The weapon had misfired. The horseman rode at him, and James was obliged to jump clear. He cocked his pistol again, and snapped it, but the priming powder was all burned, and the weapon useless. At the same moment the horseman fired his holster pistol. The heavy ball fizzed past James's left ear, grazing the tip. The explosion of the shot and the near miss at such close range had deafened him and made him lose his balance, and he staggered. Blood dripped from his ear, and in a daze he saw the horseman unholster a second great pistol, and aim it. From nowhere, as it seemed, Captain Rennie now ran at the horseman, sword in hand, and lunged. The blade went through the horseman's cloak, through his shirted front, and into his breast. It went deep, with a cleaving rasp, and it came out glistening red. The horseman made no sound, but his second pistol discharged and the ball struck the road and spun away through the branches of a tree with a whine. His mount shied, reared up, and the slack body in the saddle fell awkwardly and heavily into the road and lay still. The horse skittered clear, its eye rolling, and took off at a rein-trailing gallop toward Cobham.

'Are you wounded, James?' Rennie, over his shoulder.

'I am all right, sir. A near miss.'

'Very good.' Rennie pushed at the body on the ground with his foot, and wiped his blade on the dead man's coat.

'Sir, look out behind!'

The remaining horseman, sagging and bloody, but still mounted, had urged his horse forward, and was in the act of raising a cutlass to serve as a lance—a lance with which to cut

Rennie down. Rennie turned neatly aside, brought up his sword and tore the cutlass from the horseman's grasp with a powerful flick. He stood with his feet together a split second, in the classic point, thrust forward, and ran the man through.

A moment after, having ascertained that the man was dead, Rennie turned angrily on James: 'Now. Why did you push me to the ground?'

'I wished to have a clear line of fire, sir.'

'But you was pushing me down a second time, with your foot! Had I no right to defend myself? Why did not you allow me to rise, and fight?'

'I'm sorry, sir. My only wish was to preserve your life.'

'Did not I preserve yours, instead? When I was able? When I was let up?'

'Indeed, sir.' Himself checking that both men were dead. 'Indeed, that is so, and I thank——'

'No no, do not flatter me. I do not wish to be flattered, good God.' Wiping his blade with grass, and sheathing it.

'I am very sorry, sir, that I have offended you . . .' Stiffly.

'Well well, never mind, it is all done, and both of us live and breathe. Is anyone of you hurt?' Pushing his head into the coach.

James walked to the front of the coach, where the Clevelands stood uneasily still in the traces. There he found the coachman strangely silent in his high seat, and climbed up there. The coachman sat staring at the sky, his throat cut. His assistant was sprawled in the other seat, his skull split by a pistol butt, and blood dripping down his lifeless face. James, who had seen great injury and bloody death at sea, found himself trembling. Violent death in this peaceful, bucolic place, with the green of England all around, and birdsong, and the reassuring smell of horse-dung, was a very horrible thing to him, now that he was safe, and his hand shook as he gripped the mounting rail to climb down.

'Nobody is hurt in the coach,' said Rennie, 'excepting the other gentleman, that has a sore head.' He looked at James, and noticed his bloody ear. 'Are you badly injured? You are very waxy in the face, James.'

James told him about the coachman and his assistant. Rennie brought a flask from his coat. 'Take a pull on this, and then I will like one myself.' James drank, and handed back the flask, and Rennie took a long sucking swallow. 'This is a wretched business, by God.' Wiping his lips, and thrusting the flask away in his coat. 'We must think what to do, James, and make a plan without delay. We cannot stay here, we must get on to Portsmouth and make a report.'

⊰✥⊱

'Your coachman killed?' Admiral Bamphlett slowly reached across his desk, opened the pounce box and scattered powder on the document where he had just signed it. His expression was strained, and his face—in usual of a high colour—was pale. His appearance was in every way correct, his stock correctly tied, his waistcoat buttons shining clean, his coat brushed, yet there was about his clothes the suggestion of a not quite accurate fit. His breeches were slightly too voluminous, his coat at the shoulders a fraction too wide. There was about him too an air of apprehension, even of fear.

His appearance dismayed both Captain Rennie and Lieutenant Hayter. To them the port admiral was sadly diminished not just in his person, but in his demeanour. He had lost weight, and the bones of his face stared out, emphasized by his pallor and anxiety of expression; his movements were effortful, hesitant, slow; since they had last seen him he had grown—old.

'Your coachman killed?' he repeated. The notion seemed to bewilder him.

Rennie and James exchanged a glance.

'We was neither of us harmed, sir,' said Rennie, 'nor anyone in the coach. We made our way here without further trouble. We are ready to proceed with our commission, and to receive our sailing instructions.'

'Instructions?' The mouth open, gaping open, the hand poised above the inkstand; slowly he withdrew it.

'In course, sir, when you are ready to hand them to us. There is no pressing——'

'Ahh. Yes. Instructions. Hm. I wonder, gentlemen, I wonder—will ye be so kind as to allow me a day or two to gather together . . .' He put his hand on the edge of the desk, leaning on it for support.

'Perhaps this is an inconvenient moment, sir, to make our duty to you.' Rennie glanced again at James. 'We will not detain you now.'

'No no, Captain Rennie. No no. You must conduct your business as an honourable and dutiful sea officer, sir. And I must accommodate you, hey? Ffff . . . A sudden wince of pain, and Admiral Bamphlett stiffened. 'Ffff . . . hmm . . . Forgive me, gentlemen, it is this damned thing again. Doctor Wing attends me this morning.'

'Thomas Wing, sir?'

'Aye—your surgeon, Rennie. An admirable man, indeed. He is going to put me right this forenoon, when he comes to me from the Haslar.'

'Then you are indeed in good hands, sir. With your permission, we will leave you.' And the two officers bowed.

As they vacated the port admiral's office, Dr Wing was coming up the outside stair. His diminutive form, in new blue coat, white waistcoat and breeches, appeared to swell with pleasure as Rennie and James came toward him. He paused a moment, when warm greetings had been exchanged, to acquaint them of the port admiral's trouble.

'Yes, he is gravely afflicted,' he nodded. 'It is a stone, a bladder stone. I must relieve him of it.' He lifted his instrument case, and nodded.

'Here, at his office?' James was surprised. 'Not at the hospital?'

'At his own insistence. I should have preferred the hospital myself, but he fears that was he to cross the water to Gosport, and go in at the gate—he would never come out again.'

'How—how will you relieve such a damned painful thing as a stone?' wondered Rennie, looking askance at the instrument case.

'My own method, a slight variation upon Dr Stroud's, is to make the incision with a curved bistoury, as opposed to a straight scalpel. Cut with a curved instrument, pointed with a probe, locate the calculus, employ the forceps to open the incision, and then at once with the tenaculem hook it out— so to say—into the dish. All with the utmost swiftness, that is the essential and indeed the vital thing. The incision is then closed up . . . Are you ill, Captain Rennie?'

'I am—I am quite well, thankee. In need of air, a little, the day is close. I will just step outside.' Nodding, swallowing, nodding again. An attempted smile, that failed, and he did go outside.

When James came out into the daylight a moment later, and looked for his captain, Rennie was nowhere to be seen. He found him in ten minutes, at the coffee house on the corner of the High, drinking a large measure of brandy and his face regaining a little hint of health.

'Ah, James, there you are. I had thought you was lost.'

'Oh no, sir. Not lost.'

'Well well, we cannot waste time in idle chatter in such a place as this.' Draining his glass. 'Just pay the fellow, will you? I have forgot my purse.' And thus restored and invigorated, he strode into the street.

They went on to *Expedient*, were rowed out to her at her mooring, and jumped up the side ladder into the waist. They had come last night to Portsmouth not in the coach, but in a hired carriage, hired at Cobham and driven by a hired stablehand. The other passengers they had been obliged to leave, not entirely to themselves but in the care of the stout gentleman, when he had recovered from the blow to his head.

Rennie and James had arrived very late at Portsmouth, had slept at the Marine Hotel, and this morning had gone to the port admiral's office to make their report. Now, as they went aboard *Expedient* and glanced about at her half-dressed condition, James said:

'I am still concerned, you know, about the whole affair, the whole business. I think that perhaps we was not thorough enough in the question of reporting the assault upon us to the proper authority.'

'James, James—to whom could we have done so?' Looking aloft, then forrard, and frowning. 'To a magistrate, at Cobham? To the local squire, or the military barracks? Hm?' Peering aft now, from their position on the waist gangway. 'No no, my dear James, we did our best for our fellow passengers when we brought an end to the assault, and despatched those two blackguards to their fate. Mister—what was the fat fellow's name . . .'

'Baxter, I believe.'

'Aye, Baxter. Well well, he was clearly a man of substance and position, and so forth. It was his duty to manage things, when we had to come away.' Turning. '*Mr Tangible!*'

'Sir, I am obliged to suggest to you——'

'Y'will oblige me, James, by aiding me in getting the ship ready for the sea, now that we are come aboard. *Mr Tangible!*'

'I will find Tangible, sir, with your permission.' His hat off and on.

'Yes, thankee, James. Do so, do so. I am not satisfied with his progress, not at all.'

'But before I do, sir—if you please—should we not ask ourselves *why* we suffered such an attack? We did not discuss it last night, on that weary journey, but now . . .'

Rennie fixed his gaze on his first lieutenant, a glaring gaze, and was disposed to be fierce, but relented. 'Yes yes, yes yes—I had thought the same. *Why?* I had thought the same. But it will not do, James, simply to speculate. We do not know that they sought us out, in particular, to attack us. They saw our coats, that is all, and thought: here is rich pickings.'

'Did not one of them say: "The two officers must descend"?'

'Did he? Perhaps he did.' A pause, a decisive sniff, and: 'We cannot speculate. We must not allow ourselves to be caught up in some damned interminable investigation into a simple highway robbery. Good heaven, such depredations happen all the time. A Cabinet minister was attacked in Hyde Park not long since, threatened at pistol point, and robbed. If officers of the government itself cannot escape the attentions of these ruffians in London, how may mere sea officers do so, in the broad countryside. Hey?'

'You do not think—I mean, you do not wish even to consider that they may have had another motive? That they may have been sent—deliberately engaged and sent—to kill us?'

Rennie was dismissive: 'Ha-ha, then palpably they failed, James, since——'

'They killed the coachman and his assistant in cold blood.'

'——since the circumstances was reversed, and——'

'Did they not, sir?' Acutely, looking at Rennie.

A sigh. 'Ruthless and desperate men will do anything, James—commit bloody murder in cold blood, as you say— for a handful of gold coins.'

'Ruthless I will concede. But desperate? Those well-groomed horses were not the mounts of starving, crazed and desperate brigands, nor their cloaks and hats, that were fine made.'

'Hm. Hm. You had better find Tangible now, James, before I lose my patience.' Striding aft, clasping his hands behind his back.

'Very good, sir.'

James and Rennie had not earlier discussed the attack on them by the highwaymen—in the confusion and upset

immediately after, nor on the long, burdensome journey that
followed, at jolting, dashing speed through the gathering
night, when each had endeavoured to compose himself, and
reflect on their narrow escape from death. They had arrived
very late at the Marine Hotel, had had to rouse a grumbling
porter to admit them, and had then gone exhausted to their
beds.

Now as he went below to discover Mr Tangible, who was
not aloft, nor on deck, James felt himself more than ever
bemused, confused, out of sorts. He did not properly
understand the new commission, not yet, since he had not
listened to Sir Robert Greer's exposition at the Admiralty, and
it had scarcely been mentioned since. He was not at all
sanguine about the attack upon them at Martyr's Ground. He
missed Catherine sorely, and felt that he had left her, when he
and Rennie took ship from Weymouth, in unsatisfactory
circumstances. Their time together at Weymouth had been
marred and curtailed by Rennie's illness and Catherine's self-
imposed duties in attending on him, and then ended by the
pressing need for James and Rennie to make their way to
London and the Admiralty. He had scribbled only a brief note
to her since. He had got drunk in London at a pleasure garden,
and would readily have slept with a harlot if the opportunity
had arisen. In little he had not thought, felt, or behaved in an
husbandly way. Had he? He had not, and was troubled.

'Mr Tangible!'

He found the boatswain in the forward part of the orlop,
with lists of cordage and a lantern, and together they made
their way by the ladders to the upper deck, out of the stink of
the bilges.

'Ripe, a little, below. Hey, Mr Tangible?' As they came
into light and fresher air.

'We gets used to it, sir.'

'Indeed, we must all do so, when we begin to live in the
ship. The captain is aft, I believe, Mr Tangible, and anxious
to confer with you.'

'Do we go to the West Indies again, sir—this commission?' Dousing his light.

'Not so far away. The Mediterranean, I think.'

'The Rock is it, sir? Or t'other end, the Levant?'

'I have the notion it is convoy duty, Mr Tangible. More than that I cannot say at present.'

'Convoy? That means pirates then, don't it? Corsairs, that means, in the Med.'

'D'y'think so? They will not trouble us, I think. Was we at war, and fighting French ships, I should be concerned, but we are in the peace. There is nothing to fear from poorly armed corsairs, in the peace.'

'If you say so.' Tangible, dubiously.

James nodded, and left the boatswain with a cheerful: 'Yes, I do say so. I have dealt with corsairs before this, and they are poorly armed, frail little ships—no match for an English man-of-war.' He stepped up into the main shrouds and began to climb, and the boatswain went aft to find the captain.

From the maintop James looked out over the dockyard and the harbour, south to the square tower and the fortifications, east over the church and the town, and west across the water to Gosport, the church spires and official buildings there—the Haslar behind its walled gates, and the storehouses of the Weevil. Gulls swooped and scolded, and on riding ships pennants and signal flags streamed and flapped in the steady breeze—a topsail breeze, he reflected—and the water down at the harbour entrance glittered and ran under the cloud broad sky. Hoys ran before the breeze, and a cutter in the distance. Ashore he could see drays, carts, wagons. Bustle. Movement. The business of a great naval port.

'Should I ask Catherine to come to me?' he wondered. 'Should I take rooms at the Marine Hotel and send for her? Or must I turn my back on such things, shift my dunnage into the ship, and resume my life as a dutiful sea officer?'

'I should send for her, by all means.' A voice behind him. He turned in surprise, gripping a shroud, and:

'Tom! Tom Makepeace, by God!'

⚔

Lieutenant Tom Makepeace had last been in *Expedient* three years ago, her first commission. He had not gone in her to Jamaica on her second cruise—although he had been commissioned to do so—because of a serious family matter involving his father, who had since died. He readily supplied details of his life on the beach to James as they stood in the top and watched the great activity ashore in the yard, and all round the harbour.

'It was the very devil to work through all the papers, James, when my father died. Not a thing I would recommend. Engage lawyers, I should, when your own father dies.'

'He is quite well. And anyway, such melancholy work would fall to my brother that is a lawyer.'

'Yes, no, I didn't mean . . . Any rate, I was kept busy weeks and months together. If it had not been for Josephine I think I should've run mad.'

'Josephine?'

'My wife.'

'You are married! My dear Tom, my heartiest congratulations.' Shaking his hand.

'Thankee, James.' Pleased. 'Aye, we was wed six months ago—well, no, it is nigh on a twelve-month, to say the truth. I have brought her with me, in course.' Smiling, nodding.

'Here, to Portsmouth?'

'Yes, certainly.' Still smiling, a deep happy breath, leaning against the maintop rail. 'A man and his bride must be together, until he sails. That is why I said—just now—that you must certainly send for your own wife.'

'You propose to live out of the ship, until we weigh?'

'Well, yes . . . do not you?'

'I—I had thought of it, yes. But I don't know the captain will allow us both to—— Well, we shall see. I wonder, Tom, if you are to be second . . . I assume you are second?'

'I have my warrant, thank God.' Patting his coat pocket.

'I am very glad. I wonder, who is to be our third, d'y'know?'

'No, I do not. I have come direct from Cambridge.'

'Does Bernard Loftus come with us again as master? Does young Alan Dobie join us?'

'Dobie! I had forgot his name, and was trying to think of it in the coach. Alan Dobie, aye, the schoolmaster.'

They went through several names from memory, of former shipmates they hoped to serve with again this new commission.

'You have not seen the list, then?' asked Makepeace.

'I have only this minute come aboard, Tom, with the captain.' And he gave him an account of their narrow escape in the turnpike coach the day before, and of their earlier meeting at the Admiralty with Sir Robert Greer—but he left out all of the peculiar circumstances of his drunken evening at Vauxhall Gardens and later at Chelsea. Nor did he mention that he was commissioned again in *Expedient* as her first against his will, and that he had wished and believed himself entitled to his own command. To reveal such things was not conducive to good discipline in the ship, he thought, nor good sense.

'You have not seen the captain?' James asked Makepeace, now.

'No, I came aloft as soon as I saw who was in the top, straightway after I came up the side from the boat. But you are right, I must make my duty to him at once, and present my papers, else he will be vexed with me. How is Captain Rennie?'

And James told him about Rennie's wife.

'The poor fellow.' Subdued. 'You and I are lucky men,

James—are we not?' And he climbed down very soberly, and went below, leaving James to reflect on their luck.

⊶ ⋝◆⋝ ⊶

'Never heard a word he said, James?' Rennie frowned at him. 'Never listened to anything Sir Robert told to us?'

'No, sir. My mind was elsewhere, at the time.' Standing before the table in the great cabin, his hat under his arm.

'Good heaven, James.' Mildly but reproachfully. 'Well well, then I expect I must acquaint you with our duty myself. Indeed, it will allow me to reacquaint myself with it—with the detail. We had better have Mr Makepeace in here, too, hey?'

'Very good, sir.'

'Mr . . .' consulting a paper '. . . Mr Upward ain't yet in the ship. Or is he come?' Looking up at James.

'The third lieutenant is not yet with us, sir.'

'Hm. Hm. You know him—Upward?'

'I do not, sir.'

'Nor do I. I was informed that I should get a Mr Radcliffe as my third, but then a letter came to say he had got his own command. Clearly an officer of high connection.'

'D'y'mean—Mr Harald Radcliffe, sir?' asked James.

'Aye, James. They have made him master and commander and given him a ship sloop at Port Royal. He is welcome to that station, he is very welcome to that climate, and the fever there.'

'So Harry Radcliffe has got his own command.' A bitter sigh.

'You know him?'

'I knew him as a midshipman, sir, we berthed together. And now he has got his own command, and he's a year my junior, too . . .'

'Come, James, you must not think on things you cannot alter. Your thoughts and duties lie here, in *Expedient* —not at

Jamaica.' A sympathetic nod, eyes briefly closed. 'Just tell the sentry to pass the word for Mr Makepeace, will you?'

James did as he was told, and presently Tom Makepeace joined them, and removed his hat.

'Sit down, Mr Makepeace—you too, James. Now then, a splash of something, I think. Cutton!'

His steward appeared, hastily thrusting his shirt into his breeches. He was unshaven, and his hair stood up on his head. A waft of rum.

'A bottle of—are you ill, Cutton, or half asleep?'

'No, sir, arstin' your pardon. I was labourin' with your dunnage, sir, and——'

'Labouring with my dunnage? My dunnage was stowed as soon as I came aboard.'

'Yes, sir. It is the shirts, sir. See, I was endeavourin' to press them, sir, as they was crushed in the chest. Crushed very severe, and the mateeril of the cloth very recalcitrous to a smart appearance, requirin' that they be pressed, sir.'

'And your own appearance, Cutton? Is that recalcitrant also, in your view?'

'If you mean that I ain't pressed myself, sir—that is so, when I am signed on willing.'

'Aye, willing to make bad jokes, and not quite sober in the bargain. I will deal with you presently. Fetch along a bottle of Madeira, right quick.' A glare.

James kept his face straight, and pretended to look out of the stem gallery window.

Their duty, this commission, as outlined by Sir Robert Greer, was to sail—calling at Gibraltar—into the Mediterranean, and thence to a place on the coast of Tunisia, Rabhet, there to assemble a small convoy of ships, and subsequently escort that convoy to England.

'What is the convoy, sir?'

'D'y'mean, what is the cargo of the ships, Mr Makepeace?'

'That in part, yes, sir. But also—who owns these ships?'

'Ah. Well. That I do not know just at present, nor the cargo, neither.'

'Sir, asking your leave—ain't that strange, a little?'

'That is not for me, nor you, nor any of us to say, Mr Makepeace. What I do know is that their Lordships have seen fit to send us there—when our refitting is completed—to send us there as the strongest possible escort for these ships. In usual a ship sloop would be sent, or even just a brig sloop. In this instance, a frigate has been deemed necessary and advisable.' Lifting his chin and glancing above their heads, entirely unaware that this—in James's silent opinion—made him look slightly pompous and absurd.

'Since there is no better frigate in the Royal Navy, gentlemen,' Rennie continued, 'a fact we have proved on more than one occasion, the task has fallen to us.' Nodding, a confirming sniff.

Had Tangible been correct about the danger of pirates? wondered James, but not aloud. If not, why all this damned mystery? Well, mystery was always present if Sir Robert Greer was——

'You frown, Mr Hayter.' Rennie was looking at him.

'Was I frowning, sir? I beg your pardon, if I was.'

'Come now, that is not an answer. What troubles you? Speak plain.'

'No, sir, nothing. Nothing, I assure you—I am simply eager to get to sea.'

'As are we all, I think. Just so.' A deep breath, and he rested his hands on the spread of papers and lists before him on the table. 'Now then, is Dobie with us yet?'

'Not yet, sir.' James shook his head.

The breath exhaled in a sigh. 'Well well, I must have a clerk. I cannot proceed another day without a clerk. If Dobie don't show himself by this afternoon I must find a man in the dockyard.'

'D'y'mean to put a dockyard clerk on the ship's books, sir?' James, in surprise.

'No no, I certainly cannot press a landman clerk into sea service. I meant an useful, experienced man that can tally, and write matters down, and aid me with . . .' shuffling papers '. . . with all this burdensome work.'

'But—only until we weigh.'

'Aye, until we weigh.'

'And then, sir . . . ?'

'And then—by then—Dobie will have come. *Cutton! Where is our wine!*'

When James and Makepeace had drunk a polite glass of Madeira they left the captain to his papers in the great cabin, and went forrard into the waist.

'It is a damned odd convoy, James, that has got a fixed port of departure, but the owners do not care to tell us what their ships carry—ain't it?' Makepeace, as they went.

'Not half so odd as my own experience in London,' said James, and he told his fellow officer about his very rum encounter with the chained man at Chelsea, and the subsequent ambush of the coach on the road from London.

'You think there is a connection between the two things?'

'I don't know that I do think it—it is all so damned peculiar. We may only hope that these events are not a portent for the commission, else we shall be in troubled water from the moment we weigh.'

Makepeace now looked at him with a very sombre expression, and James laughed.

'Good heaven, Tom, I am in jest. I simply don't believe in portent.'

Makepeace smiled in relief. 'I am glad. You was beginning to make me anxious.'

'Is that Alan Dobie, in the boat?' James, peering over the side.

But it was not *Expedient*'s erstwhile schoolmaster and captain's clerk; it was merely the purser Mr Trent—the new, trimly Mr Trent—returning to the ship from the Weevil.

— ⊶ ⊰⊱ ⊷ —

Catherine had not come to Portsmouth, as James had hoped she would; he had proposed taking a small suite of rooms at the Marine Hotel, and installing her there, but Catherine had answered that Tabitha—who was growing old—could not again take care of the infant James by herself without great strain and trouble, and that to bring the baby boy to Portsmouth, to an hotel, was not a suitable thing. Reluctantly, very reluctantly, James had abandoned the proposal, and Catherine stayed at home in Winterborne. In consequence, James felt himself obliged to send for his dunnage and live aboard the ship, in the half-prepared gunroom.

Neither had Lieutenant Makepeace's plan to live ashore with his wife, Josephine, until *Expedient* was ready for the sea, been met with unfettered approval. On learning of his second officer's idea, Rennie had sent for him.

'You are aware, no doubt, that the first lieutenant is living in the ship?' Looking up from lists.

'Well, yes, sir, but I had——'

'And as you observe I myself am living in the ship, Mr Makepeace.'

'Yes, sir, I see that you are, but I——'

'D'ye think it fitting—when the ship's two most senior officers are aboard, undertaking their duties day by day—d'ye think it wholly felicitous that a junior lieutenant should make it his business to loll about in hotels ashore, sir, living a life of ease and contentment?'

'In course I do not think it, sir, when you put it like that. I would not have described myself as "lolling", under any circumstance. I merely wished to live ashore for a short time with my wife, sir. If we are to go away on foreign service, then

I had hoped you would understand my wish to do so.' Stiffly.

'Don't assume that bleating tone of voice, good God.'

'I am very sorry, sir.'

'We are called to duty in a commissioned ship of war.'

Makepeace remained silent, looking straight ahead, his back straight, his hat under his arm.

'You carry a warrant of commission, signed by the First Lord, and duly witnessed, d'y'not?'

'I do, sir.'

'Then rise up to it, Mr Makepeace. Y'may visit your wife ashore, but by God you will live in the ship. D'y'hear me?'

'Yes, sir. Thank you.'

'Very well.'

Makepeace very correctly, very stiffly, turned round and walked to the door, and was about to fix his hat square on his head, when:

'Mr Makepeace——' A self-censuring sigh, and Rennie rubbed the back of his neck.

'Sir?' Turning round.

'I did not mean to bite off your head. I am right glad we are to be together again, as *Expedients*.'

'Indeed, sir, as am I.' Unbending a little.

'You are a valuable man, a damned good sea officer.' Tapping the table. 'Well well, I will allow you to live ashore with your wife a few days, after all. Until the week's end.'

'I thank you, indeed, sir. That is most kind in you.' Warmly.

'Only until then, you mark me.'

'Oh, indeed, sir.' A brief hesitation. 'I was very sorry to hear of your loss, sir, of your bereavement.' It was the first time he had felt able to mention the death of Rennie's wife, and for a moment he was unsure how Rennie would respond. The moment became long, then:

'Thankee, Mr Makepeace.' A flick of the eyes, a nod. 'You are kind.' Another nod. 'Hm. Very good. Pass the word for Mr Trent, if you please, as you go out.'

'Aye, sir.'

Rennie watched as the cat stood on the side locker near to his desk, and without great difficulty—almost elegantly—kept its balance against the movement of the ship. At first Rennie watched the animal with casual attention, drank his tea, and busied himself with pen and journal and pounce box. Then he found himself watching the creature with more than passing interest; within a few minutes he found himself fascinated, and laid his quill aside.

The cat had been brought to him a day or two before they had weighed and and sailed from Portsmouth. Mr Adgett, the ship's carpenter, with nobody else to bid him farewell, had brought into the ship his very plain spinster sister, with whom in usual he lodged ashore during those occasions when the ship was repairing and refitting. Mr Adgett had no sweet- heart, no wife, no female companion of any kind save his sister, and at her insistence, for she wished to satisfy her curiosity, he showed her his working arrangements afloat. These had dismayed his sister, a fact that she very ably concealed by her customary tight-lipped expression, but she decided—there in the odoriferous cramped demi-darkness of the orlop storerooms—that to make her brother the gift of a cat would be most shocking unkind to the cat, that was little more than a kitten, which she had brought into the ship concealed in a wicker basket. She could not entertain the notion that the poor beast would be obliged to live in such conditions—she had caught sight of a rat scuttling away from the lantern glow—even if her brother was quite used to them. She had in course once or twice in the past been aboard the ship, but never before into the depths.

'And not never again, neither,' she told herself as she lifted her hem to go up the ladder, clutching the loop of the basket in her other hand, and endeavouring to breathe through her mouth. 'The poor creature must find a home upstairs, in the fresh air.'

On deck, amid the confusion of late-loading stores from a hoy, Mr Adgett had introduced his sister to Captain Rennie, as a courtesy. Rennie—preoccupied, searching for his clerk Alan Dobie and the purser Mr Trent both—had nodded politely, and found the wicker basket thrust into his hand. Thrust with an earnest plea:

'I would only ask, sir, that you do not think of drowning, if it do not suit. Please, sir, never do think of drowning.'

'I will not, madam. Hm. I will never like to think of that. Hm.' And in his head: 'Good God, poor Adgett, his sister is quite mad.'

And he took the basket from her with with a strained, polite grimace of kindliness. Going aft, he had called:

'Cutton! Colley Cutton, where are you!' Holding the basket away from his person. God knew, after all, what it might contain. 'Ah, now. Take this, whatever it is, basket, and——'

A plaintive mew from within.

'Yes, sir?' His steward, hovering.

Another mew, very plaintive, and insistent.

'Good heaven, is there an animal in the bloody thing?' Staring at the basket.

'I spec'late it is a cat, sir.'

'A *cat*, good God?'

'Comes in very handy in a ship, sir, cats. Right handy, when there is rats, which we has.'

'Well well, I do not want it in my ship, thankee.' Holding the basket away from him.

'If you will permit me, sir, I should very much like to care for the cat myself, sir, if——'

'No no, I cannot even consider it. It is a fact that dogs in a ship bring bad luck, and a cat is no more than an inferior dog, I am in no doubt.' Looking about him for somewhere to put the basket.

'Then—then what is to become of the poor cat, sir?' Tentatively holding out a hand, then withdrawing it.

'Eh?' As another burst of heartfelt mewing rose from the basket. 'Is not it the custom to drown unwanted cats?—No, wait, I cannot drown the wretched beast myself, else break a solemn if unwitting promise.' A sigh, and he held out the basket in front of him, and carried it into the great cabin, where he placed it on the canvas squares of the decking.

Cutton tried again. 'Asking your leave, sir, most 'umble, I should be most particular grateful if you was to permit me to——'

'Have not I just now forbidden it?' Crossly. 'It is out of the question, in all distinctions out of the question, d'y'hear?'

'Aye, sir, very good. Since you does not wish to hundertake the deed yourself, sir, then I will drown it, and end the poor creature's terrible mis'ry—at once.' Reaching for the basket.

'Damn your impudence, you will do no such thing!' Placing himself in front of the basket. 'Bring me a quart of tea, right quick. I am parched.'

'Aye, sir.' Touching his forehead, retreating.

'Sentry!'

The marine guard at the door, his back straight. 'Sir?'

'Pass the word for the doctor, and then I will like to see Mr Trent, if he has returned to the ship in the hoy.'

Presently: 'Ah, Doctor. Will y'take tea?'

Thomas Wing accepted the proffered cup, and cocked his head to one side as the sound of mewing came from behind the captain's desk.

'You have acquired a cat, sir, I see—or rather, I hear.'

'Yes, well well, I will like your opinion of the beast, Doctor.' And he brought the basket up and stood it on the desk. 'It is a—it is by way of being a gift to me, d'ye see? But I—I am not greatly knowledgeable as to cats, and I will be much obliged to you if you will look at the creature, and tell me whether or no it is diseased, so that I may decide.'

'You wish me to examine it, Captain?' Astonished.

'Well well, a decision must be reached. Will I keep the animal, if it is hale? Or will I be obliged to—to ask you to end its life, if it is not? Hey?'

'I? Kill a cat? But I—I am a surgeon to men, not beasts. I am not qualified to arrive at a medical opinion of beasts.' Shaking his head gravely, pushing away his cup. 'Nor would I consider myself adept in the taking of animal life. I have never killed cattle of any kind, at all.'

Rennie opened the basket, and after a moment the cat's head cautiously appeared, black-eared, with a patch of white over one eye, and then a black, flicking tail.

'I fear he may be vexed with you, sir.' Wing, craning his neck to see the cat. 'Perhaps he has listened to what you propose, and don't care for it.'

'Nonsense, Doctor, nonsense.' Lifting the cat out of the basket by the scruff of the neck, and holding it above the desk at arm's length. The dangling animal accepted this method of handling meekly, and gave only a hint of its consternation by a single mew. The doctor leaned forward, and peered.

'It is perfectly healthy, by the look. Clean and healthy. And . . . ahh . . . is not a he, but a she.'

'A female cat?'

'Indeed.' Peering closer to make certain. 'There can be no doubt.'

Rennie lowered the animal into the basket, and closed the wicker top. 'Well well, I expect that if the creature ain't sickly, nor savage and wild and ferocious neither, then a berth may be found for it, out of the way, in a corner.' Pushing the basket across the desk toward the doctor.

'Nay, Captain, there ain't even the smallest little corner anywhere in my quarters, that is not took up with instruments, and bottles, and the business of medicine entire.'

'Come now, Doctor, surely you can find some room for——'

'No, sir, no.' Firmly, holding up a hand. 'I must say no, emphatic. The medicinal and the feline does not mix.'

And so the cat had come to live with Rennie in the great
cabin, there to be indulged, and fed, and if not quite doted
upon then held in very considerable affection and respect by
her new master.

'What shall you call it, sir?' the first lieutenant had asked
him.

'Her, James, her. Not it, if y'please.'

'I beg your pardon, sir. What shall you call—her?'

'Well well, I had thought—Dulcima.'

James, with a straight face: 'Yes, mm, a very pretty name.'

But Dulcima was too genteel a name for Cutton to
manage, and even though he, too, nearly doted upon the
creature, she was 'Dulcie' to him, and soon to everyone in the
ship.

'Come, Dulcie, and I will give you some milk,' said Rennie
now. The cat looked at him, then sat down and began licking
a paw and running it rhythmically over her face. 'Will not you
like a little saucer of milk, hey?'

He rose, pushing back his chair. At once the cat sprang to
the deck, and followed him to the quarter gallery, where he
found a can of goat's milk, fresh from the manger that
morning. He poured a little splash of milk into a saucer, and
put it carefully down on the canvas beneath the stern gallery
window. The cat coiled through his legs, crouched before the
saucer and lapped.

Rennie was short-handed. There had been no adequate
explication at Portsmouth—where there were three and four
seamen for every berth—and his lack should have vexed him.
They had sunk the coast of England nearly a week ago; there
had been severe weather almost at once after they weighed,
necessitating a night of shelter in Cawsand Bay before they
could resume their course and beat south-west. Mr Trent
complained that the Weevil had given him whole tiers of
spoiled casks, wrongly marked and dated. There was
grumbling in the lower deck about the beer, that was said to
be sour. Mr Adgett was constantly at the door of the great

cabin, with his lists and his worried 'As I say, sir'. The extensive repair and refit required after *Expedient*'s very hard second commission—in which she had fought a desperate action—had now been found wanting in a dozen particulars, and the sea had got into the ship. The new midshipmen were an unpromising, undisciplined, uncommonly obtuse lot of boys; Rennie had retained only one from the previous commission—Mr Abey, that was brave but still very young, and could not hope to be a leader in the middies' berth. He could not make up his mind about his junior lieutenant, Mr Upward; there was something dismayingly light-hearted about him, that Rennie felt did not belong in the character of an officer in a blue coat, on the quarterdeck of a man-of-war.

Rennie should have been vexed, but filling saucers for his cat, and stroking her as she lay purring in his lap, and watching her as she bathed herself with her tongue, her head nodding and nodding busily—somehow these very little things had enabled him to put aside vexation, and upset, and difficulty; somehow the presence of this delicate, fond little creature had soothed him, and comforted him, and kept all the myriad troubles of the ship's first days at sea at one remove, not to say those deeper thoughts, of other and sadder things in his recent past, that might otherwise have assailed him.

Thomas Wing, *Expedient*'s surgeon, was not vexed, but he was downcast. Admiral Bamphlett, his old friend—who had been instrumental in getting Wing to sea—had died while under his care. Wing had performed a surgical procedure upon the admiral to remove a troublesome bladder stone, but had discovered not a calculus but a large tumour, and within days of the cutting the admiral—already much weakened by his illness—had succumbed to it. Had succumbed, in a daze of tincture—in his bed at home, having refused to allow himself to be taken to the Haslar Hospital. Just before:

'You recall . . . Thomas . . . that I . . . I said that I would not come out . . . alive . . . from the Haslar . . . if once I allowed m'self . . . be took there. Well, I have not allowed it . . . and I am . . . still alive . . . hey?' A skull's smile. And the day after, he had died, and Wing felt himself responsible. He knew that he could not have done anything to save the admiral's life, but perhaps he might have prolonged it a little, had he not cut him.

'I am cast down,' he admitted to Lieutenant Hayter. 'He was my friend.'

'Aye.' Kindly.

'We must all lose friends—God knows a ship of war is as bloody a place as any on earth, at certain times, and we must all lose friends—but he was very dear to me, in spite of the great difference in age between us, and in social standing . . . and I never expected . . .'

'Aye.' A breath. 'It is at times such as this that wine can be a solace, or grog. But in course you will not allow yourself wine . . .'

'I will not. I do not.'

'And that is a matter for you, entire, Thomas. I would only say a very small thing——'

'No, if you please, no. I am in no doubt what you are going to say to me—and it will not do.'

'In fact I was not going to say that sometimes it is worth breaking such a rule, since I know how strongly you have always felt about wine.'

'Then I beg your pardon.'

'I was going to make the suggestion that you go aloft.'

'*Aloft!*'

'Aye, Thomas, aloft. I think that you have never before been higher in the ship than the forecastle or the quarter-deck—have you?'

'I have not, and am wholly content.'

'I do not mean to suggest that you should take precipitate risk, Thomas. Merely that you might find it invigorating to go into the mizzentop, to get a different view of the ship, and of the sea—and indeed of the world altogether.'

'*Invigorating?*'

'You don't care for that word? Then—then—surprising.'

'Ahh . . . surprising. To frighten myself half to death you call surprising, eh?'

'I should go aloft with you, in course, to aid and guide you.'

'I wish for no guidance, nor assistance, at all. Thank you for your kindness . . .' holding up a hand . . . 'but no, I will not go aloft under any circumstance.'

'Then I will not attempt to persuade you any more. That would not be good manners.'

'Thank you.' A pause, and the doctor now glanced at the lieutenant. 'I am not insensible of what you attempt, in seeking to distract me. Activity of a kind unusual to a man, differing from his daily work, may well alter his thoughts, dispel doubt and sorrow and a low cast of mind. I am not insensible of that, and thank you for seeking to raise me up— except that I did not quite wish to be raised so far as that.' A smile, returned.

Although he was short-handed, Rennie knew—or thought he knew—that the discrepancy would be made right at Gibraltar, where he would take into his ship that number of men, nearly exact, presently missing from his complement. His Majesty's *Expedient* frigate should have had a com- plement—according to her papers—of 258 officers and men, 258 souls. Rennie had weighed at Spithead with 215. He was not short of topmen, thank God, not short of able nor ordinary rated seamen on the forecastle and afterguard, but he was short of idlers, boys, and the varied flotsam and jetsam of a ship's crew that made the whole a whole— servants; a loblolly boy for Thomas Wing; landsmen waisters; a shoemaker; a barber; various other lowly artisans. Men that would be needed should the ship ever be obliged—as she had been obliged on her last commission—

to fight an action. Short above two score men, he was short of guncrew.

Expedient's armament was twenty-six eighteen-pounder Armstrong pattern long guns on the gundeck, and fourteen thirty-two-pounder carronades on the upperworks—her smashers. The carronades were lighter guns, shorter, and easier handled on their transverse trucks than the long guns a deck below. But that did not mean they could be left to look after themselves, if *Expedient* came to action. Each carronade required a minimum of three men to fight it, four for preference—to load, ram, run out, aim and fire it, and powder boys to bring up cartridge, &c, &c. A thirty-two-pound roundshot could not be managed by a slip of a ship's boy; it must be carried, and handled, and loaded, by strong able-bodied men, that would not drop it in the heat of the moment. A dropped thirty-two-pound roundshot could crush a man's foot, or roll away to the opposite rail as the ship heeled on a fighting tack, and disable another man there, hauling on a fall.

'But why do I allow such vexing things to invade my head?' muttered Rennie to himself. 'We will not fight an action before Gibraltar, the notion is fantastic—fantastic and absurd. Ain't it, Dulcie?'

The cat's eyes turned upon him, and she then fell to washing her chest, a splash of sun from the stern gallery window falling on the white patch over her eye.

'Aye, you are quite right, my dear. It is absurd, and ye nod in agreement. Cutton! Tea! Jump!'

But the question remained there in the back of his head nonetheless, half-hidden among the lists of minor repairs, spoiled casks, lower deck complaints and the like that cluttered those recesses of his mind:

'Will we come to fight an action *after* Gibraltar?'

The ship survived the vagaries of Biscay, bore south to Finisterre, south and south with Lisbon away to larboard, to Cape St Vincent, where she wore and set a course east-south-east.

At seven bells of the forenoon watch, on their seventeenth day at sea, *Expedient* ran into Gibraltar Bay, the Rock towering majestic over them, gave the fort thirteen guns—smoke rushing out in balloons from the ports, and the sound echoing across the Old Town—and was answered by echoing thunder from the saluting battery. She dropped anchor just off Ragged Staff at noon.

Rennie was in two minds about eating his dinner aboard, or waiting until he was ashore—where perhaps he would be entertained. He ordered his barge hoisted out. James came with him in the boat, and Thomas Wing. The first lieutenant and the doctor had business at the Naval Hospital on the eminence above Rosia Bay, and went there by gig as soon as they landed. Rennie had business elsewhere. He must make his duty to the Governor, in course, but first he must transact something else, at the Victualling Office. He would walk there, he decided, through the Old Town. He glanced beyond the town and the fortifications, to the heights above and to the north, at the crenellations of the old Moorish Castle, then at the long arm of the Old Mole jutting out into the blue glittering circle of the bay, and beyond that the grand hills of Andalusia. Rennie sniffed the air, stretched his neck and shoulders, set his hat square, and stepped out along the narrow street. Some of the tall, narrow buildings, he noted as he walked, were even yet pocked and broken from the terrible bombardments of the Spanish fleet during the Great Siege. The street was crowded, and more than once he was pushed against a wall in the crush of traffic in the narrow thoroughfare.

'Aye, the Rock will never be abandoned,' he said to himself, 'no matter how sorely she is tried and wounded and battered.' And the thought lifted him. He must go first to the Victualling Office, and meet there a man—or men—who had important information. He must afterward see the Dockyard Commissioner, and also the master shipwright, and make known his needs in the matter of minor repair. He would

leave the business of replacing spoiled casks and revictualling
to Trent. Aye, the purser was far better equipped, in both
temperament and experience, for that difficult exercise,
where hard bargaining was required, and arm-twisting, and
other unpleasant practices of cogent compulsion, such as
bribery.

'Never was any good at bribery,' said Rennie in his head, as
he stepped up the hill to the Victualling Office, the road up
the mountain snaking away to his right. 'Don't know how.'

James Hayter and Thomas Wing, winding their way above
the fortifications and through the broad gardens and little
orchards that had sustained the Rock during the Siege,
wished to call on Dr Welbeck Mortimer at the Naval
Hospital, an acknowledged authority in the service in the
matter of tropick diseases, and other fevers. There lay at this
moment, in *Expedient*'s orlop, an ordinary seaman suffering
something very like ship fever, but enough unlike it, too,
to've caused Wing to grow anxious. Was it simply a form of
typhus, or was it . . . something else? Thomas Wing wished
to persuade Dr Mortimer to allow him to bring the sick man
to the hospital, and isolate him on a verandah and treat him
there. Lieutenant Hayter had come with Wing to add
suitable gravity to the request.

Wing was never unaware that any such request, in any
place where he was unknown, no matter his warrant from the
Sick & Hurt, and his ability to converse knowledgeably with
any medical man—however high—on procedure and treatment, Wing was never wholly unaware that the world—even
and perhaps particularly the medical world—saw him as a
dwarf first, and a surgeon second, if indeed as a surgeon at all.

'You do not need me by your side to add medical advice,
surely?' James had said when Wing put the request to him the
day previous, after divisions. 'I know nothing of medical
things, at all, Thomas.'

'You will aid me, all the same.'

'How? Will you tell me?' A quizzical frown, as he looked up from the muster book.

'If you will stand, and think a moment as you look down at me—the answer will be plain to you.' A slight flushing of his cheek, and then he held up his head, and looked James in the eye.

James did not stand. He merely nodded, and gave a little sigh of understanding. 'Yes, I see. Then you may count on my support, certainly.'

A brief half-bow of thanks.

'Thomas?' As Wing turned to walk away. He turned back, and James said: 'I will write out a formal request—to which the captain will add his signature, I am in no doubt—and carry it there in a leather fold. We will go in together as an official party from the ship, on official business.'

'Thank you, James. You are kind.'

And so it had been arranged. But fever was a troublesome thing, an awkward thing, and the physicians of naval hospitals were sometimes reluctant to admit into their premises seamen from visiting ships, in such places as Gibraltar, for fear of—plague. Was Mickleberry Bigg, rated ordinary, suffering from simple ship fever—akin to gaol fever—or was he carrying that dread and cursed disease feared from one end of the Mediterranean to the other, indeed feared everywhere?

Thomas Wing did not know the answer to that, not for certain, and he must consult Dr Mortimer's opinion. Might he, he wondered, be able to persuade Dr Mortimer to come with him to the ship at Ragged Staff, and examine the ailing man there—if he would not allow the man into his hospital? Thomas and James, very correct in their blue coats, with their official document of request, came to the hospital—a great square barrack with a central tower at the front, overlooking the fortifications on the eminence below, and below that the broad, boat-scattered Rosia Bay—and went in. Dr Mortimer welcomed them with sherry, and a sympathetic hearing. A slim, sharp-faced man with iron-grey hair and grey eyes, and spectacles sharply reflecting astride his sharp nose, he might have been a keen-edged, acerbic man altogether, taken by appearance; but in fact he was keen only in attention to what his visitors had to tell him, and in all else an humanitarian.

'In course, you was right to come, and in course I am willing to assist. If y'have not been near to North Africa, then I think it cannot be plague. You say there is no other case like it, aboard?'

'No, indeed. I have kept him in the orlop, isolated from the rest of the people.'

'Wise, very wise. However, had it been plague, there would certainly have been by now additional cases in the ship. Plague is peculiarly contagious. It is impossible, in my opinion, that the man could have lived in the ship, worked and ate and slept proximate to many other men, without he would infect in least some of them.'

'Then . . . ship fever?'

'Typhus—it is possible. And yet, from what you tell me, I doubt that it is typhus, neither. Had you thought of consumption, perhaps?'

'Well, I had considered it . . .'

'However?'

'However, I was not persuaded, entire . . .'

The two medical men began to converse in language that was as alien to James as Patagonian, earnestly jotting notes, comparing them, consulting books from a shelf behind the physician's chair, and attempting to decide between them whether or not it would be advisable for Dr Mortimer to go down to the ship and look at the man there, first, or to bring the poor fellow at once to the hospital upon a litter, and admit him to the isolation wing. James's attention began to wander, and he thought of Catherine—thought of her a little sadly, and contritely, and felt that he had not left her at home in England in quite the spirit he would on reflection have wished. He had dashed off a letter or two, before they weighed, but nothing more. He had not sent her a little gift—

a pair of earrings, or a bonnet, or a dress—with a fond dedication to her beauty and constancy. He had not made any attempt, any effort, to send her an earnest of any kind of his continuing tender and loving regard for her—for his very dear Catherine. Why not?

'I am a fool.'

The two doctors looked at him. Dr Mortimer: 'Ye've thought of something other than fever?'

'What? No, I beg your pardon. I—I was in my head, you know, lost there, and—no, nothing.' Embarrassed now, and certainly feeling himself a fool. 'Hm.'

'Ah.' Dr Mortimer continued to look at James, who saw it as his duty to make some contribution to the discussion.

'Ought we, d'y'think, Doctor—ought we to pump ship, and smoke both the bilges and 'tween decks, as a precaution?'

Captain Rennie, at the Victualling Office, suffered no such difficulty of attention. He was expected there, and was shown by the Agent Victualler's clerk into an office, with a desk, chairs, a window with a view of the steep slopes behind—and Colonel Breakspeare, of the marines. The colonel was a gentleman of Rennie's age, but stout and florid, his face matching his red dress coat. He introduced himself, and without further ceremony, but with a hint of distaste for the business, he presented Rennie with a sealed paper.

'Open it, Captain Rennie, if y'please, break the seal and open it. After that, my duty is done.'

Rennie did as he was asked, feeling perhaps—tho' he did not show it—a little affronted that he had not even been offered a biscuit, leave alone a splash of something, in this place of provisions. Having broken the seal, he opened the document up, and read:

> *By Order, to be given into the Hand of*
> *Capt. Wm RENNIE RN, at GIBRALTAR*
>
> You Capt Rennie of HM *Expedient* frigate are to take
> into your Ship at the above Station *Sgt Gosbart Host* of
> the Royal Marines, and a Party of *Forty* (40) *marines*,
> that was sent to Gibraltar by transport ship, from
> Chatham, to await yr arrival.
>
> These marines are to aid you in your present
> hazardous commission, other Details of which shall be
> conveyed to you at the time of your receipt of this
> Document, by Word of Mouth.

Rennie paused in his reading, and peered at the seal he had
just broken. It was indeed an Admiralty seal, but there was no
official Admiralty heading upon the document, nor any
names of the Lords Commissioners, nor even of the First
Secretary. The document was unheaded, and so far as Rennie
could make it entirely unofficial—aside from that seal. He did
not like it, least of all the words: 'your present hazardous
commission'. What could that mean? And why had not these
marines, over and above the contingent already in his ship,
why had they not embarked at Portsmouth, if they were
needed for this cruise?

'Forgive me, Colonel Breakspeare, but what is your own
authority in this matter?'

'My authority?' Not quite querulously, but very near to it.
'I am presently attached to the Governor's household, and I
have been asked—required—to perform this duty. My sole
association with what you hold in your hand, sir, is that I have
the honour, as do you, to serve the King. I have no knowledge
of nor influence over its content. We are met in this place to
aid us in privacy, so I am informed, in privacy and secrecy.
You see?'

'Well well, Colonel, I do not quite see, no. I am commissioned on convoy duty. I sailed from Portsmouth short-
handed, and hoped to put additional men on my books at

Gibraltar, but never expected to embark forty additional marines——'

'Forty!' The colonel stared at him. 'Forty marines in a frigate, above your official detachment?'

'Aye, from Chatham. Under a Sergeant Host.' Rennie proffered the document. The colonel at once held up a rejecting hand.

'No, no, no, thank you. I must not have sight of it. That is a secret.'

'Ha ha, well, secret. It ain't a secret any more, though, that I am to take these men off your hands, eh?'

'I know nothing of these men, that are clearly housed at the fort. Never heard of Sergeant Post, neither.'

'Host, I think.' Glancing at the paper.

'Never heard of him. I am not in usual attached here, Captain Rennie, nor have I ever been stationed at the Chatham barracks. I am seconded here from London a few months, that is all, and living at the Governor's residence.' Shaking his head, and stepping away stiffly to the rear window.

'Ah. Hah. Hm.' Rennie folded the paper with a sigh, nodded as if to clear his head, and gave a bemused little sniff.

The colonel turned to look at him, and unbent a little. He cleared his throat.

'Yes, it strikes me, Captain Rennie, that we are very dry fellows.'

'Dry, Colonel?'

'Aye, parched dry, and the noon gun fired long since. Here we stand in this provisioning office, and not a glass nor a decanter to be seen. I call that poor treatment of two serving officers. Hey? What?'

Rennie smiled. 'Poor treatment indeed, Colonel. Shall we complain, d'y'think?'

'We'll do better than that,' said the colonel, and he strode to the desk, took up a table bell and rang it vigorously. 'Complaining ain't my remedy, in anything. We must demand. Hm?'

The agent's clerk appeared at the door.

Colonel Breakspeare: 'Mr Pockley. We will like a decanter of wine, and glasses, if y'please. And some cake.'

'The storekeeper has the wine, sir, and he carries his keys upon his person.'

'What? Keys? Is there no sherry for us here, or Madeira will do, or port wine?'

'I will inquire, sir. Erm . . .' Hesitating, glancing behind him.

'Yes?' The colonel, impatiently.

'The other gentleman is here, sir.'

'Other—— Oh, yes, of course. Thank you, Pockley.' Nodding in dismissal. 'Now then, Rennie.' Turning to him. 'There is a fellow here at Gibraltar—that I have met but once—that wishes to say a word to you, as I understand it, about your commission.'

'Ah, yes . . .'

'He is arrived here now, at the Victualling Office, and waits outside.' A pause and he lowered his voice to a hoarse whisper, and leaned forward. ''Tween you and me, I do not like the cut of his coat. However, I am not party to the business, I know nothing about it. You will come to your own view of him, I am in no doubt.' A nod, and he stood back.

'Yes, thank you, Colonel.' Rennie did know about this man, had been informed about him at Portsmouth, an hour or two before weighing. The man either represented Sir Robert Greer, or was closely associated with him.

'This man will come to you at Gibraltar, and describe to you certain facts, certain particulars, without which you will not be able to fulfil your obligation.' This from Soames, Third Secretary to their Lordships, who had come to Portsmouth specifically at Sir Robert's request, and had been rowed out to the mooring. Rennie had forgotten all about that last-minute message, and Soames's evident discomfort in the boat, from wetting spray and the swell; had put it quite out of his head, and now . . .

'Good day t'ye, sir!'

. . . the fellow strode into the office, pushing the door wide and fixing Rennie with his eye.

Both Rennie and Colonel Breakspeare were startled by the abruptness of his entry, and Rennie in turn was utterly startled by his appearance.

'Ah, Colonel! Didn't see ye there, didn't know ye was to be present, at all. Good day.'

'Good day. May I introduce . . .' The colonel extended a hand and turned again to Rennie: '. . . Mr Sebastian, Captain Rennie.'

Rennie bowed stiffly.

'Captain Rennie, sir.' Mr Sebastian, bowing deeply. 'Your servant.'

Mr Sebastian was dressed—in Rennie's opinion was dressed—in as flagrantly flamboyant a manner as he had ever observed in an Englishman. Upon his head was a large round red velvet hat, sewn across with tripled circles of gold thread that gleamed as he turned this way and that. Upon his person he wore what appeared to be a great skirted dress, with voluminously sleeved arms, in a cloth of rich sewn silk, and silken gauze, and fine cotton. The colours again were rich red and gold. Upon his feet, half hidden by the sweeping dress, were elaborate pointed slippers of velvet and gold, and at his waist was a magnificent belt of ivory, worked gold and rubies, and a dagger with gold and turquoise inlaid in ivory, in a leather and gold scabbard. There wafted from him a rich and musky scent. His appearance in whole, his whole presence, was literally fantastic. His skin was a deep mahogany brown. His eyes—blue and piercing—stared from a craggy face, dominated by a great hooked nose, like mad jewels. For a few stunned moments Rennie was rendered quite speechless.

'No doubt you are wondering who I am, Captain Rennie?'

'You have come from Sir Robert Greer, have you not?' At last finding his voice, and making it unnaturally gruff and abrupt, by way of asserting himself.

'Not exact, no, sir. Not quite. I am come from t'other side, by reason of a communication.'

Rennie stared at him. Were the fellow's brains addled, in truth? Did he imagine himself to have come back from the dead? For what purpose? 'Ah. The—the other side.'

Colonel Breakspeare, seeing Rennie's puzzled look, volunteered: 'What Mr Sebastian means, I think, is that he has come from the Barbary coast of North Africa—ain't that so, Sebastian?'

'Exactly so, Colonel. I have.' A half-turn, and addressing Rennie again, shaking the great sleeves of his garment and standing with one hand on his hip, and one foot a little forward. 'Who am I?' he asked with a rhetorical flourish. 'Well. Hah. Yes. There you have me, sir. In plain language, I do not know.'

'Eh?'

'Ymm. Fffff. That will seem to you, no doubt, a very unsatisfactory reply.' Drawing in a breath and shaking his great head. 'Am I the man you see before you? Or am I some other creature entire, that merely *looks* like the present apparition.'

'Apparition?' Rennie felt that his suspicions were being wholly confirmed. Here was a Bedlamite, bedecked and raving, that had somehow contrived to——

'Sometimes that is what I am, certainly. A phantasm, a wraith, a hobgoblin, that floats and glides about the world, from place to exotic place, in the service of—what? An ideal? A principle? A notion of order and governance?'

'Well well, I——'

'Nay. Nay, sir. That will not describe me. The thing I serve, sir, is—*power*.'

'Hm. Power.' Rennie glanced at Colonel Breakspeare, who simply shrugged and turned to the window. Rennie again addressed Sebastian: 'What power? Which one? The King, d'y'mean?'

'The King! And I may ask you in turn, sir—which king?

Whose? There are many kings and regents on t'other side, you know.'

'The King of England, sir.' A humouring smile. 'Your king and mine. That is, that is, if you *are* an Englishman. But perhaps you are not. Perhaps you are instead an——'

'Have you ever heard of Rashid Bey, Captain Rennie?' Interrupting him, his demeanour now serious, and his tone far less fantastical and jovial.

'I have not.'

'He is the man in whose service I am at present engaged. It is his convoy you are to escort, sir, from the minor regency of Rabhet, on the coast of Tunis, to England. We must put to sea without further loss of time. We are to rendezvous with the cutter *Curlew*, to aid us in escort duties, at a bearing I have been given, in the letter from England I mentioned just now.'

The clerk Mr Pockley now came through the door with a brief knock, carrying a tray of sherry and glasses. Rennie scarcely noticed him.

'Did you say *Curlew*, Mr Sebastian? D'y'mean the *Curlew* cutter, that is commanded by young Lieutenant Dower?'

'I know nothing of Dower. She is at present under the command of Lieutenant Dutton Bradshaw, that is my cousin. I think she came from Jamaica when her former commander died there, and that is when Bradshaw got her.'

'Here is your wine, gentlemen, that you requested so particular.' Pockley, patiently setting the tray on the desk.

Mr Sebastian swivelled on his slippered feet, and fixed him with a blue glare. 'Y'may take that away. We have no time for such things, no time.'

Pockley shrugged, took up the tray and——

'Wait!' Rennie beckoned the clerk back. Nodded at the table, and the tray was then put down again, and the hapless Pockley retired shaking his head. Rennie poured two glasses of wine, Madeira wine, and gave one to the colonel, who took it with a grateful little jerk of his head.

'Colonel Breakspeare, a glass of wine with you, sir.' Rennie raised his glass, and the two officers drank. Rennie put down his glass. 'Now, Mr Sebastian. You say Lieutenant Dower has died? That is sad news. A capable and gentlemanlike sea officer. But I know nothing of his ship joining mine, sir, under new command. Pray show me the despatch, if y'please, with that information contained. I must peruse its contents for myself.' He held out his hand, and moved it impatiently once or twice, to indicate urgency—and the fact that here he was in command.

Mr Sebastian ignored that impatient hand, and lifted his own hand—the thumb encircled by a heavy gold and jade ring, set with emeralds and rubies—and tapped his forehead with a finger.

'That communication is already burned, Captain Rennie. It was burned the moment I had read it, and all its content is safe in my head.'

'Burned!' Outraged. 'You had a despatch directly bearing on my commission, and you presumed to burn it, good God?'

'Allah be praised, I did.' A smile, revealing strong yellow teeth. 'If you will like to accompany me now to Ragged Staff, where I think your ship lies? Then I will apprise of you of all that was in the letter, and go aboard with you so that we may sail. That is, in course, when you have drunk your wine.' Another smile, simulating good manners.

Rennie looked at him, and did not finish his wine. 'Do I understand you to mean that you are to come with me in my ship, Mr Sebastian?'

'Indeed, I am. Did not I make m'self clear t'ye? I am to be your guide, sir, your guide and mentor from this moment forward.'

'Guide? In what capacity a guide? What d'y'know of ships, sir, of handling ships at sea?'

'Ah, well, I am not a *rais*, no. But I do know the world of Islam, the world of the regencies, and all the intricacies and dangers that lie therein. These are many, Captain Rennie. May I ask: what do you yourself know of the Barbary shore?'

'That ain't the question, that ain't the question.' Knowing that in all probability it was the question, exact, and that he must submit to it very soon—but thoroughly discommoded and out of temper because of it.

⊷ ⇹⬧⇹ ⊷

Mickleberry Bigg, rated ordinary, did not in Dr Mortimer's opinion suffer from plague, nor did he suffer from ship fever. The ailing man, having been examined by Dr Mortimer— who had come to the ship—was brought from the ship to the hospital, through the palm groves and the gardens, on the road above the military barracks, where the party of seamen carrying him passed a large detachment of marines marching in the opposite direction, and admitted to a small upper ward opening on a verandah. By his name in the admissions book Dr Mortimer entered the word: 'Consumption'. However, Dr Mortimer was not entirely confident of this diagnosis. He had merely written it in the book as a means of allotting the man a bed.

'It is an expedient only,' he said to James and Dr Wing, and at once felt himself foolish. 'That is—hm—a contrivance, so to say.'

James oversaw the business, as did Thomas Wing, as a matter of duty. Although it meant leaving Bigg behind, they were satisfied they had done all they could for him, and for the ship, by putting him ashore in such capable hands. James had been privately anxious about Mickleberry Bigg, a Portsmouth man. He had said nothing of this to Wing, nor had he said anything to Rennie, but he had feared that if Bigg had been ill of a virulent contagious disease—and thank God he was not—then that might well have compromised their whole commission. James left Thomas Wing to discuss Bigg's treatment with Dr Mortimer and returned to the ship.

There were many things that demanded his attention

aboard: a long list of minor repairs; a long list of lower deck grievances about rations; the large additions of hammock and mess numbers that would in all probability be required, if Rennie was able to get on to his books the men he sought; &c., &c. As he was rowed out to the mooring he continued in his head the troubling conversation he had been conducting with himself for some little time. 'I do not perfectly understand this commission. I do not understand why we was followed in London. Nor do I know why we was attacked in the coach travelling from London to Portsmouth. Nor do I understand the absurd incident at Chelsea, where I was dazed with drink. And why did we sail short-handed? There is altogether far too much that I don't apprehend, at all.' Half an hour later these things were yet in his head . . .

'What do y'not apprehend, James?' Tom Makepeace, at his shoulder on the larboard gangway.

'Mm?' Turning. 'Oh, did I say something aloud? Only muttering, Tom, only muttering, you know.'

'Thinking of your Catherine, perhaps?'

'Eh? No . . .'

'I think very often of Josephine.' A little nod, then: 'I wonder if the captain thinks very often of his wife.'

'His late wife?' Moving aft.

'Aye. I wonder if he does think of her.'

James adjusted the blue kerchief tied about his head—he had shifted into his working clothes as soon as he returned aboard—and gave a little shrug. 'Don't know, Tom. Candidly, I have not time to ponder such things. We must make our repairs. Mr Adgett!—You there, Mr Abey.'

'Sir?' Midshipman Richard Abey, taller now than on the last commission, hurried to James as he strode aft on the quarterdeck.

'Find the carpenter, if y'please, and say that I wish to see him.'

'Aye, sir.' Hurrying away.

'He must feel her loss very acute, do not you think so?' Lieutenant Makepeace, following James aft to the taffrail.

'I expect that he does.' James leaned far out over the ported taffrail and peered down. 'No, damnation, I cannot see . . .'

'See what?'

Heaving himself up, crossing to the larboard aft rail, and again leaning and peering down: 'The rudder chains. Ah!' He heaved himself inboard again. 'I had thought one link was weakened, the last watch at sea. It ain't.' The chains had been fitted in anticipation of storms in the Bay of Biscay, and James had fretted about them ever since. 'We must unship them directly.'

'Does it trouble him at night, d'y'think? Trouble his dreams?' Touching a backstay.

'What?' Looking at him. 'Oh, you are still thinking on that? Perhaps it does, Tom. However . . .' Brushing down his jerkin, and hitching his breeches.

'However?'

'I cannot presume to introduce so sensitive a subject into conversation. It would not be good manners. Beside, there is much else to occupy our attention, as sea officers, hm?—Ah, Mr Adgett. You have your list?'

'Lists, sir, in the plurality, as I say.' Shavings fell from the shoulder of his coat as he held out the twine-tied lists with a pained expression. 'List-ss.'

'Very good. Let us go at them, Mr Adgett.' Holding out a hand to receive them, and smiling in dismissal at Tom Makepeace—who nodded and made his way forrard into the waist.

James studied the lists a moment, turning pages, then looked up briefly and watched the second lieutenant go down the ladder into the waist, his hat bobbing below the line of the deck. Was Makepeace's mind unduly troubled? By what? Thoughts of his wife? Or something else?

'Now, sir, now . . .' Mr Adgett, breathing through his mouth, sighed wafts of cheese and grog. 'We must begin, as I

say, with these troublesome leaks.' Pointing at an underlined
section.

'Indeed, Mr Adgett. We must.'

━•━ ⛧◆⛧ •━

The marines came into the ship, were given their hammock
numbers, and mess numbers; their names were added to the
quarter bills, and their dunnage stowed. James was bemused
by this sudden invasion, but their papers were in order, their
sergeant a competent man, and James came up from the hold
and oversaw their embarkation by delegating the task; he
placed the ship's marine officer, Lieutenant Quill, in charge,
and returned to other business. Returned to it until a very
peculiar person came up the side ladder, loomed a moment at
the gangway port, and bulked huge past the breast rail and on
to the quarterdeck. James, now on the forecastle, waved at
him and began to demand to know what the devil he meant
by coming unannounced into the the ship, when . . .

'Mr Hayter!' called Rennie, coming up the ladder himself
from the boat.

'Sir?' Making his way along the gangway.

'This is Mr—Where has the fellow gone to? Ah. He has
ventured aft. Just come with me, James, and I will introduce
you. Mr Sebastian! Mr Sebastian! We will go below, if
y'please.' Aside, to James: 'Was it necessary to shift into that
damned piratical rig just at this moment, James? Am I to
endure two outlandish bloody costumes in the ship? Christ's
tears.'

They went below to the great cabin, where Mr Sebastian
was made to seem larger than ever, larger than life—
certainly larger than the space-constraining life he would
lead aboard a frigate thirty-six. Having been introduced,
James tried not to stare at him. To aid himself in this he said
to Rennie:

'Are the marines the only men that will come into the ship,

sir? Are not we to have additional seamen, additional rated hands?'

'I fear not, Mr Hayter. We must make do with these redcoats, that will help crew the great guns was we to fight an action.'

'Very good, sir.'

'Mr Hayter is not dressed as he would in usual dress on an occasion of this kind, Mr Sebastian.' He poured wine. 'Those are his least impressing clothes, I fear.'

'Will you like me to shift into a blue coat, sir?' James, politely.

'Eh? No no, not now. We will drink a glass of wine, and welcome our guest. Your health, sir.' Raising his glass to Mr Sebastian, who did not raise his own, indeed did not even take it up from the table.

'I regret, Captain Rennie, that long residence in the world of Islam has caused me to lose my taste for wine.' A yellow-toothed smile of apology.

'Then will y'drink something else, sir? Tea?'

'Coffee, if you have it . . . ?'

'Alas, I never drink coffee, and so never carry any in the ship.'

'Then tea will suit me admirably.'

'Just so.—Cutton! Tea! Jump! And cake, too!'

'Erm . . . where will you like me to lay my head, Captain Rennie? Is there somewhere with a little more headroom?' Glancing at the deckhead, touching it with his hand.

'D'you join us in *Expedient*, Mr Sebastian?' James, in surprise.

'He does, Mr Hayter.' Rennie drank off his wine, and put down his glass. 'Mr Sebastian is to be entered on the books as a supernumerary. No no, drink your wine, it ain't a thing that must be done immediate.'

'Very good, sir. Is Mr Sebastian to receive victuals and grog, or does he share your table, sir?'

This was not a rude or intrusive question; a ship's books

must be signed off in every particular, as James and Rennie both knew; every shilling of every pound spent in the ship on the allocation of food and spirits must be accounted for, in a ratio of one quarter of all monies spent on the sustenance of seamen. The purser Mr Trent—like all pursers in the Royal Navy—was required by regulation to put up a bond of five hundred pounds at the commencement of each and every commission. Every shilling, every pound, that was spent above the strict allowance of monies by the Navy Board was forfeit from that bond. To take into any naval ship, therefore, any person as a supernumerary, was no small matter. The new detachment of marines were all provided for in course, their papers carried by Sergeant Host from Chatham perfectly satisfactory, since they could be taken to the Victualling Store and used like currency for provisioning. But Mr Sebastian, a very large, burly, hearty-eating man by the look of him—well, Mr Sebastian would be a costly addition—unless he proposed to pay for himself, or Rennie proposed to bear the expense out of his own pocket.

'Hm, well well, I had not yet . . .' Rennie was unsure of the exact position concerning Mr Sebastian's provisioning, since that gentleman had proposed himself as a passenger, but the captain was saved further embarrassment by his guest's intervention:

'I have took the liberty, Captain, of providing for myself. I have a great quantity of dates and other dried fruits, and ample couscous and chillies and so forth, that I will like to prepare for myself, if you will permit me the space to boil up broth for cooking, and water to brew coffee? I carry a sack of my own coffee beans. Also, I should like to bring in lambs—'

'Ye wish to cook for yourself, sir?' Rennie was startled, in spite of his resolution not to find anything his guest proposed outrageous, or discommoding, or vexing, any more.

'If it ain't too great an imposition. My diet, I may tell you, differs I should think in every particular from your own. You would not wish to eat the food I eat. Nor would I, with respect, wish to eat the food you are accustomed to. It is a question of taste, and custom, you apprehend? I have no wish to give offence.'

'Nor have I indeed, sir.' A little bow, answered by a flickering of a beringed hand to the forehead and a bow—a brief and polite salaam.

'Mr Sebastian, sir,' ventured James now, 'I wonder if I might ask you how long you have lived among Muslim peoples?'

A smile, the direct stare of blue eyes. 'You wonder, Lieutenant, do ye not, if I am become a Muslim myself? Hey?'

'That is so, I confess.' An answering smile, and a nod.

'Nay, I have not. There is many a Christian lives upon the Barbary shore, and prospers too—only he don't announce the fact of his heritage at every opportunity, nor any. You have me? He learns the customs, the traditions, the day-to-day habits and regularities of life—he learns the observances of things, and thus makes his way.'

'Yes, I see.' James hesitated. He wished to ask many further questions, but saw Rennie's disgruntled frown, drank off his glass, and desisted. Mr Sebastian, however, sensed James's curiosity about him, and now:

'Shall I take the lieutenant into my confidence, Captain Rennie . . . ?'

'Eh?'

'As to my purpose in sailing with you into the Mediterranean, finding *Curlew* there, and going on to Rabhet?'

'*Curlew*?' James interrupted, looking at him. 'You cannot mean the *Curlew* cutter, ten guns, commanded by Lieutenant Bradshaw?'

'I do mean that vessel, sir.' Nodding his great head, so that the gold circles caught the light on his velvet headdress. 'As I have already told your captain, Dutt Bradshaw is my cousin— on the distaff side,' he added.

'I have met Lieutenant Bradshaw, and know the *Curlew*. I understood him to serve only in the English Channel. One of his duties, as I have had cause to discover, is to chase down French smugglers there.'

'I know nothing of that, Mr Hayter. His duty now is to rendezvous with me in the Mediterranean and——'

Throughout this exchange Rennie had grown more and more bemused and unhappy. He felt that he was almost become a passenger in his own ship. And now his lieutenant was engaging the preposterous Sebastian in conversation, in familiar tones. Rennie did not like it, not at all.

'Cutton!' he bellowed. 'Where is the tea and cake, damn you! Ah, there you are at long last!' As Cutton edged hurriedly into the great cabin carrying a tray. 'Where the devil have y'been, when I asked most particular that you should bring the tea at once, good God.' An angry sigh, and he jerked his head at the table, where Cutton put down the tray; he was about to duck out again when Rennie seized his elbow and pushed him back to the table, and muttered at him: 'Serve the tea, pour it, pour it. Have ye no sense of your duties, y'misbegotten wretch?'

When the tea had been poured, and the now cowering Cutton had fled away, and Mr Sebastian was drinking what he endeavoured to find a pleasing brew, but clearly could not, Rennie sniffed and asked:

'How d'y'happen to know Lieutenant Bradshaw, pray?' Directing the question at James.

'Well, sir—it is a rather tangled tale——'

'Howsomever, I will like to hear it, if y'please.' Rennie, with a grim little smile, that James saw came from ominous underlying displeasure. Rennie hated to be left behind in anything.

'Very good, sir. I took passage in *Curlew*—very brief, you know—between Weymouth and Plymouth, on my way to find you at Dartmoor, sir. I never spoke of it, because it seemed——'

'Ah, so that was the circumstance. And he told you that his duty was to chase smugglers, hm?'

'Well, sir, he did not need to tell me—since we chased a smuggler in fact.'

'Ah. Ha. And did y' apprehend this smuggler?'

'No, sir. He ran away south to France.'

'Did he? Did he? That was a misfortune for Lieutenant Bradshaw, and for *Curlew*, I am in no doubt. Perhaps that is why he has been ordered to the Mediterranean, hm . . . ?' Another fierce little smile.

James knew better than to make any suggestion; he waited politely for Rennie to answer his own question.

'. . . because he was unable to fulfil his obligations in the Channel. And so their Lordships have seen fit to attach him to me, so that I might show him how such things may be managed at sea.' Smiling still, and glancing back and forth at James and Mr Sebastian.

'Such things?' Sebastian frowned and shook his head slightly.

'Aye, such things, sir. How an enemy may be run down, and challenged, and bested. If he cannot manage such tasks as defeating damned villainous dogs of smugglers, he will be of no use to me until I may be able to teach him his trade, sir.'

'Trade?'

'Trade, Mr Sebastian. Our trade in the Royal Navy is to take, or sink, or burn and destroy His Majesty's enemies, and we carry it out by superior seamanship, and superior gunnery. D'y'know what is wrote on my warrant of commission, and Mr Hayter's, and Lieutenant Bradshaw's, too? "Hereof nor you nor any of you may fail, as you will answer the contrary at your peril." Telling words, sir—telling and absolute.' A brief pause. 'And now Mr Hayter will find you a berth in the ship, Mr Sebastian, and make the necessary arrangements about stowing your dunnage. I myself must go ashore and make my duty to the Governor.'

'But I——' began Mr Sebastian.

'I will be much obliged to you, sir—and to you, Mr Hayter—if ye will join me for supper, here tomorrow night.' Taking up his hat, and moving toward the companion. 'Mr Tangible! Find my coxswain Randall South! I am going ashore!'

A hot wind had begun to blow from the south across the narrow strait, as Rennie made his way through the Old Town toward the Governor's house, a wind with the hot and exotic smells of Africa and the desert wafting in its gusts. The wind flowed from the sea over the low rocks of Europa Point, across the fortifications and the orchards, and washed in waves up over the great limestone tilt of the Rock itself, across the sawtooth of the crest to the ridges and the isthmus beyond, that linked this rocky British fortress to the broad hills of Andalusia.

As he walked Rennie found his thoughts dwelling upon his steward. Colley Cutton was a puzzle to Captain Rennie. He did not quite understand even now how the creature had come under his notice, and then under his care. Had it been Thomas Wing that had rescued him from one of the stinking taverns of the Point at Portsmouth, and brought him—his face washed, and his threadbare coat brushed—to the ship, knowing that Rennie was in need of a steward? Yes, he thought that the doctor had brought Cutton there—before they sailed for Jamaica, their last commission. But why he had agreed to put such a low, unpromising creature on the books as his steward puzzled Rennie. He could not remember, now. Cutton had come under his care, and somehow he had never summoned the severity of mind to dismiss him, in spite of an hundred transgressions. Rennie thought that he certainly did care and provide for his steward, in allowing him a berth in the ship, and victuals, grog, the means of survival, in return for a bare minimum of work. Cutton did not care for Rennie in anything but the loosest indication of the word. The daily care of Rennie's clothing, the serving of meals, &c., was never in Rennie's opinion wholly satisfactory; there was always something wanting in the way the creature managed it. Was not he frequently drunk? Was not he insolent? Was not he capable, at any time, for any motive, of the grossest mendacity and deceit? At one moment he affected a canine servility and devotion, at the next he produced a torrent of absurd self-exculpation, impudent and vexing and bumptious.

'He is repugnant and unseamanlike in his appearance,' muttered Rennie to himself, pushing past a labourer with a handcart laden with stones. 'He is without discipline, without merit of any kind.'

'Was you addressing myself, sir?' demanded the labourer. 'You pushed me, not t'other way round.'

'No no, in course I did not,' rejoined Rennie gruffly. 'The way is narrow.'

'Aye, and the navy is a bully.'

Rennie put a hand on his sword, and was about to deliver a round and ringing rebuke, then he glanced round him—at the dark stone buildings, and the unfamiliar faces—and thought better of it. He brought his hand away from the sword, adjusted his stock, lifted his chin with a dismissing sniff, and strode on.

'Why must I bear Cutton's insolence?' he said, inside his head. 'I will not bear it any more, by God.' Had not the wretch offended again that very morning? Had not Rennie said to him:

'You are a disgrace to the Service.'

'What has I done——'

'I wished to be woken with tea. Y'did not wake me with tea. And my god-damned piss-pot was nowhere to be found, neither. Where was you!'

'Ah-well-yes-ezackly-sir, the-tea-was-in-the-pot-sir, when-I-was-called-away-like, by-the——'

'Called away! Called away! You bloody dog, there is nobody in the ship that may call you away from your duty to me!'

'Nature-sir-arstin-your-pardon, but-Nature-will-never-be-denied-when-it-comes-upon-a-man-fierce-like, in-'is-newer-regions-sir, sudden-and-fierce-and-griping.'

And Rennie had been obliged to let it go. What could he say to that torrent of nonsense, without lending himself to an unseemly and unwinnable debate with a lowly cretin? He let it go. And now reflected, on the steep and narrow cobbles, that to find a replacement steward here at Gibraltar would be a most troublesome and taxing business, after all. He could not be certain of acquiring the services of an upright and hard-working man, not if the pugnacity of that damned labourer was anything to go by. And beside—Cutton was fond of Dulcie, indeed cared for the cat with tenderness and solicitude, and Rennie would not condemn him in that.

He came to the Governor's house, and was admitted by the sentry.

⋅⋅—⋅≍♦≍—⋅⋅

The Governor, Sir Havilland Gale, having ascertained that Captain Rennie had all he needed for and in his ship—the captain had only to ask if he thought of anything in addition—and having been solicitous in wine and other refreshment, listened to his guest's praise of Gibraltar, her fortitude in the bombardments of the late war, &c., and told him a favourite anecdote:

'In course you know the story of gallant Captain Fagg?'

'No, sir, I do not.' Politely cocking his head. 'I am aware, certainly, of the remarkable bravery of General Eliot at that time . . .'

'Indeed, an hero. However, Captain Fagg's exploit is very singular. May I tell it you?'

'Your Excellency is very kind.' A bow.

'Now then—in November of the year '79, the Siege had only just begun to be mounted, and Captain Fagg in his cutter *Buck* ran into Gibraltar Bay. He saw the Spanish fleet assembled, and decided he would defy them. He began to run between all of these ships, seventy-fours and the like, right under their guns. Well, naturally, they could not believe their eyes—and naturally they fired on him. Fired on him very severe, broadside after broadside, in the attempt to reduce the *Buck* to matchwood. But they reckoned without Captain Fagg's seamanship. He handled his cutter with such consummate skill that she suffered scarcely a scratch to her paint, and he brought her in safe to the mole. What d'y'think of that?'

'A remarkable story, indeed.'

'Aye, very remarkable. Not least because Captain Fagg, God save him, knew nothing of the Siege when he ventured in. His ship had run low in biscuit, sir. He was hungry, that was all, and as he made his nimble way between the Spanish ships, he thought they was firing on him by mistake! Ha-ha-ha. By *mistake*! Ain't that astonishing, Rennie, hey? Ain't that *matchless*?'

'Aye, it is. Very memorable, indeed.'

'Yes, yes, Captain Fagg, by God. Before my time, but a famous story of the Siege. Let me refill your glass, Rennie. Sea officers are always welcome here at the house.'

'. . . and so he was unaware, d'y'see, wholly unaware that the Siege was in progress. The fellow sailed right under the Spanish broadsides, thinking they had made a mistake! Bang-bang-bang! Roundshot whistling all round him, and he thought they was in error!' Rennie banged the table with the flat of his hand, making plates jump. 'When all he wanted was biscuit, the poor fellow! A capital joke!' The African wind flowed through the opened stern gallery windows as Rennie and his guests sat at their supper in the great cabin.

'D'y'think it is a true story, sir—or merely apocryphal?'

James, filling his glass and pushing the decanter to Mr Trent. Mr Sebastian bit a date in half with his great yellow teeth, and said:

'It is quite true, I assure you. I have met Captain Fagg, and he has told me the story himself.'

'You have met him?' Rennie stared at Sebastian. 'When? Where?'

'In my dealings, Captain Rennie, in my travels and my dealings, I meet many men such as Captain Fagg. His duties in the Mediterranean caused him to cross my path from time to time. He is a man incapable of dissembling, or falsehood. The account of his running the blockade is entirely true, I assure you.' He pushed the other part of the date into his mouth, and crushed it.

Mr Trent filled his glass and pushed the decanter to his left. He had not made any contribution to the conversation, save to echo the sentiments of the various toasts, &c., and did not perfectly understand why he had been invited to supper in the great cabin on this occasion. His opinion was that probably Captain Rennie had asked him out of a desire to be reassured. Mr Trent had already made a report in the matter of provisioning—in particular the provisioning for the new detachment of marines—and made it clear to Rennie that all was in order. The spoiled casks had been replaced; additional wine and spirits had been brought into the ship to replace the great quantity of soured beer; the papers brought by Sergeant Host had been honoured by the Victualling Office—Mr Trent had presented the papers himself to the storekeeper. Word had been sent from the Governor's residence to all concerned that *Expedient* was to be accommodated in every distinction, and all was well. The only possible reason, therefore, that the captain could desire his purser's presence at supper was to have by him a reliable man, to have the reassurance of that reliability. This was in turn reassuring to Mr Trent, and flattering too. He sensed—but in course did not say so—that Captain Rennie was not entirely comfortable with his new passenger, Mr Sebastian, and wished to have about him solid naval men, weighty and considerable persons of trust, that in turn lent him their weight. Mr Trent reflected that he was solid, that he was weighty—in fact he was having great difficulty in maintaining that trimmer figure he had briefly achieved at Portsmouth, under the firm direction of Dr Wing. However, Thomas Wing was not present here at supper, to make reproving remarks, nor cast reproving glances as Mr Trent cut himself another wedge of cheese, and refilled his glass with port wine. The purser smiled to himself and gave a little nod as these thoughts passed through his head, and was half startled when Rennie addressed him, as if reading those thoughts:

'Mr Trent, you are content?'

'Eh? Am I content? Indeed, I thank you, sir, I am—am content.'

'Very good.' Wiping his lips with his napkin. 'Not spoiled, hey? Nor sour, any more?'

'Ah, yes—I take your meaning, sir. Re-stored, as to that. Re-stored, and hearty. Aye.'

'Aye, Mr Trent. You have done us proud.' Transferring his gaze: 'Are you content, Mr Hayter?'

'I am replete, and content—thank you, sir.'

He in turn had made his report about the repairs to Rennie, before shifting into his blue coat for supper. He had been able to say with confidence that *Expedient* would be ready to weigh on the morrow, all of her minor repairs completed. What few materials they had required from the dockyard had been forthcoming with none of the usual haggling—they had even been given a handsome supply of new nails, unusual in dockyards away from England, where nails were ever in short supply. Spare sheets of copper had been offered, also. All mightily generous.

'Then, gentlemen, if you are content—then so am I, by God.' Raising his glass. 'A glass of wine with ye—oh, Mr Sebastian . . . I had quite forgot. You do not drink wine.' A polite smile. 'I had no wish to exclude you, when you are my guest.'

Mr Sebastian gave no indication that he was in any way disconcerted by this subtle attempt to achieve exactly that—to exclude him. He seized the water jug, filled a tumbler and raised it.

'I shall drink to anything you like, Captain Rennie, gladly.'

'Anything . . . ?'

'Gladly.'

'Then let us drink to our ship, to *Expedient*—in which we all serve.'

'To *Expedient*.' They drank.

'And to our commission—may it be carried through safe and speedy.'

They drank to that.

Other than the sturdy Mr Trent, and James and Mr Sebastian, Rennie's table was made up by Mr Loftus, the master. Until now he had said almost nothing. He was, unusually for him, flown with wine. He had encountered by chance ashore an old shipmate from the *Alarum* frigate—Bernard Loftus had been master in her during the late American war—and had in consequence already drunk deep before returning to the ship, there to find an unexpected invitation to the great cabin. He found the captain's guest a very odd fellow, and could not grasp the reason for his presence in the ship. And now an urgent consideration had presented itself. Rising from his chair:

'I beg your pardon, sir, but I muss . . . I musst . . .'

'Yes, Mr Loftus?' Rennie.

'If you will esscuse me, sir, I musst jusst . . .'

'Ah yes, I see. The quarter gallery, Mr Loftus. By all means, use my quarter gallery.'

'Thank you, sir, very kind in you . . .' Stumbling as he made his way round the chairs, pulled open the narrow door—a coat button catching as he tried to walk through square, obliging him to turn side on—and at last got himself inside.

PART TWO: THE DUTY

A splashing stream, and a heartfelt sigh. Presently the master returned to the table, buttoning his breeches. He had no clear notion why he had been summoned to supper, and nothing had informed him since they had sat down. He felt himself an inadequate guest, befuddled as he was, aware that he was not making a good impression in welcoming the captain's odd, oddly dressed passenger.

In truth Rennie had wished, by inviting the purser and the master, to conduct a thoroughly dull supper, accompanied by the dullest naval talk—since he reckoned Mr Trent and Mr Loftus two of the most supremely dull fellows in the ship—and thus take the wind out of Mr Sebastian's exotic sails. Rennie had wished James to be there so that he could squash any attempt by his first lieutenant to make a friend of Sebastian. Rennie did not like Sebastian; he felt that in spite of his extraordinary costume and his life on the Barbary shore Sebastian came from exactly the same world as Sir Robert Greer—the world of subterfuge, deceit, and ruthless manipulation in the guise of the nation's interest—and that if he was not curbed at once he would attempt to assume a place of importance in the ship both demeaning to Rennie as a man, and undermining of his position as captain. Rennie thought he could detect in Sebastian a mind and character quite as devious and greedy of power as Sir Robert's, and he was perfectly ready to deter and bamboozle him.

Having made his duty to the Governor, having seen his ship quickly and safely repaired, and quickly reprovisioned, Rennie was determined now to weigh and make sail early on the morrow, set a course for Rabhet, and there assemble the convoy in order to bring it quickly and safely to England. That was his instructed task, that was his duty of commission, and by God he would carry it out to the letter. If Mr Sebastian and Sir Robert had between them devised some other scheme, some other stratagem, of which Rennie was deliberately being kept in ignorance, then they would have to manage it without his subservient assistance. He would sail direct to Rabhet, and Mr Bradshaw in *Curlew* would have to find him on the way, and not t'other way round. He was not Bradshaw's bloody servant, after all, to seek out and make a rendezvous with his damned ten-gun cutter. He sniffed, and proposed the loyal toast.

At sea, 36 degrees 49 minutes north, and 0 degrees 17 minutes west, under a cloudless sky, the wind light from the west and the ship running with that wind on her quarter, and the main course partly in the brails, to allow the wind to flow through to the forecourse and headsails, keeping the head of the ship down a little, so that her cutwater met the blue sea cleanly and she did not pitch—a troublesome flaw in frigates if they were not accurately trimmed and handled well. Mr Loftus did handle her well, and Captain Rennie said so to him as he stood with the officer of the deck, young Lieutenant Upward. Then the captain went below.

Divisions had already been called—there had been no defaulters today—and noon declared, and the hands piped to their dinner. The large new detachment of marines, joined by the detachment already in the ship, had been paraded during the forenoon watch, and had carried out small-arms exercises. They had now gone below to the messes. At first there had been some little friction in the lower deck at Gibraltar, with so many additional men to be allotted hammock and mess numbers, but Lieutenant Quill, ably assisted by his sergeant, and Sergeant Host, had nipped it off so that it did not spark and ignite. These men would be required to man guns, and Rennie was minded to exercise the great guns during the afternoon watch.

Rennie sent for his clerk, Alan Dobie. Mr Dobie had joined the ship very late at Portsmouth, almost too late, rowed out to the mooring by a ferryman, even as Mr Soames was departing in his boat. Rennie was disposed to be severe, on that occasion.

'Where was you, Dobie, good God? In Norfolk, you say? Did not you receive the official letter?'

'I was detained by the illness of Lord Gillingham, sir.'

'Who? Lord who-is-he?'

'My late half-brother's father, sir. He wished me to be at his side in what he thought was his last days upon the earth. He—he had loved my mother, and I was the only family, so to say, that remained to him—after Lieutenant Royce was killed on our first commission, sir.'

'Ah, yes. Yes, Royce, I mind him now. But why did not ye write with this explication?'

'I did write a letter. Perhaps it may have gone astray——'

'Mmff. A fine thing, that I am obliged to delay for a clerk. Delay is very bad, Dobie, as you ought to know by now, in the navy. But in course you are not properly a man-of-war's man, hm? You are a landsman, always and for ever, with your pen and ink.'

'I have done my best to study navigation, sir, so that I might teach the boys—the mids. I have done my best to understand all naval language, I think I may say with some success, in the hope that I might more ably assist you——'

'Yes yes, well well, that's as may be, Dobie. I must not tax you beyond your limited capabilities, when you are so much in earnest.' Nodding, making a face.

Alan Dobie's slight frame had begun to quiver with indignation at these deliberate slights. He felt them keenly, not least because he had done his duty conscientiously in both of *Expedient*'s previous commissions, often in circumstances of considerable danger.

'I am sorry indeed that I do not give satisfaction, sir.'

'Come come, Mr Dobie—do not be petulant, like a servant girl that is reproved. Make your back straight, now, and look the world in the face. You have your pen? Then let us make a beginning, if y'please. I must deal with the great sheaf of vexing papers that is always occasioned by a ship newly commissioned, and provisioned, and manned, and so forth.'

'Very good, sir.' Stiffly, his pen poised.

'Met the new mids yet, have ye?' Rennie, sitting down at his desk, had endeavoured to make amends, feeling that after all Dobie was a perfectly able and willing clerk, and a more than competent schoolmaster.

'I—I have not, sir, since I am only just now come aboard.'

'Yes, well. Wretches, most of them. Oafish wretches. I look to you as schoolmaster to make them gentlemanlike, Mr Dobie, when they tread the quarterdeck. Civilized and gentlemanlike. Hey?'

And now, as Dobie came coatless to the great cabin, Rennie said to him:

'Quarter bills, Mr Dobie.'

'Yes, sir? Have not the middies done their duty? Mr Abey——'

'Middies never did what they was told in the entire history of the Service, except with inattention and muddle and damned idle negligence.'

'I had thought Mr Abey was grown into a very competent boy——'

'Aye, "boy" is the word, Mr Dobie. "Boy" describes him entire. But there is any number of boys in the ship, powder monkeys, nippers and the like, below middies. Middies must be made into men, so that they may take and pass their Board for lieutenant.'

'With respect, sir, I was not—that is, the first lieutenant in usual would take responsibility for the quarter bills, sir, would he not?'

'But he don't post them, good God. That is middies' work. Well well, never mind, Mr Dobie. It ain't *your* work, I expect.' A brief grimace, to show he did not blame his clerk. 'Where is Mr Sebastian? Have you seen him today?'

'I have not, sir. He . . .'

'Yes?'

'Well, he goes about the ship very free, sir. He might be almost anywhere on deck, or below.'

'Not on deck, I think. He ain't a man that can go unremarked on deck.'

'Then perhaps he is below.'

'Just so.' Musingly, half to himself: 'A very curious fellow. He has declined my invitation to dine regular with me in the great cabin . . .' Looking at Dobie again. 'Does he dine instead in the gunroom, I wonder?'

'No, sir.'

'Hm. My steward tells me that he prepares his own food in the forecastle.'

'I understand that is so, sir. He is very fond of chillies, I think.'

'Aye, and other—interesting comestibles. Curse-curse is one of them, I think.'

'Cous-cous, sir. It is crushed grain that is steamed over stewing meat, and spiced with chillies.'

'Just so. I am told that he brought his own killing beasts into the ship, before we weighed at Gibraltar. Lambs. I expect they was put in the manger. How will Mr Trent tell them off on his lists, hey? How will the cook distinguish them? Ha-ha, there may be a difficulty there, in the telling. Lambs have a way of getting ate very prompt.'

A shout from one of the lookouts now, and the answering shout from the deck: 'Where away!'

'I expect that is *Curlew* sighted.' Rennie nodded. 'Her commander has found us, as was his plain duty.'

'Shall you want me for anything else, sir?'

'No no, Dobie. I will say a word to Mr Hayter about the quarter bills, presently.'

A knock at the door. Rennie was expecting Lieutenant Makepeace, as officer of the deck, to inform him that *Curlew* lay ahead, but instead it was the marine sentry:

'Sir, if you please, the gentleman wishes——'

'Yes? Who is that behind you, sentry?'

And the sentry found himself shouldered aside by the bulk of Mr Sebastian, who strode in. His hands were held in front of him, tucked into the voluminous sleeves of his kaftan. He put his great head at a slight angle, and looked at Rennie with his piercing eyes past the hook of his nose.

'What d'y'mean by this intrusion, Mr Sebastian?' Looking past him: 'All right, sentry.' Frowning now at Sebastian: 'What the devil d'y'want, sir?'

'I will like to put things right between us, Captain Rennie.'

'Put things right? I am not aware that——'

'Come, sir, we are men of the world. You have felt yourself burdened by my presence in your ship, burdened and vexed, and was I in your position perhaps I might have felt the same. But the thing cannot be left like that, sir. Under the circumstances, it will not do. In course I will like to make the difficulty go away, or in least so diminish it that we may be equitable in our dealings, sir, and amiable, and able to lift ourselves to the task that confronts us.' Sebastian inclined his head, in what Rennie could only admit was a gesture of gracious goodwill, and Rennie was in turn obliged to nod.

'Hm. Hm. Very good, Mr Sebastian. Will ye sit down?'

A further interruption as a midshipman at the door informed the captain, with Mr Makepeace's compliments, that:

'The *Curlew* cutter is sighted, sir, three points off the larboard bow, and altering course.'

'Very good. Report to me again when we are within hailing distance.'

'Might I ask that your first lieutenant be present, Captain Rennie.' Mr Sebastian settled his great bulk in a chair.

'Eh? Mr Hayter? I do not see——'

'Indulge me, Captain Rennie, will you? As a favour? He is your second-in-command, and I will feel easier in my mind if the two most senior officers in the ship are in accord with me, and I with them.'

'Mr Hayter, I may tell you, will do exactly as I instruct him.' With some asperity. 'That is his duty.'

'Indeed.' Another inclination of that great head. 'Indeed, so. However, Mr Hayter is a man of considerable virtues, I think—courage, perceptiveness, an independence of spirit—that I will like whole-heartedly with me. In short, I will value his unreserving support, beyond mere duty.'

Rennie considered this a moment, decided not to take offence, and again he nodded. 'Very well. Sentry! Pass the word for Mr Hayter!'

'One further indulgence, Captain. I wonder if you will permit me to smoke?'

PART THREE: THE CORSO

Rennie and James sat with Mr Sebastian in the great cabin, the deckhead above them wreathed in tobacco smoke. The rendezvous with *Curlew* had been made, and *Curlew* now lay in line astern of *Expedient* as the two ships sailed on toward Tunisia, in light airs. *Expedient* made the sounds of all ships at sea as the three men sat together at one end of Rennie's table—a susurration of water along the wales, the creaking of timbers, the bell as each glass of the watch was turned, occasional footfalls and shouts on deck as sails were trimmed and seamen clapped on to the falls. Rennie found these sounds comforting and reassuring and easeful to him, and even a little soporific; they were the sounds that in usual drifted over him as he lay down in his hanging cot at the end of each day, and erased his cares. But now he felt himself obliged to be alert, to banish all thought of rest and sleep, and to be alert and attentive to Mr Sebastian.

'Wine, sir?' Colley Cutton, at his elbow.

'What? No no.'

'No wine with your cheese, sir?' Cutton stared in surprise.

'No, I said. Did not you hear? And I have changed my mind about the cheese. I will eat no cheese.'

'Very good, sir.'

'Take it all away, will you?' Waving at the tray his steward had brought. 'Unless you will like cheese, James, and a splash of something?'

'No, thank you, sir. I am content.'

'Will you like more coffee, Sebastian, before you begin?'

'Nothing, when I am smoking, thank you.'

'I never saw such a—such an instrument for smoking tobacco, before this.'

'It is an hookah, I believe, sir.' James, peering at Sebastian, who puffed contentedly, aromatic smoke bubbling through the water in the tall vase of the instrument and emerging from the long curved tube at his lips. 'Or *hukkah*, in the Arabic. Or *chicha*. What are you accustomed to call it, Sebastian?'

'Why, *hukkah*. You have the word exact.' Sebastian, nodding at him.

'Hm. Hm.' Rennie did his best to smile, but in truth the clouds of smoke were pernicious to him, and impeded his wind. He cleared his throat, and blinked to ease the smarting of his eyes. His cat Dulcie had crept from beneath the table, and now climbed into his lap. She shook her head in a little flurry of movement, and sneezed.

'I fear my smoking has discommoded your poor cat, Captain.' Sebastian laid aside the tube for a moment.

'Nay, she is merely settling herself to listen.' Rennie, amiably enough. 'As am I.'

'Then I will begin. I wonder, gentlemen, if you have any notion of the history of the *corso*? Is it safe for me to assume that you have little, or none?' An inquiring glance. 'I thought as much.' Sebastian nodded and settled himself in his chair, his gorgeous kaftan overflowing and settling about him, and again he took up the tube of the hookah, and began to talk. His audience of two exchanged a glance, and prepared— politely—to listen. Sebastian's tone was not hushed, or thrilling, or in any way theatrical, but calm and measured and authoritative. Yet everything he said was imbued with drama, the great drama of events, and in spite of initial scepticism, natural to practical-minded and plain-speaking sea officers, both Rennie and James found themselves drawn in.

'In the eleventh century, numbers of brave knights and

noblemen ventured from Christian Europe into the lands of the Muslim infidels on a glorious spiritual endeavour—the Crusades. But was it spiritual in anything but name? It was not. The Crusades was, in large, forays of a plundering and acquisitive nature, productive of vast fortune—under the guise of righteousness. Is it surprising, was it, that the infidels did not take kindly to this spiritual guidance?' A slow puff, and the hookah bubbled.

'A Holy War erupted between the followers of the two faiths, and there followed the emergence, and great advance, of the Ottoman Turks. They grew powerful and prosperous, and prosecuted their Holy War—*Jihad*—across the Mediterranean and into the continent of Europe.' Smoke curled and drifted in wraiths above Sebastian's head.

'By the close of the sixteenth century, the Turks could advance and expand no further. Their adventures into Europe had been repulsed. They had failed at the Siege of Vienna in 1529, they failed at Malta in 1565, and their fleet was defeated at Lepanto in 1571. We may touch in passing upon Kara Mustapha's doomed foray into Europe a century after, when the cause of Islam was crushed at Vienna in 1683, but their cause in Europe had, to say the truth, been lost by the year 1600. So much for Europe.

'In the Mediterranean, however, the Holy War continued, and was prosecuted most fiercely between the regencies established by the Turks upon the northern shores of Africa—the Barbary states—and the Christian enclaves of Malta and southern Italy, by battle and plunder at sea. The war of the corsairs.'

'Pirates,' murmured Rennie.

'No, sir, not quite pirates. Corsairs were—and are—the equivalent of the privateers licensed by your own king in time of war, to attack and take enemy shipping. The Barbary regencies of Algiers, and Tunis, and Tripoli, at last made their peace with the trading nations of Europe—England, France, Holland—because they knew very well that to continue to take and plunder the merchant ships of those Christian nations, and sell their crews into slavery, would bring down upon them naval wrath and destruction far greater than anything they could withstand. But there was an impediment to the peace. The fortress of Malta is the home of the Knights of St John of Jerusalem, the Hospitallers, who saw themselves as a separate power in the Mediterranean, prosecuting the Holy War by right, a right granted to them by the Emperor Charles V. Their powerful corsair fleets never ceased to attack Muslim ships—and in truth this greatly aided the trading nations of Europe. Their ships were free to sail from one end of the Mediterranean to t'other—from the Levant to Gibraltar—without let nor hindrance. At the same time, the trading ships of the Turkish regencies, the Barbary ships, were attacked and plundered, and their crews sold into slavery, without the Royal Navy, nor the Dutch Navy, nor the French, sending a single shot across the bows of the Christian corsairs.' A thick mist of smoke now hung all round his velvet hat.

'The rulers of the Barbary states felt—you cannot wonder at it—that this state of affairs was inequitable. They were losing position, they were losing prestige, they were losing— above all else—a great deal of money. Now then, when any powerful man finds himself put upon in this way, when he finds himself in such lamentable circumstances, he is certain to take action in his own defence. The deys and beys of the regencies had long since come to regard themselves as self-governing—quite free of Turkish command and rule—and accordingly they had long acted from self-interest. Their fortune was bound up entire with their position in Africa. They ruled as kings and princes in their own right. They had subdued the native African—and indeed ruled their own people—by armies of janissaries. And now their trading ships were being attacked—as they conceived it—by Christian corsairs that the English, and Dutch, and French navies should in all justice have suppressed——'

'You are saying that the Royal Navy was at fault in this?' Rennie interrupted.

'Not the Royal Navy itself, Captain. Officers must follow instruction, that comes from higher men—political men.'

'Ah. Yes. I have you.' He fell silent, and Sebastian continued:

'In this case the instruction was, to all purpose——'

'Do nothing.' James nodded.

'Do nothing, and see nothing.' Nodding in turn, a brief glance at the lieutenant. 'The beys and deys of the regencies therefore resumed their Holy War, by stealth. They employed admirals—men they call *rais*—to sail swift, light and deadly ships, manned by excellent seamen and ruthless janissaries, men that would not flinch from the harshest actions your imagination may tell to you, gentlemen—and worse. These corsair ships, acting singly, or in small, agile fleets, struck without warning at any and all Christian ships that plied the Mediterranean, east and west—they did not confine their activities to the Barbary coast. Not for nothing is the word "barbarian" one of the fiercest known in any language. Their cruelty was boundless. It remains so, still, for the unwary. The Barbary rulers soon reasserted their individual power through the *corso*, as countless officers and seamen and ordinary passengers, too, was taken in chains to the great slave markets of Algiers, and Tunis, and sold at the block, their ships captured and cargoes confiscated.

'A system of sea passes was established, that in theory allowed ships possessing the official printed certificate to pass unhindered and unmolested. But in course forged certificates became as common as genuine certificates . . . and the system was soon become little better than a pretence.' A shrug, and his lips pushed out in a worldly pout. 'You will ask, I expect, why neither the British Navy, nor the Dutch, nor the French, did anything to counter these new corsair assaults. The question arises, following on that: why should the British aid the French, or the Dutch the British, and so forth? Beside, the corsairs were very cunning. They struck always by stealth, swiftly, ruthlessly, almost before their prey was aware of any danger. You cannot defend against such methods by standard naval practice, I think.' Another shrug.

'The history of the conflict is long, and various, and I must not try your patience further, gentlemen. I wished merely to show you what lies behind my ideas in what we have to accomplish. I know these corsairs, you see. I have—sailed in their ships. I know the regencies, and many of the rulers. Our little convoy of ships, with but two ships of war to protect it, could never likely cross the Mediterranean intact—leave alone reach England—without we discuss my stratagems and schemes for keeping us safe.'

'Stratagems? Schemes?' Rennie frowned at him. 'Do I understand you to mean that you have naval stratagems of your own, sir? That you wish to impart to me?'

'Indeed, Captain Rennie. That is my meaning, sir.'

'Well, sir, well well.' Icily polite. 'I think I must tell you that I myself—and Lieutenant Hayter too—have very great experience, both by training and action, of any, several, and *all* such naval tactics as may be required in this or any other commission to defeat His Majesty's enemies at sea.'

'Ah, but the corsair——'

'Do not you think that a frigate thirty-six of the Royal Navy, right well handled, could blast out of the water any half-dozen of your piddling damned corsairs, Mr Sebastian? Aided by a well-handled cutter, with its own carronades, we could smash them so utterly—even an whole fleet of the wretches—they would drown in their own blood before they could draw breath. I will like to hear no more of your meddling landsman's stratagems, if y'please. Nor your tactics, neither.' Rennie looked very dark as he concluded this intemperate outburst, and sat back very stiff in his chair to bring his point home, and poor Dulcie, sensing his upset, leapt from his lap and ran away behind the desk in the corner.

Mr Sebastian said nothing for a moment. He pushed the

hookah away, and blew his nose into a large red silk kerchief. Then, lowering the kerchief and glancing at Lieutenant Hayter, he inquired gently:

'Come now, Captain Rennie, surely you are not quite so foolish as that—are you? When we may face very great danger? An attack by corsairs may be sudden and over-whelming . . .'

Rennie was nearly at the end of his patience with his presuming guest. He drew a sharp breath, and then was saved from further indiscretion by the quite unexpected arrival of the boatswain, Mr Tangible. At the door, peering in past the reluctant sentry:

'Sir, I am indeed sorry to intrude, but it cannot——'

'Yes yes, Mr Tangible. What is it?' Testily, but with a measure of relief.

'It is the fore stay, sir. We feels, myself and my mate, that it cannot be neglected further.' Coming in, removing his hat, and standing firmly on the canvas squares of the decking.

'Neglected, man? I was not aware that neglect had occurred, Mr Tangible.'

'And the fore preventer in addition, sir.'

'The *preventer*!'

'It was that squall in the Bay of Biscay, sir, if you will recall it. We was obliged to rig rudder chains, and tighten back stays, when the ship was put under very terrible strain, and was near knocked down in the sea . . .'

'But y'said preventer stay, Mr Tangible.' Now on his feet. 'I thought I heard y'say, quite distinct, that it was the fore stay?' A brief turn toward Sebastian. 'Forgive me, Sebastian, will ye? These are technical matters, but I fear I must give them my immediate attention.'

'Is there a difficulty, Captain Rennie?' Glancing at Mr Tangible, then back at Rennie.

'I fear there may be a difficulty, aye.' In answer, then: 'Very well, Mr Tangible, thank you. We will go on deck at once. James, I will like you to come with me.'

'Very good, sir.' Rising in turn.

Rennie moved toward the door, and took Mr Tangible by the arm, at his elbow. 'Had you no hint at all of this, before now?'

'None, sir.' Stoutly. 'Until today, none.'

The two sea officers accompanied Mr Tangible forrard into the waist, leaving Mr Sebastian in puzzled, frowning dismay. Presently—very soon—he abandoned his hookah, pushed his great bulk through the narrow doorway, and went forrard himself.

He found Rennie and James on the forecastle with Mr Tangible, examining the rigging in question, the fore stay, and the parallel fore preventer stay.

'Well well, that would mean taking down the crowsfeet, also,' Rennie was saying. 'And each stay would have to be tackled separate, would it not?'

'Aye, sir. In course we could not dismantle both at once.'

'You say both stays is weakened severe, and the collars, also?'

'Aye, sir.'

James had stepped up on the bowsprit, steadying himself on a strapping sheet, and was now peering closely at the collars of the stays. He frowned, leaning closer, and nodded.

'Here is the evidence, sir. It is——'

'Why was not this discovered before now?' Rennie, jerking his head at him. 'When we was at Gibraltar? Christ's blood!'

'I do not know for certain, sir. The ship was inspected thorough, as you know——'

'Yes yes, very well.' A sigh. 'Can this be managed while we are under way, Mr Tangible?'

'I should say not, sir. I should say not.' Gravely.

'It is out of the question?'

'In least so far as the fore stay isself, sir. I would not answer for the ship, was she to meet a squall when either the stay was took down, nor even the preventer, and this even with yards struck and back stays tightened to the limits, and only headsails bent. In my opinion, sir, seeing as you has arst me——'

'Very well, Mr Tangible, very well. We will heave to, and anchor, and carry out the repair.'

Mr Sebastian now came into the bow, steadying himself with a hand on the larboard knight's-head.

'Did I hear you aright, Captain Rennie? You mean to stop?'

'Aye, Mr Sebastian, I do mean that.' And to Tangible: 'What is your estimate of the time required?'

'It will take us all of three watches, I reckon, sir. By the time we has took down, repaired and rove up the stay isself, four-strand cabled—wormed, parcelled, served—and the collars—an whole day, in least. The preventer I do not know until we have took off the collars . . .'

'Then we had better allow a further watch or two for that. We must begin at once.' He moved past Mr Sebastian. 'Mr Hayter.'

'Sir?' James, stepping down from the bowsprit.

'Give Mr Tangible all the men he may require, in addition to his rigging crew. Make it so on the watch bills. We will heave to, if y'please.'

'Very good, sir.' Finding and lifting his speaking trumpet. '*Stand by to heave to!*'

'Captain Rennie, Captain Rennie.' Mr Sebastian, a hand to the captain's arm, in great consternation. 'We ought not to pause in this part of the Mediterranean. A single ship, that is obviously crippled——'

'Crippled! Crippled! We are not crippled, Mr Sebastian, we are undertaking repairs. Your hand is on my sleeve, sir.'

'I beg your pardon.' Removing his hand, but following as Rennie strode aft to the gangway amid hurrying seamen. 'I beg your pardon, but have you no conception of the danger in which you place us by stopping? Danger from corsairs? Cannot you sail on, at a moderate speed, and——'

'Mr Sebastian.' Rennie stopped abruptly on the gangway,

turned and: 'Have *you* no understanding, sir, of the danger to a square-rigged ship at sea when the fore stay is unsound? Even in a topsail breeze, leave alone a sudden squall? If my foremast went by the board we should swing beam on, and founder. Founder, sir, and every man in the ship drowned! Kindly go below now, will you, and allow me to handle my ship and my people as I see fit? Will you, like a good fellow?' And he gave Sebastian a terrible, strained, menacing grimace, in a vain attempt at amiable good manners, and marched aft with his hands clasped behind his back.

Expedient lay at anchor at 37 degrees 41 minutes north, and 6 degrees 30 minutes east, with the repairs of the fore stay and preventer stay undertaken. Roman Tangible had assembled —with the first lieutenant's assistance—a large and industrious rigging crew of seamen and landsmen idlers to carry the work through. Foremast yards had been struck, and the foretop rim and crowsfeet dismantled. The collars of the fore stay had been loosed, and the snaking, so that the whole of the stay could be taken down and the serving and parcelling removed from the cabling, to expose the trouble— the defective, strained and loosened worming.

Mr Sebastian, in spite of Rennie's request that he should go below and keep out of the way, had contrived to appear from beneath the forecastle—where he had gone to oversee the preparation of his food—and to stand by the belfry watching the whole busy, swarming, shouting and elaborate procedure. When Rennie came forrard to inspect progress, Sebastian:

'I am not clear why both these cables must be took to pieces, Captain Rennie. Could not one of them be repaired, leaving the other alone until we reach Rabhet? Every moment we delay increases the——'

'Mr Sebastian, sir.' Rennie, fixing him with a frosty gaze and a bare half-smile. 'Here you are on deck. I thought you was below, sir, attending to your dietary needs. Hey?'

'I was, Captain Rennie. I confess that in my anxiety I have ventured to climb the ladder. May I enjoin you again to——'

'Y'may not, sir.' Curtly, moving forrard.

Curlew had anchored astern of *Expedient*, on Rennie's orders. Lieutenant Bradshaw was taking the opportunity of the delay to carry out his own minor repairs on the cutter; a boat lay tethered under her transom, and there were men slung in rope harness over the side with paint-pots. All was tranquil on the slow Mediterranean swell, in continued light airs. Ripples swelled away from *Expedient*'s boats, lowered and tethered astern. Even the bustle of repair seemed tranquil in the vastness of the surrounding sea.

Rennie made his brief inspection, nodded to the boatswain, sniffed, glanced aloft, and made his way aft, ignoring Mr Sebastian. He stepped from the larboard gangway across to the quarterdeck, slapped the breast rail as he passed, and strode to the binnacle.

'We are set fair for the whole period of the repair, I believe, sir.' Mr Loftus, glancing up to the mizzentop.

'Aye, thank God. Let us hope for brisker conditions only when we are again under way.' Another brief glance over his ship, and: 'I shall be in my cabin, Mr Loftus, where I must write up my journal.'

'Very good, sir.'

And Rennie went below.

He was not left alone long. Very soon Mr Sebastian followed him there to the great cabin, accompanied—to Rennie's considerable irritation—by Lieutenant Hayter, dressed in his working clothes.

'Sir, I hope you will not take it ill when I report to you that Mr Sebastian has something valuable to contribute to our——'

'I do take it ill, Mr Hayter. Have not you duties enough, at present? I will not be badgered by you, nor Mr Sebastian— that has failed to apprehend his place in the ship.'

'Captain Rennie, I beg and implore you to listen to me for

one minute.' Sebastian moved toward Rennie's desk. 'I will not dictate anything to you, only suggest——'

'I wish neither for your supplications nor your suggestions, Mr Sebastian. They are nothing to me, sir.' Very severe.

'Will you not hear a single sensible tactical suggestion, Captain Rennie? That might save——'

'God damn your impertinence, Mr Sebastian!' An explosion of anger, and he flung down his quill pen with a black spray of ink. 'I have done my best to accommodate you in all things in my ship, but I will tolerate no more interference to my command! No, sir! No, sir!' Holding up a hand and shaking his head as Sebastian again attempted to speak. 'Do not make any further intervention now, else I shall be obliged to have you confined. Sentry! Sentry!'

'Sir?' The marine at the door, making his face blank, as if he had overheard nothing.

'Mr Sebastian is going forrard into the forecastle. You will escort him there.'

'Aye, sir.—This way, sir, if you will . . .' Holding the door open for Sebastian, who shook his massive head in turn, flicked a pained glance at James, and allowed himself to be escorted from the cabin.

'I am very sorry, sir,' began James. 'I thought——'

'No, y'did not think, Mr Hayter. In least, not careful enough. D'y'suppose I *relish* lying at anchor, repairing slow on the open sea, good God? D'y'think that I *welcome* this bloody delay? Nay, do not answer. We know the answer well enough. Now then, for Christ's sake leave your commanding officer in peace, will you? Hm?' Picking up his quill, and scattering powder from the pounce box all over the dropleted stain on his desk.

'I—I am—— Very good, sir.' Withdrawing.

⚓

The attack came at dawn. *Expedient* lay facing west at anchor, into the light prevailing wind, and from out of the east, out of the low, sea-dazzling sun, came four fast lateen-rigged galleys, with fifteen double-banked oars in each. Swiftly they slid in under *Expedient*'s stem before anyone on board was aware of what had happened. Slid round on her weather quarter, and her lee, and another vessel ahead under her prow—and she was effectively surrounded. There were lookouts in the tops, but they had allowed themselves to be lulled into near somnolence by the slow riding sea, and the isolation of the ship upon it, and had seen nothing until now. The alarm was raised simultaneously by the lookouts, and by those marines on duty, as decks were being washed by the starboard waisters of the morning watch.

'BOARDERS IN THE SHIP!'

White-clad men wielding scimitars swarmed up the ship's ladders and poured over the sides into the waist. A marine fired his musket and felled a corsair with a shot to the head. The invader pitched over the side in a spray of blood, and his companions set up a terrible shrieking howl of fury. They hacked at fleeing waisters, cutting and slicing their flesh— arms, necks, breasts—with such ferocity that a dozen men fell to the onslaught before any further shots could be fired by the few marines on deck.

Rennie woke in his sleeping cabin to the thud of feet over his head, a renewed burst of musket shots, and the frightful yells of the attackers. He tumbled from his hanging cot, flung off his nightshirt and pulled on breeches, snatched up his swordbelt and a pair of pistols he had removed from their case and cleaned last evening, and bellowed:

'*Sentry! Sentry!*'

The marine at his door did not reply, and Rennie banged out through the door, his sword at the ready and the pistols pushed into his waistband, and was confronted by a scene of shocking and bloody confusion. His sentry lay dead a little way forrard. Men milled and whirled in the waist—white clad men with curved swords, seamen of the watch, red-coated marines. Powder smoke hung in the air, and further shots were fired on the larboard gangway. Rennie dashed to the companion way ladder and up on his quarterdeck. Mr Upward, the officer of the deck, lay badly injured and senseless on his back by the binnacle. Two seamen were fighting a desperate battle with snatched-up weapons of defence—a belaying pin and a knife—against several scimitar-slashing corsairs, that had driven them aft toward the taffrail. Rennie sheathed his sword and pulled and cocked his pistols, hoping against hope they were loaded—and found they were not. He cast them aside, and again drew his sword. Felt movement at his shoulder, was about to whirl, and heard his first lieutenant's voice, low and urgent:

'I am here, sir. I am with you. Take one of my pistols, and we will advance together.'

Rennie turned and took the proffered pistol, nodded his thanks, and the two sea officers ran aft into the fray. Their pistols discharged together *crack! crack!* and two of the corsairs fell, their brains scattered bloody across the planking. The two remaining invaders leapt round and were run through, gut and breast, by two straight-thrusting blades. And they fell. But the battle for the ship was scarcely begun, and was forrard, and could certainly be lost. Rennie and James, and the two seamen, ran forrard together to the breast rail. As they did so, corsairs came in great numbers over the taffrail, swarmed up and over and into the ship, and advanced. So that now the battle was both fore and aft, with more corsairs pouring into the ship at every moment.

For a quarter of an hour everything looked very dark for *Expedient* and her people. It was clear now to Rennie that Sebastian had been right after all; that the corsairs believed his ship to be crippled, and intended to overwhelm her. And the ship was very nearly overwhelmed, except for one vital fact, one telling miscalculation on the part of the corsairs in assaulting a ship of war of the Royal Navy: they had forgotten—perhaps they had never understood—that unlike a merchant ship of comparable size, manned by a few dozen merchant seamen and filled with cargo and helpless passengers, a frigate was peopled by hundreds of belligerents, men trained in warfare, in gunnery, musketry, and hand-to-hand fighting with cutlass and pistol and pike, who would none of them give up their lives with anything but the harshest reluctance and bitterest resentment, a resentment they would visit with deadly purpose and to their last breath upon an enemy. Certainly the corsairs had had the brief advantage of surprise, and had wrought bloody havoc in the waist, but they had no advantage in overall numbers, nor superiority in weapons.

From his place at the breast rail Rennie bellowed orders—*'Beat to quarters! Open the arms chests and issue arms to every man!—'* and was hacked at, and shrieked at, and stood fast, cutting and thrusting with his sword. James fought his way below and oversaw the issuing of the arms as half-dazed men, roused from their hammocks in the lower deck, emerged to fight for their ship and defend their lives.

'Where is Sebastian?' shouted Rennie on the quarterdeck as he saw James run up the ladder with an armful of pistols. Marines now protected the captain in a narrow red line from the continued assaults of the corsairs from the stern. 'And where in the name of God is *Curlew*!'

'I have not seen him, sir. Nor have I sighted *Curlew*—she is not here any more. Fill your waist with pistols, sir.' Handing several pistols by the butt to Rennie. Rennie quickly sheathed his sword and took the weapons. Thrust three into his waist, cocked two others, and fired into the advancing corsairs. James stood at his side and fired forrard along the gangway.

Lieutenant Upward lay where he had fallen, ignored by the corsairs, and now Dr Wing appeared there at the binnacle and knelt to attend to him.

'Christ's blood, is that Wing?' Rennie, in an appalled moment. 'Why ain't he below, in an action? The damned fool will be killed, and how shall our wounded fare? *Go below, Doctor! D'y'hear me!'*

But Thomas Wing did not hear the captain—or chose to ignore him—and remained there on his knees, administering physic, and tying a bandage. Presently, glancing about him, he called to two of the marines:

'You there, corporal! And the man next you! Help me get the lieutenant below, now!'

Crack! Crack! Crack! Musket and pistol shots across the forecastle and deep in the waist now, as guncrews assembled at quarters and issued with small-arms began to make the defence of the ship tell.

Dr Wing, unassisted by the marines he had called to, began to haul his patient bodily toward the companionway ladder. Unbidden, James went to his aid.

'*Mr Hayter! Mr Hayter!'* Rennie, furiously. Again he was ignored, and the brief, dangerous task accomplished. Rennie fired another pistol into the horde of white-clad figures aft, then gave the decisive command of the battle: '*Hands to man the swivels! Fire into the enemy ships! Fire at will!'*

Expedient mounted twelve swivels along her rails, larboard and starboard, and these handy little guns—not 'great' guns, but not small-arms either—could be aimed, fired and reloaded very smartly. Mounted as they were on yoked swivels and standing gunstocks, and fitted with an aiming tiller, they could readily be angled down and discharged into surrounding craft, sending a pound of canister shot in a savage blasting pattern to kill men.

These swivels proved vital. They were aimed, fired and reloaded in a frenzy of activity by two-man crews, and larboard and starboard they killed twenty men with each small broadside:

**CRACK-CRACK   CRACK   CRACK
CRACK   CRACK**

and a blast of flame and boiling smoke from each narrow

muzzle. Three broadsides of canister from the swivels killed over half an hundred men, and wounded half an hundred more. Men climbing from the galleys, and men in them still, struck bloodily down. These lethal blows, plus individual balls from musket and pistol, cut deep into the enemy and caused him to falter, to hesitate, and Rennie:

'They are falling back, lads! Cut the bloody wretches down! Cut them to pieces, and no mercy!'

And he advanced stamping, right foot forward, along the starboard gangway, making his sword flash and glint in the early sun, and ran a corsair through the ribs with a murderous yell.

CRACK   CRACK   CRACK-CRACK

Another fizzing hail of canister, and the mortal shrieks and cries of wounded men.

'Cut them down, the bloody dogs!'

And now the corsairs began rapidly to retreat. Their fierce surprise attack had become a rout. They jumped, scrambled, fell into the galleys, and rapidly pulled east away from the ship.

'Do not cease firing!' Rennie, pointing at the galleys with a quivering finger. *'Fire! Fire! Fire! Rake them until they are out of range, or sunk!'*

The great guns could not be brought to bear with the galleys astern of the ship, but musket ball and swivel canister pursued and cracked across them until they were a cable off and more.

Rennie sniffed in a long breath, and found that he was quivering all over, shaking like the branch of a tree in a stiff breeze. He sheathed his sword with a jittery stutter of metal on metal.

'Are you wounded, sir?' James, anxiously, close at hand and peering at him.

'Nay, nay—thankee, James. Just a little done up, you know. As are we all, I am in no doubt.'

'Indeed, sir—as am I. It was a close-run thing.'

'Just so. Just so.' Another breath. 'But we prevailed, hey? And that is everything, at sea.' A nod, and a long glance away to starboard. 'And now we must find *Curlew* . . .'

———※◊≥———

Curlew had drifted in the night, having lost her best bower through poorly secured stoppers and entwining lanyards, and her other bower dragging, and by dawn had floated out of sight of *Expedient*. When her condition had been discovered—and she had hauled in her remaining cable, weighed and made her way back to *Expedient*—by then the galleys had already been defeated, had fled far to the south, and *Expedient* was again a lone ship riding the swell. Rennie was glad to see *Curlew*, glad to see her tack smartly to within hailing distance and heave to, but his relief was tempered by severity. He wished for explication, and made his signal halyard read: 'Repair aboard me without delay.'

Lieutenant Bradshaw was very apologetic, but made no attempt to excuse himself. When he heard the news of the corsair assault he was even more mortified and ashamed. He showed this by such pained rigidity of expression, and such awkward, wounded stiffness in his person, that Rennie felt for the young man, and was inclined to be less severe with him after all.

'Nay, well. We cannot, I think, in *Expedient* be condemning of you in *Curlew*, Mr Bradshaw, when we have neglected our rigging so woeful. Dragging our bowers is a hazard for any ship, and we do not always discern it at once. The sea is deceptive at night.'

'My people should have been more alert. *Expedient*'s stern lights diminishing in the darkness, my lookout——'

'Your lookout, did y'say? What of mine, hey? None of my lookouts saw a damned thing, when they should have noted *Curlew*'s absence at the first gleam of dawn. Half-asleep, the rogues. Wholly asleep.'

'You was distracted by the corsairs——'

'At any rate, no great harm was done. In truth, no harm came to you at all, other than y'lost your best bower. You was fortunate in being absent.'

'I should never wish to be absent from an action under such circumstances, sir. Such wretched ineptitude——'

'There is no shame in it, Mr Bradshaw. You did not drift away deliberate, it was . . . it was merely inadvertent. We will say no more of it.'

'Very good, sir.'

'Ye'll stay to dinner, Mr Bradshaw.' It was not an invitation in the form of a question; it was a command. Lieutenant Bradshaw bowed.

'Thank you, sir.'

'I will ask Mr Sebastian to dine with us, also. No doubt he will like to be reunited with his cousin, hey?'

'That is kind in you, sir.'

'Hm. Hm.—Sentry!'

A new marine at the door, attentive.

'Pass the word for the boatswain.—Belay that.' Putting on his oldest hat, settling it thwartwise. 'I will go on deck and find him myself.'

'The doctor is here, sir, wishing to see you. Shall I arst him——'

Thomas Wing pushed past the sentry and came into the great cabin. He carried a list, and his face had the pale, detached look of a man that has seen much suffering, and has had to place himself at one remove from it, lest he lose objectivity of purpose. He handed the list to Rennie.

'Fifteen men killed, and Lieutenant Upward badly injured.' His small frame very still.

'Fifteen, when we are short-handed in rated seamen . . . that is very bad.'

'No doubt you will reflect on the fact, Captain, that most of these unfortunate men was merely waisters.' Drily. 'As you will see . . .' nodding at the list in Rennie's hand '. . . there is a further dozen men wounded severe enough to require being excused their duties.'

'Aye, aye . . . just so.' A brief grimace, glancing at the list. 'I must go below, in due time, and look in on Mr Upward. Erm, Doctor Wing . . .' As the doctor turned to leave.

'Yes?' Pausing.

'How many enemy was killed?'

'In the ship, perhaps a dozen. Boarding, or still in their vessels, and those that fell in the sea—I cannot tell.'

'Nay, in course you was below. That is, except when you attended Mr Upward on the quarterdeck. I must say to you——'

'I do not wish for praise, when I have only done my duty, Captain.'

Rennie had not meant to praise his surgeon, but admonish him; nor did he like being addressed as 'Captain' by a warranted man who should know better; he grimaced again, said nothing, and nodded in dismissal. He waited a moment until the doctor had gone, then went on deck to discover Mr Tangible, hear progress on the stays—and attend the declaration of noon.

Mr Sebastian, Rennie discovered at dinner—as the last of the dishes were removed—had not hidden himself below during the corsairs' assault, but had defended the forecastle, and had killed a man there by the Brodie stove.

'So you was defending the stove itself, hey?' Rennie, raising his eyebrows.

'I thought that someone of us had better preserve our means of cooking. I know that the fire is put out when there is trouble at sea, but to allow the stove to be destroyed altogether by the invader was more than I could stomach.'

'Ah. Yes. That is well said.' Rennie nodded, and James

exchanged a quick glance with Lieutenant Bradshaw, and succeeded—just—in keeping his face straight.

With Rennie's permission Sebastian had brought his hookah to the great cabin. Smoke escaped Sebastian's lips and drifted up to the deckhead, where it hung in delicate layers. Between sucking at the tube and speaking he took sips from his coffee cup, always bringing either the tube or the cup to his mouth with his right hand, never his left.

'Perhaps we may return—if you will permit it, Captain Rennie—to the question of corsairs, and tactics?'

'In view of what we have endured, in course I am prepared to hear anything that may aid us in any future encounter.' Rennie, in a neutral tone. 'However, I am obliged to observe that we preserved the ship, defeated the enemy entire, and that no such attack can have success.'

'You do concede, though, Captain Rennie, that the corsair is an enemy—worthy of that name—and not a pitiful rabble?'

Rennie felt himself beginning to bristle, but did not allow his anger to master him. Instead he sniffed, and lifted his head a little. 'Not in the naval sense, he ain't. However—in the piratical dog sense, he might be a troublesome foe, at times. That I will concede, aye.' And he took a pull of wine.

'That is wise in you, Captain.' A sip of coffee, as the ship lifted on a swell, and settled, and the wine in the decanter came level. 'I have served in corsair ships myself . . .'

'So you have said . . .' Rennie put down his glass.

'Indeed, sir, indeed. As a younger man in these waters I have been a slave, chained to the bench of a corsair galley, and I have been a slave-driver, standing over the stinking rows of men with cudgel and whip, or regulating the beat of the drum to determine the rhythm of the sweeps and the speed of the vessel. Neither of these conditions is pleasant, when you must live in the stench and squalor of unwashed bodies and unpumped faeces, amid the groans and sighs of extreme suffering.'

'How came you to be both slave, and slave-driver?'
Lieutenant Bradshaw. 'Was it not——'

'I will come to that presently, if I may.' A sip of coffee, a
glance at his cousin, and: 'I have been also a commander of
janissaries in corsair ships, and have led assaults upon many
unwary merchant vessels. On occasion we used stealth—such
as our adversaries did this day—but in usual the trick was to
fly out of nowhere with a sudden tremendous thunder of
noise. Your janissaries set up a terrifying clatter of scimitars
and shields against the sides of the ship, and a blood-curdling
cacophony of shrieks and and yells. Your prey is at once
intimidated, all thought of flight is made impotent by the
malevolent uproar, and before he can collect himself to
resist—he is lost.'

'But how came you to this occupation——'

'All in good time, my dear Dutton.' Another brief nod at
his cousin. Smoke drifted from his mouth and he took in the
others with an encompassing glance, and continued: 'I have
been an intermediary between corsair *rais* and the merchants
of the great slave markets of Algiers and Tunis, and an
intermediary between slaves and financiers, in the arranging
of ransom. Have you any notion of the value of slavery to the
Barbary states? It is enormous. It is tremendous. The whole
of their prosperity would fall without it. Thus . . .' a worldly
shrug '. . . thus, any man that finds himself enslaved, and
wishes to be free again, must first find the means. It is a
question of business. He must strike a bargain.'

Another suck of smoke, and the gurgle in the jar. The
sound of the bell echoed through the ship from the forecastle
as Sebastian, his head wreathed in smoke:

'In due course, I was able to make for myself a modest
fortune, and my activities came to the attention of Rashid
Bey. He believed at first—for I let him believe it—that I was
a Circassian. Only later did he learn that I was English by
birth, but even then I felt it wise to assume the role of an
apostate, a convert to Islam. As time went on, and I was able

to be of greater and greater use to him—as adviser, and counsellor—he ceased to care what might be my religious beliefs. His chief and only concern was my loyalty to him.'

'And . . . ?' Rennie, his head cocked a little to the side.

'Am I loyal to him? Is that what you ask?' A sip of coffee, an inquiring look.

Rennie could not quite get used to Sebastian's assumption, his subtle but irksome assumption—to Rennie—of superiority in these discussions. He did not care for Sebastian's manner. But again he contrived to hold his wrath in check, and to be agreeable. He made himself smile, and waited for the answer to his question.

The smile was returned. The smile, and nothing more—until presently:

'If I may iterate, Captain Rennie—it is a matter of tactics. Yes, a question of tactics.'

'Eh? What is, sir?'

'Our purpose. Our whole venture. I will like to lay my proposed tactics before you—in case of further attack, that may well be more concerted and determined than the assault we have suffered today. You will hear me out . . . ?' A quizzical look.

Damn the fellow, thought Rennie, but he said: 'I will, in course, I will. But I must say this to you, before I listen. I am not obliged in the ship to adopt any tactics that I do not believe to be sensible, and worthwhile. I am in sole command, which ain't a right—it is my duty and obligation, upon my oath to the King. You apprehend me?' And he made himself smile again.

'You are very direct, Captain Rennie, and I thank you for that. I propose this: At the moment of the future attack all of Sergeant Host's marines will rise up in the ship, clad in white, and white turbans, and brandishing scimitars. As the attacking corsairs approach——'

'Forgive me, Mr Sebastian, for interrupting you, but you appear so entirely certain that this further attack will come that I wonder if you have direct intelligence of it, that I do not . . . ?'

'Allow me to say only that I am quite certain it will come, at a time following on our departure in convoy from Rabhet. I cannot be more exact.—May I proceed?'

Rennie gave an impatient little sigh. 'Has this intelligence come to you from Sir Robert Greer? Or from another source, here in the Mediterranean, or on the Barbary shore?'

The great head turned, and Mr Sebastian in turn gave a little sigh. 'I cannot be more exact,' he repeated, 'I have told you all that I am able at present. Will that suffice . . . ?'

'No, sir, it will not.' Bluntly.

'No?—No.—However, I may say no more . . .'

And now Rennie could contain his irritation no longer. He sniffed in a great breath, rose from the table, gripped the back of his chair—and bellowed:

'Cutton! Colley Cutton! I am going on deck! Bring me a can of tea there! And *jump*, by God!' And without further word, without explication of any kind to his guests, he banged out of the great cabin, and banged up the companionway ladder.

⚓

Noon of the following day, and *Expedient* at last under way— the two fore stays again whole and sound, after the interruption of the corsair attack—and *Curlew* at two cables distance in line astern. The beginning of the new day declared, and the ship's position fixed by the duty midshipmen and the master at 37 degrees 53 minutes north, 11 degrees 12 minutes east.

Captain Rennie—having kept to himself for most of four-and-twenty hours—addressed the assembled ship's company. The boats were again towing astern to make room in the waist. For the occasion Rennie wore his dress coat and his dress sword, his cockaded hat firmly athwart his head. A burial service for the dead would follow; the shrouded corpses lay in a line by the waist guns.

'As we are all sorrowful aware we have lost some of our shipmates, in the cowardly and unprovoked attack upon us yestermorn by piratical dogs. We defeated those damned mongrel wretches, and showed them what is the consequence when they attack stout-hearted Englishmen, in one of His Majesty's fighting ships.'

A murmur of approval.

'We will proceed to the coast of Tunisia and the port for which we are designed: Rabhet. I will like to make all possible speed, now that we have completed our repairs. But first we will honour and bury our dead. I will read from the Book of Common Prayer.'

He took off his hat, and the ship's company bared heads, and bowed them.

On deck Rennie stood apart from the hands of the first watch, aft in darkness at the weather side of the taffrail. Hammocks had been piped down long since, and the ship was quiet. Rennie felt the light, steady wind on his face, and allowed all of the upheaval and upset of the last two days to slip away astern, and was tranquil. Light from the stern gallery window cast a glow over the folding green lace of the wake. Beyond this framed glow on the water, wisps and sparklings of phosphorescence flashed across the darker sea. Rennie took a deep breath, leaned back against the rail, and looked aloft at his spanker curving up to the gaff. Far forrard on the forecastle a seaman lifted his voice in a lament, and the words came drifting:

> Oh my darling, I am gone from you
> Oh my dear, I'm far away
> And I yearn for you as night descends

> Love, more than I can say
> Yes, you and I must wait awhile
> Wait long and many days
> For my ship to bring me back again
> Into your sweet embrace.

And Rennie was at once struck—and utterly overcome. Tears filled his eyes and dripped on his cheeks. His throat tightened. He felt as if something had broken within him, and he sobbed helplessly and had to turn away toward the quiet dark sea.

'Oh, Christ . . .'

His love not only far away, but lost and gone for ever. Lost with the house on the wide wild moor, and all their life that might have been. Everything came in on him from the darkness, flying into his heart on the wind, on the notes of the song, and he felt physically weakened, bodily beaten and broken by the force of his emotions. All of his previous life was dross, aside from that brief intervening golden time, a few months when hope had been within his grasp, glad and warm, when he had held his love in his arms and read love in her eyes. And now—now all of his life stretching ahead could only be dark and dead. What could lie there that was not cast over by the black shadow of his loss? Were not all the oceans and seas, all headlands lifting out of the horizon, all fiery dawns and fire-dying sunsets, broad across the world—were not they all dimmed and hid by perpetual dark drear mist?

> Oh my darling, I am gone from you
> Oh my dear, I'm far away . . .

'God help me,' wept Rennie, and he had to grip the rail to prevent himself from falling. 'Oh, I am lost—lost certain and for ever without my dear sweet Susan . . .'

'Sir?' A figure by the wheel, peering aft. Lieutenant Hayter.

Rennie shook his head, dashed tears from his eyes, and blew his nose. He turned and faced forrard. He must betray no sign of weakness, nothing of lowering emotion or weakness. He swallowed, cleared his throat, and:

'Yes, Mr Hayter, y'may come aft.'

James approached, his hat under his arm. 'Mr Sebastian has asked me to convey to you how sorry he was to have offended you, yesterday. In course, also, he wishes you to know that he will be our friend at Rabhet, in all particulars. He wishes to give us assistance in everything there—and after. That was always his intention. His purpose was never to seek to usurp your authority.'

'Ah. Ah. Thank you, Mr Hayter. That is . . . hm . . . that is welcome news. I may perhaps . . . hm . . . I may perhaps have been a little harsh in my behaviour toward him, and to you, James, and young Bradshaw, in leaving you all so abrupt at dinner yesterday. I—I have had much on my mind.'

'Mr Sebastian wished to know if you would shake hands, sir.' Waiting.

'Eh? Shake hands? No no, there is no need of that. Tell him—tell him that I accept his apology, that I am glad, and so forth. Tell him that I shall speak to him in the morning. I am—in need of further air, just at present.'

'Very good, sir.' Slightly puzzled. 'Good night'

'Good night, James.' Turning away to the rail.

Rennie had set himself a task. He had done so to alleviate his despondency and gloom, that had persisted through the night, long after James had come on deck to tell him of Sebastian's decision to aid and assist the commission at Rabhet and after. He had lain in his hanging cot—listening to Mr Sebastian's stertorous snores rumbling from the coach—tossing and turning, and seeing in his head the moor falling away in a long green slope from Belveer Crag, far down to

Lower Tor and the valley of the River Dart to the south. Had walked there again, with Susan at his side, her shawl lifted from her shoulder by the wind, the soft sighing wind, and their dogs running ahead, flushing birds from clumps of gorse and bracken. Had walked there, and heard the distant mewing of buzzards rising and falling on the air, across the places of his heart.

And at last had risen—at six bells of the morning watch, to the rhythmic swishing of holystones along the decks—and begun to assemble his lists. This was his task: to assemble the entire written-out duties of the ship's day, with every man's name in its place at stations, quarters, divisions, &c.; the mess numbers, hammock numbers, guncrew numbers. As hammocks were piped up in hurrying clatter at seven bells, he had summoned his clerk, and his first lieutenant.

'Mr Dobie, you have got your pen?'

'In course, yes . . .' fumbling, a cough, pushing back tangled hair '. . . yes, I have got it.'

'Are you indisposed, Mr Dobie?'

'No, sir.'

'Then tuck in your shirt, sir.'

'I'm sorry . . . I have only just woke.'

'It is natural in man that he should wake in the morning, Mr Dobie. But this is a ship of war, and we cannot waste time dashing the sleep from our eyes, and adjusting our clothes, when we may be called to action at any moment. Hey?'

'No, sir. I am ready.' Holding up his notebook, and his pen.

'Very good. I am settled upon a new method of organization . . . y'may sit as you write, Dobie.'

'Thank you, sir.' Sitting at the table, placing ink and pad before him, holding his pen poised.

'I am settled on a Duty Book, that will be drawn from all of the lists available to us in the ship, having as its foundation the ship's books themselves.'

'. . . ship's books themselves.' Dobie, dipping and scratching.

'Each man, from the lowliest landsman idler to the highest—so to say—the highest topman petty officer shall be included, according to his several duties, in the Duty Book. And all of the others in the ship, naturally. Including midshipmen, warrant officers, and commissioned officers.'

'And the marines, sir?'

'Yes yes, in course the marines.'

'. . . and marines . . . both men and officers . . .' Scratching rapidly.

'The duty quartermaster for each watch; the helmsmen for each watch—both weather and lee; the master's mate; foretopmen, maintopmen, mizzentopmen; forecastlemen; afterguard waisters; and the parts of the watches, and so forth—nay, do not write "and so forth".'

'No, sir.' Sighing, scratching a line through.

'It must include—or shall I say encompass? Yes, encompass. It shall encompass all of the differing exigencies, for all circumstances. Stations for weighing or unmooring, and leaving harbour. Stations for going about through the wind. For wearing. Everything. Ah, Mr Hayter. Was you delayed?'

'I was, sir, briefly. I beg your pardon.' James stood at the door in his working rig.

'Come in, come in. We are busy with our Duty Book.'

'Duty Book, sir?' Coming in and joining them at the table.

'Aye, you heard me right. Each day, for each man, there is his duty—his several duties, multiplied by several circumstances that may arise—and they must all be wrote out.'

'Are they not wrote out already, sir, with respect? Divisions, watches, parts of watches, stations, quarter bills, and the like?'

'Yes, but it is all a very great muddle of individual lists, individual papers and lists. It must be regulated and set down all at once for each man, in the new Duty Book. It is my object to make it so, and I will not be deflected nor thwarted.' A warning glance.

'Aye, sir. Very good. What is my duty in this?'

'Eh? Well well, it is to—to assist.' Nodding, as if this ought to have been perfectly plain.

'Yes, sir.' Waiting politely.

'Do you wish for a egg, sir? Hor two eggs?' Colley Cutton, emerging from the cramped larboard quarter gallery, which he had converted into a temporary pantry now that Mr Sebastian occupied the coach. Steam rose from the lamp-heated kettle behind him. Dulcie the cat came from beneath the table, and at once began to push her head against his ankles. Rennie glared at him.

'Why d'you interrupt me when I am at work, Colley Cutton? Cannot you see that I am, good God? Have you fed my cat?'

'Not today, sir, no, has yet. I was about to do so, following behind of your breakfast, sir . . . Will it be one egg, hor two, sir?'

'Two then, two. In half a glass. Not before half a glass.'

'Aye, sir. Two, sir.' Backing into the quarter gallery, pulling shut the narrow door and excluding Dulcie, that fell to licking her chest in vexed dips of her head. Presently the door was opened a trifle to admit her, but she disdained this offer and fell to washing her tail.

'Is it because we are short-handed, sir?' James now asked. 'Even more so, since the attack?'

'No no. Well—yes and no, yes and no. I have had it in my mind some considerable time, but since Gibraltar and the new detachment of marines—and indeed the corsair attack— I have had additional incentive. The new marines have had to be accommodated in the ship, assigned mess numbers, hammock numbers, and guncrew divisions, and so forth, and this has concentrated my mind. However, it is a scheme much older than this commission, you know.'

'Yes, sir?'

'Yes yes, indeed.' Warming to his theme. 'The Duty Book is a notion I have entertained since I was in command of

Mystic in '82. It will answer for all ships in the Service, I think, from first rate down to sixth and below. It is a question of system, d'y'see, and method. A system by which everything and every man is fitted into place. It works like a—well, like a clock, with all of its intricate parts precise and efficient—tick-tick-tick. You have me?'

'I—I think so, sir.'

'The Duty Book is the ship's clock.'

'Like the chronometer? Do not we have two chronometers, sir?'

'I meant—as a metaphor.'

'Ah.' Nodding.

Something in this nod irked Rennie. He shot James another warning glance, and:

'I will not like any kind of slovenly, lubberly, deliberately reluctant conduct in this, I will not tolerate nor countenance ill-will in the performance of duty.'

'No, indeed, sir.' A frown of surprise.

'I shall expect from my officers whole-hearted support.'

'Yes, sir.'

'And in future I will like all officers that come to the great cabin to shift into a blue coat before.'

'Very good, sir.' James, glancing down at his working clothes.

'Very well. Mr Dobie, you will assemble the whole by the declaration on this day, and present it to me on the quarterdeck, bound with twine, and the title plain upon the cover in black ink.'

Alan Dobie stared at the captain appalled, his pen between inkwell and notebook. 'The Duty Book—entire?'

'Are y'deaf, Mr Dobie?'

'No, sir.'

'No, you are not. You may set to work in your own quarters. Take the lists with you.' A nod of dismissal.

Dobie gathered up the massed lists, bills and muster books from the captain's table, and hurried out.

'Was it wise to be so severe with Mr Dobie, sir?' began James. 'After all——'

'Mr Hayter.'

'Sir?'

'Who is in command of this ship?'

'In course—you are, sir.'

'Then ye've answered your own question. Good morning.—*Cutton! Breakfast!*'

But James could not allow himself to be dismissed without first:

'Sir, if you recall, I said last night that Mr Sebastian had agreed to assist us in everything at Rabhet and after. In fact he gave me his proposed plan of action for the defence of the convoy, that he had wrote out, and I had meant to pass it to you, sir . . .'

'Well?' Curtly.

'When may I give it you, sir?'

'You have it?'

'It is in my cabin, sir—in my blue coat.'

'Then y'may go to your cabin, shift into your coat, and bring back the plan—to breakfast.'

'Thank you, sir.'

PART FOUR: RABHET

The minor regency of Rabhet, in Tunisia, lay in the region south of Mahdia, on the northernmost reaches of the Gulf of Gabes. It was founded in AD 904 on the site of a ruined Roman fort, and its wealth came from trading in the products of extensive olive groves, first established by the Romans, and then revived. By the middle of the tenth century Rabhet was rich, the town and the port grew, a large and impressive medina was established, and the Great Mosque built—its towers and courtyard, and *qibla* wall, reckoned the finest in all Islam.

In the upheavals of the twelfth century Rabhet was attacked by Christians, and fell in 1152. The Rabhetans were intent on revolt, but were circumspect rather than precipitate in their actions. They planned and schemed for two years. On New Year's Eve in 1155, as fireworks exploded over the town, the insurgents spread through the squares and along the waterfront in the guise of beggars. As the celebrations reached their height the beggars cast off their rags, drew their swords and overran the Christian fortifications. The rout was total, accompanied by the blood-freezing shrieks of the attackers, and there was terrible slaughter. The dazzling Christian procession through the town—of bejewelled saints and gold-decorated horses—provided the victors with the means to rebuild their medina and the Great Mosque, sacked during the invasion. The central part of the city was known thereafter as the Square of the Golden Horse.

In 1549, Rabhet became a separate regency in Tunisia under the ruthless Bey El Hakkan. Pirates, adventurers, Christian corsairs all attempted over the following two centuries to invade this most prosperous of the minor regencies—that traded all over the Barbary coast, and into the Levant—but all were repulsed. The original Bey's descendants and wider family maintained their control, and now under Rashid Bey Rabhet prospered still. However, powerful neighbours now threatened his independence; larger fleets than his, and greater armies, were gathering to invade, and Rashid Bey was in need of friends.

All this Mr Sebastian conveyed to Captain Rennie and Lieutenant Hayter in the hours preceding *Expedient*'s arrival at Rabhet.

The city of Rabhet, and the port and harbour, lay in a half-circle of low hills, facing east. On the north a jutting eminence fell down in gentle terraces of olives to a long south-turning tongue of land, low and rocky, on which stood the harbour fortifications—a castle and a fort. Further harbour defences included an inner wall of rocks that stretched in a curve from the southern shore, protecting the entrance. The city itself stretched away in a sun-brightened white and yellow sprawl up the shallow incline from the port, the towers of the Great Mosque and other prominent buildings visible from a league and more out to sea. Further fortifications lay along the waterfront, protecting the stone wharves and piers.

Within the harbour great numbers of ships lay moored: galleots, tartanes, pinques, chebecs, misticous, lateen-rigged barques, feluccas, polacres, saiques. James noted all of them in his glass as *Expedient* and *Curlew* ran in toward the harbour entrance. *Expedient* saluted the fort with her starboard battery, thirteen guns blank-loaded with Mr Storey's special 'glory smoke' powder.

BANG   BANG   BANG   BANG   BANG

The fort answered with its own battery of heavy guns.

BOOM   BOOM   BOOM

Smoke hung in lazily expanding clouds above the rocky ground at the fort, and across the breeze-ruffled water to leeward of *Expedient*, creating dramatic shadows as it drifted away. The vessels at the harbour entrance—a pair of armed barques—cleared a road. *Expedient*, under topsails and head-sails in the breeze, slipped in and dropped anchor. *Curlew* followed.

Rennie ordered his launch hoisted out, but Mr Sebastian:

'Nay, Captain Rennie, Rashid Bey will send his galley. You have no need of your own boat in Rabhet harbour.'

Rashid Bey did send his galley, and Rennie and Sebastian were rowed in to the pier—not quite a mole—and there landed. Rennie was uncomfortably hot in his dress coat, and his tasselled dress sword caught on a rope as he stepped out of the galley on to the stone stair of the pier on the lift of the sea. He nearly stumbled, and was acutely aware that to have measured his length in these circumstances—the Bey's large entourage awaited him in great solemnity on the pier—would have been a wretchedly inauspicious beginning. Mr Sebastian caught Rennie's elbow at the vital moment, and prevented ignominy.

Rennie glanced at him as they ascended the stair—the watery light reflected in the gold circles on Sebastian's hat—and nodded his thanks.

'Do we go to the castle on the spit there, Mr Sebastian?' asked Rennie.

'No, Captain, no. Nor to the fort, neither. We go to the palace in the medina.'

To Rennie's surprise they were to ride to the medina not in a carriage but upon horses. The animals were lined up, held at the bridle by a row of white-clad grooms. The horses

were greys, and to Rennie's dismay were evidently spirited
beasts, tossing their heads and rolling their eyes nervously.
What if he was thrown? Good God, that would be even more
ignominious. At the best of times Rennie was not an accomplished horseman. He rode when it was absolutely necessary.
He had ridden when he lived on the moor. But in usual,
through all his life, he never went near to a horse except to
ride in a gig, sociable, or coach.

'Are those horses for us, Mr Sebastian?' Knowing the
answer, dreading it.

'They are, Captain. Mine is the sturdiest mare—you see
her, at the far end?'

'Ah, yes. Tell me . . . ?'

'Yes?'

'Which animal will I be expected to mount? They do not
quite have the look of amiable beasts, Mr Sebastian. They
have a skittish, unruly, wilful look, hm?'

'They are fine horses, Captain, never fear. Once you are
up—all will be well.'

'Once I am up, indeed. But which beast has been chosen
for me? Or—or may I choose my own?'

'I think not. I think that very probably the horse two away
from my own in the line is the mount that is designed for
you.' Nodding at a horse with golden harness.

'Are you certain?' Regarding the animal with deep
suspicion. 'D'y'know, Sebastian, I have decided to walk to the
palace, after all. Yes, I have a mind to stretch my legs.'

'That will never answer, Captain. We must ride to the
medina, with due ceremony and dignity.'

The medina and palace at Rabhet were built in a rough
square, not quite an oblong, at the centre of the city. The
gates—a later addition—were in the Ottoman style, with
minaret towers, flanked by tall bearded palms. The palace
itself had been built and rebuilt over the centuries; first in the
twelfth century following on the Christian invasion and
sacking; then later in the fifteenth and sixteenth centuries, as

the power and wealth of the city grew. Hints of the Italianate style were clear in the two grandest pavilions. But it was the extensive gardens—of olives, cedars, and cork oak—that were truly exceptional, with deep groves and avenues that might have been found in Paradise itself. Here under the spreading branches could be imagined scenes of great luxury and ease and elegance, where the harsh sun was ameliorated and softened by Umbrian shade, and there were pools of clear water. The mounted entourage rode at a steady pace from the gardens to the palace. The great tower of the main pavilion, Rennie thought as he gazed up at it, would not have been out of place in . . . where? Florence? Venice?

'But I have never seen Florence,' said Rennie to himself. 'Nor Venice, neither.'

'You have rode here without discomfort or alarum, after all?' inquired Sebastian, riding up beside him now on his sturdy mare.

'I had feared the girthing strap was loose—but I have come to no harm, thankee.'

'I have always found that it is wisest to grip with the knees, in such a case. And as a last resort, to grip the mane.'

'With my knees, good God?'

Rashid Bey was not nearly so gorgeously dressed as Mr Sebastian. Nor was he as tall or imposing a figure as his principal adviser. A man in early middle life, guessed Rennie, perhaps in his middle thirties, fine-featured, with intelligent dark eyes, Rashid Bey wore instead of a fabulous kaftan a simple white costume. White turban, white blouse, white pantaloons. His only concessions to vanity of appearance were a pair of red and gold slippers, and a gold thumb ring set with rubies. He received Rennie and Sebastian in a long cool room of symmetrical arches and angles, tiled in mosaics, and floored in patterned tile. A gallery ran round the entire room at an upper level, with elaborate calligraphy set into the walls. Rennie had on Mr Sebastian's instruction removed his sword and his buckled shoes, and retained his hat, which in usual he would have removed upon entering any building, leave alone so grand a building as a palace. They all sat on the tiled floor, Rashid Bey and Sebastian beside him in complete ease and apparent comfort, Rennie with awkward, knee-jutting discomfort; before long he was nearly crippled by his aching back and aching joints, and had to make a concerted effort not to show any pain or displeasure in his face.

Before Rashid Bey on the tiled floor lay a pen-holder, ink and a loose roll of paper, on which had been inscribed—in scrupulously neat and intricate calligraphy—a list. In a surprisingly deep voice, and accentless English, Rashid Bey:

'You are come direct from England, Captain Rennie?'

'I am, sir—that is, with a short stay at Gibraltar.'

'Ah, yes, to meet Mr Sebastian. I wonder have you heard of a Mr Richard Amiss, of London?'

'I . . . do not know that I have, sir. Amiss? No, I think not. Is he a sea officer?'

'Sea officer . . . ?' Shaking his head, glancing at Sebastian.

'A naval man, effendi.'

'Ah, a *rais*.' A nod to Sebastian, and he smiled at Rennie. 'No, Captain, not a man such as yourself. He is a man that makes an implement for the mouth.'

'The mouth? Hm.' Politely.

'Yes, he has made this implement to his own design, from bone, and the bristle of the hog. Well, that is unclean, but perhaps another bristle might be found. From another beast.'

'Ah. Hm.' A fixed smile.

'It is a most ingenious notion, this implement. If only we could find a different bristle, then I would have my craftsmen construct one for my own use.'

'Indeed, sir . . . ?' A polite nod, disguising utter bewilderment.

'Yes, for my mouth, you see. To cleanse all of my teeth, cleanse them of particles of food after eating. He has called his invention a "mouth brush".'

'Has he? Has he? That is—that is excellent news.'

'It is, I think so, yes. I have had to use a stick my whole life, sharpened quite fine, and it is apt to prick the tongue. And most vexingly slow, as a method.'

'Indeed?' Raising his eyebrows. Was he hearing quite right, wondered Rennie, in these strange stone-and-tile surroundings?

'Ah well, you cannot enlighten me further then, as to Mr Amiss?'

'I—I fear I cannot, sir.'

Rashid Bey leaned and with a neat stroke of the pen eliminated an item from his list. Laying down the pen: 'If I may inquire, Captain Rennie—do not think me intruding—what is your own method, in your ship?'

'Method, sir? You mean, in handling her?'

'To refresh your mouth—at sea.'

'Ah. Well well—I am accustomed to tea, in the morning. That refreshes my mouth, you know, and brings me wholly awake.'

'You do not wash your mouth? You do not cleanse your teeth?' Surprised.

'Well, sir, hm. I am not acquainted with Mr Amiss and his—his machine—so therefore I cannot say that I am accustomed to his methods.' A glance at Sebastian, who gave the merest nod of support.

'Thank you for indulging my curiosity, Captain. I hope I did not offend your sensibilities by such inquiry?' Rashid Bey again took up his pen.

'Not at all, sir, not at all.' Relieved to be released from dental inquisition.

'We will now proceed to the business of your visit.' Marking an item, putting the pen aside.

⚜

Lieutenant Hayter, aboard *Expedient* in Rabhet harbour,

wrote up his journal; he included quick, accurate sketches of the harbour and surrounds, the fort and castle, and other defences, and the rocky eminence with its descending olive terraces. It was a habit he had acquired as a midshipman, and had maintained since his first commission, a practice encouraged in the navy because it taught sea officers how to be accurate in observation, as an adjunct to navigation; further, it taught them to sketch each and every landfall in the wider interest of the nation. The eighteenth century had been a century of war, most particularly of war with the French. It was as well for the Lords Commissioners of the Admiralty, and the Government, to have at their disposal as great a breadth of information about foreign ports of call as could be produced—should the nation be obliged again to go to war.

When he had laid aside his pen he carried out a detailed inspection of the ship, a duty he and Rennie had agreed upon before the captain went ashore. He inspected both the running and standing rigging—the cable-laid ropes beginning to drip tar in the African heat—and assessed the condition of repair of all masts and yards. He required the standing officers—the gunner, carpenter, and boatswain—to give him accurate reports of their stores. He looked at the sail lockers with the sailmaker. He drank coffee, and chewed a biscuit, and with a sigh settled to the task of listing defaulters in the book for punishment. The heat was not quite intolerable, but the merest increase of intensity would make it so. His cabin was very close, the whole of the gunroom and the lower deck was close, and airless, and noisome. Presently he went on deck.

Awnings had been rigged, and the gratings over the hatches in theory should have provided some circulation of air—but in truth did not. Hammocks had been washed, and hung triced up the length of the ship.

'Mr Tangible!'

The boatswain came to him in the waist. 'Sir?'

'I will like windsails rigged at the hatches, Mr Tangible. We must endeavour to get some cooler air below.'

'Aye, sir.' Glancing about, and wiping his brow. 'I don't know that we shall be able to cool this air, sir. It is Africk air, when all is said.'

'We must get some air 'tween decks, Mr Tangible. Tomorrow, I think, we shall wash and smoke. The ship is damned ripe below, and the captain . . .'

'Aye, the captain don't like bilge reek, sir.'

'He does not. Let us make a start with the windsails, at any rate.'

'Mr Hayter?' From aft. The first lieutenant turned to look from the sun-dazzled waist into the comparative gloom below the quarterdeck, as the boatswain left him and went forrard.

'I am here.'

Alan Dobie came to him from the demi-darkness. 'May I speak to you privately?'

'Is it a private matter, Alan?'

'Not exact, but——'

'I am very busy, you know.' Tying his blue kerchief round his head.

'Yes, I can see that you are. However . . .'

'Yes?' Impatiently.

'I think that I must say what I have to say—in private.' Lowering his voice, glancing round at the hands in the waist.

'Oh, very well. We'll jump up to the quarterdeck, and go to the taffrail. Will that suit?' And without waiting for a reply he did jump up the ladder, and Alan Dobie followed.

At the taffrail James stood looking at the many other ships in the harbour, and leaned out to observe *Expedient*'s stern cable—she was moored fore and aft—and the anchor buoy. Turning: 'Well, Alan?'

'You recall the captain's idea for a Duty Book?'

'I do.'

'I fear that I was unable—unable to complete the task. In

truth I was lost before I had begun. There was too many lists and papers. He has said no more about it to me, since that day. But I am in a quandary. What should I do about it? Am I to pretend that I still contrive to complete it? Or must I confess that it is beyond my capabilities?'

'Good heaven, Alan, is *that* all you wished to ask me? It is really a very little thing——'

'I ask you only because the captain wished you to be present when he set us this task.'

'Us?' Frowning now. 'How d'you arrive at "us"?'

'He wished you to assist, did he not?'

'Ah, I see. Very well. You mentioned two possibilities, hey? Pretend that you are still at work, or confess that you are not. There is a third.'

'Yes?'

'Yes. Say nothing.'

'You think so?'

'Certainly. In all likelihood he will say nothing to you, if you say nothing to him. It was a whim, a fancy, and he has forgot all about it.'

'You think that?' Dubiously.

'Frankly I do. And now, I hope that has put your mind at rest, Alan.' Turning forrard.

'Wait—there is something else.'

'Eh?' Turning back.

'I have overheard something.' Looking very serious, again lowering his voice. 'Something that concerns the future safety of the ship. I do not like to carry tales, to be a common informer, but I think this may be very important. That is why I wished to talk privately . . .'

'What did you hear?' Taking his arm, and bringing him to the corner of the rail. 'Do not hesitate, Alan. In view of all that has happened, it is your plain duty to speak up.'

'Nay, I must keep my voice down.' A near whisper. 'I heard some of the marines—the Chatham marines, that are not properly part of the ship's complement—I heard them say that when the time came they was intent on going into the boats, escaping to *Curlew*, and running away in her.'

'Did you hear them say when that time might be?'

'No, I did not. The gist of their conversation, the snatch that I heard, was that they had not took the shilling to be disembowelled by infidel savages, nor to be pressed into slavery. They was not cowards, one of them said, but this was not a fate they would suffer willing—to be made slaves, in a further attack by more determined corsairs.'

'When did you hear this?' Gripping Dobie's elbow, bending closer to listen.

'Last night. I was making my way to the heads, and heard it through a grating in the waist.'

'You are certain it was marines?'

'Aye, I could see the red sleeve of a coat, with the little badge particular to the Chatham marines, the little insignia, sewed there.'

'Yes, I have seen the device.—You heard nothing more?'

'No, nothing.—I was right to tell you?'

'Indeed you was, Alan, and thank you. I will inform the captain as soon as he returns. Until then, say nothing of this to anyone else.'

'And now I will like to show you something of our way of life here at Rabhet,' said Rashid Bey. To Rennie's great relief he was getting up on his legs. He did so easily, and Mr Sebastian followed suit, with a surprising suppleness of movement. Seeing Rennie's difficulty—his aching joints had half-crippled him—Sebastian offered his hand to Rennie, who took it and was brought quickly and smoothly to a standing position.

'Thankee, Sebastian.'

A brief bow, not quite a salaam.

'Later we will see the medina, and the fort,' said Rashid

Bey. 'But for now we will go to the hammam.' And he led the way out of the room, walking with a quick, lithe step.

'Hammam?' Rennie, aside to Sebastian.

'The bath.'

'Ah. Ah. It is a ruin? An ancient site?'

'Ruin? No, it is not a ruin.'

'Surely it is like the Roman baths at—at Bath?'

'Well, perhaps. The purpose is the same.'

They followed Rashid Bey through a succession of long, cool, beautifully tiled rooms, and came to an arched door. A servant bowed low as Rashid Bey entered and a waft of steam eddied round his head. Rennie held back a moment.

'Is this bath in use?' Puzzled. 'I had no notion that it was in use . . .'

'Not just in use, Captain,' said Sebastian with a great-toothed smile. 'It has been made ready for us.'

'Us!'

'Indeed, it is the custom at this hour to repair to the hammam.'

'Good God.—You mean that *I* must submit to this?' Following Sebastian through the steam.

'It is the custom.'

The room they had entered was divided by tall pillars, and through the wafting clouds of steam shafts of sunlight from small windows in the domed roof made glowing pools on the wide stone floor. Rennie made out stone benches, and a deep, steaming bath. Pails of cold water stood at the edge.

'You must disrobe, Captain, if you please.'

Rashid Bey was already divesting himself of his blouse behind a strip of cloth held up by a servant. Sebastian, attended by a second servant with a cloth, began to shrug himself out of his voluminous kaftan. He pulled off his velvet hat, revealing close-cropped black hair. A third servant approached Rennie, holding up a length of cloth.

'Now then, Mr Sebastian,' began Rennie in what he hoped was an authoritative tone, 'it is all very fine being shown these quaint things in a foreign place, but I am an officer in His Majesty's service, that must maintain dignity fitting my position, and——'

'You must disrobe, Captain Rennie,' quietly and firmly, 'else give grave offence to your host.'

And Rennie, with much misgiving and embarrassment, did as he was told, and undressed behind the cloth held for him by the servant. When he was naked the servant—his eyes averted—held out for Rennie a white towel.

'Yes yes,' said Sebastian behind him, 'take the *fouta* from the *tayyeb*, and place it round your waist. It ain't the thing to be quite naked in the hammam. You must cover your private parts.'

'Yes, I see.' Taking the towel. 'The *fouta* is simply a towel?'

'Simply a towel. And the *tayyeb* is your personal servant for the pummelling, and the scrub.'

'Pummelling, good God? Did I hear you right?'

'You did. Do not be alarmed.' Donning his *fouta* and stepping from behind the cloth, and making his way to the bench. 'The body entire is pummelled very vigorous, but not painfully so. As you sweat you are then scrubbed down with the *lufa*, and then you plunge your person in the hot bath, and afterward sluice yourself down with cold water—should you desire it.'

'All this?' Fastening his own *fouta* and following Sebastian to the bench, where Rashid Bey sat already. 'I must submit to all of this?'

'You will discover, Captain Rennie,' said Rashid Bey with a polite wave of his hand over the water, 'that all this—the pleasures of the hammam—far outrun the discomforts. You will emerge after the passage of an hour infinitely refreshed, lifted up, and made into a new man. Will he not, Mr Sebastian?'

'He will, effendi.'

Rennie gritted his teeth and sniffed in a long breath. 'If I am not a dead man,' he said—but not aloud.

*

When they came from the bath an hour later Rennie had to acknowledge that he did feel better. His step was lighter, and his mind easier. The pummelling and scrubbing and steaming, and the subsequent plunging and rinsing, had lifted him. His unease about the commission; his lingering displeasure with Sebastian; his doubts about what lay underneath, and behind, in the minds of Sir Robert Greer and his allies in London; his negating sense and feeling about the convoy and what might happen in the event of an attack: all these things seemed less important, less pressing in upon him, and his brow as they stepped into the fresh air was unfurrowed for the first time in weeks.

Rashid Bey proposed that they should walk through the crowded medina to the souk, where all manner of goods and artefacts were for sale in the narrow, rich-smelling streets.

People fell back, and humbled themselves on the ground as Rashid Bey passed. 'We will find you a *chechia*, Captain Rennie,' he said. 'I will like to make you a small gift of a *chechia*.'

'A hat,' advised Mr Sebastian, at Rennie's side.

Rennie was duly presented with a hat by Rashid Bey, a handsome *chechia* in red felt. He accepted it with a bow and a polite smile, but inwardly felt himself at a distinct disadvantage. He had not thought—as certainly he should have thought—of bringing a gift for his host. As if sensing this, Mr Sebastian said quietly:

'Do not trouble yourself, Captain. Rashid Bey does not expect anything in return. You are his guest, his honoured guest, and you are to do him a great service in due course.'

From the medina they rode to the fort on the point. In the remains of the Roman fort at the base of the newer, greater structure—square and crenellated—Rennie made appropriate sounds of appreciation as he viewed the fine Roman mosaics of gods and goddesses and chariots, in beautiful tinted glass. They climbed to the top of the fort, and from the crenellations Rennie could make out his ship in the distance, riding at anchor in the late afternoon light. He was growing anxious to return. However, Mr Sebastian now proposed:

'In course you will spend the night as Rashid Bey's guest, under his roof.' This in a quiet aside as Rashid Bey spoke to the fort commander. Rennie was at first unsettled by the suggestion.

'Sleep ashore, did y'say? Nay, Sebastian, that is quite out of the question. I must return to my ship.'

'Why?'

'Eh? Why? The reason is entirely obvious. I am the captain, and I must behave as the captain. We are in a foreign place, and my people look to me for everything—leadership, strength of purpose, and so forth. In a foreign place, my place is in my ship. I must set the example.'

'Example? My dear Captain Rennie, your place today, and tonight too, is by Rashid Bey's side, as his guest. He wishes to convey to you all of the information you will need in escorting his convoy of ships.'

'Ah, I see—tonight?' Nodding. 'Well well, that I am eager to learn. I must send a message to Mr Hayter, else he will grow uneasy at my absence.'

'Certainly. We will send it from the palace, wrote in your hand, by special messenger.'

Rashid Bey left the commander and rejoined Rennie and Sebastian.

'It is settled. Upon your departure in a few days, Captain— when the convoy has been assembled—the fort will salute you with thirteen guns. That matches your own salute in your frigate, yes?'

'Indeed, sir, it does.'

'Yes. And now we will return to the palace. Tomorrow we will travel to the desert,' pointing to the fire of the setting sun, the features of his face burnished like metal, 'and I will show to you the great oasis in the Chott el Hakkan.'

And he took Rennie's arm.

━┅━ ≊✦≊ ━┅━

As James ate his supper in the gunroom with Lieutenants Makepeace and Upward, and the lieutenant of marines, Mr Quill, the message from Rennie was brought to him. When he had read it he asked the ship's boy if the messenger was yet on board, and was told:

'He has went away, sir, in the boat. He were in a great hurry.'

'Damnation. I wished to send a reply. Never mind.' He dismissed the boy, and read the message through again. In Rennie's neat, rather cramped hand:

> I am detained o/night, as the honoured guest of Rashid Bey. In the morning we are to visit an oasis, that will require a journey of some many miles, in the desert. Pray continue with the detailed duties that was discussed before my departure. I shall return as soon as I am able.
>
> Wm Rennie

'Is there a difficulty . . . ?' Tom Makepeace, cutting cheese.

'No. No, not exact. But I must reply to this, and send a messenger of my own from the ship.'

'You mean, a ship's boy?'

'Good heaven, no. In a strange foreign port? Most certainly not.'

'I should be happy to send a small party of marines, Hayter.' Mr Quill refilled his glass.

'Thankee, John, but redcoats in such a place will not answer, neither. Armed men might provoke resentment, even hostility.'

'Then who will you send, instead?'

'I had better go myself, I think.'

'Cannot it wait until morning?' Lieutenant Quill was surprised, as were the other officers.

'Are you sure there ain't a difficulty, James?' Makepeace looked at him closely.

'No.' Curtly. Then, thinking he had been rude: 'No, Tom, there is just one or two things I must discuss with the captain, you know, about our stores. He was most particular in his instruction to me, since we cannot store here as we would at a more familiar landfall.' This was largely invention, but James did not wish to confide in his fellow officers about the overheard snatch of conversation Alan Dobie had reported to him. He rose, and went on deck.

'Mr Tangible!'

'The boatswain is in the forecastle, sir.' A member of the anchor watch, touching his forehead.

'Very good. Jump forrard and ask him to come to me at once.'

'Aye, sir.' Another touch, and his bare feet padded away along the gangway.

Presently Mr Tangible came to James, smelling of tobacco and rum. He was not quite sober. He endeavoured to be alert and attentive, and to make straight his back. 'Sir?'

'I shall need a boat, Mr Tangible, I am going ashore. Hoist out the small cutter, if y'please.'

'You go ashore . . . now, sir?' Swaying very slightly.

'Yes. Yes, I do go ashore, Mr Tangible, thank you.'

'Aye, sir.'

———— ≍♦≍ ————

James was brought to Captain Rennie at the palace, after some little difficulty. The palace guards, recognizing him as an officer from the visiting English ship, were suitably deferential—but absolutely refused him admittance until they had kept him waiting half an hour. A fierce turbaned figure led him through a courtyard, and a bewildering series of lamp-lit passages, and at last he was delivered into Rennie's presence, in what were clearly his sleeping quarters, large connecting rooms, with luxurious hangings, and a great cushioned divan in a corner, and trays of coffee pots, sweetmeats, dates, &c. James was astonished by his captain's appearance—his new apparel—with which the captain was evidently not yet quite at his ease.

'Was it necessary to come to me, James, at this hour?' Rennie was distinctly put out. He put a hand to his head, and removed his *chechia*. He glanced down at his white tunic-blouse, and his white pantaloons, and gold slippers, and was uncomfortable.

'Since you go into the desert on the morrow, sir—I felt that it was necessary to see you before, yes. Tonight was my only opportunity, after I had received your message.'

'Well well, you have had an entirely wasted journey, James. There is nothing that cannot wait until I have come back from the desert. We are here at the command of Rashid Bey, and it is his convenience we must observe, and obey.'

'Surely—their Lordships, and Sir Robert Greer?'

'Eh?' Pulling at a sleeve, and endeavouring to hide the gold slippers under the bottoms of the pantaloons. 'What say?'

'Do not they command us, sir?'

'Hm. It is late, James, and I must be awake early tomorrow.' Brusquely. 'By the by—does he take good care of her?'

'Sir?'

'Cutton.'

'Oh, Cutton. D'y'mean—your cat, sir?'

'In course I mean the cat, good God. Dulcie. Is he kind and attentive?'

'I—I think so, sir. If you please, I must convey something to you, tonight. That is why I have come ashore, and——'

'Have not I just said to you there is nothing that cannot wait?'

'We face rebellion, sir.' Determined to be heard. 'Mutinous rebellion in the ship.'

'What? Nonsense.' Straightening the other sleeve.

'Mr Dobie overheard a conversation by chance, between two of the Chatham marines. They are set upon seizing the ship's boats, sir, when we are again at sea, and making off in *Curlew*.'

'Dobie heard this?'

'He did, sir.'

'When? No, pray do not tell me.—In the dead of night.'

'Sir, with respect, this ain't a matter for jesting——'

'What does Lieutenant Quill say?' Impatiently.

'Lieutenant Quill has overall command of the marines, but he don't know these Chatham men, sir. His non-commissioned officers——'

'And Dobie came to you with this, did he? I know why, too. He does not wish to trouble himself with the Duty Book. It is his method for avoiding and pushing aside my Duty Book. Yes yes. No no. I have not forgot the Duty Book, James, and you should not think that I have, neither of you.'

'Sir, with the greatest respect, Alan Dobie——'

'James, this is mischief. It is Dobie's mischief, because he is a fanciful fellow. Clever and capable in his way, you know, and useful, but inclined on occasion to entertain nonsense. The Chatham marines will not in course be mutinous, they will do their duty as ordered. We are now at the disposal of Rashid Bey, and presently, when he is ready, we will assemble his convoy of ships, and we will do *our* duty, as sea officers.'

'We was fortunate to prevail against those corsairs, but I can understand why some of the marines might have got it in their heads that they could be made slaves——'

'Fortunate! We was nothing of the kind. We cut them to ribbons, and put them to rout. As we shall again if need be.' Holding up a hand and shaking his head as James again attempted to speak. 'James, James—I have been very patient with you. I am sorry that ye've had a wasted trip in the boat,

but it is late at night, and I must make an early start
tomorrow. So now I will like to go to my bed, and I will like
you to return to the ship, if y'please.'

'Sir, I really think——'

'Christ's blood, Mr Hayter! Will you *do as you are told*, sir!'

———— ⊯⊹⊒ ————

A line of palms, diminishing into the distance, stretched
across the gleaming crust of the Chott el Hakkan, showing
the safe way through the forty miles of salt that lay before the
party. Today they rode camels, tall, rolling, humped and
grumbling creatures not at all to Rennie's taste—in comfort
or pleasure. When he had first seen the camels standing in a
train under the trees beyond the palace wall, he had admired
them as majestic animals. When he had learned that he was
expected to ride one, he had smiled glassily and asked:

'Surely, sir, I am to ride an horse?'

'Oh no, Captain Rennie. We will all ride camels today.
The journey is long, and we must move at a quick and steady
pace across the lake.' And Rashid Bey had smiled benignly.
'You will find your mount most satisfactory, I promise you.
Her gait is not dissimilar to the movements of a ship, I think.'

'Ship?' Staring at the animal.

'The ship of the desert,' said Mr Sebastian.

And so Rennie had submitted—what choice had he?—to
the business of seating himself cross-legged upon the
creature—that he was certain had fixed him with a disdaining
eye as he approached—and absorbing instruction as to
clicking his tongue, flicking the beast with his cane, &c.,
urging her to lift herself snorting and groaning up on her tall
legs and great flat feet, and go forward. Soon all of Rennie's
pleasant new feelings of comradeship and admiration for
Rashid Bey had vanished, and keeping his voice low he turned
his head to address Sebastian:

'Why must we go by the palms? Why must we go across

this wasteland at all? How came it to be called a lake? It is so dry and harsh only a madman would call it a lake.' Rennie's buttocks were already paining him, his back ached, his knees, his ankles.

'It floods once a year, in the raining season, and then the camels must stay on the line of palms, that is the only dry route. Further, even when the lake is dry—as it is now—it is unwise to venture off the known path, the Path of Palms. Under the surface salt, you see, is an ooze of black mud that will swallow a man and his camel in a few moments.'

'Ah. Hm.' Grimacing as he tried to find a more comfortable position. 'I may tell you, Sebastian, a camel ain't like a ship, in any particular. Would that it was the raining season now, and we could get across the damned place by boat.'

'I fear not, Captain, not even then. The water is not deep enough to permit the use of boats.'

'Hm. Hm.' Blackly, a suffering sniff. And presently, keeping his voice low so as not to give offence to Rashid Bey at the front of the party: 'Why *does* he take us on this journey, Sebastian? What can be gained by going all this way, across a corner of Gehenna, when my proper work is at sea— assembling the convoy, for Christ's sake, and putting to sea? When will he tell me of his final plan for the convoy? We have had a great many discussions, but nothing at all has been decided upon. When will these decisions be reached? When!'

'You must not grow agitated, Captain, nor be impatient. You must not interpret this journey as anything other than a very great compliment to an honoured and valued guest. It is the custom to offer to esteemed friends the gift of hospitality, and a visit to the oasis is its supreme expression.'

'Supreme, hey? The top part of flattery? Well well, my bottom parts will likely never recover.'

Soon afterward Rashid Bey ordered the pace of the party to be lifted, and as the camels loped along under the burning sun, on and on into the quivering, glittering expanse, Rennie fell into grim-faced, jolting despair.

----- ✦ -----

On board *Expedient* Lieutenant Hayter continued with his duties. There was activity in the ship: the minor repairs always undertaken when a ship is in harbour after a period at sea; the instruction of midshipmen in navigation; the drilling of parties of marines; but none of this activity was prosecuted with a very earnest will. Shore liberty had not been granted. The air was hot, and the ship 'tween decks foetid and oppressive. Men grew fractious, and deliberately slow in obedience.

'Tom.' James beckoned the second lieutenant. They were on the quarterdeck, under the rigged awning, James in working clothes, Makepeace in his shirt-sleeves.

'Yes, James?'

'Is young Upward well enough to take his place at quarters, d'y'suppose?'

'He is still mending, I think. Are we to beat to quarters here at the mooring?'

'Ask him—if he is able—to come to me here on the quarterdeck, will you? I will like to see to him for myself, up on his legs and on deck, and assess his progress.'

'Very good.'

'And no, Tom, we will not beat to quarters inside the harbour. I mean to weigh, put to sea, and stand off the coast.'

'So we may pump ship in the open sea? That will certainly sweeten things below.'

'We will decide on that afterward.'

'Very good. When does the captain come on board?'

'The captain is in the desert, Tom, as I told you last night. He don't come back on board before tomorrow, at the earliest.'

'You . . . you mean to weigh and make sail . . . going without him?'

'Don't look so disapproving, Tom, good heaven. It is time the people had something vigorous to occupy them, and bring them back on their toes. They are grown listless and unwilling, and they must be brought back to their proper work.'

'Proper work? You mean, pumping ship . . .?' Puzzled.

'As guncrew, Tom, fighting the guns. This is not a damned merchant ship. His Majesty's *Expedient* frigate is a man-of-war. Very soon she is to assume her responsibilities as a convoy escort. It is time she was brought up to a fighting condition, and I mean to do it by exercising the great guns until both batteries are proficient. We don't need the captain to tell us our plain duty in that, hey?'

'Aye, very good. I—I will just go below and look in on Upward, and see if he is——'

'Yes, on second thought, get him out of his cot at all cost. He cannot lie there for ever, I need him to return to duty and take his place at his gun division. Y'may throw a bucket of water over him, if he ain't keen to rise.'

'Very good.' Hurrying below.

'Mr Tangible! We will weigh and make sail in one glass! Hoist out the boats to tow astern! Mr Abey!'

'Sir?' Attending.

'Make a signal to *Curlew* that she is to weigh and take station in line astern as we leave harbour.'

'Aye, sir.'

'And, Mr Abey . . .'

'Yes, sir?'

'Your hat off and on to me, when I give you an order on deck.'

Richard Abey's slight hesitation—as he stared at Lieutenant Hayter's piratical working rig, and the blue kerchief tied round his head—was followed at once by:

'I am very sorry, sir,' as he lifted his hat and made his obedience.

The stern anchor already hauled in, and now hands to the capstan to take in the bower, standing to the bars and turning to a rhythmic chant. The long loop of the messenger turned to the lower whelps of the main capstan on the upper deck, led forrard to be fixed by the nipper boys to the cable. The cable itself, heavy and dripping and stinking, hauled from the ooze of the harbour bottom through the hawse hole in the bow. At the main hatch the nippers taken off, and the cable fed below to the cable tier in the orlop. Arduous work, back-straining, arm-straining, arduous work, and sweat dripped from the men's backs in the Africk heat.

At last the cable vertical and taut at the bow.

'Up and down, sir!' Mr Tangible.

'Very good. Pipe to weigh, Mr Tangible.'

The boatswain's call, and the great dripping ring of the anchor broke the surface. The forecastle men at the cathead, under their petty officer, waiting for his shout:

'Hook up!'

And the anchor lifted up by the tackle to the cathead, carefully lifted, lest the heavy flukes damage the ship's side. As the ship swung slowly free, foretopsail sheeted home:

'Bring her to the wind!' James Hayter's speaking trumpet gleaming in the sun. Away to larboard *Curlew* was already coming to the wind, the breeze from the west, warm and steady. 'Loose the maintopsail!'

'A fine topsail breeze for leaving harbour,' said Bernard Loftus to James.

'Aye, we shall run east when we clear the mouth, with the wind two points on our larboard quarter, stand off the coast, and come about to run nor-east into the open sea. We will then——'

'Ships blocking the harbour mouth, sir!' An alert midship-man at the rail, pointing.

A diminutive figure appeared at the waist ladder, and came up on the quarterdeck. 'If you please, Mr Hayter, I——'

'Not now, Doctor.' Curtly.

'I must speak to you on an important matter, if you pl——'

'Not *now*, d'y'hear me!' Jumping up into the mizzen shrouds, unslinging and focusing his glass.

'I cannot permit Mr Upward to be thrown out of his hanging cot when he is not yet fully recovered from his injuries——'

'Two barques, blocking our way! Damn their insolence!' James, hanging in the shrouds, and peering through his glass.

And now there was a flash on the side of the nearest barque, a puff of smoke, and immediately thereafter the *BANG* of the gun.

'I fear we may not be exercising our great guns today.' Mr Loftus, quietly to Midshipman Abey, who stood by with his signal book. 'Nor anything else, neither.'

In the early morning at the oasis the sun stared low across the quiet water. No wading birds stalked or rode there in these summer days. Only the faintest zephyr ruffled the surface, rippling across and dissolving the perfect reflected symmetry of the great dark tents and the clump of bearded palms. Beyond the tents a camel groaned, acknowledging the dawn with complaint. And at the edge of things—hidden low and secret on the horizon—heat crouched like a lion.

Rennie woke longing for tea, a craving so strong it was like an ache in his guts. He struggled to a sitting position, peering in the darkness of the tent, and briefly wondered:

'Where am I, in the name of Christ . . . ?'

A grunt nearby, and the sound of coverings thrown off. 'You are at the oasis in the Chott el Hakkan—in the name of Allah.'

As memory returned: 'Sebastian? Is that you? What o'clock is it?' Turning blindly in the direction of the voice.

'It is early o'clock, Captain. Far too early o'clock. My advice is to——'

'Nay, I don't want your advice at this hour, thank you. I want a pot of tea. Last night I was obliged to drink coffee, very strong coffee it was, and I lay awake with my thoughts spinning and tumbling and my belly nearly on fire. Is there no possibility of my being given tea in this godforsaken place?'

From outside came the sound of the camel groaning under the trees.

'There, d'y'hear? Even the poor beasts want tea. They are weary of coffee and dates, as am I.'

'Some of the camel drivers drink tea, I believe. If you will wait half an hour they will no doubt give you a cup of their brew, after they have been at prayer.'

'They seem to pray a lot, do not they, in this country?'

'Five times daily, Captain. First, at sunset. Then again when darkness has fallen, and again at dawn, noon, and mid-afternoon.'

'At sunset—first—did y'say?'

'The Islamic day begins at sunset, as rigorously as your shipboard day begins at noon.'

'Are we expected to follow these rituals, Mr Sebastian?'

A sigh, and Sebastian struck a light, resigned to rousing himself and beginning the day. 'No, Captain. Rashid Bey is entirely sensible of your beliefs, and would not—as a matter of good manners—seek to impose his own upon you.'

'And you, Mr Sebastian . . .?' Looking at him in the flickering light of the oil lamp.

'I observe, Captain . . . I observe.' Neutrally.

'I see. Will you tell me a little about it? I fear that not only have I no understanding of their religion, but that I know nothing of it whatsoever.'

Another sigh. 'If you wish . . .' Pouring water into a basin, and washing his face.

'They believe in God, certainly, yes?'

'Allah. There is no God but God, and Mohammed is His Prophet. That is the first—the principal thing—and all else follows. Prayer five times daily, facing in the direction of Mecca. The *hajj*. Ramadan. And lastly, the giving of alms. It is a sin to ignore the poor, or the needy.'

'*Hajj?* What is *hajj*?'

'The yearly pilgrimage to Mecca. As the Christian faithful in England once went to Canterbury, you know. Prayer is always preceded by the ritual washing, and the feet must be bared. The central and most oft repeated phrase is *Allah-o-Akbar*. "God is great." The——'

'God is great? Hm. Not dissimilar entire to Almighty God, in our own faith.'

'The fast of Ramadan takes place in the ninth month of the calendar. During the hours of daylight, for the period of one month, no food nor drink may pass the lips of the faithful between dawn and sunset.'

'Nothing all day? Damned uncomfortable, I should think.'

'You have never practised the same—at Lent?'

'Lent? Well well, that is a wholly different thing. Absolutely a different thing. We don't go about all the day depriving ourselves of food and drink.'

'No, but you do abstain from certain pleasures—wine, as an instance—for the whole of Lent, d'y'not? Forty days, ain't it? Ash Wednesday to Easter Eve?'

'Well well, put like that—you have made your point.' Nodding. 'And now I want my tea.'

'I must warn you, Captain, that the tea drunk here in Rabhet is a great deal stronger even than coffee. It is a brew——'

'No tea can be so poisonous as that damned coffee,' muttered Rennie.

'It is a brew made by boiling very strong leaf in water for several minutes, then adding a great quantity of sugar—blocks of sugar into the open kettle. The whole is then allowed to simmer upon the fire, to simmer and stew, for upward of three and four hours at a time, or even overnight. The result is a liquor of such ferocious intensity I have never managed more than the merest sip, that I was obliged to spit out at once.'

'And this is called tea?'

'It is.'

'Well well,' a sigh, and he lay back down on his cushion, 'in least it ain't coffee. I shall be glad of it for that alone.'

But when he tried to drink the brew the camel drivers provided, half an hour after, he found that what Sebastian had said was true, and he was unable to swallow a single mouthful. Rashid Bey came to stand beside him at the water's edge, as Rennie endeavoured to cleanse his mouth of the disgusting, powerfully tannic and sickly sweet taste.

'The wading birds have alas departed to the north at this season.'

'Ah. Ah.' Nodding. 'I wonder, sir, I wonder if we might discuss——'

'If you are interested in other birds, there is a great variety of larks and finches, most pretty and delicate creatures, to the lover of such things.'

'Ah. Hm. My first lieutenant is the man for such things as birds, sir.'

'You are not?'

'It ain't that I am against them, you know. Birds have their uses, and so forth, as creatures of the air. However, I am not a close student of their activity. Unlike my lieutenant, that is a countryman.—I wonder if we might dis——'

'Tell me your interests, will you, Captain? What absorbs and delights you? Are you a lover of music, as so many Europeans are?'

'I—I am not much interested in music.'

'You are not?'

'Very little. Sir, with respect, do not you think it time——'

'Then—books? You are interested in literature?'

'Shakespeare, a little.'
'Yes, Shakespeare . . .

"What a piece of work is a man! How noble in reason! how infinite in faculty! in form, in moving, how express and admirable! in action how like an angel! in apprehension how like a god! the beauty of the world! the paragon of animals!"'

Rennie, surprised, waited a moment, then added:
'But to complete that passage—it is *Hamlet*, I think—does not he say that we are but dust? Quintessence of dust?'
'You are right. He does.' Quietly, looking across the tranquil water of the oasis at the palms grouped like silent men on the far side. ' "Man delights not me." Does he delight you, Captain Rennie?' Glancing at him.
'In the round, sir, d'y'mean? In the whole?' Aware that this question was probably the last in what had constituted an elaborate test. That the entire trip to the oasis had been a test of . . . what? His character? His trustworthiness? His education?
'Do you take men as you find them? Or as you find them out?'
'Ah. Ah. That is very well expressed, sir.' Carefully. 'The latter—if you press me.'
'So?' Another glance, and again Rashid Bey contemplated the quiet water. 'So.' At last, and Rennie was relieved of inner anxiety; he had passed the test, he thought.
'So,' repeated Rashid Bey, taking Rennie's arm. 'And now we will talk of your service to me . . .' They began walking back to the tents. '. . . and why I wish it. And of the service I shall provide, in return, to your king.'

━◆━

James Hayter wrote up his journal, and recorded the events

following the blocking of the harbour entrance, and *Expedient*'s detention within the harbour. The ship lay once more at her mooring.

The larger barque had sent a boat. This larger ship was lateen-rigged at the foremast, and square-rigged at the main and mizzen, and was ported for twenty guns. She had an overhanging transom stern and a slightly raised quarterdeck. There was provision for sweeps, James noted. In the boat, standing in the stern sheets, came a man in very curious apparel. Over white blouse and pantaloons he wore a large blue frock coat of a European cut. On his head was a hat very similar to that worn by Mr Sebastian, but blue in colour, and without decoration of any kind save a large jewel that glittered and winked in the sun—a central emerald surrounded by a circle of rubies, set in gold.

The boat came to *Expedient*'s side, and the man came nimbly up the ladder. James made him welcome, treating him exactly as he would treat any senior officer, any important visitor. He took off his hat and bowed. The visitor regarded James, and in heavily accented English announced himself:

'I am *Rais* Ahmed el Ali, commander of Rashid Bey's fleet, and I have come to guide and assist you.'

James introduced himself, and explained that Captain Rennie was ashore.

'I am aware that he is. That is why you need guidance, Lieutenant.'

'I am not sure that I understand you, sir . . .' Politely. 'May I give you coffee, below?'

They went below, James taking it upon himself to usher his visitor into the great cabin, where Rennie's steward prepared coffee, taken from Mr Sebastian's stores. The *rais* examined the cabin, no doubt comparing it with his own quarters, then when the two men were seated with their coffee, James repeated:

'I do not quite understand you, sir, when you say that we need guidance . . .'

'Yes. I feel certain that your captain would not wish you to leave harbour without him. To depart from Rabhet without him, against orders.'

'I had not intended to depart, sir. I had intended merely to conduct an exercise upon the open sea, and then to return.'

'Exercise?' Sipping his coffee.

'Yes, I wished to exercise the great guns. To practise our gunnery.'

A frown, and a dubious stare. 'This is not completely true, is it, Lieutenant? You are an English ship of war, and already your gunnery is excellent. I know this of English ships. Always the gunnery is excellent. That is why you have come here. That is why you are chosen.'

'Forgive me, but our gunnery cannot remain excellent if we do not practise. Unless we exercise the great guns very frequent we grow lax and incompetent. We must practise. We must.'

'You must fire your guns?'

'No, not exact. It is a drill, an exercise, to keep the guncrews at the peak of their skills. We do not always need to fire the guns, if we wish to save powder.'

'If you do not fire the guns—then why leave harbour, Lieutenant?' Laying down his coffee cup as if he had answered his own question.

'Well, sir, it ain't just a question of running out our guns, you know. The open sea provides us with the opportunity to tack, and go about, and run at the enemy, so to say. To handle the ship in simulation of attack. That is part of the exercise, at sea.'

'Has Captain Rennie decided this?' Another scrutinizing stare.

'On this occasion, d'y'mean? Well, no, he is in the desert. I undertook the exercise upon my own authority, in his absence. Since we are to be convoy escort——'

'Yes, he is in the desert. I think that you may exercise your guns without firing them—inside the harbour, Lieutenant. That is my guidance.'

'Very good, sir.'

'When Captain Rennie returns he will discuss such things with me. Until then . . .'

And he rose, salaamed, returned to his boat, and to his ship.

James wrote it all in his journal, as near word for word as he could recall it, then went on deck. If exercising the great guns could only take place at anchor, in the harbour, then so be it. However, in spite of what he had told *Rais* Ahmed el Ali, there was nothing to stop him from——

'Mr Tangible! We will clear the ship for action! Mr Storey! We will worm all of our guns, and reload with blank! Let us give our hosts a taste of what the Royal Navy may do! Glory smoke, Mr Storey! Let us have glory smoke in our cartridge!'

And presently, echoing and cracking and thudding round the fortifications:

BANG   BANG   BANG BANG   BANG   BANG

and clouds of dense drifting smoke, rolling and tumbling like stormclouds, made dark shadows over the calm harbour water.

＊＊＊

'What the bloody hell was you thinking, Mr Hayter! What the hell was you about, sir! Hey! Hey! God damn your presumption!'

Captain Rennie trembled with anger. He could not hold his tea without spilling it, so great was his wrath. Poor Dulcie, that had been eager to greet him when he returned to the ship, and climb into his lap, fled under the table. Lieutenant Hayter stood his ground.

'If I have given offence—then in course I must apologize, sir. I do not see that firing our guns in exercise, with blank cartridge, could be seen as an offence, however. We are a man-of-war, after all, and must soon undertake convoy duty. Therefore, I thought——'

'Yes? Yes? What *did* you think? Firing our guns to salute the fort, as we approached the harbour, was one thing. To fire them inside the harbour, without notice, other ships all round you, is quite another! It is wanton, reckless lunacy! Not only a damned insult to Rashid Bey and his admiral, but you might have been fired upon y'self, y'fool! The ship severely damaged, and men killed!'

'I do not think any other ship would wish to fire on us in harbour, sir. I do not think they would dare.'

'*Dare! Dare!* In their own harbour, thinking they was fired on by a ship they had trusted as a friend—they would not *dare*! My God, you *are* mad! Stark crazy!' Banging down his teacup and breaking it.

'Sir, with respect, that ain't quite a fair judgement, when they did not in fact fire——'

'Allow me to decide what is fair, sir. Allow me to make judgement as to your conduct.'

'I am very sorry indeed, sir, that I have caused you distress.'

'It ain't a question of whether or not I am distressed, Mr Hayter. You have distressed Rashid Bey, just when I have gained his trust. You have distressed his admiral, Ahmoud el—— whatever the fellow's name is. You have distressed them both.'

'Admiral Ahmed el Ali, sir.'

'He came to *Expedient*, did he not?'

'He did, sir.'

'And quite rightly prevented you from putting to sea?'

'He did, sir, but I——'

'And you did not like it, hey? You thought that it was not the place of some damned foreigner officer to order you about? Yes?'

'I would not—would not put it in quite those terms, sir——'

'Oh? Would y'not? Ah-hah. Well well, those are the terms

I would use. Certainly they are. You deliberately sought to discommode the admiral. You deliberately sought to undermine his authority, and insult him.'

'I wished to exercise the great guns inside the harbour, sir, as the *rais* advised me to do.'

'*He* advised you to fire a broadside of guns?'

'In truth he did not advise that, sir. I wished merely to——'

'You wished? You wished? I wish you had not wished, Mr Hayter! It ain't your place to wish, when we undertake demanding duties, far from home, as guests of a foreign power. My orders will be your whole and only consideration, by God. The wish to *obey*.'

'Very good, sir.'

'You will go to the admiral's ship, and make your apology direct to him. And then you will come with me to the palace, and make your apology to Rashid Bey.' A sniff. And he shook his head.

Lieutenant Hayter duly went to the admiral's barque in *Expedient*'s small cutter, returned, and duly went with Captain Rennie in the launch ashore, and accompanied him to the palace. To Rennie's surprise Rashid Bey expressed no anger at all about the battery of guns fired in his harbour, and was entirely understanding of the lieutenant's actions.

'You are a diligent and dutiful friend, Lieutenant, and I thank you for your close attention to detail, exhibited by your desire to practise with your guns. You have grasped instinctively the importance I attach to your visit, and to your assistance. As I have explained to Captain Rennie,' taking James's arm, and walking with him down the arched passage, 'and will now explain to you, Rabhet is not one of the most powerful regencies. We are prosperous, Allah be praised, but we are small, and vulnerable.'

'Your admiral is a very dutiful officer, sir, and you have fighting ships . . .' James, politely.

'Yes, you have met my *rais*, and you are right, he is dutiful and brave. But our fleet is small, and may be profitably engaged only in protecting the port. To our north we have a powerful enemy. The Dey of Tunis, Suleiman el Hassad, has designs on us. He has engaged a new *rais*, a man named Zamoril. You have heard of him?'

'Zamoril? No, I cannot say that I have, sir.' A glance at Rennie, who shook his head.

'No? He is a corsair from Algiers, and rose from obscurity to a position of some power and influence in that place. Some say that he came from the Levant, others that he came from Istanbul, others again that he was a Christian from Portugal, that apostasized, and came to our faith. I do not know the truth of his origins. What I do know is that he is entirely ruthless, and is now in command of a very powerful fleet of twenty ships and more, including barques, xebecs, and fast galleys. He also has at his disposal a thousand janissaries.'

'And—you think it is likely that he will attack our convoy, sir?'

'Not with his entire fleet, but even half of it is formidable. Mr Sebastian has prepared a plan, and Captain Rennie has discussed it with him, and with me—while we were in the desert. I think you have seen this plan, Lieutenant?'

'I have, sir.'

'It is ingenious, I think. Also, our only chance of breaking through.'

'You come with us, sir? You return with us to England?' Surprised.

'It is a matter for the greatest discretion, Lieutenant. I must go to England for—for consultation. I will return very soon. My people must not be aware of my absence.'

'Very good, sir.'

'Thank you, Lieutenant. And now there are things I must discuss with your captain. If you will please excuse us, I hope that before we leave Rabhet, you will be my guest at the hammam.'

'Thank you, sir, I shall be delighted.'

'Wait for me at the wharf, James, if you please.' Rennie nodded to his lieutenant in dismissal. As James was shown the way to the gates he reflected that if Rashid Bey was so understanding and approving of his desire to exercise *Expedient*'s great guns, it was very curious that his admiral was not. He guessed—further—that *Rais* Ahmed el Ali was not nearly so important in Rashid Bey's eyes as he wished himself to be, and that this rankled. James was beginning to tire of the seemingly endless delays and unspoken tensions in the regency, and wished that they could assemble the convoy without delay, and be gone. If they were to face great trial, if the convoy was likely to suffer attack, as *Expedient* had suffered attack, at least let it come on the open sea, where a vigorous defence might be mounted. As he walked along the stone wharf, passing the stone storehouses, and came toward *Expedient*'s boat, he was troubled by further thoughts. Why was Rashid Bey proposing to depart in a convoy and go to England? Why did he wish it, at a time when he feared an attack by superior forces from the north? And how could his people fail to notice his absence, fail to blame him for it, should such an attack come—an attack that could not likely be repulsed by the small defending fleet?

'It ain't my business, I expect,' he muttered to himself as he descended the stone stairs. 'When all is said, I do not really care about Rabhet, nor Rashid Bey, nor Sebastian, neither.'

'You wishes to return to the ship, sir?' Randall South, the captain's coxswain, knocking out his clay pipe.

'Eh?' Stepping into the stern sheets. 'No, not yet, Randall. We must wait.' Sitting down with a sigh. 'Wait, wait . . .'

Randall South shook his head at the boat's crew from behind the seated lieutenant, and refilled his pipe, and the boat swung a little, lifting the mooring rope and sending a ripple across the stone-shadowed water.

PART FIVE: DANGER

At sea, 12 degrees 35 minutes east, 34 degrees 51 minutes north, east of the Kerkennah Isles, and sailing north-east by north and a point north, the wind from the south, but very light, and progress slow thus far.

The convoy was small, much smaller than Captain Rennie had imagined—indeed had been led to believe by Mr Sebastian—only six ships in all, with *Expedient* to protect them, aided by *Curlew*. A poor-sailing, lateen-rigged xebec was consistently slower than the rest, from the moment of leaving harbour, and *Curlew* was consequently obliged to husband this ship, to go about and run south of the convoy to bring her back into the fold.

'She is a bagging, sagging-off, leewardly whore of a ship,' Rennie had muttered to himself more than once, stamping aft on his quarterdeck, and glaring astern over the taffrail.

It worried him, and his first lieutenant too, because if—even in these light, following airs—the damned xebec fell so easily behind, what would happen when the wind freshened and the convoy began to make brisker time? What would happen if the wind swung contrary, and they had to beat into it close-hauled? Their concern was compounded and exacerbated by the staring fact that the xebec was the ship that Rashid Bey had chosen for himself, boarding her in darkness in the harbour to aid concealment. She was, as the regent's ship, heavily laden with a great retinue of servants, beasts and personal effects, far beyond what a trading xebec would in usual carry. None of Rashid Bey's small fleet of armed ships of war—his armed barques and the like—had been permitted to accompany the convoy. He had insisted that all warships should remain at Rabhet, under *Rais* Ahmed el Ali, to protect the harbour, port and city in his absence. Rennie had endeavoured to reason with him.

'But surely, sir, you will sail with me as my guest? Sail in *Expedient*?'

'No, Captain, no. I thank you for your kindness, but it is fitting that I have my own ship.'

'Then—then will not you go aboard one of your barques, sir? I judge them good sea boats, weatherly sea boats, that can keep up.'

Rennie's efforts had been fruitless. The regent simply grew more determined to follow his own counsel, and Mr Sebastian—aside—murmured to Rennie:

'Rashid Bey ain't accustomed to contradiction, Captain Rennie,' and gave a little shake of the head, a scarcely perceptible quiver of his velvet hat, and that was that. The regent had boarded his slow-sailing xebec, and slowly she had sailed.

They had made poor time, and Rennie had posted lookouts in the crosstrees to watch for any sails of ships, with sharp instruction to quarter the horizon. To James Hayter he said:

'We will double-shot our guns, Mr Hayter, and load with full allowance.'

'That has already been done, sir.'

'Done? When?'

'Before we weighed, sir, at Rabhet.' Very correct.

'On whose instruction? I gave no such instruction, that I recollect.'

'It was done on my own initiative, sir.' Beginning to be fearful that in doing so he had again overstepped his authority in the question of gunnery. 'I—I thought it prudent.'

'Prudent?'

James waited, certain that he would be savagely admonished, but instead:

'Well well, it was prudent, James, thankee.' Flexing his knees as the ship rolled a little to leeward. 'Y'did right.'

'Very good, sir.'

'Mr Abey! Mr Cutforth!'

'Sir.'—'Sir.' Both midshipmen attending. Mr Cutforth was a year Richard Abey's senior, and very solidly made, with a thatch of hair so fair it was nearly white against his pink skin. His blue eyes were a fraction too close together. The effect overall was unprepossessing, and Rennie had to make repeated pledges to himself to be less censorious of the boy in his head. No human creature could be thought responsible for his appearance, after all—unless it was by fault of dress, or glumness and futility of expression, or outright sullen defiance. Mr Cutforth displayed none of these lamentable errors. The boy was upright, clean, obedient, and his coat had been made by a reputable tailor. Rennie liked young Abey, could find no fault in him, and so began with him:

'Make a signal to *Curlew*, Mr Abey. She is to bring that damned straggling xebec back to her position yet again. Nay, I must not curse the ship, she is the regent's vessel. Make: "The single ship astern is to take station with the convoy immediate."'

'Aye, sir.' His hat off and on, and he hurried aft to the flag lockers.

'Mr Cutworth, you will go aloft to the main crosstrees, relieve the lookout, then quarter the horizon and make a report. Jump now.'

'Aye, sir.'

'Nay, wait. Where is your long glass, Mr Cutforth?'

'I have not—I do not possess a long glass, sir.' Failing to meet Rennie's eye as he said it.

'Now that is nonsense, Mr Cutforth. I have seen ye with the glass myself, slung on your back as y'went aloft. Where is it?'

'I—I . . . no longer possess the glass, sir.'

'No longer possess it? Have you lost the glass?'

'Yes, sir. That is . . . in away.'

'Come come, Mr Cutforth, we are at sea in a man-of-war, with no time for dissimulation. Speak plain on the quarter-deck, if y'please.'

'I lost the glass in a wager, sir.'

'A wager, hey? Over what?' Frowning.

'I had rather—rather not say, if you please, sir.'

'Very well, I cannot oblige you to say more, on a debt of honour. How will you quarter the horizon, Mr Cutforth? That is the question.'

The boy was silent a moment, his face deeply flushed, a flush that made his fair hair vivid against the skin of his forehead. Then he said:

'I—I could take one of the glasses from the binnacle, sir.'

'All in use, I think.' Glancing there. 'No no, y'may borrow my own glass.'

'Thank you, sir.' Relieved.

'Sling it careful on your back, Mr Cutforth. Do not drop it. It is a Dollond, the finest-lensed long glass to be had in England, for which I paid a small fortune.' Handing him the cased glass by the leather strap.

'I shall be very careful of it, sir.' Taking the glass.

'You have seen the first lieutenant slide to the deck by a back stay, I expect? From high aloft?'

'I have seen him, sir.'

'Do not attempt emulation, Mr Cutforth. You will go aloft in the shrouds, and return by the same method. You have me?'

'Aye, sir.'

'Very well.' In dismissal.

                         —•—⚒—•—

Mr Sebastian had removed himself and his dunnage from *Expedient* at Rabhet, and was now aboard Rashid Bey's xebec. There he was in daily close consultation with the regent, as his adviser. Rennie sent an invitation to Rashid Bey to dine with him in *Expedient*—sent it by Lieutenant Bradshaw—but received no formal response. Rennie wished to conduct exercises along the lines of Mr Sebastian's plan of defence in the event of the convoy's being attacked, and was both perturbed and put out when no answer came from the xebec. Further, he was anxious because the xebec was so damned slow; nothing he could say or do, apparently, would correct in the xebec's captain the tendency to stray from the course, lag behind, and intolerably hinder the progress of the convoy as a whole.

'Is not the convoy really Rashid Bey's, and not ours, sir?' James Hayter asked Rennie.

'What? Yes yes, it is his convoy, in course. But I am responsible for it, and for him.'

Rennie summoned Lieutenant Bradshaw again, and again sent him to the xebec, to implore his cousin to use his influence with Rashid Bey, and the captain of the ship, to keep up—and to request an immediate meeting with Sebastian to review their tactics. Lieutenant Bradshaw returned in *Curlew*, flying up and coming about very stylishly under *Expedient*'s stem, and with a great show of agility leaping from his cutter up a rope ladder into the ship. He reported to Captain Rennie that:

'Mr Sebastian is unable to accept your invitation just at present, sir.'

'Unable? Unable to accept?'

'He is in consultation all the time with Rashid Bey. He sends his humblest regrets.'

'Does he, indeed? What do they talk of, I wonder, that does not include me? Am I not in command of this fucking convoy, Mr Bradshaw? Hey? Do not answer.' Grimly, pacing to the taffrail. Turning back: 'What do they talk of? What do they discuss? Was you able to hear any of it?'

'With your permission, sir, allow me to say that Mr Sebastian is my cousin by blood.' Almost brusquely, very upright in his bearing. 'I do not think in all consience you will expect me to be party to overhearing his private conversations, nor overviewing any of his private activity.'

'I have not asked you to spy on him—have I?' Nettled.

Lieutenant Bradshaw was silent, lifting his head to stare at a point near the larboard vang.

'So you do think that?' Rennie was now very irritated. 'Y'think that I would require you to perform a duty intolerable to your sense of family honour, in sum? Hey?'

'I must say to you that I do not understand why you would wish it, else.' Again very stiffly, his lean frame upright, only a muscle twitching at his temple betraying his own anger.

'Do you know where you are, sir? Do you know who you are talking to?' Furious, now.

'I have the honour to address an officer in the service of His Majesty. From whom I am entitled to expect in turn the highest observance of honour and propriety.'

'Entitled to expect! You pompous young prig! You have the honour to make your obedience to me, sir, and nothing more!'

'I do not think that I will allow myself——' began the lieutenant.

'Be *quiet* sir!' Shaking with anger. 'You damned impertinent dog, you will beg my pardon, or know the consequence!'

'I do not think I will tolerate that word. I will not be called a dog.' Turning away.

'You'll be called any bloody thing I choose, sir! *Do not walk away! How dare you walk away when I address you!*'

Lieutenant Bradshaw paused, turned back, and regarded Rennie with what Rennie saw as open contempt. Both men were now exceedingly, intemperately angry, and on dangerous ground.

'I do not think I am obliged to stand still and listen to any more insults to my family and my character, sir. In other circumstances I should be obliged——'

'There are no other circumstances, Mr Bradshaw, but these! You will beg my pardon!'

Lieutenant Bradshaw stood very still, very straight—and said no word.

'You refuse, do you? Very well, very well.' A great sniffing breath, and a stride or two forrard, his hands clasped behind his back. 'Mr Quill! Mr Quill, here!'

Presently the lieutenant of marines came to the quarter-deck, where Rennie stood apart from Lieutenant Bradshaw. He glanced at the two men, sensed hostility, then made his obedience:

'Sir?' His hat off to Rennie.

'Mr Quill, you will conduct Lieutenant Bradshaw below, and confine him in one of the storerooms of the orlop.'

'Am I under arrest!' Bradshaw now took a step toward Rennie. 'On what charge?'

'Be *quiet*, sir! You had your chance to speak, and you refused it! You will go with Mr Quill, quiet and decent, or by God ye'll be manhandled below! D'y'*hear me*?'

'I have the right to know with what offence I am charged!' Pale with anger and humiliation. 'I am commander of my own ship! On what charge am I removed from my command!'

Rennie ignored him, and sent for his second lieutenant, then walked aft. Reluctantly, but with a show of injured dignity, Lieutenant Bradshaw accompanied an embarrassed Mr Quill below. Presently Lieutenant Makepeace attended on the captain, and smartly removed his hat.

'Ah, Tom. I must relieve you of your duties in *Expedient*.'

'Relieve me, sir?' Dismayed, his confident expression fading.

'Aye, Tom. You will remove yourself into *Curlew*, and take command. When you have done it, you will repair to the xebec astern of us, and require Mr Sebastian to attend on me immediate in *Expedient*. I will give you a letter to take.'

'Take command of *Curlew* . . . ? Has Lieutenant Bradshaw fallen ill, sir?'

'Nay, he has not fallen ill. He has fallen foul of me. Mr Dobie!'

'I am here, Captain.' Hurrying up the ladder from the waist.

'Pen? Paper? Very well.' And he dictated the letter.

A distant yellowish tinge to the sky to the east, and a blurring of the horizon there, made the sailing master Bernard Loftus uneasy. He did not like the look of that sky, and there was on the sea a peculiar, slow, surging swell, quite unlike the usual Mediterranean swell that was scarcely more than a meditative quiet lifting along the wales. He was uneasy because the convoy seemed to him recklessly exposed; slow and vulnerable and incapable, should an emergency arise. His attempts to say so had been brushed aside by his preoccupied captain.

A system of signals had been arranged before the convoy weighed at Rabhet, based upon Rennie's own signals book and the contents of his flag lockers, and *Curlew*'s. Each ship in the convoy had been issued with rudimentary copies of the signals book, prepared in great haste—but with fair accuracy —by Alan Dobie, assisted by Midshipman Abey. Flags had not been issued to the convoy ships, with the exception of Rashid Bey's xebec; his ship had been provided a set of duplicate flags sufficient to make signals of her own, and reply to those hoisted by *Expedient* and repeated by *Curlew*.

A signal came from the xebec now: 'Request the convoy heave to.'

Mr Makepeace had not yet gone into *Curlew*—the cutter keeping close attendance on *Expedient*—when this signal was hoisted and read, and in response to it Rennie signalled that he understood, and gave the order.

'Heave to, sir?' The sailing master came from his place by the weather helm to Rennie's side. 'I do not care for that sky to the east, and——'

'Noted, Mr Loftus,' said Rennie, very curt and dismissive. Turning to his first lieutenant: 'We must settle the thing right quick, here and now, today. It should in course have *been* settled at Rabhet, before we weighed, but it was not. That was my fault, I confess. I should have been stronger in my determination, but I allowed myself to be took for granted. So then, we must get down to it now, and resolve the question.'

'What must be resolved, sir? Has not everything been managed about the convoy, everything that could be managed? Or . . . perhaps you have reconsidered that conversation I reported to you, of the Chatham marines . . .' Lowering his voice.

'No, James, I had dismissed that long since.' Moving to the rail. 'No, I had thought it was merely a question of assembling, and setting our course, and making a plan to avoid attack, and so forth. Hey? Well well, it was not, I may tell you.' A sniff, and he lifted his glass and focused it on the xebec. 'It wasn't, and it ain't.'

'Then—what is the question, sir?' Bracing himself as the main topsail yard was brought round and braced, and the ship began to pitch a little as her progress slowed, and roll on the swell. Rennie answered him by lowering his glass and giving him a quick, silent, significant stare. Then:

'Mr Abey! Make a signal to the xebec that I am coming aboard! Mr Tangible! We will hoist out the launch!'

The convoy ships rode together, hove to, as *Expedient*'s boat—having delivered Lieutenant Makepeace to *Curlew*—was rowed double-banked to Rashid Bey's xebec. Some of the ships, lateen-rigged, drifted untidily apart, attempting to maintain station by the use of sweeps. It was clear to Mr Loftus on *Expedient*'s quarterdeck that if this meeting aboard the xebec took more than a very little time—fifteen or twenty minutes, half an hour at most—then the riding ships might drift apart to the extent that the convoy would in effect break up. This was certainly a possibility if the wind came gusting and blasting from the east, out of that murky yellow sky.

'I don't like it, Mr Abey,' and Richard Abey felt himself almost a man, addressed thus. The master moved to the rail, looked aloft, paced aft, paced to the binnacle, then made some notes as the bell was struck and the glass turned by the marine on duty. 'Nay, don't like it at all,' said the master, putting aside his notebook. He sent the midshipman below for charts, and consulted them.

'If a gale struck us we should have to run north, or risk being driven on a lee shore.' Half to himself, but by a brief turn of his head including Richard Abey. 'That would certainly scatter our ships, we could not hope to stay together, and when the wind fell—who knows how long after?—it might take a week to find all of our charges.'

'What is the cargo of the ships, sir?'

'I had thought it was to be olive oil, but we never saw any casks hoisted into the ships. In short I don't know what they carry.'

'Might not it be many things, sir? Spices, dyes, hides? All these things are stored in the warehouses along the wharf.'

'Aye, but we saw none of them loaded in. The ships was simply assembled, and then we weighed.'

'Surely they must carry cargo of some kind, sir? Why have they come with us . . . ?'

'If there is anything else, I have not been informed of it. But we are lowly men, Mr Abey. We ain't privy to all of the business of this little cruise, and must do our duty without prying inquiry.'

'Yes, sir.'

'Patiently do our duty.' A deep breath, exhaled through his nose. Glancing again to the east. 'So long as we are able.'

Rennie's boat now returned, rowed in great haste, and as soon as he had jumped up the ladder into his ship, he ordered the convoy to get under way. When the boatswain began the procedure for hoisting in the launch, Rennie countermanded him:

'No thank you, Mr Tangible, the launch is to tow. There ain't time to hoist in, now. Mr Loftus, we will set a course due north. We must clear Cape Bon, and outrun that storm to the east of us.'

As soon as they were under way he went below, and summoned his first lieutenant to the great cabin. James, in working rig—having forgotten his captain's earlier edict that he should shift into a blue coat when he came to the cabin—found Rennie examining charts, corner-weighted with leads on the table. Rennie ignored his lieutenant's dress, perhaps did not notice it.

'I have elicited all the facts, James, from Rashid Bey and Sebastian. In least, as many of them as bear direct on us in *Expedient*, and our task in bringing this damned convoy to England and safety. I have also established that I am in sole command, at sea. Sebastian in course protested my treatment of his cousin Mr Bradshaw, but I prevailed. There can only be one commander at sea, else no convoy could proceed. Cutton!'

Colley Cutton emerged from the quarter gallery, Dulcie darting under his feet, and he stumbled and cursed the animal under his breath. Rennie bristled.

'What's that y'say? Do not abuse a mute creature, that cannot answer you in kind. Bring me some tea, right quick. Will you drink tea, James?'

'Nothing, thank you, sir.'

'A glass of wine?'

'Thank you, no.'

'Very good.' To Cutton: 'Are you still there, flat-footed and agape? Tea, man.' And when his hapless steward had disappeared into the gallery, Rennie's tone grew fond, and cajoling:

'Dulcie . . . Dulcie . . . will not you favour me with a look, in least?'

Dulcie sat beneath the far end of the table, contorted herself into a leg-jutting posture, and began to bathe herself with her pink tongue.

'She has not yet forgiven me for going away into the desert without her.' He gazed at her a moment, and drew a self-busying breath. 'Now then, James.'

'I am here, sir.'

'Yes. What I am going to tell you must be in confidence between us.'

'As always, you have my word on it.'

'Thankee, James.' A breath, and a look. 'Rashid Bey is a man of very definite opinion. I find myself divided in my opinion of him, but we will put that aside. He requires of his immediate circle, and of his allies, absolute trust and dedication to his cause. That is understandable, given what is at stake. His cause is to treat with His Majesty's Government so that Britain will provide him with a squadron of ships and a large detachment of marines, to protect Rabhet from his enemies, in particular the Dey of Tunis. In return Rashid Bey will grant Britain the right to establish a permanent naval base and dockyard at Rabhet—the harbour and wharf is ideal —to serve the Mediterranean Fleet. That is all straightforward. However, I have discovered that he brings with him to England the whole of his personal treasure. This vast fortune is in his xebec in large, but part of it—in artefacts and goods—is in the other ships. Two feluccas, two misticous, a pinque and a polacre, all bar the polacre lateen-rigged, and the xebec is lateen-rigged. When we come to sail by the wind they cannot hope to keep up to a fair rate of knots, and his damned xebec is the worst, as we have already seen, heavy-laden as she is. It is damned folly, to speak plain. He could have brought his treasure with him in *Expedient*, and *Curlew*, and one or two of his armed barques, that is faster ships, but he wished only to listen to his own counsel——'

'Surely Mr Sebastian is his adviser, sir, his counsel? Did not

Sebastian tell him just what you have said, exact? Did not
he——'

'Perhaps he did, very likely.' Rennie, holding up a hand.
'But Rashid Bey ain't a fellow to cross, James, as Sebastian has
made clear to me. Until I made him understand that I was not
his *rais*, to command and subjugate as he pleased, but instead
served King George, he was entirely indifferent to per-
suasion. However, I did make him understand—I was obliged
to make my back straight, and speak forceful—and we are
now in accord as to my seamanship, and my command of the
convoy.'

'Forgive my interposing again, sir—but why has he
brought his treasure with him? Surely he does not mean to
attempt to buy the King's goodwill? In fact, why does he
come to England at all? Could not all of this have been
negotiated by an intermediary, an ambassador or pleni-
potentiary, sent from London?'

'Rashid Bey has given to me the bare facts necessary, from
his understanding of the business, conveyed by Sir Robert
Greer in correspondence with Sebastian. I am not privy to
Rashid Bey's innermost thoughts, nor indeed am I a party to
this affair, except as naval escort. I do not concern myself with
anything but the simple, practical task of bringing the convoy
to England, and nor should you. It will require all of our
efforts as sea officers to accomplish it, leave alone we should
cram our heads with speculation. Hey?'

'In least it is clear why Britain would wish to make this
treaty. It is in case of future conflict between ourselves and
France, to protect our own interests in the Mediterranean,
rather than Rashid Bey's alone—is not that the truth of it,
sir?'

'Future conflict between ourselves and France.' Nodding.
'That is a possibility.'

'In light of the recent developments and upheavals in
France, that must be rather more a probability, would not
you say, sir?'

'I know nothing of politics, James. I am a sea officer, under the command of their Lordships and the King. I do as I am told. Should France again become our enemy, then I am ready to do my duty.'

'As am I.—I should find it regrettable, since France has much to offer the world . . . but I am bound by my oath.'

Rennie frowned, and was about to make a remark when Cutton brought his tea. He frowned instead at Cutton, and waited until he was gone. Then:

'I hope that it was not, James, but that sounded like reluctance, just now . . . ?' Pouring tea.

'I am always reluctant to think of war, sir. What sane man can be otherwise than reluctant, when our two nations are the greatest the civilized world has known? When so much may be put at risk, should we come again to war—bloody, wasteful, barbarous war. And yet I am not one to shrink from war, should it come. We did not shrink from it on our last commission—even if it was a small, private battle, fought far at sea.'

'We was both wounded—lucky to suffer only that.' Rennie did not frown any more, but looked at his lieutenant with affection, and understanding. 'Aye, we have seen action together, and know what it is. I did not mean to doubt you—not at all.'

'Sails of ships on the larboard bow!' Midshipman Cutforth's cracking basso and falsetto bawl from high aloft at the mainmast crosstrees. 'Many ships, hull down!'

Rennie and James ran immediately to the companion, jumped up, and ran on deck.

'So many ships together can only be another convoy—or the corsair fleet of *Rais* Zamoril, of Tunis,' said Rennie. He and James both attempted to make out the ships from the quarterdeck, but were defeated. The wind had risen from the east, and the ship was rolling on the swell, as were all their charges; only *Curlew* seemed able to run cleanly through the sea, dashing hither and thither under

Lieutenant Makepeace's firm command, rounding up the flock.

'Go aloft, will ye, James? Spy them out right quick.' Rennie did not often go aloft himself.

'Aye, sir.' James jumped forrard and into the weather main shrouds, climbed quickly and easily hand over hand aloft, and presently joined young Mr Cutforth in the crosstrees. Unslinging his glass:

'Where away now, Mr Cutforth? Point them out to me.' The mast beginning to sway with the wind and the swell, so that the perspective was one of a narrow deck far beneath, glimpsed between bellying canvas, a great expanse of white-flecked sea, and the sense of being on a very high swing flung back and forth. Mr Cutforth's straw hair was whipping about his ears, he was getting green about the nose and mouth, and his blue eyes had a desperate staring look as he grimly clung, and managed to point to the north. James hooked an arm round a t'ga'nt shroud, focused his glass, and:

'Aye—I have them.' His words half-lost in a whack of wind.

Far to the north, at the horizon's edge, hull down, a dozen sail of ships. Nay, fifteen.

'That ain't a convoy, Mr Cutforth.'

'No, sir?' Clinging, endeavouring to keep his voice strong, and confident—not quite succeeding. The mast swung far to leeward, swung back, the narrow deck far below. Fore-shortened figures hauled on falls there, and the sea rippled and licked and creamed along the lee wales, and boiled aft. James:

'No. Where is the escort? I see no escorting frigate, nor brig, among those ships. No man-of-war among them, at all. They are corsairs . . . and we may well see action this day.'

He slung his glass inside his jerkin, smiled at Midshipman Cutforth, and without further word stepped off the crosstrees and plunged straight to the deck.

The corsairs came nearly within range of *Expedient*'s guns at four bells of the afternoon watch, in hazy air and a chopping swell, the wind blustery and troubling. Nearly within range, but not quite. There were fifteen corsair ships, among them armed barques and xebecs, part square- and part lateen-rigged, and lateen-rigged galleys, narrow fast vessels with no heavy armament.

'Unless you count those white clad, turbaned devils of janissaries as armament,' said Rennie, peering at the ships through his glass. 'Their task is one of intimidation, James. Well well, they shall not intimidate us, hey?'

'I think that if we follow Mr Sebastian's stratagem the reverse will be true, sir.'

'Boy! Find Mr Quill, and ask him to attend on me as soon as he is able.'

'Aye, sir.' The boy dashed away, his bare feet crunching on the sanded deck.

The ship had been cleared for action and had stood ready at quarters three glasses, now, and in the heat of the region the men grew thirsty. Rennie had sent boys to the guncrews with monkeys of water at each turning of the glass, so that they would not suffer, waiting by their guns.

'Sir?' Mr Quill, correctly dressed, sweating in his red coat, his hat under his arm.

'Are your marines ready, Mr Quill?'

'They are dressed as you ordered, sir, in white, and we have made turbans out of extra cloth from the slops chest, and from bandages. Dr Wing was not very happy about the bandages. His entire store has been used up.' A smile.

'Yes, well, they may be returned to him soon enough, when we come to action, Mr Quill. But why are not you wearing white yourself?'

'Wear white, sir? You require me to wear white—an officer of the Royal Marines?'

'Perhaps you have not appreciated the tactics we wish to employ, Mr Quill. The Chatham detachment, and your own marines, wear white—as if they was janissaries. How will that look, if they are commanded by a fellow that is dressed in a glaring red coat? Do not answer. They will look like damned theatricals, commanded by a buffoon.'

'I am very sorry, sir.'

'You will shift into white at once, if y'please.'

'Very good, sir. However, I do not think it quite just to be called a buffoon——'

'I did not say you *was* a buffoon, Mr Quill. I said you would *look* like one, in red.'

'With respect, sir—you are not wearing white yourself. Nor is Mr Hayter——'

'Kindly do as you are told, sir.' Curtly, turning away to the rail. Presently: 'Mr Hayter.'

James came from the binnacle, glancing east, and joined Rennie at the rail. A big shivering sea ran under the ship at an angle, and showered both men with a dumping sluice of spray.

'Sir?' Wiping his face.

'We had better shift out of our coats, I think, and tie a bandage or two about our heads. If we are to present a convincing appearance to those damned blackguardly corsairs, we had better look exactly as they do.'

'You have often remarked, sir, that in my working clothes I do already resemble a corsair.'

'Yes, but a Malta corsair, James, a Christian—not an Arab. We must resemble Barbary men this day.'

'Very good, sir.' Making to go below. Rennie held up a retaining hand, a finger cocked:

'I had meant to ask Lieutenant Quill. Have the marines been issued with cutlasses, and instructed to brandish them, and strike them against the ship's rail, and so forth, and to bellow '*Allah-o-Akbar!* at the top of their lungs?'

'Mr Quill and his sergeant, and Sergeant Host, have all issued such instruction, sir. Some of the marines, I fear, have difficulty in recalling the Muslim phrase, exact——'

'But they must recall it, James! That is the essence of our deception!'

'I have said to Mr Quill that they might simply bellow *Aaaagh! Aaaagh! Aaaagh!* as loud as they are able.' James had a sudden impulse to laugh at the absurdity of this, but managed to keep his face straight. 'I—I am sure that will suffice, sir.'

'Hm, I am in no doubt that it will. Very well. Mr Upward!' To the junior lieutenant, now sufficiently recovered to take his place at quarters: 'Mr Upward—starboard battery ready! Keep yourselves concealed! Mr Loftus, bring me a point closer to the wind, if y'please, and lay me closer in!—And now let us see what these infamous wretches are made of.'

Captain Rennie grimly shrugged off his blue coat, called for bandages, wound them round his head—and drew his sword.

* * *

By design *Expedient* had sailed ahead of the convoy, flying her Colours Confused, an ensign and pennant of Rennie's devising, consisting in squares and strips of bright colours sewn together, representing no nation, no navy. Rennie now ran straight at the leading ships of the corsair fleet, two barques and a large armed xebec. This large xebec was presumably *Rais* Zamoril's ship, although Rennie could not make out the admiral in his glass. Crowded in her waist were a great number of white clad janissaries, and there were seamen aloft. All was ominously silent in the corsair ships, and Rennie felt a twinge of unease in his bladder. Would they wait until he was abreast of them, and unleash a storm of metal into his ship?

'We must hold our nerve, and proceed with our plan of action,' he told himself, and aloud:

'Courses in the brails, Mr Loftus, if y'please.'

Expedient was now within pistol-shot of the xebec, a

handsome vessel with a beaked head, flat-steeved bowsprit, overhanging stern, a lateen-rigged foremast and square-rigged main and mizzen. Rennie counted ports for twelve guns per side. If this was Zamoril's ship, what were his guns? Nine pounders, twelves? Iron, or brass? What shot would he use? Round, bar, grape? The answers would be plain soon enough. By a prearranged signal to Mr Quill, of a raised hand, the disguised marines were now brought bellowing to their feet. '*Haagh! Haagh! Allah!*' they bellowed—a serviceable approximation of the required cry, thought James, as he too bellowed, and brandished a cutlass. Noise echoed and rang from every part of *Expedient*. Cutlasses were smacked and rattled against great guns and banged against rails, and below decks every man from the cook to the carpenter's mate struck metal against metal—pots, kettles, tools—setting up a loud, crashing clatter that mingled with the yelling cries of the marines to create a roaring, ringing, menacing din.

No shots were fired by any of the corsair ships. Of the many vessels—xebecs, barques, tartanes, pinques—there was not one that was not ported for guns, and yet none of them fired. The astonishment upon the faces of the seamen in the leading xebec was plainly apparent. They hung motionless in the shrouds and on the spars, and those handling the great lateen sail froze on the steep angle of the yard, staring at *Expedient*. The surprise tactic had worked.

'*Starboard battery . . . FIRE!*' Rennie shouted through James's speaking trumpet.

Thirteen guns erupted in flame and smoke along *Expedient*'s side, blasting out a tremendous doubled weight of roundshot. The side of the xebec exploded in fragments, the lateen yard was cut to pieces, and the mainmast shuddered, toppled, and went by the board in a rending crash of timber, shrouds and canvas. Screams burst in the muffling smoke, mortal anguish in the devastated waist of the xebec. Splinters pocked and riddled the surrounding sea, thrashing the water into foam.

'*Reload with grape!*' James ran along the gangway, cutlass in hand. '*Marksmen, fire at will!*'

Four or five cables distant, out to larboard, *Curlew* cut across the rear of the corsair line, and loosed her carronades.

BOOM BOOM BOOM BOOM BOOM

Two pinques were hit simultaneously by the eighteen-pound roundshot from *Curlew*'s carronades, the first suffering three hits to her stern, and losing her rudder, the second suffering the loss of her lateen-rigged foremast. *Curlew* came about in a rapid, heeling curve, and ran down the line of the fleet, loosing her other broadside into a barque. The barque at once lost way, men could be seen leaping for their lives into the sea, and a gaping wound in the vessel's side began to gulp water by the ton. She sagged, twisted, heeled drunkenly and sank by the stern, in a tangle of masts and rigging, with a rapidity that even to Lieutenant Makepeace on *Curlew*'s quarterdeck was very shocking.

Crack! Crack! Crack! Crack! Sharpshooters in *Expedient*'s tops fired into the xebec, cutting down janissaries as they strove to gather themselves, and recover from their initial appalled surprise and dismay. Some few of them attempted to launch fire arrows, but these missiles fell flaming into the sea, trailing black smoke.

The Chatham marines, having performed their role as mock janissaries, had immediately after taken their places at the great guns, making up the full complement for the starboard battery crews of 130 men all told. The carronades on the forecastle and quarterdeck had not been deployed; Rennie had preferred to concentrate his guncrews at the eighteen-pounder guns. The carronades were, however, loaded and ready, should they be needed, should circumstances grow dire, and smashers be required.

Lieutenant Upward, white clad—his head still bandaged white—reported to James: 'Starboard battery reloaded, full allowance and grape!'

At the same moment the corsair fleet appeared collectively to recall itself to its purpose, and to counter-attack with a stuttering roar and crash of guns. A tightly ordered line of ships—barques, pinques, tartanes—had formed to reply to *Expedient*'s and *Curlew*'s opening salvoes, and Rennie, standing upright on his quarterdeck, saw his ship injured. Blocks fell, rigging parted, sails were shot through in great buffeting rents. Over the blasts of the guns came also now the the blood-curdling yells of the janisseries, echoing those of the Chatham marines, and outdoing them in sheer ferocity and power—yells, shrieks, and the loud, rattling concussions of scimitars upon shields.

Expedient was now abreast of a tartane and a pinque, and fired across their decks on the lift.

BANG   BANG-BANG   BOOM-BANG
BANG BANG BANG BANG

Grapeshot whistled across the half-cable's width between the ships, fizzed in a scattering hail through rope, timber fittings, canvas, and cut men in half—chopped them, dismembered them, smashed open their skulls. Smoke rushed in fiery rings, and puffing expanding clouds. The bellicose yells of janissaries became their dying shrieks, their dying moans.

Rennie, alert on his quarterdeck, now strode to the larboard rail to look for *Curlew*. Nearly too late—almost beyond the moment when he could make a defence—he saw that a long, low galley, with a sharp battering-ram bowsprit, and a hundred janissaries crowded in the body of the vessel, curved scimitars at the ready, had slipped up to *Expedient* from astern and now lay on her larboard quarter. The galley had a single mast with a lateen sail hauled up in the brails, and was powered by dozens of slaves at long sweeps. At the stern, under a curved awning, an imposing figure stood near to the rudder. A figure dressed all in black, save for a vivid red wound of a hat, and in his hand a long black staff—an ebony staff.

'By God, that is Zamoril . . .' Rennie, under his breath. 'He has outfooted us.' A moment of stunned indecision, then: 'Mr Tangible! We are under attack! Hands to repel boarders! Mr Hayter! Mr Upward! Guncrews to man the larboard carronades! *Jump, now, every man!*'

Even as he shouted these commands, he saw out of the corner of his eye, away to sternward, another galley rushing in a flurry of sweeps alongside Rashid Bey's unprotected xebec, saw janisseries leap and swarm up the xebec's side and into the ship.

'God damn them! Mr Loftus! We must go about! Sink and destroy these bloody wretches, go about, and save Rashid Bey!'

The words scarcely out of his mouth before they were snatched away in a sudden whoomp of wind, his hat snatched from his head, and the once distant yellow storm now rushed from the east across them, dark and furious across the corsair line, across *Expedient*, the galleys and the convoy on the riding sea, and plunged them all into a new and even more desperate battle—the battle to survive.

With the assault of wind came the first horizontal spatters of rain, cold pellets on the gusting air, stinging Rennie's face as the ship heeled steep under his legs, and he clapped on to a shroud to steady himself. Over his shoulder he saw that the towing launch had been cut loose of its rope and set adrift by the corsair galley. He saw it lift high on a wave, beam on, already filling with water as the wave crested, saw water swim over the thole pins, saw the boat wallow and settle in the mass of the wave, then with a brief glimpse of its white-leaded bottom roll sinking and disappear. Another blast of wind, and Rennie turned and sucked in a breath:

'Bring her head to the wind!'

But even as he gave the order he knew that it must be futile to attempt to do it. The helmsmen briefly did their best, clinging and straining at the spokes, weather and lee, but *Expedient* was reluctant, she was sluggish and unwilling, and immense waves were already beginning to loom and drive at her from the turbulent east. Rennie saw that if he persisted in trying to bring her head up to the gale, he risked exposing her weather side too long, risked a massive wave breaking over the waist, surging over the gangway, the hances, the skids, and flooding through the ship. In short he risked drowning her, with all souls, as quickly and dismayingly as the launch had drowned a moment ago.

'Belay that! We must run before, and save ourselves! Mr Tangible! Hands to shorten sail!'

The galley had already broken off the attack, and with a much-reefed sail was now running before the wind, the figure of *Rais* Zamoril diminishing in her diminishing stern, her immense rudder fighting to keep the ship from swinging beam on, and being pushed on her beam ends to certain destruction. Rennie again glanced astern, but could not see Rashid Bey's xebec, nor the other galley. The storm had filled the air with spray, and rain, and the waves were seething and huge all around. Wind howled like a madman in the rigging, an enormous sea rode up aft, tipping the ship forward, burying her bowsprit, and Rennie clung for his life.

'WE MUST HAND SAIL!' he bellowed in his most carrying quarterdeck, but in the wild screaming of the wind he could scarcely hear the words himself. 'TRIPLE REEFED TOP-SAILS, FORE AND MAIN! MR LOFTUS! MR LOFTUS!' But he could not see Bernard Loftus on deck.

'Permission to double-bowse all great guns, sir?' A voice directly in his ear. James's voice.

'Yes, James, yes! Double-bowse all guns! Find Mr Storey! Mr Quill and the marines to assist you!' Another massive wave, and both men were lifted off their feet as water seethed round them. Rennie clung to the shroud, and James clung to a backstay, until the mass of water had passed over and through, and the ship righted herself, streaming. 'Are the hatches battened!'

'Aye――' A whack of wind tore the remainder of his reply into nothing, and both men had to turn their heads into the shoulders of their coats to escape the cutting force of the tempest. Rain began to slash across the deck, whipping and cutting like icy razors. Lightning flickered across the sky, illuminating the poles of the masts as high as the trucktops. Thunder immediately followed, thudding and booming so loud it made their ears hum.

'Did you have sight of *Curlew*, James?' Rennie, directly into James's ear, his head bent.

James shook his head, glancing at Rennie. Water ran down their faces, streamed from their hair, half-blinded them. 'No, sir! She was――' Wind defeated him, then: 'She was away to larboard, I think, when we was attacked! I must go forrard, and find Mr Storey!'

A shivering shock through all the ship's timbers as another wave smashed against her, and James lurched away forrard, pulling himself by newly rigged lifelines, and ducking his head.

Topmen clung to the yards, balanced on the footropes and horses, reefing topsails in the near impossible conditions, and the helmsmen brought *Expedient* off the wind to run before. Mountainous seas broke over the ship as this manoeuvre was carried out, but she was battened, and bowsed, and strong, and she did run, and run well. Below decks conditions were very poor. Men fell and squashed against each other; boys fell and crawled on all fours in the tumult of the messes; kids fell, pots fell, food and drink were spilled, and vomit joined the frothy, pooling dregs upon the deck timbers, stinking and sliding with the lurching of the ship. The fouled air was filled with groans and curses, and imprecations to the heavens, and the cook and his mates despaired.

The ship ran west and west before the roaring wind, until Rennie judged that unless he wore, and clawed back some sea room, beating into the tempest, they would be driven in upon the Tunis coast. Darkness fell just as he wore, and even as he did the wind veered through 180 degrees, and began to blast from the west. Rennie was again obliged to run before, now to the east, *Expedient* scudding under bare poles save for close-reefed topsails at fore and main. In the black night, lit only by the electrical flashes of the storm, Rennie calculated that they might run due east for a few hours only, lest they be driven in turn against the lee of Pantelleria Isle, that was proximate to them if they followed their present course, and would smash them to fragments if he was negligent in his seamanship.

At midnight and half a glass, as Rennie dozed fitfully in his hanging cot below—having snatched a chance to rest— lightning struck the spanker gaff, there was a tremendous crash, a brief flaring of flames, and the gaff fell on the quarterdeck, breaking in pieces and trailing smouldering vangs and blocks. The crash woke Rennie, and he stumbled forrard to the waist in his shirt and breeches, wrapping himself in his oilskin. As he put a foot on the first rung of the waist ladder a huge wave flooded over the taffrail, seethed forward, sucked the weather helmsman from his place at the wheel, and dragged him over the lee rail, as if he had been no more substantial than a rat. His hopeless scream was smothered at once in the mass of the wave, and he was drowned in darkness, deep astern of the heeling ship. Rennie himself was inundated by the flooding of seawater under the quarterdeck, and clung to the ladder there, quite unaware of the little tragedy that had just happened. When he was able to climb to the quarterdeck a minute after, he found the lee helmsman, that had had the foresight to lash himself to the spokes, hanging there gasping but alive.

'Alfred Gunn is drowned, sir. He were swep' away. Dear God.' Distressed.

'You are certain?' Over the wind and the clatter of the smashed gaff sliding across the deck.

'Aye, sir. He did not lash hisself, and he is drowned, poor bugger.' Standing now.

'Where is Mr Loftus?' Glancing aloft at the snapped-off gaff, and aft at the wreckage.

'I has not seen the master this watch, sir.'

'Very well. Hold her so, as you are able, and I will send another man. Mr Loftus!' Moving forrard, his oilskin glistening in the glow of the storm lantern. 'Mr Loftus! We must repair the gaff!'

Mr Loftus did not appear, and could not be found in the ship, and Rennie sent for his first lieutenant. James came on deck in his working rig, turning his head away from the stinging spray.

'There is no officer on watch, Mr Hayter. The ship was not being conned. Where in Christ's name is Mr Upward, and Mr Loftus, and the master's mate, good God? Are we to lapse into damned idle indiscipline merely because we have struck a modicum of bad weather? Hey?'

James's reply was lost in a rumbling clap of thunder, and he repeated himself over the hissing whip of the wind as the thunder died:

'I was in the hold, sir, where we was securing a line of shifting casks——'

'Are they secured, now?'

'Aye, sir. There was some small leakage, but we——'

'Never mind, never mind. You have secured them. I wish to know who is officer of the watch.'

'I was certain that Mr Loftus was to take this watch, sir, with Mr Cutforth and Mr Abey.' Cupping his hand to his mouth.

'Well well, they are none of them on deck. What has become of my ship? Cannot I go below a few minutes, to look at my charts, without——'

'Have a care, now!' bellowed James, and ran at his captain, and buffeted him bodily across the quarterdeck, so that they both fell in a sprawl. The peak halyard block, that had been swinging loose aloft since the gaff broke, now fell with a lethal thud—exactly where Rennie had been standing. The block skidded away in a snaking of rope between two double-bowsed carronades, and Rennie scrambled to his feet, touching the back of his skull.

'Are you all right, sir?' James, getting to his own feet.

'Aye, James, thankee.' Rennie nodded at him—nodded again, and: 'Thankee, indeed.' A sniff, and: 'We must ride this out, then make the attempt to gather the convoy, and find *Curlew*—if she ain't with the other ships. We will make a start, if y'please, by restoring discipline upon the quarter-deck.' Straightening his oilskin on his shoulders, and lifting his head against the wind.

In the space of a further half-glass, during which the wind dropped a little, Mr Upward was summoned, and asked why he had not remained on deck with his middies when the watch changed, if Mr Loftus had not then relieved him. He replied that as the captain surely recalled he had himself sent Mr Upward below, suffering as he was with a severe headache, with instruction to remain in his cabin until the doctor could attend on him.

'And has Dr Wing attended you, Mr Upward?' Over a sudden renewed gust of wind.

'No, sir. I understand he is very busy below, as there are a great many injuries to the people. I am very sorry, sir, but I fear I am going to be sick . . .' And he ran to the rail.

'Good God, good God.' Rennie, glancing again at James, then: 'I must recall Lieutenant Bradshaw to duty, I think.—Who is that skulking by the binnacle there! Come aft, now, and show yourselves!'

Two bedraggled midshipmen, very pale and miserable, came aft as ordered. They were Mr Cutforth and Mr Abey, who should long since have presented themselves for duty.

'Well well, where are your hats and coats, gentlemen?'

'They are very wet, sir. Our berth is very wet, and very disgusting.' Mr Cutforth, suppressing a retch. Both youths were in breeches and shirts, their shirts stained with puke.

'A man-of-war is very wet, in a storm at sea.' Grimly. 'We are all very wet. Eh, Mr Hayter?'

James turned from the binnacle, and came aft, wringing out his sodden blue kerchief, and tying it back on his head.

'Aye, sir, very wet. We are yet running near due east, sir. May I make the suggestion, given the break in the weather, that we should attempt to make some northing? Lest we fall on the island shore in darkness?'

'Break in the weather? It don't look very friendly to me. What o'clock is it?' As he asked two bells sounded. He sighed. 'Very well, Mr Hayter, we will wear, and attempt to run north—in the hope that the convoy is somewhere there ahead of us, under *Curlew*'s care.'

'Very good, sir. You there, Mr Abey! Find Mr Tangible right quick!—Mr Upward, y'may go below. Mr Cutforth, find the master-at-arms, and tell him to release Mr Bradshaw to my custody upon the quarterdeck! Then rouse the carpenter, Mr Adgett, and say I wish to see him at once, so that we may repair the spanker gaff! Jump, now!' Striding to the breast rail, raising his speaking trumpet: 'HANDS TO WEAR SHIP!'

Expedient shivered as a big sea rode up under the larboard quarterlights, washed the rim rail and sash lights, and rolled heavily forrard along the sheerline and the gunports. Captain Rennie breathed out through his nose, planted his feet apart, and set his mouth.

'All is not lost quite yet,' he said, but not aloud. All was not lost, but what if *Curlew* and the convoy were, and Rashid Bey himself? What then?

--- ✤ ---

Seven bells of the middle watch, and James Hayter could only guess at the ship's position. Lightning flashes lit the coastline to starboard now, as *Expedient* clawed her way north—clawed but did not greatly advance—and it became clear to him that the ship was being driven south-east. Not by the wind so much—that came from the west—but by a fierce current, running from the north-west, and forcing *Expedient* sternward toward that ominous coast, that could only be Pantelleria.

He had doubled the men on the helm, with two on the weather, two on the lee. The spanker gaff had been effortfully replaced, the throat of the new spar fixed to the mast and the vangs and braces rove up—the heaving, spray-swept quarterdeck and the pendulum-arcing mizzen-top not an ideal environment for the carrying-out of such a repair—and Mr Adgett and his mate and crew had retired below with an extra ration of grog. Mr Bradshaw had not come on deck, had in fact refused to do so, since he claimed to be desperately ill. Since James could not contradict a fellow officer without calling him a liar, he had been obliged to take the watch himself. Bernard Loftus had not been found—could not be found—and Rennie had quietly said to James, before going below to his cabin, that in his opinion the master was lost overboard.

'Mr Abey!'

Midshipman Abey, still very wet and subdued, but wrapped now in a foul-weather jacket, and resigned to seeing out the watch, attended the first lieutenant.

'Sir?'

'Go below to the great cabin and wake the captain, with my apologies, and inform him that we have an island on our lee, and must alter course to stand off and give ourselves some sea room, with his permission. Jump now. Oh, and Mr Abey——'

'Sir?'

'Bring me my flask from my cabin, will you, when you return? The silver flask, that is in my undress coat.'

'Very good, sir.'

'Y'may take a nip from the flask yourself, Richard Abey. It will lift you.'

'Aye, sir, thank you.' And he ran forrard to the waist ladder. The companionway hatch was battened down because of the storm.

Presently Rennie came on deck, complaining: 'Why was I not woke before this, Mr Hayter? I left instruction I was to be woke at four bells, and— Good heaven, is that the land?' As a lightning flash showed the coastline less than a league to starboard.

'It is Pantelleria Isle, sir. There is a strong current driving us, so that we are all leeway, making no headway at all. I fear that we may have to boxhaul her, else be driven in.'

'Why was I was not informed! Why was I not woke before this!'

'I was not aware of our predicament until the lightning showed me the coast, sir.' James, very formal and correct.

'Yes yes, very well. We will boxhaul, if y'please, right quick. You there, boy! Bring me my boat cloak, and a flask. Jump!'

They would boxhaul: however, it soon became clear that since the ship was already being driven sternward, and had little sail bent, she could not efficiently nor effectively be boxhauled, with her foreyards braced round and sails aback, but must instead be clubhauled, if she was to be saved. The first lieutenant accordingly conferred with his captain— hastily conferred, in the wind and flash of the quarterdeck— and the commands were duly given. Topmen raced aloft to the yards. A spring hawser was attached to the lee bower, to be run from a port adjacent to the lee mainbrace shear, and:

'Forecastle, there! Lee bower away! Let go! Helmsmen, put your helm hard down now!'

As the cable and hawser were paid out together, and brought up at the stopper, *Expedient*'s head came round into the wind, and the crucial further commands were bellowed; first:

'Slip your cable!'

then, a few anxious moments after:

'Cut your spring!'

and a strong young seaman of the afterguard wielded his sea axe, chopped through the hawser in three fierce downward blows, and the ship was free.

'Haul of all!' Yards braced, sail loosed, and *Expedient*— fighting the current, and gaining on it by the power of the wind now drawing her sails—clawed her way off the island, her masts and canvas made bright in electrical instants, and the sea flowing in lacy dark mounds along her wales.

'My people are seamen, by God,' said Rennie with a nod, just loud enough for James to hear him, and understand that the compliment applied as much to him as to the men. 'We have lost a best bower, but saved our ship.'

'May I suggest an extra ration of grog at the change of watch, sir?'

'Indeed y'may, James. They have earned it. Make it so.' Another nod, and bracing himself he trod aft, and breathed a great sigh of relief, his face hidden.

'A little less lost.' Murmured. Then he called his lieutenant to him again:

'Mr Hayter.'

'Sir?' Attending.

'What of Mr Loftus? Anything?'

'No, sir. Unless he has hid himself—and I do not think that a possibility—then I believe he is lost.'

'As I had thought.' A sniffing sigh, and he turned his face into the wind briefly, allowed the wind to whip away the last of that sigh, and: 'Why is Mr Bradshaw not on deck?'

'He is ill, sir.'

'Ill! He ain't ill, the fellow, he is shamming because I confined him. You ordered him to duty?'

'I sent him my compliments, sir, and required him to take his watch.'

'Aye, just so.—Mr Cutforth!'

'Sir?'

'Go below to Mr Quill. Rouse him, and say to him that I wish Mr Bradshaw to be brought to me on the quarterdeck

forthwith. He is to do so with a party of marines, just so many
as may be required to carry Mr Bradshaw up the bloody
ladder, should he decline to come of his own accord! Ye have
me, Mr Cutforth?'

'Aye, sir.'

'Jump then.'

At daybreak, the storm abating—the sky densely overcast
still, and the sea unruly, with a ten-foot pitching swell—
Expedient had been driven far to the south-east, round the
southern tip of Pantelleria Isle and into the open sea, by the
wind and current combined. Part of the morning watch on
their knees with holystones, scrubbing the decks. A rigging
crew splicing and serving under a croak-voiced Tangible.
And Mr Bradshaw reluctantly on the quarterdeck, under the
watchful—not to say humiliating—eyes of a pair of marines,
and the barely averted gaze of the two midshipmen of the
watch, in turn deeply embarrassed by his predicament. Mr
Bradshaw snapped at them, sent them on errands, made them
work every minute, repeating the task of reeling out the
logline twice every half-glass, &c., because he found their
work unsatisfactory, and they felt his displeasure—as inferior
beings have always felt the wrath of their superiors in ships,
since men first nailed timbers together in frame and beam
and planking and launched themselves upon the immensity of
the sea, uncertain of their fate.

Rennie came on deck, muzzed with sleep, and in a not very
much better temper than Lieutenant Bradshaw. He dismissed the marines, and:

'I will like to see your glass-by-glass notations, if y'please,
Mr Bradshaw.'

'Very good, sir.' Gruffly. 'You there, Mr Thomas, fetch the
glass-by——'

'Ye'll fetch them yourself, Mr Bradshaw, when I require it
of you,' snapped Rennie. 'Unless you wish to be broke back
to midshipman?'

Rennie in truth had not that power, but Mr Bradshaw could certainly again find himself confined in the orlop, a prospect he did not relish. The orlop stank, and was cramped and dark. In fact he had found as the watch progressed that the fresh air of the deck was welcome, and the return to duty, albeit on an unfamiliar quarterdeck, not altogether irksome to him. And so the lieutenant obeyed, fetched the notations from the binnacle, and brought them to Rennie. The captain did not even glance at them, but merely said:

'In course we cannot yet know our position, only guess at it.'

Mr Bradshaw was silent, since he did not think the captain wished a response. He was wrong.

'Hey, Mr Bradshaw?'

'Eh?—No, sir, indeed.'

'We have run at a brisk rate of knots in darkness, though.'

'Aye, sir, we have.' Unbending a little. 'Seven and eight knots, as noted.'

'God knows what has become of our convoy, of Rashid Bey. All of the ships are scattered, no doubt. Are they to the north? Or the east? Is *Curlew* with them? We do not know that, neither.'

Mr Bradshaw winced at the mention of his ship, and did not know if Rennie had meant him to wince, or had spoken of *Curlew* in the lieutenant's presence without thinking what it might mean to her erstwhile commander to hear her name. To bring his mind away from a painful subject he pointed out something in the notes:

'As you will see, sir, Mr Loftus ain't lost, after all. He is——'

'Not lost! Mr Loftus is safe! Why did ye not inform me at once, good God?'

'I—I did not understand the urgency . . .'

'Well? Well? Where is he, for Christ's sake!'

'He—he had a fall in the sailroom, sir, when he went there to look for foul-weather canvas, and he struck his head, and was buried under mending canvas, where he lay undetected all the middle watch, I believe. Dr Wing is presently tending to his injury.'

'I should have been informed of this the moment it was known, good heaven!' A harsh, exasperated sigh. 'Is he able to return to duty?'

'I do not know that, sir. I heard it from the mess steward, that brought me a wedge of pie, and so I added the information to my notes——'

'Well well, I will like to see the doctor, then. Perhaps he may be able to tell me whether or no the sailing master is hale. Boy!'

And he sent a ship's boy below to find Thomas Wing. Presently the surgeon came up the ladder.

'Yes, Captain?'

'You must address me as "sir", you know. Certainly you cannot have forgot that, when we have sailed together three commissions?'

'I beg your pardon—sir.' A polite inclination of his head. Thomas Wing did not like to bow, except in the most obligating circumstance; his very small stature made bowing, for him, a diminishing exercise, in that bodily it made him even lower than he was already, and in self-estimation he felt himself lowered by it altogether. His origins had been humble in the extreme; he had begun his career as a porter in the Haslar Hospital at Gosport, carrying death-soiled sheets and bandages to the laundry, carrying the dead to the mortuary and laying out the corpses, carrying carboys of physick upon his handcart, &c., &c. These duties had eventually led to his being trusted by the great Haslar physician Dr Stroud to carry his instrument cases, and in turn to lay out the instruments, clean and polish them after surgical procedures, and number and label the myriad bottles in the pharmacy storerooms. Without formal education of any kind, save that provided by the perceptive Dr Stroud, and by his own assiduous daily reading, Thomas

Wing—a dwarfish man, with mild countenance but exceptional physical strength—had become to all intent and purpose a surgeon in his own right. He had treated the port admiral at Plymouth, Admiral Bamphlett, they had become friends, and this in turn had led Wing to his heart's desire—the chance to go to sea as a surgeon in the Royal Navy. That chance had come with *Expedient*'s first commission, and he had been with the ship ever since. So that now, when Rennie admonished him over a minor question of etiquette, he took it lightly enough, knowing that Rennie liked and admired him, and was merely reminding him of his place in the hierarchy of the ship. 'You wished to see me—sir?'

'I did, Thomas Wing, I do. Is Mr Loftus fit for duty?'

'Not quite. Not quite yet.'

'Damnation to "not quite", Doctor. Do not be dainty, if y'please. When may he take his watch?'

'Not . . . quite yet.' Moving his head from side to side a little, and giving the merest shrug—that said: I will not be bullied in this.

'Hm.' Glancing at him sidelong. 'Hm. Very well. Y'may say to your patient, Doctor, that I will require him to take his watch tonight. He may rest today, but at the beginning of the first watch tonight he must present himself.'

A day, and a night, and noon declared on the day following before the first limping ships of the convoy were sighted— two feluccas, both battered by the storm but swimming, and their lateen sails bent. Of the other ships, including Rashid Bey's heavy-laden xebec, there was no sign. *Expedient* lay on a bearing of 36 degrees 41 minutes north, and 12 degrees 49 minutes east, at the declaration. The sea was calm, the day sunny, and there was a light southerly topsail breeze.

Rennie signalled the ships, and hove to. Presently Lieutenant Hayter went in the pinnace to the leading felucca, where he found Rashid Bey and Mr Sebastian, the latter with his arm bound up and resting in a sling. Rashid Bey looked haggard, and older, but was unharmed.

'I am most pleased to see you, Lieutenant,' he said, and made salaam.

James removed his hat and made a leg, and was nearly swamped by a sudden lifting wave, that drenched his coat. Wiping his wet face: 'And I am most pleased—and greatly relieved—to find you well, sir.' Turning: 'Mr Sebastian, I trust your wound ain't too painful.'

'Nothing to the wound I inflicted upon the wretch that gave me this, Mr Hayter. In truth, he did not live long enough to know pain.' A show of his yellow teeth.

'Alas, Lieutenant, as you see—I have lost my own ship.' Rashid Bey stood near the rudder of the felucca, in the shade of an awning.

'Captain Rennie sends his compliments, sir, and most earnestly begs you to repair aboard *Expedient*, and join him.' Including Sebastian with a glance.

'Yes, of course. We must confer.'

The three men returned to *Expedient* in the pinnace, and the much-reduced convoy again got under way. James went to his cabin to shift his sodden clothes, then to the great cabin to hear Rashid Bey reveal his dismaying news to Rennie:

'My entire fortune is lost, Captain Rennie. Sebastian and I took refuge in a boat when my ship was attacked, and came into the felucca and thus survived, but lost everything excepting our lives.' Rashid Bey's face was stricken with anguish and shame. He first refused the coffee brewed by Colley Cutton from beans brought by Mr Sebastian, then with a sigh accepted a cup and sipped mutely, his dark gaze lost in reverie for moments together. Rennie did not—could not—allow himself to say that he had warned Rashid Bey of the very great folly of bringing all of his riches with him, in a slow-sailing ship—but he thought it, all the same. Thought it, and was vindicated, though without comfort of any kind; it was comfortless and empty triumph to have been proved right in prediction of calamity. The depth and extent of Rashid Bey's predicament were clear, and terrible.

'How can I face my people now? How can I tell them what has happened?'

Rennie obliged himself to remain silent. Since he could offer no solace, silence was best.

'Yes . . . yes . . .' A sigh, heartfelt. 'I have lost all of my gold, all of my precious things—all of Rabhet's precious things. Everything in my xebec has gone to *Rais* Zamoril and Tunis—and very probably the other ships also, if they have not foundered in the storm. It is all gone, everything . . .'

Rennie could restrain himself no longer:

'Sir, if only you had not put it all at risk! Why? For what reason, good heaven?'

'I wished to preserve my fortune from the depredations of Suleiman el Hassad, the Dey of Tunis, should he invade.'

'Could not you have hid your gold—indeed, all of your precious goods—away in the desert? At Chott el Hakkan?'

'Perhaps, in hindsight, I might wish that I had done so—but I was persuaded otherwise.'

'Persuaded, sir? Was not this your own decision?'

'Nay, it was not. In least, not entire, it was not.'

'Then—if not yours . . . ?'

'I was persuaded that my gold would be safest in England, in an English bank. The English banks are like fortresses, impregnable places, where no evil force may penetrate, where gold is held safe for ever.'

'Ah, yes. Yes. However, banks ain't always completely safe, sir. Banks may fail.'

'Fail!'

'Indeed. Fail. A bank is an enterprise, like any other. Should it make unwise loans, or investments, and become over-extended, well . . .'

'This I was *not* told! Of this I was *not* made aware!' Almost fiercely, then the truth of his predicament again came in upon him, and what might have been—however negative and dismaying—was not so dismaying as the reality, and he slumped in his chair.

'Might I inquire, sir, who persuaded you about English banks?'

'The very man that agreed to send British ships, in return for the use of my harbour and port. That I had thought was a wise and honourable man——'

'Sir Robert Greer, hey?' Quietly. 'Was it?'

'Sir Robert Greer.' The merest nod.

'Indeed.' Grimly, with a grim little glance at Mr Sebastian. 'Sir Robert Greer, the fellow.'

'You do not trust him?' Rashid Bey lifted his head to regard Rennie. 'But he has sent you here. He has sent you here to escort my convoy of ships.' A momentary flicker of his eyes toward Mr Sebastian, then he returned his puzzled, suspicious stare to Rennie.

Rennie sniffed deep, looked away, then met that stare. 'Sir, it cannot matter to you now what I may feel about Sir Robert Greer, when your fortune has been lost to Suleiman el Hassad—or perhaps to the sea itself, since *Rais* Zamoril and all his fleet may possibly have met a stormy fate. I have lost *Curlew*, and a valued officer in Lieutenant Makepeace, and I have absolutely failed in my commission—to preserve your convoy and bring it safe to England. In least I must now endeavour to preserve your life, by carrying you there. You, and Mr Sebastian.'

'No, but I wish to go to Rabhet, Captain Rennie. My people must hear the worst, and decide my future. They may not forgive the loss of my treasure, but certainly they will not forgive a coward that flees from their judgement and hides in England.'

'Mr Sebastian, a word with you in private.' Rennie stood.

'Anything you say to me must be said before the Regent.'

'Very well——'

A bellow from the quarterdeck immediately above: 'BEAT TO QUARTERS!'

Rennie broke off, snatched up his sword, and dashed for the companion-way ladder.

Zamoril came at them this time not in galleys but in heavily armed, lateen-rigged barques, from astern of the little convoy. There were four barques, each ported for six guns a side, and chasers mounted in the bows. There were fifty or sixty janissaries in each ship, waiting for the chance to board and fight hand to hand. Zamoril's tactic was to divide his small fleet into four individual units of attack, and run at *Expedient* from four different directions at once, ignoring the two feluccas—for the moment, at least.

Rennie saw at once, as he gained the quarterdeck, that *Expedient* was in trouble. Certainly either one of her batteries in broadside could destroy any one of these attacking vessels—that were by comparison with an English man-of-war inconsiderable and fragile ships. But four such ships, with the ability to come about and manoeuvre very fast—and forty-eight guns between them—could maul a frigate, fatally maul her, if she allowed herself to be caught.

'Broadsides, starboard and larboard!' bawled Rennie. 'Short crews also to man the carronades! We must smash and run, lads, or be bested!'

The nearest barque, coming at *Expedient* from the south under all three lateen sails, now fired her chaser. A puff of smoke from her bow, and the ball hissed harmlessly over *Expedient*'s spanker gaff, and made a splash far off. The other ships came at *Expedient* from the north-east, the east, and the south-east, with the frigate four points large on the larboard tack.

'Stand by to go about! Larboard battery, out tompions!'

Expedient swung through the wind, yards bracing, sails backed, and came up on the new heading, running square— as nearly square as possible—across the attacking line, and fired her larboard battery of guns at the converging corsairs, each section angled on the breeching ropes to reach one ship.

Blasts of flame and furious balloons of smoke. Then part of
each guncrew ran up the waist ladder to the larboard
quarterdeck carronades, manned them, and turned and aimed
them on their transverse trucks at the fast-closing barque
coming from the south. But the barque now tacked sharp to
starboard, and the carronades' crews had to leap down from
the quarterdeck to man the starboard battery of long guns, as
Expedient swung a little further on her arc of direction, and
her starboard battery was brought to bear.

BOOM BANG   BOOM-BANG   BANG BANG
BANG BANG   BOOM

The barque was caught by the full weight of metal of that
broadside, caught square amidships, and shattered. Her main
and mizzen collapsed, dragging the triangular lateen sails on
their wide yards down to the rail in a massed slumping of
canvas. The vessel slewed, her waist splintered by roundshot,
and hampered there by the extra weight of janissaries. She
began to sink by the stern. A man struggled from the
quarterlight in the stern, flailing and squirming in
desperation as he tried to free himself, and was submerged.
Screams and cries echoed across the water. Even as she sank,
some of her forrard guns were fired, but the balls skipped and
skimmed harmlessly wide. The long steeved bow of the
barque jutted skyward in a mist of gunsmoke, there was a last
horrible groaning of timbers, and rolling on her beam ends
she went down.

'God help them,' muttered Rennie, lowering his glass.
Then, sniffing in a breath, he turned and asked aloud: 'Was
Zamoril in her? Did anyone see him, the villain?'

His question went unanswered, for *Expedient* herself now
came under threat of murderous assault. Her first broadside
had not greatly impaired any of the advancing corsairs to the
east, widely separated as they had been, and now they had
closed in a tight line, making their foreshortened hulls
difficult targets, and Rennie saw what was their purpose: to

lay in alongside him, port and starboard, and the third ship astern, to rake *Expedient* where she was most vulnerable—as were all fighting ships when cleared for action. Unless . . .

Unless he could swing right round through his present arc, and head nor'-east, the wind on his quarter, before the corsair line divided. Then he could rake them, as *Expedient* ran briefly close and parallel to them, rake them all with both long gun battery and carronade broadsides. He bawled the orders, and the ship began to heel as men pulled their weight on the falls. Guncrews reloaded, the sea hissed and rippled up in surging white along her lee wales, and she was in position.

Before Rennie could order his guncrews to fire their guns as they bore, a withering broadside from all three corsair ships whipped, cracked, fizzed and smashed into *Expedient*'s starboard side. Great guns were flung off their trucks. Men fell, screaming. Blood sluiced across the quarterdeck. Appalled, Rennie saw two roundshot, linked by a whirling length of chain, behead a seaman securing a line to a cleat, saw the head bounce in a spray of blood over the rail, and the corpse crumple slack on the deck. Rennie sucked in a savage breath:

'FIRE AS THEY BEAR! FIRE! FIRE! FIRE! FIRE!'

Half of the long-gun battery responded, and all but one of the carronades. The deck was lost in a boiling storm of smoke, and Rennie ran forrard to the breast rail, half-deafened.

'RELOAD, LADS! RELOAD AND SMASH THOSE WRETCHES!' His voice was muffled in his ears.

Something whined past Rennie's head, and instinctively he ducked. As he did so, a fragment of chain struck him on the temple, tore a hank of hair and skin bloodily from his head, and he fell senseless to the deck, sand spilling round him from a smashed bucket. Mr Loftus, returned to his duties as sailing master, ran to Rennie's side, knelt beside him and saw his bloody head, and called for assistance:

'The captain is shot! Fetch the doctor!'

In the din of firing and screams and falling blocks he was

unheard, and came to his feet, staring about urgently for someone to send below for the surgeon. He saw James Hayter, now in working rig and kerchief, jump into the starboard mizzen shrouds with his glass and peer through the smoke at the corsair ships. Saw him flinch as he was struck by a musket ball, and drop his glass. Saw him topple from the shrouds on the lift of the sea, and fall through the smoke over the side, apparently lifeless.

'James! James!' shouted the master in terrible dismay. This would not do. *Expedient* could not lose both her captain and first lieutenant at the same lethal moment. Mr Loftus ran to the rail, peered anxiously down into the sliding rush of the sea, and saw nothing. He looked aft, and saw only the undulating swell and the washing wake.

'This is a sad, bad day . . .' In anguish.

'Is that you, Mr Loftus?' Rennie's voice, rasping and weak, but certainly living.

'Thank God.' Bernard Loftus returned at once to his side. 'Thank God you are alive, sir. But Mr Hayter is lost——'

'What! James!' Struggling to his feet, blood trickling and dripping on his face and shoulder. 'When? When was he lost?'

'He went over the side just now, sir. Shot, I think——'

'Good God, it ain't possible.' Shocked and disbelieving. 'Not James.' Coming to himself. 'Did you order the ship to heave to, Mr Loftus? Did you raise the alarm?'

'No, sir. It has only just happened——'

'Then, Christ's blood, man, we must stop, and send a boat! *MAN OVERBOARD! MAN OVERBOARD!*'

But further fire from the corsairs now raked *Expedient*, zipping and fizzing through the rigging, traversing the decks, thudding into her planking, and both Captain Rennie and Mr Loftus were obliged to crouch down behind the hammock cranes to save their lives.

━◆━

James woke with a searing headache, a pain that seemed to
dart down like fire into his limbs, and he was aware of the
sound of the sea. The eternal sea, washing and flushing along
the hull of a ship. A ship that, by force of logic, he must
himself lie within. He sat up, and his head thudded with
excruciating pain, as if he had been struck a blow. His neck
was stiff, his whole left side, and in a peculiar flashing dream
he saw himself in *Expedient*, fighting a French frigate in the
West Indies, when he had been hit by a musket ball in the
shoulder. But in the next instant he was altogether aware that
he was not in *Expedient*, that the sea action with the French
ship had happened long since, that he was now in another
ship, entire. In darkness.

He reached out with his undamaged arm, his right arm,
and felt around him. He was not in a hanging cot, but lying
on a straw palliasse on decking, or timber platform—perhaps
the forrard orlop of the ship. He felt a lurch as the ship
pitched in the swell of the sea. What ship was this, good
heaven? How had he come here?

'How was I injured?' he muttered. He felt with his right
hand the place where the stiffness and pain was most acute,
and found a rough bandage wound round his neck. His
fingers strayed gingerly under the folds of the bandage,
touched stickiness—an ointment, or poultice of some kind—
and a ragged wound. Icy needles of pain shot through his
shoulder, and arm, and up into his head, and he brought his
hand hastily away. He had been struck, then, in the left side
of his neck. By what? The edge of a cutlass, or a sword? Or by
a musket ball? He did not know. He could not remember
anything.

'How came I here, into this ship?' He contrived to sit up
further—and ignoring the pain this movement caused him—
to touch a bulkhead, or the deckhead above him. The
susurrating wash of the sea, rinsing and sluicing and rushing,
was very close. He was either below the waterline, or nearly
level with it.

And now he heard voices. Should he call out? The voices became more distinct, and he heard footfalls accompanying them, the clatter of men descending a ladder. They were coming below to him. A light, flickering and glowing, showed him that he was near to the bow of the ship, in a storeroom of the forepeak, perhaps . . . but only if he was in a frigate. Was he in a frigate? A further—dismaying—thought now assailed him. He was injured, lying here injured and in darkness. Was he a prisoner? His head ached with confusion, and deep weariness, and he was aware also of a consuming thirst. A thirst so utter that he felt that his throat would seize up if he did not drink at once.

'I am here!' he called, careless now of the consequences. But in course they must know he was here, else why would they be coming below with a light?

'I am here, and awake! Will you bring me some water? I am desperate thirsty . . .'

The light came nearer, leaping and flickering over the timbers, and now there were men before him, leaning and peering in on him in his confined space. An exchange in a tongue he did not understand, then a deep, fricative voice:

'You are well, English?'

'I am not well. I am damned thirsty. Will you give me water, in the name of God?'

'In the name of Allah—certainly.' In the dimness beyond the light a head turned and a rapid command was given. Presently a beaker of water was handed to James, and he took it, half sitting, and gulped down the contents.

'Thank you. You are kind.'

Soon afterward James was helped to his feet and led aft, up a ladder and along a low deck, and taken into a well-appointed but exotically decorated cabin. There were elaborate hangings draped in the stead of bulkheads and doors, and the decking timbers were covered in rugs of the most intricate pattern and design: of birds and beasts, eagles, waterfowl, lions, in peculiar geometric shapes; of symmetrical symbols and figures and arches, all in the most brilliant reds and blues and golden yellows. There was the smell of incense, disguising the usual odours of ships at sea. There were piles of cushions, low tables, and a collection of tremendous swords and scimitars. The man who had commanded that water be given to James sat in a position of prominence near to what—in a frigate—would have been the stern gallery window, but in this ship was a painted, glassless transom. He was dressed all in black, with a vivid red hat, on which a single sapphire burned like an icy eye. His eyes were very dark, his skin pale, his features not quite coarse. His mouth was generous, but firm. This was the face of a man used to command, and the power of command.

That deep voice: 'My surgeon will dress your wound again, English, when you have told me all I wish to know.'

'Thank you, sir. I will tell you that my name is James Hayter, and that I hold the rank of lieutenant in the Royal Navy.' He inclined his head in a polite bow, instantly regretted. He grimaced in pain, and covered his mouth and coughed to disguise it.

'May—may I know your name, sir?' Determined not to show weakness.

'I am *Rais* Zamoril.' Motioning James to sit down on one of the red cushions. When James had done so: 'But you are not dressed as an officer of your navy, English. You are dressed as a seaman.'

'I call these my working clothes, sir. You must take my word as a gentleman on the rest.'

'Very well.' A nearly imperceptible nod.

'May I know how I came into your ship, sir?'

'Your frigate has fought clear of me—this time—you will no doubt be pleased to hear. As for your question. How came you here, into this ship? It was written.'

'Written?' Touching the bandage at his neck.

'You fell from your frigate into the sea, and by the will of Allah you drifted into the path of my ship, and were dragged from the water and saved from drowning, and you were then treated by my surgeon—a well-schooled and able man.'

'I—I do not recall any of this . . .' Rubbing his forehead.

'No, because until a few moments ago you lay senseless below.'

'You said my frigate had fought clear. D'y'mean— *Expedient*?'

'Yes, *Expedient*. Your crew are brave, and they fight courageously, and your *rais* has escaped—this time. There will be another.' A slight movement of his head to one side. 'Yes, there will be another. It is written.' The dark eyes on James.

'I am most grateful to you for saving my life.'

'You will not remain grateful long, English, when you learn what I intend for you.' The eyes.

'What is that, sir?'

'You will be imprisoned in the Grand Bagno at Tunis with slaves, and a price put on your head for ransom. A very heavy price, English. You and your frigate have caused me great loss, and that I do not forget, nor easily forgive.'

'May I know—how heavy a price, sir?'

'In English pounds, or French francs?'

'In pounds.'

'Let us say—five thousand.'

'Five thousand pound!' His determination to express nothing of his emotion defeated by this daunting sum.

'I see that it impresses you, this price. You are a valuable man, English.'

'Five thousand sterling of money . . . is a very great deal, sir. I do not know how I will pay it.'

'Then you will be sold into slavery at the block.' Again the slight movement of his head to one side, the same dark dispassionate gaze.

'I am glad you think it amusing—but I cannot find it so, I fear, when my freedom is at stake.'

'I do not think it amusing, not at all. I am in earnest. Unless five thousand pounds is paid to me, you will end your days at the sweep of a galley, or in the stone quarries.'

'It does not seem that I am very valuable after all, if I am to spend my life so miserably.'

'You are valuable to me, English, if you—or your friends—will pay me my price. If that price cannot be found, if the money cannot be raised, you are as nothing to me, then. Less than the pit of an olive.'

'May I ask you a question? You spoke just now of loss. But have not you took from Rashid Bey's ships a great quantity of gold and precious things? Are you not content with that?'

Rais Zamoril made no reply, but simply stared at James a long moment, then turned his head and gave an order in his own tongue. Returning his black gaze to James:

'Do you drink coffee, English?'

'Thank you, sir, I do.'

'We will drink coffee together. Or perhaps you will like wine . . . ?'

'Wine? You carry wine in your ship?'

'Naturally, why do you ask?—Ah, I see. You think that as a devout Muslim I should not countenance wine. That I should—what is the polite expression?—that I should *eschew* it?'

'That is not for me to say, sir, when I am your prisoner.'

'Yes, you are my prisoner, but I am not a barbarian, and I will like to converse with an officer that has fought bravely in battle as one civilized man to another, and take refreshment. What is your preference?'

'Coffee, if you please. I fear that wine would not improve my headache.'

The ship now heeled a little and shuddered, her timbers creaking and groaning, as a large wave rolled under her keel.

'Another storm may come tonight,' said Zamoril. 'And then we are simply seamen together, is it not so, praying that the tempest will not tear apart the ship, and suck us down to a cold and terrible death?'

'You put it very eloquent, sir.'

As they drank their coffee—rich, dark, and for James reviving—the two began to talk, not as enemies, not as captor and prisoner, but as sea officers, man to man. Without hard prompting from James, *Rais* Zamoril revealed considerable facts of his background, that he spoke of with a mixture of pride and regret.

'I was born in the Levant, at Latakia, of a Maltese father and a part-Turkish, part-Circassian mother, a great beauty. However, I grew up in Algiers, where my father was a merchant, but he was lost at sea in a storm when I was still a boy, and my mother was sold into slavery over his debts——'

'Your mother was sold into slavery?'

'She was.' A brief dark glance over his coffee cup, and a sideways tilt of his head, that James saw now was a kind of shrug, accepting, worldly, matter-of-fact.

'Did not you find that a very dreadful thing?'

Another glance. 'I had to make my way, and tears will not bring a man his fortune. I went to sea in a corsair ship, very young.'

'Ah, yes.' Nodding. 'Very young, yes.'

'You also were at sea as a boy?'

'I was, sir. Twelve years old. The ship was *Gargoyle*, seventy-four—it was a rude awakening. But forgive me, please go on . . .'

'I was a mere ten years old when I went to sea for the first time. As you say, it was a "rude awakening" for me also. Very hard, very cruel, and I saw things that were . . .' The head tilted, a small sigh, and: 'I survived, and by long endeavour I was able to gather a little money for myself, and after ten years I came to my own command.'

'At twenty? You had your own ship at twenty?'

'A small ship, a felucca. Because it was so small merchant-men did not fear it—and I took many prizes, by stealth, and surprise. Surprise at sea is a very powerful weapon, no?'

'Indeed, it is.—May I ask, where did you learn to speak English? You speak it right well.'

'My father spoke it, because he dealt with many English traders in ships. And I liked to read books, also.'

'Indeed? Then we share that singular pleasure. I myself am a lover of books.'

'So?' The dark gaze. Was there a hint of sympathy, of fellow warmth in that regarding stare? wondered James. Perhaps not. He must be careful to make no assumptions, to build up no false hopes of release. 'So?' repeated Zamoril, and drank off his cup.

'If you was an Algiers corsair, how came you to Tunis, sir?'

'By a chance, an opportunity. It was written. The Dey of Hone, a small regency on the coast of Algiers, had lost his *rais* in a storm at the Bay of Calles, and he had heard of my exploits. He offered me a xebec of twelve guns, and a small fleet of galleys, to pursue his interests in the Mediterranean in taking trading ships. I lost the xebec almost at once, by the most fundamental error of seamanship. My anchors dragged in the night, we drifted in upon a rocky shore, and the ship broke up. Naturally, this was a disgrace, and I had to flee. I fled to Tunis, and threw myself upon the mercy of the Dey, Suleiman el Hassad.'

'Why to Tunis, sir?'

'It was near.' A glance, that said he did not care for further interjection. 'I was fortunate in my choice, for the Dey of Tunis had also heard of my earlier successes. He was just then assembling a new fleet of corsair ships, and in need of a second-in-command. He employed me, under his *rais*—who, alas, died of a fever before he could take the new fleet to sea. Most unfortunate. So naturally it fell to me to take his place, and——'

'Your rivals seem often to have met with conveniently unfortunate ends, sir.' James, drily.

'What do you mean by that remark, English?' The dark

stare now cold and menacing, and his voice very cold and hard.

'Nothing—I meant nothing at all by it.'

'You wish to lose your head?'

'I—no, indeed.'

'I could have you beheaded in a moment, English. I will summon my slave-driver, that is a man of uncommon height and strength, and keeps his scimitar sharp-honed. All I need do is wave my hand, and your head will roll upon the deck in gouting blood. Yes?'

'I—I hope not, sir.'

'No?'

Swallowing. 'No.'

'You wish to hear the rest of my story, then?'

'I—I should be most happy to hear it.'

'You will not interrupt me again with your intruding English "wit"?'

'I shall keep silent.' Very correct.

'Good.' Pouring coffee. 'It was written, then, that I should succeed as Suleiman el Hassad's *rais*. My fleet had great good fortune, and I made the Dey rich. I will not deny'—the head tilted—'that I too became rich, in his service. Nor do I wish to boast unduly, but I came to be seen as one of the most feared—and most fearless—of seafarers on the Barbary coasts.'

And now James saw a way—as he thought—of gaining Zamoril's favourable opinion of him, and he risked asking a question:

'Was you able to rescue her, sir?'

Looking up from his coffee: 'Rescue—who?'

'Your mother, when you had become rich. Did you offer ransom money?'

For a few seconds James believed he had instead of gaining favour sealed his doom. *Rais* Zamoril stared at him in what James assumed was speechless wrath. A long moment, then he put down the coffee cup with a bleak click, and turned his face away.

'Jesu Christ.' James, but not aloud. 'Now he will call his executioner . . .'

A groan, very subdued, and Zamoril brought his head up again, and James saw with surprise that his eyes were filled with tears.

'It was too late . . . too late . . .' In a whisper. 'She had died . . .'

'I am very sorry.'

'You must forgive me, English, for this display . . .'

'It is I that must ask your forgiveness—for reviving so painful a memory.' Quietly, and sincerely.

'I could have attempted to find her sooner . . . but I was angry with her for abandoning me, as I believed then, to a bitter life. I did not know until years after I went to sea that she was a slave, and by then it was hopeless. I did not know where she had gone, where she was enslaved, and when at last I did discover the place—she had died a year since.'

'I am very sorry indeed,' repeated James.

A breath, and with grimacing effort Zamoril composed himself. 'Does your mother live, English?'

'I am fortunate. She does.'

'And your father?'

'He also.'

'So? Yes, you are fortunate.' A sip of coffee, and he resumed his dark unrelenting stare. 'Tell me, he is a rich man?'

'My father?' Looking at him. 'Ah, I see. You think that he will pay you the five thousand pound.'

'You are an officer, and a gentleman. Your father is no doubt proud of you, and would wish to preserve you from harm. I think that he will pay.'

'And I think, sir, that you do not understand the English rule of primogeniture. My father's estates and income are bound up, entailed. He is obliged to pass on his fortune to my eldest brother, Charles. I am merely a third son, and there will be no money for me when my father dies. So, you see . .

.' a shrug '. . . applying to my father would be entirely useless.'

'You have no money of your own?'

'None, other than my pay as a lieutenant RN, that is very little indeed.' Thankful that he had revealed nothing of his marriage and family life at Birch Cottage. He would not call on his property, and jeopardize the future of his wife and son.

'Then your own *rais* must find the money.'

'Captain Rennie? Good heaven, he has only his pay, like myself. His wife is dead, lawyers have took his house in England, and he has no family at all.'

'Someone must find it, English—else you will suffer very hard.'

'We make now for Tunis?'

Zamoril made no reply.

'I can only say that I will endeavour to send a message from Tunis, if we go there now. Perhaps some of the money might be raised in England, in my behalf—but I do not have high expectation, I fear.'

'Then you will be a slave, and of no further interest.' Curtly, rising easily to his feet. James struggled to a standing position, his neck and side very painful. To his surprise Zamoril leaned and gave him his arm for support.

'Thank you, sir. You are kind.'

'I must go on deck. You will be escorted below, there to think of a way to pay me.'

'Sir, might I prevail upon you to allow me a few minutes on deck with you?' Contriving to lean heavily on that supporting arm, and to wince.

'Why should I permit it?'

'I think that you will not wish to deprive a fellow sea officer of fresh air, and the opportunity to see how your ship points up, how she is handled. I have never before been aboard a fast corsair . . .'

'Do not think of leaping into the sea, English, to make your escape.'

'I give you my word that I will not do that, sir. I am injured, and much weakened, and would certainly drown.'

'Then I will permit it, for a short time.' Moving forrard, bracing himself against the heeling of the ship. 'I will let you see that it is not only the English that take pride in their ships.'

And the two sea officers—disparate in culture and tradition, and in allegiance, but together in the sure eternal things of water, wind, timber, rope and canvas—went together on deck and trod there in the saline smell of their chosen world, a world that makes of sailors a race distinct.

'You will be blindfolded.'

James heard this pronouncement with anger, supplanted at once by mortal fear. Blindfolding too often heralded a violent and untimely death.

'There is no need of that. I am injured, and cannot attempt escape.' Endeavouring to keep his voice calm and reasonable.

'The blindfold will be removed when we reach the Bagno.' The janissary officer motioned to two of his men, who seized James by the arms and bound his hands behind him with a hide rope that bit into his wrists. Pain shot through his left arm, his entire left side. He gritted his teeth and refrained— just—from crying out in agony. The blindfold, of rough dark cloth, was now tied over his eyes, and his world became intimate stumbling night.

'Why d'you humiliate me thus?' he complained as he was thrust forward and pushed up the ladder.

'Do you wish to be gagged also, English?' The distinctive voice now of *Rais* Zamoril, above on deck.

James stumbled up the ladder, felt the air on his face and neck, and was aware that the ship was running into her mooring in a busy harbour. Creaking timbers, rippling water, distant shouts, closer shouts, the sound of a splash and a hawser running out, wide clatter and echo—all spoke of a bustling port. Most distinct of all was the smell—of hides, vinegar, tallow, oil, spices, dung—all mingling and floating on the air, a heady exotic reek.

'We are at Tunis?' James, turning his head to where he thought Zamoril stood.

'We are. Only you will not see it, English.'

'Sir, I appeal to you as a fellow sea officer. Please to make them remove the blindfold, when I am bound and helpless. What harm can there be for me to see Tunis, when I am in it?'

'No more questions, now.' Curtly.

Firm hands gripped James's arms, and he felt himself pushed toward. 'Wait! Wait a moment.' He felt the grip ease, and knew that Zamoril must have nodded to the men who held him. 'Sir, will you allow me to ask one last thing of you? If I cannot raise the sum you ask—will you allow me to speak to you again?'

'That is not possible.' Again curtly.

'Perhaps, rather than allowing me to be sold into slavery— you would consider taking me into your employ.'

'You, English! You ask that I employ you, my enemy?'

'As an officer in your ship.'

'The notion is absurd. Put him in the boat.'

'In least if I was aboard your ship I could be of some use to you! Sea officers are not made to be slaves!'

'Be silent!' Hands again gripped James's arms, then he heard, closer and quieter: 'Be sensible, English, and do as you are bidden, as I must do as I am bidden, by the Dey. Things will go hard for you if you struggle and resist.'

'Sir. *Rais* Zamoril. If you have any pity for me, you will allow me to speak to you before I am sold. In least make me that promise.'

A brief sigh, and a brief pressure of fingers on James's shoulder. 'God go with thee.' James was now led to the rail, and guided roughly down the ladder into the boat. He tripped on the gunwhale and nearly upset the boat, and was pushed down with a curse on a thwart, the boat was pushed off, and began to move with a gurgling suck of sweeps.

—•— ⚑◈⚑ —•—

The sounds of crowded, narrow streets, and the odours of beasts and human beings, gave James a mental picture of the city through which he was being brought, in what he supposed was some kind of covered cart, that jolted and rattled over cobbles and ruts, and made his pinned arms a torture of needling pain. He felt nauseous, at the end of his strength, and was fearful that he could not withstand the rigours of the prison that awaited him.

The cart jolted to a stop, there were shouts ahead, and next instant the blindfold was torn from his head. He blinked, stared about him, and was pulled from the back of the cart— a cart drawn, he saw now, by two slaves in loincloths. The Grand Bagno immediately beyond resembled a medina, a market square, except that here the gates were taller and made of stouter metal, and manned by keepers so ferocious in appearance they might have been guarding the gates of Hell.

Across the square he could make out, through the smoke of innumerable small fires, stalls selling all manner of goods and foodstuffs. To his considerable surprise in this Islamic setting there were many small bars, little more than trestled tables on which drink was served, round which there slouched, strolled and idled janissaries, seamen, traders, and those slaves who had at their disposal sufficient money to buy arak and wine. James was hurried across the square by his two escorting janissaries to the house of the concierge on the far side, next to a second great archway and gate. Many of the buildings lining the square had towers, some square, others round, and nearly all of the myriad casements and doorways had rounded arches. The size of the square—more properly a rectangle, noted James with his sea officer's eye for detail—was very considerable, perhaps three hundred yards by two hundred.

A great host of people had gathered on the far side, and as James was escorted past he saw a raised platform on which stood some two or three dozen people in chains.

'Christ's blood,' to himself, 'that is the damned block, and the poor wretches are offered for sale.'

And his heart went out to the poor creatures. Many of them were young women, some stripped to the waist, and very miserable of countenance.

'Who are those women?' he asked his escort, turning from one to the other. Neither replied, but merely pushed him on and into the gateway of the concierge's house. The concierge himself was not present, and the escorting janissaries were obliged to wait with James to hand over their prisoner. They waited in a walled stone courtyard, with stables at the far end. James could see asses there, and goats, and a line of amphoras against the inner wall.

The concierge, when he returned, looked to James like one of the traders of the market, with a busy, slightly self-important air, a clean blouse over a beginning paunch, neat pantaloons, slippers and hat, and a wide venal nose over a dark beard. His eyes appraised James with the detached acumen of commerce. To James's surprise the concierge spoke English, with a French accent. He took James by the arm and guided him into his private office and parlour, a long cool stone room with a hint of vinegar on the air. The janissaries he left outside. In a hoarse, husky voice:

'Do not think of me as a gaoler. Instead think of me as a banker, with additional responsibilities. Apply to me when you have raised the required sum. You are poorly dressed today, but surely this is a disguise? If you wish it, no doubt more agreeable quarters than the common Bagno may be found for you—for a consideration.'

'I have no money at all.'

'No?' Doubtfully. 'None?'

'I have been brought direct from *Rais* Zamoril's ship.'

'How will you eat, and live?'

'I have not the smallest notion. I have been brought to this place against my will, after all.' With spirit, pulling himself up, and painfully making his back straight.

'You will starve, without money to pay for victuals.'

'Then how d'y'expect me to raise the ransom, good heaven, in a starving condition? It ain't a sensible indication to starve your captive, and at the same moment require of him that he be active in gathering up a large sum to gain his release. You had better feed me, and treat me decent, else suffer *Rais* Zamoril's wrath. He will not thank nor commend you for starving so valuable a source of revenue, hey?'

The bluff—a very daring conceit given James's parlous plight—had its desired effect.

'Why did not *Rais* Zamoril send you to the private quarters of the Bagno, instead of to me?'

'You had better ask those two fellows that brought me here. Eh?' James had begun to play up to the role of important hostage, and to emphasize an officerlike manner and bearing. 'I have spent my time aboard the admiral's ship more as his guest than his prisoner. We discussed his greatest triumphs at sea. He was kind enough to order his own surgeon to dress my wound. He gave me his personal assurance that I would be well treated at Tunis, whilst I made my arrangements. And now I should like to be taken to the private quarters, if y'please. By the by, I should be obliged to you if y'will just cut these damned bindings, hey? I gave my word to the admiral, in course, that as an officer I would not seek to escape.'

The concierge cut the bindings with his own knife, and gave James coffee.

'Who are those women in the square outside?' James asked as he drank off the grateful reviving coffee, and rubbed his aching wrists.

'Women, effendi? No women are permitted in the—— Ahh, you refer to the female slaves, at the block? They have been captured at sea, from a merchant ship that had no certificate.'

'They was ordinary passengers in the ship?'

'*Mais oui, certainement*. And they are offered for sale to the highest bidder—unless they can find the money to buy their freedom.'

'Surely they are European women?'

'Perhaps they are European.' A shrug. 'Such female slaves are highly prized in the households of the great merchants.'

'It seems very harsh to sell European women into slavery at all, don't it?'

'Whatever may be their origin, or their nation, they are now merely slaves for sale. Unless they may pay.'

'Like myself, hey?' A smile.

'Indeed, like yourself, effendi.'

'But I will never likely be offered for sale at the block, I think.'

'Perhaps not. But we cannot feed and keep you for long, here at the Grand Bagno, without reward. Unless *Rais* Zamoril himself would send word that he will vouchsafe for your—your daily needs.'

'But, good heaven, man—the admiral has already sent word.' Taking an even greater risk with this bald lie.

'Not to me, effendi . . .'

'You doubt my word?'

'Ah, well, alas . . . we are in the confines of the Bagno . . . and in here words are plentiful and cheap.'

'Listen, now—bring those two fellows in here. Keep one of them here, and send the other back to the admiral's ship. Within the hour you will hold the admiral's written instruction in your hand.'

But this time the bluff did not quite work. Something in James's voice must have been a little too urgent, something in the way he bent forward a little too like supplication, and the concierge put his head on one side, regarded James a long moment, and said:

'You know, effendi, I think that *Rais* Zamoril would have sent such instruction with you from his ship, and that I would already hold it in my hand—had he ever intended to write it. You see?'

'You refuse?'

'Let us say—that I doubt.' And he turned his head to the door, and raising his hoarse voice gave an unmistakably harsh command.

＊—‒ ⪥◆⪤ —＊

When James was delivered, not to the entrance of the private quarters, but to the entrance of the common lodgings, all his senses were assaulted at once. The stench, noise, wretchedness and squalor of the lodgings were far worse than anything he had imagined. The building was divided into three parts. The central wing was evidently a temple, a place of worship of some kind, and the eastern and western wings the slave accommodations. James was in the eastern wing.

When his eyes had grown accustomed to the comparative darkness of the interior after the bright sunlight of the square, James saw that the wing was itself divided into three long spaces. Against the walls on either side were great tiers of bunks, suspended one above the other by ropes, like an immense arrangement of hanging cots. Between these rows of tiers was a long central space dense with the smoke of cooking fires, and loud with the drunken wrangling of hundreds of slaves, most of them in filthy rags.

The two janissaries escorting James pushed him forward into this place, this abominable eastern wing, and having delivered their charge retreated in haste, eager to be clear of the din and stink, and the scrabbling hands that were now thrust out at them from all sides. They quickly disappeared into the square, and James was left to fend for himself. He saw two men fighting over a loaf of bread, in a writhing, screeching, lunatic battle of both will and bodily strength. The loaf was torn in two, and both halves fell to the filthy straw-covered cobbles and were there crushed underfoot at once. The men continued to fight, swaying, gouging, biting, in a frenzy of violent loathing. The taller of the two gouged at the eyes of the other, and an eyeball, hanging by a slimy string, fell on the cheek of his opponent in a spill of blood. The man screamed like a beast at slaughter.

'If they fight thus over bread, what must they do when there is real dispute?' wondered James silently, appalled and sickened.

He sensed that none of his experiences in the Royal Navy, not even his harshest difficulties the first year in *Gargoyle* as a midshipman, had been nearly so degrading and demeaning as the sufferings he was about to know.

'I must stiffen myself, and get through the next four-and-twenty hours, come what may.'

The lodge-keeper—himself a slave, but one that had made for himself an enterprise by exacting from fellow inmates small amounts in money and goods, in exchange for favours—found for James a bunk, and bread and coffee sufficient for one meagre meal. The keeper provided this service strictly upon the promise of funds to be paid on the morrow. James knew that he had no such funds, that he had no hope of obtaining them—unless he could appeal again to *Rais* Zamoril to vouch for him a few days while he attempted to arrange the ransom money. Surely it would be in the admiral's interests to keep James alive while he made that attempt? But even if Zamoril did vouch for him, how in God's name was he to find the ransom? To whom might he appeal from this Godforsaken rats' den, far from home, far from friends? A further twinge of hopelessness ran through his guts. Such twinges, such intimations of doom, had become frequent since his arrival at the lodgings. 'I must not flinch, I must not despair, nor sink into stupefying self-pity. I must keep my wits sharp, and thus survive.' Closing his eyes, breathing deep.

He went out into the square, and found a French-speaking seaman at one of the stalls where liquor was sold, and enjoined him to take a message to Zamoril's ship.

'Who will pay me for this service?' the seaman asked.

'Listen now. You will be paid by *Rais* Zamoril's men when you reach his ship, that lies in the harbour.'

'You say that, sir, you say that you are an officer—but how do I know?'

'Will you take the message, or no? Or must I find someone else?' Standing straight, lifting his chin, looking the man in the eye.

'I will take it.'

The seaman departed, but he did not return.

Dusk, and night. And for James only the smoke-thick bedlam of the lodgings, the returning pain of his wound, and black thoughts.

PART SIX: DILEMMA

'I make this offering most sincerely.' Rashid Bey looked very earnestly at Captain Rennie. 'I have very little left, so you must excuse the——'

'Sir, I do not ask for anything from you.' Stiffly. 'I had thought that you must have known by now that my sole desire in this is to do my duty.'

'You have always done that, Captain Rennie.'

'I hope that I have.' A sniff.

'So that is why I will like to reward you.'

'Have not I just said that I do not wish any reward, sir!' Bristling again.

'I think what Rashid Bey is attempting to say, Captain Rennie, is that——'

But now Rashid Bey put a hand on Mr Sebastian's arm, glanced at him, and his adviser closed his mouth and was silent.

'I most certainly did not wish to insult you by offering a bribe, Captain.'

'Very good.'

'I wished instead to make you a gift, a most sincere and heartfelt gift, in recognition of your courage, and your kindness to me.'

'Ah. Hm. Well well, then I beg your pardon, sir.' Unbending a fraction. 'I was mistook.'

'Yes, I do wish it. When Mr Sebastian and I escaped from my ship, I brought with me some few pretty trifles, that I was able to carry easily. All else was lost. Mr Sebastian, you have the box by you?'

'It is here, effendi. I have it.' Bringing a green jade box to Rennie's table. The sides and the lid were decorated with beautiful gold flowers, and delicate gold dots.

'Please to open it.'

Mr Sebastian did as he was asked, slipping the gold hook that secured the lid, and lifting the lid open.

'Tip it, tip out the contents.' Rashid Bey, nodding encouragement.

Sebastian tipped the box carefully, and out on the table slid and jostled the most astonishing set of chess pieces Rennie had ever seen. They were of carved rock crystal, and set with large emeralds and rubies in worked gold flowers, gleaming in the light. Sebastian stood them in their correct rows, emeralds and rubies in opposing ranks.

'Unfortunately, I have no chessboard to give you,' Rashid Bey, glancing at Rennie. 'I was able only to bring the box, containing the Istanbul Crystal Men. But a board may be easily obtained, I think.'

'They are—they are very beautiful, sir. I cannot in conscience accept the set, however. I could not presume to deprive you of so valuable——'

He broke off as he saw Sebastian's warning frown. Rashid Bey smiled and closed his eyes.

'But you do not deprive me, Captain Rennie. I willingly offer you this gift, as a token of my great admiration, and friendship. You will not deny me that honour, and pleasure . . . ?' Opening his eyes.

'Indeed, I would not wish to offend you, sir.' Embarrassed now, as well as reluctant.

'Then please to accept the Crystal Men, and the box, in the spirit with which they are offered—the spirit of unconditional esteem.'

'I—I am most grateful to you, sir.'

The eyes briefly closed again, a brief silence, then Rashid

Bey asked, in a much more businesslike tone:

'Soon we will arrive at Rabhet. Yes?'

'On the morrow, sir. Yes.'

'Yes. You are not yet persuaded that I should return, Captain Rennie.' A statement rather than a question, and by not looking directly at Rennie Rashid Bey was able to convey both his understanding of Rennie, and his impatience with him.

'I—I am not persuaded entire, sir, no. However—it is a matter for you, and I am obedient.'

Still without looking at Rennie Rashid Bey gave the merest answering nod, and Rennie saw that in effect he was being dismissed, and that he had better go on deck. He felt, strongly felt—and it rankled—that in spite of Rashid Bey's assurances to the contrary the chess set, with its beautifully made individual men, its gleaming gold and precious stones, was in effect . . . a bribe. A bribe that he had been coerced into accepting, that he had been constrained to accept. He bowed, took up his hat, and went on deck.

At Rabhet he would be obliged to advise Rashid Bey on how best to defend his harbour and city from the attempt to invade that would almost certainly come. He would be obliged to make *Expedient* in effect the flagship of the Rabhetan navy— that is, if the regent's own *rais* did not object.

'If only *Curlew* had not been lost,' muttered Rennie to himself, striding to the taffrail and staring astern over the wake. 'I could send her to Gibraltar, to ask for assistance. Or clear to England.' He would not allow himself to think, let alone dwell upon, the bitter loss of James Hayter.

'With your permission, sir . . .' Midshipman Cutforth, with the logship, line and glass.

'What? Oh. Aye, very well, Mr Cutforth, y'may find out the speed of the ship.'

'Thank you, sir. Richard, the glass.'

Mr Abey came aft and stood by his side, and took the half-minute glass.

'What ships sighted this watch, Mr Abey?' Rennie brought his long glass from under his arm.

'None, sir.'

'Not even small trading vessels, or fishermen?'

'No, sir, we have seen nothing at all.' Embarrassed that he had nothing to report, wishing with all his heart that he could make it otherwise.

'We could do with *Curlew*, now, hey?'

'Oh, indeed, sir.'

'However, we must make do without her.' Sniffing deep, turning to look forrard and aloft. Presently: 'What speed do we make, Mr Cutforth?'

'Six knots, sir.' The line in his hand, and lying taut over the rail and down.

'Very well. Only it will not do.' Marching forward. 'Mr Tangible! Weather stunsails, high and low! Let us crack on!'

He wished to crack on, and reach Rabhet, and make a stratagem. He wished to act, and be free of all troubling, debilitating, deep, dark musings, all sorrow and regret and doubt.

'Cheerly now, lads! Show me you are seamen, in a flying man-of-war!'

———— ☲❖☲ ————

James Hayter stood scratching himself under his filthy shirt at the gate of the concierge's house, in a group of slaves. The squalor of the lodging was very repellent to him. All his life he had had a loathing of personal uncleanness, had deplored in the navy the existence of 'itching ships' that crawled with vermin, and now to find himself living in the equivalent ashore made him more determined than ever to remove himself from this hellish place, where there was not a free-standing water pump anywhere to be found, and the stink of excrement hung on the hazy air.

Presently the concierge appeared and at once singled

James out, and allowed him into the courtyard.

'So, you have found the money, eh? You can pay me?'

'No, in fact I cannot. The man I sent away yesternight did not return. I have come to ask you——'

'You cannot pay me anything?' The hoarse voice harsh, the eyes hard.

'No. As I told you, the messenger I sent——'

'You have lied to me, effendi.' Pronouncing the courtesy with ironic emphasis.

'No, I have not. I did send a man to *Rais* Zamoril's ship, but clearly he was waylaid, and——'

'Waylaid? What word is this, waylaid?'

'Either that, or perhaps he met with an accident. All I am asking of you——'

'You may ask nothing further of me, effendi.' Again the sarcastic emphasis. 'You have lied to me, you cannot pay to me what you owe for your victuals, and now you must work. Like all those damnable wretches that skulk at my gate, and try to cheat me with sweet words, in the hope of favour——'

'Listen now, I know nothing of their business with you', with some spirit, 'but you must not equate me with them. I am an officer in the Royal Navy, and you must treat me with respect. I demand that you send a man to *Rais* Zamoril's ship yourself.'

'You demand, effendi? You demand? Hhhh-hhhh.' A waft of cloacal breath as the concierge laughed in scorn. 'Allow me to explain to you what I demand. Today you will work, or suffer.'

'Work?'

'Yes, you will work.' Pointing at the gate. 'As they will work. If you do not, if you refuse, you will be beaten, and starved.'

'You will regret it, by God, if you treat me ill!'

'Hhhh-hhhh. With an empty stomach you make threats? You are a very great fool. Effendi.' Turning his head he barked an order. Two hulking men with aprons of hide emerged from the stables at the far end of the courtyard, and approached.

'My men will take you to your work,' said the concierge in dismissal.

And James saw—and felt, and knew—that to resist was folly. His heart sank within him, and something very like despair flooded his breast.

'Mr Bradshaw sends his compliments, sir, and requests that you come on deck as soon as you find it convenient.'

The midshipman, a diminutive boy called Skillow, whose breathless voice was not yet broken, was very excited. Rennie, roused from his hanging cot in his sleeping cabin only five minutes since, was yet muzzed with sleep, and half dressed. Through the half-open door, he inquired:

'What does he want, Mr Skillow?' A slurp of tea.

'I think—I think that he wishes you to see his ship, sir, as we approach Rabhet.'

'See his—— d'y'mean *Curlew*, good God?'

'Aye, sir. *Curlew*, that is moored in the harbour.'

'Good heaven, then she has survived. He is certain it is *Curlew*, and not some other cutter?'

'Oh, yes, sir.'

'Very well, Mr Skillow, thankee. Y'may say to Mr Bradshaw that I will join him on deck directly.'

'Very good, sir.' And the boy dashed away.

'Cutton! Colley Cutton! More tea, for the love of God! And what has become of my razor? Where is my razor, and my shaving glass? Are ye awake, there!' Presently, with another draught of tea inside him, and clean-shaven—with only one small cut—Rennie came on his quarterdeck, and focused his long Dollond glass. There beyond the harbour wall, riding on the mirror of the harbour, was *Curlew*—anchored fore and aft, and so far as Rennie could make out, undamaged.

Lowering his glass: 'Well well, Mr Bradshaw, a welcome sight, very welcome. Hey?'

'Indeed, sir.' Jerking his head, swallowing. 'The most welcome thing I have seen—these many days.'

'Let us hope Mr Makepeace fares as well as his vessel—that is, your vessel, Mr Bradshaw.'

'Indeed, sir.' Nodding vigorously, swallowing again, and blinking.

'I am of a mind to return you to your own quarterdeck, as soon as may be practicable. I will like Mr Makepeace by me in *Expedient*.'

'Very good, sir. Thank you.'

'Mr Skillow!'

'Sir?' Attending.

'Are you able to use the signal book?'

'I—I think so, sir.'

'"Think so" will not answer, Mr Skillow. Make y'back straight, if y'please. You are on the quarterdeck of a man-of-war. Now then. Signal book?' Not harshly.

'I—I can make any signal that you request, sir.'

'Very well. Make to *Curlew*: "Prepare to receive your commanding officer."'

'Aye, sir.' Hurrying aft to the flag lockers.

'Mr Storey!—You there, boy! Find the gunner and say to him that I want glory smoke in our guns. We will give Rabhet thirteen, a full broadside of our starboard battery, as we approach.'

The ship's boy ran forrard, and jumped down the ladder into the waist.

'Mr Tangible!'

The boatswain came to his captain, and touched his forehead.

'Mr Tangible, we will dress the ship, in honour of our distinguished guest's return.'

'Very good, sir.'

He turned and found that Rashid Bey and Mr Sebastian

had joined him on the quarterdeck, having been at their prayers. They stood with Rennie as *Expedient* came about to enter the harbour, the two barques guarding the entrance standing apart to allow her passage. Rashid Bey made the request that the ship should not be dressed in his honour, but should come to her mooring without display of any kind. He was very quiet in his demeanour, in what Rennie thought was an uneasy mingling in his mind of relief to be again at home, and regret that he came with such dismal news. Today he was dressed not in his customary white, but in dark clothes, and a nondescript dark head-covering—almost as if he was in disguise.

Expedient ran in, put her topsails aback, her courses in the brails, and dropped anchor on the bearing taken and noted upon her first visit, within a cable or two of *Curlew*. Mr Bradshaw went at once to her in Rennie's gig, took possession as her commander once more, and Lieutenant Makepeace returned in the boat.

'I am right glad to see you alive, sir.' Coming up the side ladder, and greeting his captain at the breast rail.

'As am I to see you, Tom Makepeace. And *Curlew*, by God. How came you to return here? I will like you to come to supper, and tell me all about it.'

'I will with pleasure, sir.'

'You too, Mr Loftus. We will all like to hear it, hey?'

'Thank you, sir, indeed we will.' Bernard Loftus moved from the rail and shook Lieutenant Makepeace's hand warmly. 'Is your dunnage in the boat?'

'Captain Rennie . . . ?' Sebastian, approaching.

'Yes, Mr Sebastian.'

'I think that the Regent himself would like to be present at your supper—if you are minded to invite him.' Sebastian gestured toward Rashid Bey, who stood away from the little group at the breast rail, aft of the mizzen mast, looking ashore.

'Eh? Invite him? Ain't he going ashore at once, Mr

Sebastian? Surely he has most pressing matters to attend to there, don't he? Will he not be fully occupied with——'

'The Regent feels that to rush ashore precipitate might perhaps be unwise. To slip ashore at a later hour might be better suited to his—to his predicament.'

'Ah. Ah. In darkness, hey? Well well, then I shall be most happy to include him. By all means. And you, Mr Sebastian.'

'Thank you, Captain Rennie.' A salaam, and he went aft.

James lifted his head, straightened his aching back, and mopped at his dripping face and neck with his kerchief. He retied the kerchief on his head, his only protection from the beating sun. He felt weakened, and nauseous. His wound pained him, he was hollow with hunger, and the work—of splitting blocks of stone with a hammer and wedges—was arduous and draining in the extreme. The concierge had explained where James would work, and a little of the history of the place, with the air of a man who relishes the explication of harsh duty to others, from a position of protected ease:

'The quarries are to the north, beyond the Christian graveyard, effendi. They are the source of the stone from which the massive fortifications of the city are built. The fortifications were not always so extensive. Before the Ottomans came, Tunis had been a great Arab trading metropolis. Under the Hafsids, Tunis was at the centre of the great trading routes between the Islamic East and Christian Europe, it was a place certainly the equal of Cairo or Morocco. The Great Mosque of Zitouna was surrounded by mederasas full of learned men, innumerable traders in the souks, a thriving cultural life unrivalled anywhere in the Mediterranean. Then with the coming of the Ottoman Turks, Tunis changed. It became a fortress. A more exacting regime was established, and became dominant.' A shrug. 'That is the way of the world, effendi, no? The beautiful civilized metropolis gave way to a world of regents, and janissaries, and pirates—the world of the *corso*, and countless captured slaves. And now, alas, you are one of them. Yes, you are one of them.'

'I am one of them . . .' sighed James to himself. He looked at his blistered palms. A shadow fell over them. The slave-driver, behind him, flicked James about the shoulders and neck with his whip, and barked an order in Arabic.

'*Allah-o-Akbar*,' James intoned, inclining his head. Then he made the gesture of drinking, lifting his hand to his mouth. The slave-driver scowled at him, then jerked his head toward the well.

The slave at the well, a scrawny creature with sores all over his face, attempted to charge James for water, but James pretended not to understand him, and reached past him for the leather bucket, clapping on to the rope. The slave again angrily demanded payment, but James pushed him aside with a look of such murderous utterness that the creature gave way, stepped back and allowed James to lift the bucket unhindered and gulp water down. When he had drunk James lifted the bucket higher and poured water over his burning head. The slave at once began to protest, and James wordlessly thrust the empty bucket at him and walked away.

As noon approached the slave-driver indicated that there would be a respite from their work for the faithful to pray. The sound of the muezzin echoed across the quarry from the mosque to the south. James sat slumped in the shade of a low wall, his head aching, his back, his arms, every part of him. Blearily he became aware of a figure standing in front of him. Sandals, pantaloons, a blouse—and a boy's voice, speaking in French.

'You wish me to take a message for you, monsieur?'

'I cannot pay you.' Curtly, in French.

'I will take a message for you, monsieur.'

'I cannot pay.' Exasperated. 'Do not pester me. *Allez!*'

'But you will pay me later, monsieur. No?'

And now James did look up, squinting against the sun. *'Ensuite?'*

'Oui, monsieur, ensuite. D'accord.'

'Then—perhaps you can help me, after all. I will like a message took to *Rais* Zamoril's ship, lying in the harbour. You have heard of——'

'Certainly, monsieur, I know the admiral's ship.'

Presently, as the others ritually washed their feet and prostrated themselves in prayer, the boy slipped unobtrusively out of the quarry and away, carrying James's message.

When he came back with the slave gang in chains to the Grand Bagno, late in the afternoon, faint with hunger and exhaustion, James had no way of knowing if the boy had reached Zamoril's ship. Bread and coffee were all that interested him, and grateful, deadened sleep.

To his surprise he and all of the gang of returning slaves were fed cous-cous, and coffee, and dates. He had expected nothing more than the stale bread he had been given the night before. As soon as he had eaten James retired to his bunk in the tiers, and oblivious of the smoke and din of the lodging fell into dreamless slumber.

He woke in the dim light of the small hours, the lodging house illuminated only by the dying embers of cooking fires, and an oil lamp at the entrance. Balanced on the edge of his bunk, having climbed up by the ropes, was the boy he had sent to the harbour with his message. The boy was shaking him. Whispering:

'Monsieur, monsieur . . . you must wake.'

'I—I am awake.' James raised himself on an elbow, blinking at the boy. 'Have you an answer for me?' Also whispering.

'I have, monsieur. The admiral's ship has sailed.'

'You did not see him, then?' The news was like a blow to the stomach, knocking all the wind out of him.

'I did not, monsieur. However . . .'

'Damnation to this cursed place! It will destroy me!'

'No, monsieur, I do not think so . . .'

'What?'

'Your message has gone to an English ship. I gave it to a seaman from the ship, who swore he would pass it to the captain.'

'What ship? A merchantman? Tell me the name.' A flicker of hope in his breast.

'I do not know the name, monsieur. A trading ship, loading oil, and hides. I know it was an English ship, because the seaman spoke English, and all the men in her. She lay alongside the wharf.'

'You spoke to this seaman in English?'

'No, monsieur. He spoke to me in French, when I asked after *Rais* Zamoril's ship. He swore that he would give your message to his captain.'

'Ah, yes. Thank you. Seamen will swear to anything, if they are so minded. But, you know . . . I cannot pay you for your trouble, now. Had I been able to move to the private lodgings, and there arrange temporary finances, I could have paid you then. But now I cannot. *Je regrette . . .*'

'You have nothing for me, monsieur?'

'Only a few dates, that I have not eaten.' He gave them to the boy, who fell on them ravenously. James began to feel sorry for the boy, who was clearly starving.

'Tell me your name, will you?'

'Hamdan.'

'I am sorry that I cannot pay you, Hamdan. Here, finish the dates.'

James thought: He is like to an animal, a starveling puppy, or a kitten, that has crept from its hiding place into a dwelling, to beg for its supper.

'Where d'you live, Hamdan?'

'Anywhere, monsieur. Nowhere.'

'You have no mother, no father?'

'My mother is dead. My father I have never seen. I think he was a seaman, a corsair.'

'A corsair, you say? With *Rais* Hamidou's fleet?'

'I do not know for certain.'

'How came you to me, at the stone quarry?'

'I heard in the square that you wished a message to be brought to the harbour.'

'Who told you this?'

A shrug of the pinched shoulders. 'I heard it, monsieur.'

'Where will you sleep tonight?'

'In the square.'

'With no bedding?'

'I have no money for straw. I sleep where I am able.'

'Then you had better stay here tonight, and come with me to the concierge in the morning. I am determined to spend no further time in this damned place, and I will——'

'No, monsieur! I will not go to the concierge! He is a cruel man, a fiend and a blasphemer!' Before James could say anything further to dissuade him, the boy swarmed down the ropes of the tier and scurried away out of the lodging into the square.

James made to descend himself, then thought that he would never find the boy in the darkness of the square, and desisted. Fatigue once more overwhelmed him, he was seized by a yawn, lay down in his bunk and was at once asleep.

He dreamed of Catherine, who came running past him, carrying her child—his son—bundled up in a blanket clutched to her breast and shoulder. He tried to call out to her, to arrest her headlong rush, but she did not hear him, did not see him at all. His arms outstretched, his hands clutching at the air, he could not speak, and could not move. Catherine ran away from down a long grassy slope, ran and ran, her dress flapping and catching at her ankles. At the bottom of the slope, rising as it were out of the depths, the sea stretched to the horizon—a horizon that seemed strangely high.

'If she runs to the edge, she will fall.'

He could not say it aloud. He could not run after her,

toward the far-down edge of the slope, toward the blue-grey sea, stretching up to the horizon and the strange subdued light of the sky.

'Cathy—Cathy—why do you run from me?'

He woke with a cry in the near darkness, to the smell of hemp and filthy straw, and stale smoke, and the aches and pains of his limbs, and a sense of desolation and loss.

'I must escape. I must make my way home to England, and my family. Damnation to this miserable place, and this whole miserable commission. Somehow, I must escape.'

And at that moment, deep within him, deep resolve rose and burned, and in a moment more was branded on his heart: I *will* be free.

⊨◆⊒

Rennie sat in the great cabin with Rashid Bey and Mr Sebastian, and the master Mr Loftus, with Alan Dobie as clerk to take notes of anything that Rennie thought important enough to transcribe as they listened to Lieutenant Makepeace conclude his tale:

'I expected at any moment to run up against one of the corsair ships, or several of them together, flying at me out of the tempest, and to have to make a fight of it. I could not take a reading at any point, so had no idea of our true position. Thank God, when the storm at last blew itself out, and the cloud broke, I was able to take sightings at noon, and later calculate by my pocket watch—there was no chronometer in *Curlew*—and the lunars, my exact position, and realized that we were proximate to Rabhet, if we made enough westing. And so I decided to make Rabhet my design, and carry out such repairs as were needed, and make a plan—and then, very happily, you came in *Expedient*.'

'Excellent, Tom, thankee for so comprehensive an account. A glass of wine.'

He and Makepeace and Mr Loftus raised their glasses, and

Rashid Bey and Mr Sebastian politely sipped water from tumblers.

'Naturally I have wrote it all out in my journal, sir, and will copy it out for my written report to you.'

'Dobie will do it. Hey, Dobie?' A brief glance in Alan Dobie's direction. 'Just give your journal to him, Tom.'

Alan Dobie nodded in compliance, and managed a smile. He had not been included in any of the toasts, nor offered wine at all, and he felt himself injured by this slight. Was not he a full member of the gunroom mess? Was not he thus a guest in the great cabin? He made a note in his book with his pen, and emphatically underlined it with a fierce scratch of the quill.

'Thank you for a most absorbing account, Lieutenant Makepeace,' said Rashid Bey now, putting down his water glass. 'I so much enjoyed your word picture of the seabirds alighting in exhaustion in your rigging at the height of the storm. It shows us what remarkably practical creatures they are, in dangerous and extreme circumstance, no?'

'I have known birds fly from ship to ship, in truth, sir. I have heard of one instance where letters was exchanged between two ships in a gale, by tying a packet to a seabird's leg, and flinging the bird high to leeward, and it was carried clear to the other ship upon the wind, and the letters thus safely delivered. Quite remarkable.'

'Yes, remarkable.' A little intake of breath, a brief pause, and: 'Whilst we are all gathered together, Captain Rennie, I wish to make a proposal—that is, a request.'

'Sir?' Rennie was amiable and steadfast in his facial expression, knowing what was likely coming.

'I wish that you and your ship will aid me in making a defence of Rabhet, of my harbour and port. An assault is certain to come, led by *Rais* Zamoril, under instruction from Suleiman el Hassad. I had hoped as you know to reach England and there arrange for a fleet of English ships to aid me, but events have moved against us. Zamoril will not wait very long, I think.'

'May I make a proposal of my own, sir?'

'Certainly, Captain Rennie.'

'I will send *Curlew* to England, flying fast, never losing a moment, carrying an urgent despatch requesting that a squadron of ships be sent at once to Rabhet. With luck, and favourable winds, she will reach England in a fortnight, three weeks at most.'

'Gibraltar is much closer, sir.' Lieutenant Makepeace. '*Curlew* could be at Gibraltar in a few days.'

'No, Tom, I considered it, but there ain't enough ships at Gibraltar for our purpose here. Beside, the Governor would not likely give us what few ships are there, without authority from London. No, the squadron must come from England, and——'

'Gentlemen, Rabhet cannot wait so long as two or three weeks for a message to arrive in England, and another two or three weeks for ships to come. That is at least a month. Zamoril will attack within days.'

'So he might, sir,' said Rennie. 'So he might. We must have the ships, one way or t'other. Even if Zamoril was to prevail at first, break through your defences and take the city—we shall need the ships, and the men in them, to take it back again.'

'Will not your small ship—your *Curlew*—will not she risk capture or destruction, if she sails alone?'

'That is a risk all ships of war must take, sir, in hazardous waters. It cannot be helped. I am in no doubt your cousin is well aware of such risk, Mr Sebastian, and decidedly able to rise up to the challenge. Hey?' Turning to the bulky adviser.

'Dutt Bradshaw will rise to it.'

'Just so. He is a sea officer in the Royal Navy, and he will do his duty.'

'Then—when will you send *Curlew*, Captain? Tonight?' Rashid Bey glanced out of the stem gallery window at the dark harbour.

'Nay, sir, not tonight, you know. On the morrow, when

Lieutenant Bradshaw has completed his few repairs, and I have had time to write his sailing orders, and——'

'You said without losing a moment. Could not you give Lieutenant Bradshaw his orders now, Captain, tonight? Why delay?'

Rennie took a breath, and held his temper in check. 'Sir, with respect, I must write the sailing orders, and I must write in addition an accompanying letter to their Lordships. Such a letter requires——'

'But your scribe is here with us, now. Why not write the letter at once?'

Rennie smiled—he hoped not frostily—and said: 'Sir, you have asked for my help, and I will certainly give it, willingly give it—to the highest of my ability. But I really must have time to gather my thoughts.'

'Yes yes, but——'

Rennie shook his head, held up a hand, and firmly: 'Forgive me, sir. I must again remind you that I am not in your employ, but in the employ of His Majesty King George. It is his interests I serve, by my solemn oath, above all others. *Curlew* will sail on the morrow. And now, gentlemen, if you will excuse me, I have much to do . . .'

And he rose, pushing back his chair.

At noon on the following day, with his orders and the letter to their Lordships safely in his hand, Lieutenant Bradshaw gave the order to weigh, brought *Curlew* to the wind, and put to sea.

Having seen *Curlew* safe departed, Rennie returned to his great cabin and sat awaiting the arrival of *Rais* Ahmed el Ali, Rashid Bey's fleet commander. In keeping with his decision to take a firm stand with Rashid Bey—as to his allegiance and duty to King George—Rennie had made it plain to him that the stratagem to be employed in defence of Rabhet must come from *Expedient*, from Rennie, and not from Ahmed el Ali.

'Was I high-handed in this?' he wondered aloud. 'Hey, Dulcie?'

His cat, that he had seen so little of these last days, answered with a miaow, and now leapt into his lap, where she lay purring with her eyes closed. He scratched her ears—one black, one white—and stroked her shining fur. There was still a great deal of work to be done, but as Rennie gazed upon the little creature, indulgently and fondly gazed, his spare frame relaxed in the chair, the lines on his forehead and face softened a little, and he was briefly at ease. There was much to deepen those lines on his forehead. His present predicament, the near total failure of the commission. The ever present sadness of his being a widower. The new sadness of having lost his most able officer and staunchest friend, James Hayter, with whom he had sailed to the far corners of the earth, borne much hardship and danger, and fought side by side in fierce and deadly action.

He sighed. 'Ah, Dulcie, dear Dulcie . . . in least I have you by me.'

'As you has me, sir, always and eternal.' Behind him.

'What?'

'Always ready, sir, at your command—as you knows well.'

Rennie turned his head to look at Colley Cutton. 'Have you been drinking?'

'Oo, me, sir? Ho no, sir, noooh.—Tea, sir, izzit?' Leaning forward in a show of eager servility, and swaying very slightly.

'You have been drinking, by God.'

'I will not like to contra . . . dict but you are m'stook, sir. Tea, sir?' Raising his eyebrows with an ingratiating smile.

'Yes yes, very well. Tea. Have you fed my cat?'

'I has already done it. Thus, for why the cat is content—as you see, sir.'

'Very well, very well. Only do not spill my tea, will you? I should be vexed was my tea to be spilled, to scald me or my cat. Or both of us together.'

'I always takes care, sir.' Backing into the quarter gallery, and closing the door.

'And when you have brought my tea, y'may shift yourself out of that quarter gallery, and back to the coach, now that my guests have gone out of the ship.' Calling over his shoulder through the closed door. 'D'y'hear?'

A clatter of kettles and dishes.

'The wretch is drunk.'

The sound of the boatswain's call roused him to his duty, and Rennie gently lifted the cat from his lap and placed her on the deck.

'Cutton! Colley Cutton! Ye'd better brew some coffee, as well. D'y'hear me?'

And he stood up, straightened his shoulders, and waited for the sentry to knock on the door, heralding the arrival of *Rais* Ahmed el Ali.

Rais Ahmed el Ali was accompanied, to Rennie's surprise, by Mr Sebastian. Was Sebastian there as the instrument of his master's will? wondered Rennie.

'I am to act as interpreter,' said Sebastian, as if in answer to Rennie's unspoken question.

'The Admiral feels that his English is inadequate . . .'

'Ah, very good, Mr Sebastian.' He offered his guests coffee, and himself drank the tea Cutton brought to him on a separate tray. When the coffee came Rennie noticed that both of his guests lifted the cup with the right hand, always carefully and fastidiously with the right hand. It had puzzled him previously, and now before they got down to their business he asked Sebastian:

'I am curious, Mr Sebastian—why d'you always lift the cup with the right hand only? Is it an article of Islamic faith, an observance of some religious principle?'

'The left hand is unclean.'

'Unclean?' Puzzled. 'How, more so than the right?'

'Bluntly, it is the hand used to wipe the breech.'

'Ah. Ah.' Nodding politely.

Coffee and tea drunk, and polite formalities dispensed with, they set to their business.

'Y'may say to the *rais* that as I see it, the key to everything is gunnery,' Rennie began. He waited as Sebastian translated, and continued: 'Zamoril will bring his full fleet, I am in no doubt. However, I do not think he will risk his all in one blasting assault from the east. I think that instead he will attempt to land shore parties—his janissaries—upon the coast to the north, at some little distance from the harbour and port. From there they will march upon the city in darkness, and attack from the rear before dawn, both the city and the fort. At the same moment his main force of ships will bombard the harbour defences—the fort and walls—thus obliging us to defend several points at once.'

Rais Ahmed el Ali now interrupted, and through Mr Sebastian asked a question:

'How do you know that this is what Zamoril will do?'

Rennie listened, then: 'It is how I would make the attack myself. Shore parties in darkness, to skirmish to the rear of the city, and the fort, and attack from the west. Send in the fleet in line of battle and begin a full broadside bombardment from the front, from the east. We must prepare our defences accordingly.' He waited while Sebastian translated, then continued: 'I propose guns to the rear of the city, loaded with canister, and additional men at the fort with swivels—that I will provide—also loaded with canister, to fire down upon the assaulting troops. We must have red-hot shot for the east-firing great guns at the fort, to fire into the attacking line of ships.'

Again the *rais* interposed a question, through Sebastian:

'Where will your ship be placed during the battle? At what position in the harbour?'

'Yes, I was about to come to that myself. *Expedient* will not lie in the harbour at all. She will stand off the coast, awaiting the arrival of the attacking fleet from the north.

When the attack upon Rabhet has begun, *Expedient* will stand in and attack from the east, with the prevailing wind.'

Rais Ahmed el Ali was not wholly pleased by this answer. In truth he found it dismaying. Through Sebastian:

'Surely your ship must defend the harbour from within. *Expedient* is a frigate, a large ship, with the best armament.'

Rennie responded with a nod. 'Aye, sir, exact. And that is why I wish to attack from the east. To take Zamoril by surprise, and sink and destroy as many of his ships as I am able, before he can defend himself.'

The *rais*'s reply was forceful and succinct. 'This is madness. It is folly. The harbour and city must be defended from within. I demand that your frigate assist me.'

Rennie maintained his composure, and even contrived to nod and smile. 'I understand your anxieties, as to your harbour and city, sir. However, we will follow my stratagem to the letter, if you please. We must arrange a system of signals, by rocket. Just so soon as the attack has been begun on the city and fort, rockets are to be fired. I will then sail from the east, and the internal defence of the city and fort will proceed.'

'But what is the role of my fleet?' The *rais* was now greatly agitated. In his dismay and anger he knocked his coffee cup to the deck, where it smashed; he did not notice. 'Am I to lie alone in the harbour, and do nothing!'

Seeing his anger, Rennie became placatory. 'In course, Admiral, your role is vital to our cause. You will—when the attack upon the city and fort from the west has been thwarted—you will make a foray from the harbour and attack the enemy line. By then I shall have begun to smash Zamoril from behind, from the east. When you attack him from the west—well well, his time will be up, d'y'see?'

'I must wait until after the attack, then? You expect me to wait until after the main attack?'

'I expect you to be *in at the kill*!' And Rennie lifted his tea, and swallowed off the now lukewarm liquid in an emphatic gulp.

*

Long days of waiting, and no sign of Zamoril's fleet. *Rais* Ahmed el Ali placated, and reconciled, and if not quite subservient then certainly accommodating of Rennie's wishes. The guns in position along the rear walls of the city; the additional guns at the fort—the swivels—in position. Powder and shot laid in. The fleet in the harbour now entirely familiar with their required movements once the first wave of the attack had been subdued. Rennie's own people brought to a pitch so near perfection in the daily exercising of the great guns that Rennie could not fault them.

'What holds Zamoril back, the fellow?' wondered Rennie aloud, pacing his quarterdeck.

'Ahoy the boat!' cried Midshipman Cutforth, leaning over the side. 'Who are you?'

'What, another message from the admiral?' said Rennie. 'What now, I wonder?' Glancing across the water towards the *rais*'s barque.

'No, sir.' Young Cutforth. 'The man has come from the wharf.'

'Then it is another message from the Regent, I expect. Asking yet again: are we ready?'

'I do not think so, sir.' Peering over the side. 'It is a very small boat, and the man looks like a beggar.'

'Then warn him off, Mr Cutforth.'

'He waves a piece of paper, sir.'

'Eh?' Rennie himself came to the rail, and looked down. A small brown man stood in a very humble vessel, little more than a raft. He held up a scrap of paper, and waved it.

'No no,' called Rennie. 'We want nothing from you. Stand away now, if y'please.' Aside, to the middy: 'You was right, Mr Cutforth. He is a beggar, in rags. Very probably he is diseased.'

He was about to push back from the rail and resume his pacing, when the man in the boat called out.

'*Capitaine Rennie!*'

'Eh? Did he call my name?' Glancing at young Cutforth.

'I think that he did, sir.'

'*Capitaine Rennie!*' And then a long and hoarsely enunciated passage of French, and the paper waved repeatedly.

'What does he say? D'y'understand him, Mr Cutforth?'

'I—I think he says that it is a message from Tunis, sir. Something about *Rais* Zamoril, and the Bagno . . .'

'Zamoril? What can this starveling fellow know of Zamoril, good God?'

And then there came to Rennie's ears a word—a name—that he had never expected to hear again.

'Did he say Hayter? Did you hear him say the name Hayter?' His heart lifting.

'I did, sir.' Midshipman Cutforth's face flushed with excitement as he turned to Rennie, then cupped his ear to listen to the man in the boat. 'He says—he says that it is Lieutenant Hayter that is in the Grand Bagno at Tunis, sir—and that he—he appealed to *Rais* Zamoril for assistance—I cannot quite follow the rest, sir. His French is garbled, and my own French is imperfect . . .'

'Appealed to Zamoril? Why would James appeal to him?—Unless . . . unless it was Zamoril put him in the Bagno. That must be it.' Nodding. 'Ask the fellow to come aboard, Mr Cutforth, if y'please. Bring him to me directly.—Mr Dobie! Mr Dobie! Where is my clerk when I want him!'

Presently, in the great cabin:

'You speak French, d'y'not, Mr Dobie?'

'A little, sir, yes.'

'Pray ask this man for the paper he carries, that I saw in his hand before he came aboard. Say that I will reward him with gold.'

Alan Dobie turned to the little brown raggedy man standing barefoot on the decking canvas. He addressed him in halting French, and the crumpled, dirty scrap of paper was handed over. Rennie took it and perused it eagerly. In a shaky but recognizable hand:

Rais Zamoril—to be given into his hand

Sir,

I am held, as you are aware, in the Grand Bagno, but I am not held in the private quarters. I am held in the common lodgings, in very squalid conditions. I beg you to intercede, so that I may shift at once into the private quarters. Only there can I make the attempt to raise the five thousand pound you ask. In here I am very ill-treated and fear for my life. Certainly neither you nor the Dey can wish me dead, before I have paid you.

James Hayter, Lt RN

'By God, it is James's hand! He is alive! He is alive! Thank God!' Rennie's eyes prickled, and his vision was momentarily blurred. He turned away, cleared his wind, and sniffed. And soon:

'Mr Dobie, ask him how he came by this, will you? And how long since?'

Alan Dobie again spoke to the barefoot man in French, listened to his brief reply, and:

'He requests that you pay him his reward, sir.'

'Yes yes, very well.' Rennie searched in his desk, found gold coins and gave then to the man, who examined them, turning them over in his hands, and acknowledged their worth with a toothless grin.

'Very well. Ask him again, Mr Dobie. How did he get this paper, and when?'

A brief conversation in French as Rennie waited, glancing again at the letter in that familiar hand. Alan Dobie turned to his captain:

'It came from a seaman in Tunis, sir.'

'From Zamoril's ship?'

'I do not think so, sir. He says that the seaman was in a brawl ashore, and was arrested and imprisoned, and gave out the paper to try to raise money for his fine. Or so this man was told, sir.'

'Told? Told? How came he by it, is my question.' Waving the paper.

Another brief exchange in French, and:

'I fear that he is unwilling to say, sir.'

'Hm. How did he know to bring it to *Expedient*? How did he know where *Expedient* lay?'

Again an exchange, and Dobie nodded.

'That is easily explained, sir. Mr Hayter is clearly identified in the letter as RN. *Expedient* is the only one of His Majesty's ships in these waters, and news of such things spreads up and down the coast and into the humblest quarters of Tunis. This man made his way here in the hope of reward.'

'And he has had it. But how did he come? By what means?'

Dobie asked the visitor this question, and was able to tell Rennie: 'He took passage in a trading pinque at Tunis, in which his cousin is cook. He was put ashore some distance to the north of Rabhet, where the pinque took in cargo, and has made his way some many miles south on foot. He is very weary and hungry——'

'Yes yes, I am in no doubt.' Rennie, over him, impatiently. 'See that he is fed, Mr Dobie, and thank him . . .' turning to the man '. . . Thank you, thank you. *Merci, monsieur. Bon,* indeed, *bon.*' To Dobie: 'And now escort him out of my quarters, if y'please. His odour is very penetrating.'

＊━━━━━━━━━━━━＊

Lieutenant Quill, *Expedient*'s marine officer, stood on the quarterdeck with the third lieutenant, Mr Upward. In the gunroom they had had a discussion as to the best method for boarding an enemy ship in attack. Lieutenant Quill wished to demonstrate his own preferred method.

'You do not advance into the enemy ship with your sword drawn,' he began.

'Oh, that is very bad,' interjected Mr Upward, shaking his head. 'You must advance with your sword at point.'

'Now, that is nonsense, you know.' Lieutenant Quill, shaking his head in turn.

'Eh? It ain't nonsense, not at all. It is the approved——'

'Good heaven, Upward, I do not entertain the "approved" in this. My method is anything but "approved". It is the effective method. Step back, will you? Allow me to show you. So . . . you do not draw your sword. In truth there is nothing in your hand until you light on the enemy's deck. Then— only then—you take from your sword belt the first of your four pistols.'

'Four! Did y'say four pistols?'

'Aye, four. You grip the pistol by the butt, not with one hand alone, but with both hands.'

'What did y'say—*both* hands?'

'Please do not interrupt me so frequent, hey? Let me show it to you.' He took up the sea pistol he had carried to the quarterdeck, gripped the butt in his right hand, then folded his left hand round his right in a double grip, raised and pointed the pistol in one swift movement.

'Bang!' He pretended to cast the pistol aside on the deck and to draw a second from his waist, and mimed the same action, gripping the butt with both hands, raising, pointing, firing.

'Bang!—And the same a third and fourth time. Then— only then—having cast aside your fourth pistol, you draw your sword and advance. Thus.' And he put up the pistol, and drew his sword.

'Yes, very admirable,' said Mr Upward, rocking his head from side to side. 'Admirable, but far too particular, you know. By the time you had aimed and fired all these damned pistols, you'd've been run through.'

'By whom, pray?'

'By your opponent, in course. Or your several opponents.'

'By no means, not at all. Four men would lie dead, all of them shot. Any further opponents would likely fall back from such a determined assault, and you may then advance, sword drawn.' Thrusting once or twice with his blade, and sheathing it.

'Will I tell you why I think your method would fail? It would fail because you could not hope, in all the haste and confusion of boarding, to aim your pistols accurate. Yes, you may well fire off four charges, but will you hit a single opponent? Bluntly, Quill, I think you will not.' Again shaking his head.

'You are wrong. Flat wrong. And I will prove it to you. Mr Skillow!'

'Sir?' The midshipman, attending.

'Tear out a sheet from your notebook, will you?'

'Very good, sir.' Fumbling in his pocket, finding the book, and tearing out the required sheet.

'Now then, make a central black square with your pencil.'

'Yes, sir.' He made the mark on the paper.

'Very good. Move aft to the taffrail, will you, and hold out the paper at arm's length, with the square facing me.'

'May I—may I ask why, sir?'

'The square is my target,' answered Lieutenant Quill, and again his pistol was in his hand.

'What!' Mr Upward. 'You are not proposing to shoot at the boy, are you!'

'Good Lord, no, not at the lad. At the target.'

'Sir, if you please—I had rather not stand as you ask . . .'

'Nonsense, Mr Skillow. No harm will come to you, I am an excellent shot.'

'Look here, now, Quill—this will not do.' Lieutenant Upward, keeping his voice at an amiable pitch, attempted gently to remove the pistol from Lieutenant Quill's hand. 'God damn me, you will blow the poor boy's brains out.'

'No no, I will not. Kindly stand aside—and watch. Mr

Skillow! Hold out the paper, if y'please! Let me see my target clear!'

'Aye, sir . . .' Very fearfully the boy held out the sheet of paper with the black square at the centre. He closed his eyes, screwed up tight.

Lieutenant Quill pushed the pistol down into his sword belt, and stood calmly a moment.

'Give me the word, will you, Upward?'

'Oh, very well. If you are determined on this foolishness, let us get it over with. *Now!*'

Lieutenant Quill smoothly drew the pistol from his belt and brought it rapidly up, his left hand cocking the lock as he did so, gripped the butt in both hands, and as the barrel came level he fired. The paper in the boy's hand jerked, and where the black square had been a neat round hole was evident. The whole exercise had taken a fraction over one second. Midshipman Skillow stared at the perforated paper in his hand in relieved wonder.

'There, d'y'see?' said Quill easily, lowering the pistol to his side. 'Supposing that was a man's forehead, his brains would now be scattered into our wake. I reckon the distance at ten paces.'

'And you are confident you could achieve that marksmanship four times in as many seconds?' asked Upward.

'I have done so many times, at practice. Deadly fire is all practice, and a cool head.'

'I confess I had not thought it possible,' admitted Upward. 'Are you all right, Mr Skillow?'

'Yes, thank you, sir.' And the boy sat down suddenly on the deck, very white in the face.

'Was that a pistol shot on the quarterdeck?' Rennie glanced up at the deckhead from his desk. 'Did you hear it, Mr Dobie?'

'It is the marines at practice, I think, sir.' Coming into the great cabin from his cubby-hole forrard of the coach. 'Lieutenant Quill.'

'On my quarterdeck? Pistols? I don't care for that. I shall certainly speak to him.—Well well, have you wrote the letter out, Mr Dobie?'

'Aye, sir. As instructed, and it requires only your signature before sealing.'

'Very good. Show it to me.' Reaching for the letter. Alan Dobie gave it to him, and stood waiting as he perused it. Rennie nodded, sniffed, reached for his quill and signed the letter, then folded it and sealed it with wax. He held the letter in his hand, and:

'The beggar fellow will take it?'

'He will, sir—for a consideration.'

'Yes yes, in course. For a further consideration.' He made to hand the letter to Dobie. 'Wait, though. I will make it a packet, a despatch packet.' And he found a roll of canvas in his desk, cut off a length, folded the letter neatly inside it, and tied and sealed the packet. Dobie waited patiently, but still the captain would not give up the letter. Staring at it, he shook his head.

'I am dubious that such a fellow will bring the letter to the Dey's palace at Tunis, you know.' And he looked away out of the stern gallery window, tapped the packet with a finger, and laid it down on the desk again. 'What is to prevent him taking my gold, discarding the letter, and running away? Hm?' Glancing at Dobie.

'He brought Lieutenant Hayter's letter, did not he? In expectation of reward? Sir, why not say to him—if I may make the suggestion—that he will be rewarded with gold at Tunis?'

'Give him no further gold now, d'y'mean? Myself? Trust the Dey to reward him?'

'Exact. Say to him that his reward will come at Tunis, as it came when he brought Lieutenant Hayter's letter to you here.'

'Very good, Dobie. Yes, then that is what we will do. Say so to him.' Nodding, and handing the despatch packet to his clerk. He rose, and shrugged into his coat. 'I must go ashore and see Rashid Bey. No doubt he will wish me to accompany him to the hammam.'

'Yes, sir. May I ask . . . ?'

'What?' Taking up his sword belt.

'May I ask—is the experience beneficial, would you say?'

'The hammam? Was you thinking of it for yourself?'

'Well, sir—I had thought of it, yes.'

'If ye can withstand fierce heat, head-benumbing heat, and sudden plunging cold, and a sound thrashing at the hands of an adept, then by all means, Alan Dobie. Avail y'self, by all means. See that y'give the letter to the beggar fellow before, though, will ye? I will not like it was you to be so prostrated by the bath that the letter was forgot. Hey?' A grim little smile.

'Is this boy your servant—or your catamite?' The concierge's hoarse voice was insinuating and lubricious as he asked the question, his calculus bead eyes slyly suggestive. James had to clench his teeth a moment before he allowed himself to reply.

'He is neither.'

'But he is always with you, I think?'

'That is his choice. I neither pay him, nor enjoin him to remain. I have nothing to offer.'

'Then . . . why does he stay with you in such a place as the Bagno? He is not imprisoned.'

'I expect that it is because I am the only person in this entire wretched place that has not kicked him away like a rat.'

'So? Why so?'

'Why did I not kick him away? Because I am a Christian.' Essentially an untruth, since he had no religious beliefs, having discarded them at Cambridge.

'Ah, a Christian. It is your obligation to show him kindness and charity, then?'

'Charity I cannot offer. I am penniless, as you know.'

'But he pleases you, no?'

'He neither pleases nor displeases me.' An impatient jerk of his head. 'Why have you had me brought to you?'

They were standing in the courtyard of the concierge's house. James had been summoned there, and escorted out of the line of slaves about to go to the quarries by the concierge's two guards.

'I wish only to be of service to you, effendi. I am here to aid and assist. Let us go inside, where it is cooler. The boy will wait here.'

'He is thirsty, as am I. Will you give him water?'

'Yes, he may have water. It will be brought to him while he waits.'

James nodded to Hamdan, and the boy at once sat down by the wall. The concierge led James inside to the cool long room where he conducted his business. He turned and smiled:

'Word has come to me that your ransom will be paid.'

'What! Paid!' James raised a hand to his head as dizziness briefly surged, and as it receded he felt his heart jumping and thudding in his breast. 'Who—who will pay it, five thousand pound?'

'The offer has come to the Dey, from the south. As soon as the money is in hand, you will be released.'

'From the south? D'y'mean—from Rabhet?'

'I do not know from what source, effendi. I have been informed of the simple facts, and know nothing of the detail.'

'Perhaps it is Rashid Bey. Yes, it must be Rashid Bey. He has took pity on me.—But how has he heard of my plight?' All this musingly, aloud.

'I do not know, effendi. However, I have been instructed to take you immediately to the private quarters, and to provide you with anything you may require to make your—your remaining time comfortable. I can——'

'Remaining time! Surely I am to be released at once?'

'No, effendi, you have not listened. I said that you would be released as soon as the money had been paid.'

'Christ's blood, if word has come that it is to be paid, then it will be paid! I will give you my word that——'

'Ahh. Ahh-hahh.' Shaking his head. 'Sadly, effendi, I must say no to you. You will understand—it is a delicate question altogether, the question of money. No?'

'The Dey believes it. He believes that the money will be paid, else you and I would not now be engaged in this discussion!'

'I will ask you please, effendi, not to put your hand upon my person. I will ask you to remove your hand from my blouse, if you please . . .'

James released the bunched cloth of the concierge's blouse, and stood back. 'I am sorry. I did not mean to become violent. I meant only to draw your attention to my position, and——'

'But I am wholly aware of your position. I know your position exactly and entirely. You very naturally wish to be released. I am simply following instructions when I take you to the private quarters. Please, effendi, it will be easier if you will accompany me, rather than submitting yourself to the humiliation of being bound and carried there by my men. Yes?'

James accompanied the concierge to the private quarters. He made the request that Hamdan be allowed to go there with him, and the request was at first refused. As James followed the concierge between high, narrow walls, and paused while a heavy iron gate was unlocked:

'Listen now, I will not go there to the damned private quarters unless the boy may be permitted to go there with me. D'y'hear?'

The concierge turned, the heavy key in his hand. 'He is your catamite, this boy—is he not? Your regard for him is . . . pressing, yes? I think so.'

'Y'may think what you wish. My regard for him is that he

is a vulnerable child, that I do not wish to abandon. A child that has done me a service, and will likely starve if I do not protect him. Well?'

'Hh-hm-hm, yes.' A smirk. 'That is as good an explication as any, I suppose, hm-hm. Very well, the boy may come.' He beckoned, and the boy was allowed to slip along the alley to the gate.

When they reached the entrance of the private quarters, beyond which a private courtyard with a fountain and a small garden could be glimpsed through a kind of cloister, the concierge:

'Anything you wish, effendi, is yours. I can summon a tailor, I can provide wine, and various fine foodstuffs, or even . . . but no, you have your boy. It remains only for me to request that you sign a paper, that will ensure I am reimbursed for all expenses. Yes?'

The concierge led James into a cubby-hole at the foot of a stair near the entrance to the cloister. He indicated pen-box and ink on a desk. James took up the pen, dipped it in the inkwell, and was about to sign the paper pushed across the desk by the concierge, but he paused.

'May I send a message by the boy to the Dey's palace?'

'First you must sign.' Pushing the paper.

'Yes, I will like to sign when the boy has took my message. Hamdan!'

Hamdan came at once and stood by the desk. The concierge firmly pushed the boy aside, and:

'You must sign now.'

'I think you did not hear me. I will sign when the boy has gone with the message, and returned to say that he has delivered it.'

The smirk faded from the concierge's face, and was replaced by a frown. 'Now, effendi, this will not do——'

'Then I will not sign.' James pushed the paper away from him, and laid the pen down in the open pen-box, and shut the lid of the well. At once the concierge became conciliatory, and ingratiating. His frown became an obsequious smile.

'I understand, effendi. Yes, I understand perfectly. You are anxious to know if the message I have given you is an accurate one, that it is true. You wish to establish beyond doubt that you are to be set free—upon payment of the money. Hm-hm, of course, it is natural in you to wish it, hm-hm-hm. But effendi . . . effendi . . .' spreading his hands '. . . I can do nothing unless the regulations are observed. You see, I must have your name on the paper indemnifying me against all expense incurred by yourself. It is the rule of the Grand Bagno . . .' Widening his smile, and tipping his head slightly to one side.

'May I tell you my own rule, damn your blood?' Mildly, but with a glinting eye. 'It is this: I will do nothing at all to accommodate you, nor your bloody regulations, until the boy has gone away and returned. *D'yhave me?* Very good. And now I will like coffee.'

The concierge shrugged—reluctantly shrugged, to make a show—and reluctantly agreed. James took up the pen, wrote his message, and sent the boy away. The concierge gave an order brusquely to a servant, resumed his patient and acceding smile—and coffee was brought.

James knew that for the second time in the Bagno he was taking a great risk. His demeanour, his language, his attitude—of command, of having the advantage, of taking the wind gage—were entirely assumed, since he could be sure of nothing and no one so long as he remained here. How would the ransom be paid? Had not all of Rashid Bey's treasure been stolen by the Dey of Tunis? How could Rashid Bey produce five thousand pound in gold? Or was the offer merely a ploy? Were Rashid Bey and Rennie together plotting to—what? Make a daring raid upon Tunis, and release the prisoner by force of arms? Well, that was nonsense; no such scheme could conceivably be brought to success against the fortifications and numbers of men the Dey had at his disposal.

Then perhaps Rennie proposed a version of the cutting-out party, a shore party in the ship's boats at night, slipping into the harbour and stealing ashore with a party of marines disguised as janissaries, or beggars, and coming to the Bagno quietly through the alleys.

'No no,' sighed James to himself. He pushed away his empty coffee cup, and shifted in the low chair to ease the ache in his neck.

'You are troubled, effendi?' The concierge peered at him in the dim light of the cubby-hole. 'You do not trust this boy to return, after all?'

'In course I do trust him.' Curtly. 'He has took the message, and will come back with the reply.'

They waited long, and James had all but given up hope by mid-afternoon, and then the boy returned. He had been kept waiting at the palace, he said, and the guards had been harsh, making him stand in the sun . . . but he had the hoped-for reply, tied in a parchment packet. James tore open the packet, and found a letter addressed in Rennie's hand to: 'His Supreme Excellency Suleiman el Hassad, Dey of Tunis'.

James's heart lifted as he read.

Your Excellency,

I have in my possession objects that I am informed must be of the greatest interest to Your Excellency, which I am pleased to offer as payment for the release from your custody of Lieutenant James Hayter RN. The objects in question are a full set of chess men, very old and valuable, of crystal and gold and jewels, that was made in Istanbul for Sultan Selim the First. I am told this set, that is known as the Crystal Men, is nearly priceless. Certainly, Your Excellency, it is of a value exceeding five thousand pound sterling of money, that you ask for the release of Lieutenant Hayter. May I take it, therefore, that just as soon as the Crystal Men may be conveyed to you—by an arrangement suitable to the convenience of Your Excellency—Lieutenant Hayter will be released, & given Safe Passage?

May I ask that you send a reply to me as soon as may be possible, to my ship at anchor in the harbour at Rabhet?

I have the honour to remain, sir, your humble and obedient servant,

Captain William Rennie RN   HMS Expedient

With the letter in the packet was a paper confirming that a reply had been despatched to Rabhet, cordially assenting to the Crystal Men in lieu of monies as payment for Lieutenant Hayter's release. James signed the document the concierge again placed before him. James was then shown into his private quarters—three small rooms—his spirits if not high then at least raised a little above their recent level. Hamdan came with him as his servant.

'I cannot pay you,' James told the boy. 'Even when the ransom has been received by the Dey at his palace, I will have no money at all.'

'I do not wish payment, effendi.'

'I cannot pay for these quarters, nor our victuals neither, even if I have signed that damned paper promising to do so.'

'Will not the Dey take care of us, effendi?'

'D'y'mean pay the charges? Certainly not. Oh, I shall be released at his command—and likely arrested again at once for debt by the concierge, or his officials.' A bleak smile.

'I do not think they will dare to disobey the wishes of the Dey.'

'And I do not think I will dare to celebrate my freedom before it has come, Hamdan.'

But he thought that it would come, he felt that it would, and that he could overturn any difficulty about the concierge's money. He allowed himself another little smile, and asked Hamdan to bring him more coffee.

━━ ☰◈☰ ━━

'Rashid Bey is angry with me,' said Captain Rennie.

'Does his anger bear upon the—upon those chess men, sir?' Alan Dobie was never quite sure how far he might pursue this kind of query with Rennie. The captain was inclined to be peppery, and bristling, upon the mildest interrogation on any subject, even those subjects he had raised himself. Since Dobie had made a fair copy of the letter to the Dey of Tunis, detailing Rennie's proposal about the Crystal Men, and was fully conversant with Rennie's motives, he felt obliged to make sympathetic inquiry. But he quaked in his shoes lest Rennie's response should be hostile, and condemning, and reproachful.

'Hm, well well, I fear that it does. I fear that it does bear on the chess men, Mr Dobie.' A nod.

Dobie felt a little burst of relief in his breast, and made his face pleasantly alert as Rennie continued:

'He had made the gift to me, he said, in a moment of great emotion, in a moment of great affection toward and for me—after all we had endured together, and survived. I had thought he meant to bribe me, you know, into staying at Rabhet, but now I see it was more than that.'

'Surely, sir, he must understand your desire to free Lieutenant Hayter——'

'Ain't a question of Mr Hayter, d'y'see, in Rashid Bey's eyes. It is a question of humiliation at the hands of Suleiman el Hassad.'

'Humiliation?'

'Aye, Mr Dobie. Rashid Bey feels that I had no business allowing those chess men to go out of my possession, when they was coveted by Suleiman el Hassad these many years. Wished for by him beyond measure.' A glance at Dobie, a sniff, and he walked to the stern gallery window, his hands clasped behind.

'But—you was not to know that, sir.'

'Nay, I was not. I did not know it. But a gift of that kind, you know, a gift of such immense value is not bestowed lightly. I was meant to keep it all my life, value it above all things as recognition of the esteem for me and friendship and emotion Rashid Bey had felt as he gave it. In his estimation I have betrayed him.'

'Oh no, sir, surely not betrayed? What is a set of chess men against Mr Hayter's life?'

'In course, that is what I asked myself before I wrote to the Dey, exact. It was a box of crystals that could set free a man I value above all others, and hold dear. That was all the value of the set to me, the value of a man's life.' A sigh. 'Rashid Bey cannot see that. He cannot.'

'Perhaps when he has had time to reflect——'

'No no, he will not reflect. He is angry, and men do not reflect wisely when they are angry. They stir their minds with sharpened dirks, and add bitter potions to the mixture.' Turning from the window. 'Suleiman el Hassad has coveted the Crystal Men since he learned they was here in Rabhet, and has prized them above all Rashid Bey's other treasure. They are unique in all Islam, no other set has been fashioned quite like them since chess came to the region from India a thousand years ago.—No, I will not be forgiven, and not just because I sent the chess men to Suleiman el Hassad . . . but because I sent them in the care of Mr Sebastian.'

'Mr Sebastian took them!' Astonished. 'And said nothing to his master?'

'Rashid Bey ain't Sebastian's master, you know, not quite. No no, Sebastian has another and higher master, that is not in the palace here at Rabhet but in England. He is my master, and yours, Mr Dobie. He is the King, to whom every Englishman owes his allegiance. When I had reminded Sebastian of that, that it was his duty to assist in restoring

Lieutenant Hayter to freedom, well well, he went willing enough.'

Alan Dobie did not perfectly understand the logic behind this, but he did not say so. Instead:

'Are we to depart Rabhet, sir?'

'Eh? Depart?'

'If Rashid Bey is angry and will not forgive you, will not he wish us to go away?'

'No, he will not. He is not so foolish that he will wish to fight Zamoril and his janissaries without our help. We are at the heart of his defence.'

'Then—will Mr Sebastian and Lieutenant Hayter return to Rabhet, sir, when payment of the ransom has been made?'

'That is my hope and wish—and my instruction to Sebastian. He has gone there to Tunis in disguise, and he is to return with Mr Hayter, both of them disguised. Sebastian will not give up the ransom until Mr Hayter has been given up. He goes to the Dey's palace and will offer to remain there until he has had word of the release, at which moment he will convey the location of the hidden Crystal Men to the Dey. Afterward, he and James will meet and steal away from Tunis in the ship that brought Sebastian there, in darkness. It is a most careful and thorough-plotted scheme, and I have every expectation of its success. It is time we had success this commission, when we have had nothing but failure until now.'

'I am sure the plan will succeed, sir.'

'Yes. Yes.' Nodding, gripping the back of a chair. 'In course we may fail overall.' Quietly.

'Fail? Oh, I do not think——'

'If *Rais* Zamoril should attack before Sebastian and James return, then very probably we shall never see them again. The attack, I may tell you, will likely be pressed home very hard. It is not impossible that all of Rashid Bey's ships will be took, sunk, or burned, that *Expedient* will be lost with them, and that Rabhet will fall.'

'Will not *Curlew*——'

Over him, grimly: 'Even if *Curlew* does get through, Mr Dobie, even if a squadron of ships is sent from England, it will almost certainly be too late for *Expedient* and her people—too late to save us. You see?'

━・━ ⚔ ━ ・━

'You are free to go, effendi.'

James roused himself on the divan, and sat up, blinked dazzled in a shaft of sunlight, and saw the concierge leaning over him. Hamdan hovered by the door, holding the coffee pot. As soon as he saw that James was awake, Hamdan came forward, but the concierge blocked his path, hit him on the side of the head with the flat of his hand, and pushed him away.

'Why d'you strike the boy?' James, angrily. He swung his legs to the floor, and stood.

'The boy is not released. The boy must work here, until you have paid to me my charges for the private quarters.'

'Who says this? The Dey?'

'I say it, effendi.' The awful obsequious smile. 'It is only just, when I have been so accommodating to you. No?'

'No, and no. The boy will come with me. I will send the money on to you.'

'Ahh, ahh, but that will not satisfy me, effendi. Unless you can pay me now, then I fear I must summon my men. You will be escorted to the Bagno gate, and the boy will remain.'

'What will be his duties, exact? Hey?' Suspiciously.

'Ahh. Well, he is a pretty boy, very pretty, as of course you have observed. I will give him light duties only, and keep him close by me . . . yes?'

'Christ's blood, what a wretched place!' Half under his breath, then: 'Who brought the message that I was to be released? Is he still here? If he is, I want him to return to the

Dey with the request that the boy be released with me, under my care.'

'Alas, the messenger has gone away . . .' A shrug, a spreading of the hands, that smile.

'Very well, then I suppose I must leave without the boy. But I shall return for him, you mark me?'

'Yes, yes, of course you will come back for him, effendi. He is very pretty.'

'Enough! Do not say that to me again!'

'You are *jaloux*, effendi . . . hhhh-hhhh? Have no fear, I shall not touch him—for now.'

'Yes, and I will run you through, on my honour!' James, under his breath, turning away to pull on his clothes. Aloud: 'Hamdan, never fear, now. I will come back for you. This man will not harm you. He will not dare to do so.' And he gave the concierge a smile in his turn of such stark warning that the man took a step back, and flinched.

'I think that I will ask my men to escort you to the gate, in any case.' His voice shaking a little, either with fear or indignation, or both.

'There is no need of that.' Curtly. 'I have the use of my legs.'

'I wish it for my peace of mind.'

'I doubt any man not a blackguard could find peace of mind, in a place like this. Call them then.'

A few minutes after, as James was turned out of the Grand Bagno gate into the medina proper, he saw a figure detach itself from the knot of people under an awning, emerge from the shadow into the sunlight and become—Mr Sebastian.

'Good God—it is you, then . . .'

'Aye, Lieutenant—it is.'

And he made salaam. James, during his time in the Bagno, had learned and become familiar with certain customs, and now said without thinking '*Allah-o-Akbar*', and himself made salaam. A look of surprise on Sebastian's face was at once replaced by a great-toothed smile.

'You will need feeding up, Lieutenant. The prison has not been kind to your corporeal self.'

James glanced down at himself. 'Perhaps I am a trifle thin, and these rags are not what I would wish to wear longer than I must—but we should not talk of me. There is a poor, half-starved urchin boy in the prison, that I wish to have released. Have you any money?' As Sebastian began moving away across the medina.

'Money? But the ransom has been paid. Word has gone to the palace about the Crystal Men, that was being held for me by a merchant, and they have now been given to the Dey's guards. You are free, entire.' Beckoning to James to follow him. They walked on a little way, and:

'I do not ask for myself. It is the boy concerns me. God knows what will be his fate if he is not released to my care, d'y'see.' James glanced back toward the Bagno gate. Sebastian gestured across the broad medina, at the teeming activity of commerce, and people, and light and shadow, and the sounds of turning wheels and hurrying feet and voices that rose jostling and roiling on the dusty air.

'Look about you, Lieutenant. You are *free*. And now we cannot waste time. We must make our way to the harbour.'

'You have a ship?'

'A ship of sorts. A small trading felucca, nothing to be remarked. Part of the bargain is that we must slip away discreet.'

'You mean that I cannot return for the boy?'

Sebastian now seized James, seized him by the shoulders and thrust him under the shadow of an awning. 'You do not quite understand, I think. This has been a debt of ransom, honourably paid. You are free, and we can now make our way to our ship, and be gone. However—' looking directly into James's face, into his eyes '—however, if we do not go away at once, out of Tunis, that will be a very foolish risk.'

'You said that the debt had been honourably paid. What of my own debt—to that boy? Must I not pay that, honourably?

Have not you even a few coins about you? It will not take a moment for me to cut back across the square to the gate, and pay for the boy's freedom . . .'

Sebastian tightened his grip. 'I will say this once more, and then be silent. You must come with me now, direct to the ship, and we will then make sail. We must be gone from here within the hour.'

'Else . . . ?'

'For the love of Allah! We are attached to Rashid Bey, that is the enemy of the Dey! Should we delay a moment longer than is thought fitting, our ship will be seized, we shall be taken, and we shall lose our heads! I am fond of my head, you know, Lieutenant. I am very much attached to it. I hope that you are fond enough of your own to allow it to reason with you. Yes?'

'I cannot simply abandon——'

'Look! Is that not the boy there!' Pointing. James looked, and was at once struck a stunning blow, lifted senseless on broad shoulders, and carried bodily away through the alleys toward the harbour and the waiting ship.

—◦—◦═◊═◦—◦—

'I am in two minds, Mr Storey.'

'I fancy red will be the more easily seen, sir, at a distance.'

'You think that, do you? Red? Hm. Hm.' Putting a hand to the back of his neck, Rennie frowned at his gunner, turned away briefly and stared across the harbour, then:

'I had thought blue—but I have changed my mind. Red will be seen better in daylight. Red, or blue—at night—would answer equally well. But blue during the hours of daylight will not show near so distinct. Red then, Mr Storey, if y'please.'

'Very good, sir.' The gunner went below to begin making a batch of rockets, to burst red on the sky as soon as the enemy fleet was sighted.

Rennie had pondered a system of flag signals to be relayed overland along the coast, from lookout points to the north. But after initial experiment he had found that the signals could not be seen quite so clearly as he had hoped, and he had decided to replace flags with rockets.

'Mr Makepeace!'

Tom Makepeace came from the waist, where he had been inspecting the starboard battery, to make sure that lead aprons had been placed over all flintlocks. As acting first lieutenant he was in undress coat, and sweating. He removed his hat as he came up the ladder.

'Sir?'

'Good heaven, Tom, are ye in your coat?'

'I am hot, sir, I will admit.'

'Then throw it off, by all means. And your waistcoat, too. We must not be stiff and formal and over-correct, in this heat.'

'Thank you, sir.' And he removed his coat and waistcoat with relief.

'Mark you, I do not altogether approve of Mr Hayter's notions of dress for officers, that he is pleased to call his "working clothes". I hope you will not think of following his example.'

'When do you expect Lieutenant Hayter, sir?'

'Daily, hourly, at any time.' Gesturing away to the north, beyond the harbour wall. 'He is there somewhere, at sea, he and Sebastian together. May God protect them and their ship.'

'Indeed, sir.' With feeling.

'May they come through safe, evading that devil Zamoril.' Another glance to the north. 'Now then—red.'

'Sir?'

'I have decided that we are to have red rockets, not blue. Mr Storey is assembling them. Just as soon as he has them ready, you are to despatch them to the lookout posts to the north, by the horsemen that wait ashore. The arranged signal is by a flash of my looking glass, from the quarterdeck. As soon as that is seen a boat will be sent to the ship, and the rockets are to be put into the boat at once.'

'Should I take them ashore myself, sir?'

'No no, send one of the mids. Mr Cutforth. You are to remain aboard, Mr Makepeace, while I go ashore to inform the Regent about the rockets.'

'Very good, sir.'

'To send a message will not suffice. He is a man who insists on the correct form of things. He will like to hear it direct from me.'

'Very good, sir.'

'All our guns are double-shotted?'

'Aye, sir.'

'Full allowance?'

'Full allowance, sir.'

'Very well. The ship is yours, Mr Makepeace.'

'Aye, sir. May I ask . . .'

'Well?'

'May I ask how long you will remain ashore, sir?'

'It may probably be some time, I think. Rashid Bey does not like to be consulted, nor informed, in haste. He is angry with me about the ransom I sent to free Mr Hayter, and will likely keep me waiting for an audience, then insist on going to the *hammam*, and so forth.'

'Yes, sir. It has occurred to me that if you was ashore after the rockets had been despatched to the north, and then Mr Hayter's ship was sighted—is there any means of recognition, so that his ship ain't mistook for an enemy vessel?'

'Aye, there is such means. I gave Mr Sebastian instruction to hang a fishing net from the beak, as far forrard as may be possible, trailing in the water.'

'Very good, sir.' A smiling nod. Rennie was very adept at such invention. A fishing net was such a commonplace thing, yet hung in this way it became the equivalent of colours. 'Oh, forgive me, sir—one last thing . . .'

'Yes, what is it?' Growing impatient.

'It has just entered my mind, sir. If you was still ashore and the rockets was fired—to warn of the approach of Zamoril's fleet—am I to wait for you, sir, or put to sea?'

'You are to weigh, make sail, put to sea without the loss of a moment, and leave me behind. You know the stratagem I wish to employ, Tom. You are to follow it just as we have discussed. Stand off, then attack Zamoril from the east—you should have the wind gage if the wind comes steady from the east. Attack him as he attacks the harbour.'

'Very good, sir.'

And Rennie ran down the side ladder into his gig, and went ashore.

The felucca ran south, in a light easterly wind. Like most lateen-rigged vessels she was able to run closer to the wind by a point or two than a square-rigged ship, by balancing the trapezoidal sails, with the yards to leeward on the short single-spar masts, and run a little faster. In these conditions, with the wind on her beam, there was no great advantage. In fact, as James quickly came to realize when the wind freshened, the ship was inclined to fractiousness, and had constantly to be managed, and brought true, and made obedient in direction.

'Let us hope that we do not fall foul of corsairs on our way south,' Mr Sebastian said, when James drew his attention to these shortcomings.

'Surely *Rais* Zamoril will leave us alone, when the ransom has been paid?' James felt his jaw where Mr Sebastian's fist had made contact, and he tried not to think of abandoned Hamdan.

'Zamoril ain't the only corsair in these waters, though. As we have discovered before this.'

'We ain't such a prize for any corsair.' James glanced

forrard from where they stood on the raised, steep quarterdeck, abaft the short mizzenmast. A knot of seamen stood in
the waist, ready to swarm up the main lateen yard and take in
a reef. The long flat-steeved bowsprit jutting from the
beakhead seemed naked to James, lacking a headsail as it was.

'We are a ship, a lone ship, and any corsair will likely
assume that we carry cargo, and passengers. We are
unarmed.'

'Hell and fire, then we must crack on.' Pacing nervously
from weather rail to lee, and peering critically at the great
curved leeches of the sails. 'If only we had gaffs and booms,
or in least a headsail, with the foot loose on the sheet, we
should be a great deal abler to keep her true.'

'Ah. Yes. Should we?' Sebastian nodded, wishing to agree,
but only half-comprehending what he was agreeing with.
Despite his own time in corsair ships, he was no seaman.

Presently a ship was sighted to the east, standing well off
and making south. The felucca had more or less clung to the
coast on the journey south, so close in to the ochre hills and
sandy shore that James had at times feared they might be
driven in upon it, should the wind again increase. Lacking a
glass he could not hope to identify the ship from the tiny
quarterdeck of the felucca, and he decided to swarm up the
mainsail yard, just as he had seen the felucca's people climb,
and try to observe the other ship from as far aloft as he was
able to go.

He went forrard into the waist, and forrard again to the
block securing the yard on the lee, clapped on, hands and
feet, and begun to jump up the yard. Mr Sebastian watched
him, fascinated. It never ceased to surprise him how other
men in ships could jump, leap, cling, and climb almost
anywhere, up any mast, any form of rigging, without
hesitation or fear. His great bulk closed any such activity to
him, and now, in wondering admiration:

'He is a monkey. A leaping nimble Africk monkey . . .'

James did not pause until he had reached the highest band

of the yard, beyond which the knobbed cap rode against the sky. He lifted his chest off the yard, clinging with his legs athwart, and looked to the east, shading his eyes, his hair whipping about his head in the wind. And there was the ship, two leagues off, clearer from this height. He saw that she was a single-masted vessel—a cutter. She was altering course.

'By God . . . it is *Curlew*.' An astonished murmur. He looked again to make sure, shading his eyes. Then filled his lungs and bellowed:

'D-e-e-e-ck, there! Mr Sebastian! She is *Curlew*! *Curlew*!'

He came slithering down the yard, and jumped aft, to the consternation of the felucca's master, a frowning wizened man who had begun to wonder whether or not he was still in command.

Sebastian met James as he jumped up to the quarterdeck from the waist. 'You are certain she is *Curlew*?'

'As nearly certain as I can be without my glass. She has altered course, and I think she will like to speak.'

'This is very strange, you know.' Gravely, taking James's arm and turning aft.

'Eh?'

'When we returned to Rabhet in *Expedient*, after the loss of Rashid Bey's ship, *Curlew* was already there, and Captain Rennie sent her away to England under my nephew's command.'

'Lieutenant Bradshaw? Not Lieutenant Makepeace?'

'Dutt Bradshaw took her, and set sail for England. Why then is he sailing south? Why is he not far to the north of us, sailing west across the Mediterranean toward Gibraltar?'

'Perhaps he has suffered damage, and is returning to Rabhet to repair . . . or wait, perhaps . . .'

They looked at each other, the same thought coming into their heads.

'She has been took!' James. 'Aye, she has been took by corsairs, and is now herself a corsair ship!'

The master of the felucca now came aft and began to speak

to Mr Sebastian in Arabic, in great agitation, volubly and at length, with gestures in turn imploring and assertive. Sebastian listened, and turning to James:

'He is anxious to know who is in command. He wishes to know this because he does not know how to behave toward you, when you are constantly dashing about his ship, going aloft, shouting and disturbing his crew. Accordingly, he will like——'

James, over him, with authority: 'Y'may say to him that I am taking command, Mr Sebastian. Say that he will be handsome rewarded when we reach Rabhet, but that from this moment he is to take his orders from me, and convey them to his people. D'y'have me?'

'Is this wise, d'y'think, Lieutenant——'

'Mr Sebastian, we have not time to argue and debate. We cannot outrun *Curlew* in this slow-sailing ship. We must therefore make a stratagem to outwit the villains that have seized her.'

Mr Sebastian put his head dubiously on one side, dubiously assented, and conveyed James's decision to the master, who regarded James with puzzled consternation, not to say alarm. James gave him what he hoped was a reassuring smile and an encouraging nod, and:

'Mr Sebastian, I wish you to ask him this: has he a black flag aboard, or a plain black garment of any kind?'

This inquiry was duly put to the puzzled master, who grew more puzzled still, and glanced at James with a rolling eye— as if James might be quite irretrievably mad, and about to bring the ship to irretrievable calamity. His reply to Mr Sebastian was even more voluble than his first troubled query, and Sebastian translated it:

'He has no such costume nor flag, and begs you to allow him run in close to shore, if we fear the other ship is a corsair. He knows these waters well, and the coastline, and he believes it best to run in there and——'

'No. No.' James shook his head firmly. 'I mean to stand

away, to stand off. Ask him again, has he any kind of black
cloth at all in the ship, in his stores—an awning will answer.
Cheerly now, I must have it right quick.'

'May I ask——'

'Then he is to order one of his men to double himself over
the waist, to hang right down over the side, dressed in white,
as if he had collapsed there and died. Better still, two men.
Aye, two.'

Sebastian dutifully translated, and the master shrugged and
in turn gave a series of orders in Arabic. James glanced aloft,
and forrard, and peered again at the advancing *Curlew*—still
some distance to the east. The black awning was now brought
on deck, rather torn and tattered, but roughly approximate in
shape and size to a large black flag.

'Mr Sebastian!'

'Yes, Lieutenant?' Joining him at the weather rail.

'The awning is to be run up to the head of the mizzen yard,
and fixed there. The two men are to prostrate themselves
over the side—dressed in white, mind, so they are plainly
discernible—and every man in the ship is to set up a cry, as
Curlew approaches.'

'A cry . . .?'

'Indeed, a cry. It is this: "*La fièvre! La fièvre! La fièvre!*" And
as they cry out thus they are to wave their arms as vigorous as
they are able.—You begin to see?'

Sebastian smiled, shook his great head, then laughed aloud:
'I do see, Lieutenant, I do.' And he conveyed this instruction
to the master, and assured James that the master understood.

Soon all was in place. The black awning hung from the
mizzen, the two men in white hung down over the side in
plain view, and the rest of the crew set up the cry of fever, and
began waving and flapping their arms as if in distress.

As *Curlew* approached, James gave his final instruction:

'The master is to allow his main yard to fall to the deck,
very clumsy, and allow his ship to begin to drift, as if helpless.'

Mr Sebastian translated, then:

'Lieutenant . . . ?'

'Well?'

'I am obliged to ask—supposing they do not believe your deception? Supposing they are not persuaded that we carry plague? What then?'

'Then we shall be blown to pieces, Mr Sebastian, I am in no doubt.'

PART SEVEN: ACTION

The rocket was fired in error, early in the morning of the day following. *Rais* Zamoril's fleet had not been sighted by the lookout high on the eminence to the north of the city. The lookout, a young man anxious to be proficient whenever the sighting should be made, had risen early and begun to practise with his tinderbox. He had practised too assiduously, the touchpaper on one of the rockets prepared by Mr Storey had ignited, and the rocket had soared into the sky, trailing smoke and sparks. It exploded in red flashes high on the morning air.

The reaction, at Rabhet, was immediate. Defences were hastily manned, cannon run out on wall and battlement, and the ships of Rashid Bey's fleet bustled into life in the harbour. Captain Rennie, who had returned to *Expedient* from the palace late at night, was roused at once from sleep, and came on deck bleary and unshaven in his nightshirt.

'You are certain, Mr Makepeace?'

'There can be no doubt, sir.' Lieutenant Makepeace had the deck. Full watches were being kept in anticipation of a call to action at any time. 'A red rocket to the north, very clear on the sky.'

'Lookout, there!' Rennie's voice, not yet lubricated to full strength by tea, was a rasping croak. He cleared his throat, and took hold of the speaking trumpet the lieutenant held out to him, and bellowed to the lookout in the main crosstrees:

'*Lookout there! Do you see any sails of ships!*'

'Noooo, sir! No ships to the north, nor eeeast, nor sooouth!' Echoing down, and the sound of that echo washed round the harbour wall.

'*Keep a sharp eye, d'y'hear me?*'

'Aye, sir!'

Rennie handed the trumpet back to Lieutenant Make- peace, strode to the rail and looked across at Rashid Bey's small fleet of ships.

'Very well, Mr Makepeace, we will prepare to leave harbour and put to sea. We must assume the damned fleet is there, standing away to the north, else the rocket would not have been fired. *Rais* Ahmed el Ali knows what to do, and I must leave him here to do it.—Cutton! Colley Cutton, where are you! Tea!'

In half a glass *Expedient* had weighed, had bent topsails and courses—yards braced to harness the breeze—and was putting to sea, when a horseman flew down from the hills to the north, galloping in a line of dust, and reached the fort. A minute after, the fort fired one of its heavy cannon, a boat put off from the shore, and news of the mistake was brought to the fleet, and signalled to *Expedient*.

The ship returned to the harbour, and to her mooring.

'I confess I am a little relieved, Mr Makepeace.' Rennie, newly shaven, and refreshed by a quart of tea. 'I want Mr Hayter back safe with us in the ship, before we are obliged to come to action.'

'Indeed, sir.' Tom Makepeace smiled briefly and politely.

'Oh—oh—I did not mean that you was not fully capable as my acting first, Tom. That you would not serve admirable well. No, no, I meant only that Mr Hayter's rightful place is here with us. Hey?'

'Indeed, sir. *Expedient* is the poorer without him.'

An agitated Lieutenant Quill now came on deck and asked permission to speak to the captain.

'Yes, Mr Quill?'

'Some of the Chatham marines are missing, sir.'

'Missing? Why was not I told?'

'It was not noticed until now, sir, in all the haste to leave harbour. Sergeant Host——'

'Well?'

'Sergeant Host was bound hand and foot, sir, and locked in the breadroom.'

'Good God. Where is he now? Why has he not come with you, Mr Quill, to make his report?'

'Dr Wing is tending to him below, sir. He has an injury to his head.'

'Christ's blood, is there no end to the failures and stupidities of this commission!'

'He was struck a blow that left him senseless. He is not yet himself, sir.' Stiffly.

'Yes yes, I did not mean to blame Sergeant Host—nor you, Mr Quill. Is there a boat gone, has a boat been took?—*Mr Tangible!*'

No boat was missing from *Expedient*, but presently a report came that a small boat was missing from the wharf.

'They likely slipped clear of the harbour in darkness, sir. A small boat might do that easy enough, undetected.' Roman Tangible, touching his hat.

'Yes, very well, Mr Tangible. Thank you.' Looking toward the harbour entrance, and the two barques guarding it. 'Well well, they cannot go far, I think.' A moment, then: 'Had the boat stepping and sails, or merely sweeps?'

'That I do not know, sir.'

'Then we had better discover it, Mr Tangible, right quick. If they was able to bend canvas, that would give them a great advantage of distance achieved before daylight.'

'I don't know those marines is right seamen, sir. I don't know as they could work sails——'

'They stole a boat, Mr Tangible, and escaped undetected from a heavy-defended harbour. They are clearly resourceful, and determined.' A sniff. 'But they will hang, certainly they will hang.' He lifted his head, and clasped his hands

behind him—and remembered that some little time since
Alan Dobie had warned him—having first alerted James
Hayter, who had conveyed the information—that a party of
marines might attempt to escape. He went below, summoned
his clerk, and questioned him closely.

'What had ye heard recent?'

'I had heard nothing more of the scheme, sir. Nothing
after the whispered conversation that I described to Lieutenant Hayter, and then to you, sir.'

'They did not—in that conversation you heard—mention
any direction they might sail?'

'No, sir.'

'Nor that they might expect help from the shore?'

'From the shore?'

'Yes yes, from men on the wharf, Arab men.'

'I heard nothing of that, sir. Only that they meant to steal
a boat, and go into *Curlew*.'

'Well well, they have stole a boat, but not from *Expedient*,
thank God, when we have already lost our launch. And
Curlew has gone away, so they cannot be in her.'

'Will they get very far, d'you think?'

'Don't know.' A sniff. 'No, I shouldn't think they will, Mr
Dobie. If they are not took by corsairs, and sold into slavery,
or their throats cut—they will likely perish at sea. Failing
that, they will come limping back to Rabhet, in the hope that
I will show them mercy. I will not.'

'They have been very misdirected in their actions——'

'Misdirected! They are mutinous dogs, that will be
hanged!'

'I should not like to think that I have informed on men—
that will be hanged.'

'Ye've done nothing you need feel ashamed in, Mr Dobie.
You did your duty, you did right.'

'I cannot be easy in my mind—as executioner.'

'Mr Dobie.' Looking at him gravely. 'Think now, will you?
Had you not informed on them, had you said nothing at all,

would their circumstances be at all altered? They have run away in a stolen boat. They are deserters and mutineers. Whether or no you had spoke, they would hang. You see?'

'It—don't sit right with me, Captain Rennie, all the same.'

'Well well, you are not properly a hardened seaman, in course. You are a man of books, and thoughts, and so forth. I do not mean to be disparaging of you, but you do not see things in quite the way the navy does, hey? There is no fault in that, for a man of your temperament and position. In a way it is admirable that you harbour such fellow feeling, even when men are villains and dogs.'

'Thank you, sir.'

'I am not an unfeeling man myself. There is much in the world that is—unfortunate. However, I cannot allow anomaly and doubt to inform my conscience. And in this case, of these damned deserting marines, I am in no doubt at all: they are condemned by their actions.'

Alan Dobie said nothing.

'We will attempt to make order of the ship's books, Mr Dobie, now that we are again idle. You have pen and paper? Let us sit down, and begin.'

And relieved of the burden of examining their souls, the two very different men set to work.

All but three of the fleeing marines came back by chance to Rabhet with Lieutenant Hayter and Mr Sebastian in their felucca. The stolen boat, limping and half-swamped, had lost mast and sail in a squall, and the marines' meagre provisions had spoiled. Three of them had drowned. The wallowing craft was nearly run down by the felucca at first light, in chopping seas. James had willingly taken in the surviving men, and had only then recognized some of them as marines from *Expedient*. Upon being questioned they admitted everything. Because they were in a very low condition James knew that they were not minded to try to wrest control of the felucca from his command. They were aware that in returning to Rabhet they faced inevitable punishment, severe punishment, but appeared to accept their fate, grateful as they were to be safe, and dry, and fed.

James questioned the most senior among them, a Corporal Henning, more closely than the others, at the lee rail on the narrow quarterdeck.

'What was you thinking of, a non-commissioned officer, attempting to cross the sea in an open boat? Why did you desert the ship?'

'We did not wish to fight them barbarians no more. We feared we would never see England again, sir.'

'But good heaven, you are Royal Marines. You are fighting men that have took the King's shilling and sworn to defend him. And you was well treated in *Expedient*.'

'None of us was ever attached to a ship before, sir. We never even knew each other, took as we was from various companies at Chatham, in ones and twos. Aye, we expected to go into ships, but we did not bargain on serving foreign devils in foreign ports, and fighting heathen barbarians afar from home.'

'But you knew when you took your oath that you would likely be sent abroad, to the West Indies, or Gibraltar, or to the East. You knew it, and signed on willing.'

'We never reckoned on no barbarian foe, no demon corsairs, that will cut a man's throat and eat his liver.' Sullenly.

'If you feared that fate, then why did y'set sail in an open boat in corsair-infested waters, y'damn fool? Hey?' A sigh. 'Very well, Corporal, you are much cast down and exhausted, and your spirit is broke, so I will not chastise you any more.'

'Thank you, sir.'

'Nay, you will not thank me when we approach Rabhet. Captain Rennie will not be kind to you.'

'We knows that, sir. Only . . .'

'Yes?' Impatiently, clapping on to a stay to steady himself as the felucca pitched through a steep swell.

'Since you has rescued us—might I ask that you speak in our behalf, sir?'

'I cannot do that, you know. You had better ask Lieutenant Quill.'

'He ain't our officer, properly. We has no officer, only Sergeant Host.'

'Then you had better throw yourself on the sergeant's mercy, had not you?'

'I fear—we cannot do that, sir.'

'Oh?'

The corporal described what had been done to Sergeant Host.

'Ah.' A grim nod.

At noon the felucca came within sight of Rabhet, and according to Rennie's instruction a fishing net was hung from the beak. The felucca was recognized and signalled by the fort to stand in and enter the harbour. Soon she glided in, and dropped anchor.

Rennie was greatly pleased and relieved to see his first lieutenant safe at last, although he noted James's ragged and nearly gaunt appearance after his time in the Bagno, an appearance Rennie did not, however, remark. He sought to be kind, and welcoming, and glad-faced—in the slightly effortful and laboured way those that have not suffered tend to greet those that have. The two men shook hands warmly, Rennie pumping and wringing James's hand, and smiling heartily. Beyond, the marine prisoners filed head-down into the waist.

Rennie took James—and Mr Sebastian—below to the great cabin. Wine was quickly brought, and opened.

'You did not sight Zamoril's fleet?' Rennie glanced from one to the other. James answered:

'No, sir. We had brief sight of *Curlew*, that had fallen into corsair hands.' And he described their encounter with the cutter, concluding his account: 'And when they saw the two men hanging over the side, that did convince them, and *Curlew* sheered off and ran.'

'You—you do not know the fate of Lieutenant Bradshaw, I expect?'

'No, sir.'

Mr Sebastian was silent, looking down at the decking, and Rennie said with a sigh:

'Then I fear he may be lost to us, and all the poor devils with him. Not to mention *Curlew* herself, and her mission. I am very sorry you have lost your cousin, Mr Sebastian.'

'He may perhaps have survived. He may be held to ransom.' Lifting his head a little.

'Indeed, indeed, we must hope that he has survived, as you say. Hm. Y'did well to deceive those corsairs, James, and escape their ferocious intent. I will like to hear a thorough account of all your experiences, including your estimation of Zamoril as an opponent—when you are recovered from your ordeal. You are the only one of us that has met with him face to face. I will deal with those wretches of marines in due course, that you brought back with you.'

'I am able to give a full account now, sir, if you wish. I am quite recovered from the Bagno. The sea air on the journey south has revived me.—I—I wished to say at once how grateful I am to you for paying the ransom——'

'No no, a small price.' Rennie held up a hand.

'Five thousand pound ain't small, though——'

'No. No.' Rennie shook his head. 'It was not specie, in any case, but merely a few trinkets that had come to me by chance. We will not speak of it again, if y'please, James. You are returned to *Expedient*, where ye belong. That is my reward, that I wished for with all my heart.' He now looked down a moment, swallowed, and cleared his throat. 'Hm.'

'Very good, sir.'

Rennie lifted his head again, and made a great show of smiling, and banging the table with the flat of his hand.

'Good. Just so. Well well, here we find ourselves, James, at

Rabhet. In a damned vexing fix, too. You will not like the fix we are in, James, when I tell it to you. You may wish you had not come back. Eh, Mr Sebastian?'

'I took the liberty of explication, when we was at sea,' said Sebastian now. 'I think Lieutenant Hayter is possessed of all the facts.'

'And I am not down-hearted, sir, in the smallest particular. I had far rather be here, in a fighting ship, with my sword and a brace of pistols, and eighteen-pounder guns, than sitting on my arse in a hellish damned festering slave prison. Let Zamoril do his worst. We have in least a good fighting chance.'

'Well said, James. We are of one mind. A glass of wine, and then I will like to hear your report.'

Rennie lifted his glass, and was about to drink when:

'*Red rockets to the nooorth! Rockets on the sky!*'

In great haste *Expedient* weighed and put to sea, and cleared for action; this time there could be no mistake about the rockets. Now Rennie saw to his dismay that *Rais* Zamoril— had not only confounded him by not attacking at night, and not landing shore parties from the north to circle behind the city, then running in close with his main force of ships to bombard the harbour and defences, but had landed no men at all, and had instead approached in two large but separate squadrons, in full daylight. The first squadron came from the north, hugging the coast, and the second came direct from the east. James jumped aloft to the main crosstrees, swept the sea with his glass, assessed the positions and numbers of ships, and slid to the deck by a back stay. He reported all he had seen, and Rennie:

'We must run wide to the south-east in a long sweep, continue until we are clear, then run in from due east, behind the second squadron.'

James looked closely at his captain, attempting to judge his mood, and ventured: 'By then, sir—by then, will not both corsair squadrons have run in and took Rabhet?'

'Nay, James, do not be down-hearted. All the defences was planned long since. Men are in the fort, and along the west walls of the city. Large numbers of armed men, and heavy guns.'

'Very good, sir.'

'I thought that certainly he would attack at night—but no matter. We are well prepared.'

'Yes, sir, I am in no doubt. However . . . however . . .'

'Well?' Turning to face James on the quarterdeck.

'I do not perfectly understand, I confess, the defence of the west walls of the city—when the assault will surely come from the north and the east.'

Rennie drew breath, then did not reply. He paced aft to the taffrail and stood there alone. He was further dismayed when the lookouts bawled down that the squadron to the east was forming into a long crescent, the ships sailing side by side westward, and not in line ahead. This effectively destroyed Rennie's tactic of running in a sweep to the south-east. If he attempted that now he would be caught, surrounded, raked and smashed.

The truth of this predicament flooded in upon Rennie, swirled invisibly about his head, and for a time he was thoroughly bemused. He ordered the ship to lose way, and for half a glass he stood motionless at the taffrail. Lookouts bellowed the positions of Zamoril's ships to the deck, and the eastern squadron came nearer and nearer in a long fanning line. *Expedient* lay with her topsails aback, the picture of indecision, rolling on the slow swell.

James had again jumped aloft, this time into the mizzen crosstrees, and after half a glass came sliding down a back stay to the deck. 'Sir, surely we must now go straight at them? Straight at them, and attempt to break through?'

Rennie shook his head, sniffed in a deep breath, and:

'We will run due south. Mr Loftus! Mr Tangible!'

And the captain issued his orders in a sharp, crisp, concise fashion, hands clasped behind him, and his hat firmly athwart his head. *Expedient* braced her yards, sheeted home, and ran south, and south, and then swiftly came about—it was very handsome done—and tacked diagonally north-east, to intercept the crescent of corsair ships at an acute, piercing angle.

'Mr Hayter!'

The first lieutenant came jumping up to the quarterdeck from overseeing the batteries on the main deck, having shifted into his working clothes.

'James, ye've heard of Captain Douglas? Sir Charles Douglas, that was Rodney's First Captain in *Formidable* at the Saints?'

'I have heard of him, sir . . .' Puzzled, a little.

'Just so. He invented a scheme for breeching ropes that enabled his great guns to be fired through ninety degrees of angle——'

'So that is what those wider-spaced tackle rings is about, on the gundeck!'

'Aye, with the sprung breeching ropes. I decided to employ Douglas's scheme in *Expedient*, as near as we was able at short notice. And in course I had meant to inform you, but there was no time before this.—*Mr Storey! Mr Storey!* Where is my gunner when I want him!'

'I think he is below, sir, in the forrard magazine.'

'You there, boy, find the gunner below and tell him I want him right quick. Jump now!'

The boy dashed down the ladder into the waist, and soon afterward Mr Storey appeared in his leather apron, direct from the filling room, where he had been supervising the making of cartridges. Rennie asked him to explain Captain Douglas's methods in greater detail to James, but almost as soon as the gunner had begun, Rennie interrupted him with a question, to which Mr Storey replied, with a barely suppressed sigh:

'Aye, sir, all cartridge I am making is flannel-cased—as we has discussed on more than one occasion, I b'lieve.'

'Just so, Mr Storey.' Glancing away over the rail. 'Just so. I wished to be reassured that we are entirely prepared, entirely ready. Goose-quill priming tubes, fine grain mixed with spirits of wine, and flannel cartridge. Hey?'

'Everything is just as we has discussed it, sir, to your requirement. According to Captain Douglas of *Formidable*— at the Saints.'

'Indeed, Mr Storey. We was not shipmates then, but I was at the Saints, you know, and saw things for myself.'

'As you say, sir.' Wiping his hands with a piece of cotton waste and raising his eyebrows; clearly he wished to return to his filling room.

'Very good, Mr Storey. Thank you. Just go with Mr Storey, James, will you? He will tell you all the detail, and so forth, as you return to your duties.' He gave a nod of dismissal, stepped aft and looked aloft, and:

'Mr Loftus!'

Bernard Loftus had the conn, and now came from the binnacle. 'Sir?'

'We will cut through them without losing way. I will not like the loss of a single knot of speed. We will cut through, firing broadsides larboard and starboard, and never give the blackguards time for a clear shot at us as we fly along. You have me?'

'Aye, sir.'

'Very good.—Yes, Cutton, what is it?' Impatiently, as Colley Cutton's head appeared at the companion way.

'I cannot find Dulcie, sir. In usual when we clears for action she stays by me, but I ain't seen her at all today.'

'What? Not today? Do not cringe there half-hid, like a timid rat. Come on deck.'

Cutton emerged. 'I seen her last evening, sir, laying in your cot, but never since. I laid out her food, like always. It has not been ate. She has vanished.'

'Well well, that is damned nonsense, Colley Cutton. She is in the ship. You must look for her, and discover her.—You was not unkind to her?' Severely, a penetrating glance.

'I am aggrieved you should think that of me, sir, when I am as fond of Dulcie as yourself.'

'Do not be insolent. Go below and send word to me as soon as she is found, d'y'hear?'

'Aye, sir.'

'Mr Hayter!' Stepping toward the breast rail.

'Sir?' James again came up the ladder from the waist.

'Those damned wretches of deserting marines, that you brought back with you in the felucca . . .'

'Aye, sir?'

'I believe we may need them on deck. We shall need them as guncrew.'

'I am glad. I was going to suggest it myself, sir.'

'Very good. Say to the master-at-arms that I wish them released immediate. With this proviso: should any of them attempt again to escape, or shirk their duty in any way, they will be hanged from the fore yard at noon on the morrow.'

'Very good, sir.'

The ship's boats were already towing, and now *sauve-tête* netting was rigged over the waist as the deserter marines— released from the orlop—came blinking on deck, and with quick rope's-end encouragement from the bosun's mate took their places at quarters.

'Hold her steady, hold her just so.' Mr Loftus, by the wheel, the anchor buttons of his coat gleaming and winking in the sun as he turned one way, turned the other, and stared critically aloft at his canvas. The helmsman, feeling the ship swim under his hands, made small adjustments of direction to his living charge, half a spoke at a time, and kept her true.

The wind, moderately brisk, came now from the south-east on *Expedient*'s starboard beam and quarter as she ran nor'east at four points large toward the crescent of Zamoril's

squadron, which ran steadily due west. Zamoril's ship, a large
xebec, was the centre of the crescent. James counted off the
ships in his glass: eighteen. Three xebecs—including
Zamoril's—of three masts, the foremasts fore-angled and
lateen-rigged, the main and mizzen square, fast and well-
armed ships of twenty guns; four brigantines, small, low,
lateen-rigged ships, lightly armed, with many sweeps to aid
speed in action; five feluccas, with large square fore-and-aft
mainsails, each vessel packed to the gunnels with janissaries;
two galleots; and four lateen-rigged barques of ten guns each,
and sixty janissaries. It was a formidable fleet for one ship to
engage, even an oak-built English frigate of thirty-six guns—
a weatherly, well-handled, stout sea boat.

'We will need everything of luck, in addition to all of our
skill and courage,' said James, but not aloud. Captain Rennie,
as if reading his lieutenant's thoughts:

'The odds as may be are against us today, Mr Hayter. But
odds do not count against one of His Majesty's fighting ships,
they do not signify against our seamanship, and our gunnery,
when we mean to prevail.' Loudly enough for the afterguard
to hear, and the carronade crews, and the helmsman. Loudly
enough to stiffen backs, and lift hearts, and put the villain
Death firm in his place.

The creaking of yards and tiller ropes, of parrals and cleated
lines, and the frothing rush of the sea along the wales, to swirl
and fold away astern in the long straight line of the wake. And
on deck an anxious, breath-holding quiet now, across the
forecastle, over the waist and along the quarterdeck—as men
waited, and waited, and tried to think of nothing but their
tasks, their immediate duties, factual and deliberate things
that held them fast, and steadfast.

James had twice inspected all gun sections, reported all
ready to Rennie, and now stood with his glass at the weather
rail, abaft the mizzen. His own guts churned within him, and
he had to fight off a wave of dizziness—legacy of his time in

the Bagno. He heard Rennie speak:

'Again, Mr Hayter, tell me how many they are, will you?' The captain stood square, facing forrard, his hands behind his back, his glass under one arm, a picture of calm confidence.

James lifted his glass again. 'The count is eighteen, sir. The nearest are a galleot, light-armed, a barque of ten guns, and a xebec of twenty. *Rais* Zamoril's ship is at the heart of the crescent of ships, the heart of the squadron. I saw his red hat amidships a moment or two since, and then again on his quarterdeck.'

'Very well, thank you. We will not mind the galleot, I think.' Looking at the squadron through his own glass. 'No, we must run between the barque and the xebec, and smash them both with broadsides, larboard and starboard, fired near simultaneous. All guns are double-shotted?'

'As ordered, sir.'

'Full allowance?'

'As ordered.'

'Indeed, just so. As soon as we have smashed the barque and the xebec both, by running direct between, we will tack east through the wind, reload, and come at Zamoril's xebec from windward, straight at him *bang* before he has the chance to make his move. We shall have the wind gage, and the advantage of superior weight of metal. I do not think he will have above nine-pounders in his ship. Even if he has twelves, that is 120 pound in his broadside to our 468 double-shotted. With our carronades, we have got above 600 pound to throw at him. His ship is lighter built, too. We will make him suffer, Mr Hayter! We will make him fear us, by God, and curse the day he provoked an action with the Royal Navy!' This last very loud and defiant, and James—playing his part—responded:

'Very good, sir! Let us smash them, larboard and starboard! Smash them to splinters!'

The distance between the attacking ship and the crescent narrowed, and narrowed, but there was no sign from any of Zamoril's ships that *Expedient* had been seen. They meant to ignore her.

*

Expedient closed with the outermost larboard ship of the crescent, sailing directly at her. At the last moment the xebec was obliged to tack to larboard to avoid a collision, and as she did so, *Expedient* passed between her and the barque.

James lifted his speaking trumpet and:

'*Starboard battery, fire as they bear!*'

BANG BANG   BANG-BANG   BANG BANG BANG-BANG

The eighteen-pounders.

THUD   THUD   THUD   THUD-THUD

The carronades.

Expedient shook from rabbet to sternpost with the tremendous shuddering concussions of her guns, and her decks and side were lost in dense expanding clouds of smoke.

A moment of rippling quiet, and *Expedient* bore down on the barque, running away from great wafts of smoke that swirled aft of her. The barque's captain, his astonished face clear to Rennie in his glass, shrieked an order, and his ship veered hard to starboard. At that moment:

'*Larboard battery . . . Fire! Fire! Fire!*'

BANG-BANG-BANG   THUD-BANG   THUD-BANG   BANG-BANG-BANG

'*Stand by to go about! Reload your guns!*'

The xebec, in attempting to defend herself, had fired her guns, but in the din of *Expedient*'s assault their noise had been deadened, and their effect was similar. None of the xebec's roundshot had hit *Expedient*. Most of *Expedient*'s shot, however, had found its mark. The xebec lay listing, crippled and dismasted, her sails and rigging trailing over the side, and the torn bodies of men.

The barque, *Expedient*'s second target, had never had a

chance to fire anything. The frigate's full larboard broadside, 660 pounds' weight of iron, had cut her in half, and she sank at once. Men struggled to swim amid the debris, and were hidden by drifting smoke, as *Expedient* turned through the wind, tacks and sheets off, yards bracing, mainsail hauling, and beat briefly south of east. Almost as soon as she was on the new heading she tacked again, coming about with the wind on her quarter, and ran in behind Zamoril's xebec.

'Now I have him, by the grace of God!' Rennie whispered fiercely, his glass focused at his eye. 'I have him, the blackguard!'

Then this happened:

A hail of flaming arrows rained on *Expedient*—a hundred, two hundred, three hundred, blazing missiles dropping out of the sun, as if the sun itself had loosed all of its rays upon the earth in fiery form. The points dug into the rails, the hammock cranes, the decking, dug and clung, and within moments *Expedient* was candled from bowsprit to taffrail, and wreathed in drifting black tendrils of smoke.

The ships immediately near to Zamoril's xebec had in them hundreds of janissaries, and these men had loosed the fire arrows. Zamoril himself—having behaved until now as if nothing would deflect him from his purpose of standing in relentlessly to Rabhet and attacking the port—put his helm down, tacking to larboard, and defended himself. To Rennie's dismay—compounding the dismay of finding his ship afire—Zamoril carried not nine-pounder guns in his ship, nor twelves, but eighteen-pounders, and they were not loaded with roundshot, but with grape.

A broadside of grape slashed and whirred through *Expedient*'s rigging, cut jeers, cut halyards, cut shrouds and stays, and cut off the right hand of the helmsman as he lifted it from a spoke. He stared at the bloody stump of his wrist, at the blood pulsing there and splashing down in attenuated drools upon the deck, stared in astonishment, and:

'Stand away from the wheel, John Penning!' bellowed Mr

Loftus, his own neck splinter-grazed and bleeding, and his hat swept away over the rail by the wind of a grape ball. 'Mr Cutforth! Stand to the wheel and steer!'

Penning stepped in a daze from the wheel, his foot snagged in a tangle of rigging, and he fell to the deck and lay in a dead faint. Smoke from the fire arrows now enveloped the ship, and each small individual conflagration strove in flaring, swerving leaps to join the next, and doom *Expedient*, doom her to that most horrible of fates—burning to the waterline at sea.

'*Fire buckets!*' bawled Rennie. '*Fire buckets and hoses, fore and aft!*'

'*Larboard battery, stand clear of your guns, and make a relay line!*' James, running along the larboard gangway. '*Waisters to man the pumps! Jump now!*'

Pump cocks were opened, and hoses brought up. Many of the arrows, though flaming hot, were not tenaciously firm where they had struck, and could easily be kicked clear, or stamped out. Hosemen sprayed water along the gun deck, and over the forecastle and quarterdeck, but not before a powder box by one of the carronades, with its load of squat cartridge, had exploded, dislodging the gun on its transverse carriage, and killing two of the crew outright.

Rennie, knocked to the deck by the force of the blast, stumbled to his feet and lurched forrard to the breast rail. He felt his head, and found that his hat was still firmly wedged upon it. Absurdly, this heartened him. All about him his ship was burning, men lay injured and dying, and those that were not were in mortal peril—and yet he knew in his bones that he would not die this day, and nor would his ship.

Expedient's people, under the close supervision of her officers, boatswain, and midshipmen, succeeded in dousing the flames that had threatened to engulf her. The courses were in the brails, but the maintopsail caught fire and might have doomed the ship, had not quick-thinking Richard Abey—once desperate afraid to go aloft—jumped up the shrouds with three topmen and cut the yard down. The fire was crushed out partly by the collapsing of the canvas, and partly by the action of the hosemen on the deck below, who sent a stream of water into the top at the midshipman's shouted instruction, just enough water to render embers and smoke into steam. All of this activity came at a price. The ship's guncrews were obliged to neglect their guns for long minutes together, and in those minutes Zamoril sought to drive home his advantage. He sent further broadsides—of grape and chain—across *Expedient*'s decks, severely damaging her rigging and canvas, and impairing her ability to manoeuvre. His low, fast brigantines, made faster by sweeps, were able to run alongside the frigate—with the clear intention of sending the massed janissaries in their waists up *Expedient*'s sides and into her, to take her as a prize.

Rennie saw—in a moment of clarity as he helped to handle a heavy hose, and heave it across the quarterdeck with seamen of the afterguard, toward the burning flag lockers—Rennie saw exactly what Zamoril had done, and meant to do.

'He did not mean to destroy us by fire, nor by broadsides of guns. Nay, he meant only to distract us, and impair us, and then make us his captives, the bloody wretch!' To himself. A last heave of the percolating canvas tube, and he turned and bawled:

'*Hands to man the guns! Fire into those damned sweep-ships! Smash them at pistol shot! Cheerly now, lads! We must smash and run!—Mr Tangible!*'

'Sir?' Roman Tangible, bleeding from a deep gash to his forehead, and limping.

'We must run from this, or be took! I will not be took by a damned impudent corsair! We must go about, even as we fire our guns, and run north!'

'Aye, sir.' He touched his forehead with bloodied fingers, and lifted his call.

James, on the larboard gangway, was fully exposed both to Zamoril's great guns and to any men in the xebec with small-arms, but he was not hit. Through the smoke, away to the west, he saw the second squadron of Zamoril's fleet as it closed on the harbour at Rabhet. The guns of the fort were firing, but to no discernible effect. The few ships of *Rais* Ahmed el Ali's fleet, lying defensively within the harbour wall, would be no match for the advancing ships with their guns and hordes of janissaries. Rabhet would fall.

Clapping on to a stay James turned to bawl an instruction to the men below him in the waist. Through the drifting smoke he glimpsed *Rais* Zamoril, standing tall on his quarter-deck in his red hat. At the same moment Zamoril glanced across and saw James, and at a distance of perhaps one cable the two men acknowledged each other in a brief salaam. It might have been an absurd gesture in the heat of battle—but neither man felt that it was absurd, nor in any way ironic, nor trivial. Smoke at once obscured each from the other's gaze as *Expedient* began to come about, and to fire her guns. Half-crippled as she was, with much of her rigging shot away, or lying tangled over the still smouldering hammock cranes, limping and struggling she was able to break clear because of those two broadsides of guns, fired on the fall of the sea.

BOOM-BANG   BANG-BANG-BANG-BANG BOOM   BOOM-BOOM-BANG   BOOM

The two brigantines, to her starboard and larboard, were stove-in, shattered, broken into whirling and tumbling fragments of timber, in fountaining eruptions of spray. Water poured through the smashed sides, drowning men, drowning guns, overwhelming everything of those light vessels, and sending all beneath the boiling sea. *Expedient* was clear, and tacked north, torn and broken, the wind on her quarter and rippling through her tattered colours, high on the halyard.

Expedient was free, but the cause for which she had fought, everything she had attempted to protect and defend—was lost.

Expedient at 37 degrees 16 minutes north, and 8 degrees 27 minutes east, in nearly calm conditions, with a slow swell. The ship entirely alone on the sea, and slowly westing toward Gibraltar, repairing as best she could. Mr Adgett's crew greatly increased to aid him and his mate in bringing *Expedient*'s shattered rails, shattered bitts, fife rails, and binnacle into something approaching a serviceable condition. Men dangling over the sides in roped harness to make good her wounds, where scattering grape had splintered and torn away long spikes from her planking and wales. Mr Tangible supervising a similarly extensive repair of the rigging. Waisters employed to white-lead and paint the boats, and the catheads, forehead rails, and hances. There was not a man or boy in the ship that did not have employment in assisting refurbishment. The sailmaker, again with extended crew, patched and mended and stitched. The lieutenants were everywhere in the ship, encouraging, inspecting, instructing.

Captain Rennie, excepting when duty absolutely called him on deck—to bury the dead, and hear noon declared—kept to his great cabin, and did not like to be disturbed. James Hayter knew, or thought that he knew, the reason for the captain's withdrawal. He did his best to alleviate his captain's suffering, and was rebuked.

'Did I send word to you, Mr Hayter?'

'No, sir. You did not. I thought merely——'

'I did not, and when I will like you to break into my thoughts, and my solitary hours, when I must write my journal, and letters, and all manner of perplexing but essential lists, and so forth—well well, I will send word. Until that moment, pray do not trouble yourself to disturb me again.'

'Very good, sir.' Carefully correct. 'I am sorry.'

'Sorry? What?' Glaring.

'To have disturbed you inadvertent, sir.'

'Oh. Ah. Hm.' Turning away again in his chair, as James retreated and carefully closed the cabin door.

The marines were now officerless. Lieutenant Quill, with

four pistols thrust into his belt, had fallen in the first fire, shot
through the forehead by a musket ball, or perhaps a pistol
ball; no one could be certain where the shot had come from.
The lieutenant and twenty-three other *Expedient*s had lost
their lives in the action, and had been duly buried at noon of
the following day, the ship briefly heaving to for the
melancholy ritual, all of her people assembled with their
heads bared and bowed under the burning sun to witness the
tipping of weighted shrouds into the sea, the slow-swelled,
riding, eternal sea. Rennie had presided, had read the service
in a firm, steady voice, but had been observed by those
nearest to him at the breast rail to be very pale, very waxy, and
his eyes flat in his head.

That was two days ago, and the captain had scarcely
ventured out from his cabin since.

The gunroom, at Lieutenant Hayter's instigation, made
the captain an invitation to dine. If the captain would not
permit intrusion into his own quarters, perhaps he could be
drawn out of himself, as it were, by being obliged to eat his
dinner in a different location.

The invitation was refused.

'Refused?' Lieutenant Makepeace was greatly surprised.
'He has refused to dine in the gunroom mess?'

'He ain't himself, Tom, and must not be blamed for
appearing to slight us. It is unthinking in him, he is
preoccupied, and cast down.'

'I know that he is dismayed by what we suffered, as are we
all, but surely——'

'I said he might not wish to come, did not I? Hey?'

'There is no need to be brusque with me, James—is there?'
And Tom Makepeace smiled.

'Nay, forgive me, Tom.' Returning the smile. 'In course I
did not wish to bite off your head.'

'As I say, sir, it is a little matter of a quite urgent nature.'
Mr Adgett, appearing in the waist, where the two officers
were talking.

'What is, Mr Adgett?' James, turning to him. As always the carpenter was disconcerted by the first lieutenant's working dress that he privately thought made him look ruffianly, and un-officerlike.

'Whether you wishes—or the captain wishes—the main topsail yard proper rescarfed, sir, that was damaged severe when it was cut down to the top, and scorched.'

'If it must be done, then it must, Mr Adgett.'

'Only it will be consuming of time, sir, as I say. The sooner the better. We must dismantle both trees of the yard, examine them thorough, then coak the new scarfing together, before we may fix the new tye. We cannot be doing very long w'out our main topsail, can we, sir?'

'No no, you are quite right. Make it so, Mr Adgett. I will inform the captain.'

'Very good, sir, thank you. As I say, I did not like to disturb him, when he is——'

'When he is what?'

'He—he does not like to be spoke to at present, I reckon . . .'

'Yes yes, very well. Y'may leave it to me, Mr Adgett. I will see that he is informed.'

Mr Adgett retreated, making a note in pencil and pushing it into his hat. James, believing it was his certain duty, straightway went aft and did duly inform Rennie about this important repair. And was again rebuked.

'Did not I tell you that I was not to be interrupted, good God?' Rennie's eyes were red-rimmed, either from lack of sleep—or was it weeping? James wondered.

'I am very sorry, sir, but a repair of this kind——'

'Christ's blood, could not you have wrote it out in your report?' His voice catching, and rasping in his throat.

'I—I will do as you suggest, sir.' Again very formal and correct. He put on his hat, and made to leave. Rennie stopped him.

'A moment, if y'please, Mr Hayter. James. Stay a moment, will you?' Clearing his throat.

'Willingly, sir.' Returning to the table. A wide-bottomed decanter of wine stood untouched next to a pair of glasses.

'Sit down, James. I must say something to you.'

James sat down quietly, and was attentive. For a long moment Rennie said nothing, then:

'I think that I must expect grave consequences for my failure, James. I do not think their Lordships will seek to blame you, in least not direct. However, because you are attached to me, and we have sailed together three commissions, there may be coincidental consequences for you, also. Nay—' raising a hand as James opened his mouth to speak '—hear me out. I cannot conceal from you my very great apprehension and disquiet as to our future employment in His Majesty's service.'

'But good heaven, sir,' James broke in, unable to keep silent, 'how can you or I be blamed for what has happened? We was one ship, against——'

'We was two ships, don't forget.' A sharp glance, and a nod. 'Two ships, at first.'

'Sir, we was lucky to break clear and escape. Had *Curlew* been with us she would have had to do just the same—flee, and save herself.'

'We lost Rashid Bey's fortune, James. Lost it at sea. We have lost Rabhet to the same enemy, and to the King. There will never be a base for the Royal Navy at Rabhet, after this. And Rashid Bey himself will never recover. Likely he will be put to death, or sold into slavery, and Mr Sebastian with him. In addition, I sent *Curlew* away, and lost her. The commission entire has been nothing but calamity upon calamity, since we sank Gibraltar. Altogether a disaster, James.'

'I repeat, sir—I do not think we can, nor should be, blamed. We have done all that we could, against all of the odds. In any case', shaking his head, 'we was never told the whole truth about this commission. From the beginning there was sinister and devious things behind.'

'Eh?'

'Do not you recall them, sir? The man that followed us, in London. That strange, half-crippled, stinking fellow at the hospital at Chelsea. The damned peculiar attack by those well-mounted highwaymen, on our way overnight to Portsmouth.'

'Hm. I had not put them together in quite the way you have done, James. I had not minded them at all in recent days, I confess.'

'Might not they have a bearing on everything that has happened . . . ?'

'Eh?' Again. 'How so?'

'I do not know, exact. It is just a sense . . . an apprehension of something behind. Sir Robert Greer sent us, after all. He is not a man to say the whole truth in anything, not even "Pass the butter". He is as like to say "Pass that dish, that is concealed by its cover".'

'Ha-ha-ha! By God, James you have a wonderful gift for seeing the absurd side of a difficulty. Hhhh—concealed by its cover—ha-ha-ha. Indeed, indeed—that is Greer to a nicety, the fellow.' Sobering, and a sigh. 'But we cannot ignore the peril in which we will likely find ourselves, at home. It may be that this will be our last commission together, in *Expedient*.' Glancing about the great cabin. A further sigh. 'It may be that we will find ourselves on the beach, on half-pay, the rest of our days.'

'I do not believe that, sir.'

'Do y'not, James? I wish I could believe you was right.' A sniff, and he raised his eyebrows.

'Well well, it ain't an hearty toast, but let us drink to that faint hope, shall we?' And he poured two glasses of wine. It seemed to James as they drank that some little tinge of colour had returned to Rennie's cheeks.

Expedient did not call at Gibraltar on the homeward leg. She completed her repairing—enough to enable her to venture

into the Atlantick—and turned north through the Bay of
Biscay for England.

Rennie's one consolation, as *Expedient* beat into a Channel
westerly a fortnight after, and rounded the Isle of Wight to
make her signals, and drop anchor on a bearing at Spithead—
was that his cat Dulcie had been found, hiding in a storeroom
in the orlop, and had now resumed life as the mistress of the
great cabin.

There were no others.

PART EIGHT: HOME

James Hayter did not call at Melton House, his father's family seat at Shaftesbury in Dorset, on his way to Birch Cottage at Winterborne Keep. He travelled straight through on the turnpike coach, and alighted at Blandford, where he hired a horse to ride the last few miles to his house. He was tired but elated as he rode down past the tower of the Norman church, past the inn and the castle ruins, and turned the horse's head down the drive to the paved court. No one came out from the house when he called:

'Catherine! Cathy!'

He dismounted, and called out her name again, but was greeted by silence. He went inside, and found the house empty. Puzzled, he made his way to the stable at the rear, and found that his horse Jaunter was not there; nor was the stable lad that had used to come daily from the village. James returned to the village and inquired at the inn. No one there knew the whereabouts of the boy, nor had anyone known of Catherine's absence from the house. Now thoroughly bemused, James came back to Birch Cottage and waited. He waited an hour, two hours, and another half-glass. At last, in growing disquiet, he decided to go to Melton, after all. He washed his face in the cool water of the stable trough, and led the hack round to the front.

'Cathy is there at Melton. She must certainly be there, and I shall go to her.'

And he mounted the hack, rode away up the drive, and

turned north on the road. He reached Melton House late in the evening. His mother Lady Hayter was overjoyed to see her son safe, gladdened him by her hugs and kisses, but disconcerted him by saying, in answer to his immediate question:

'Nay, Catherine is not here with us, my dear. She is at Winterborne.'

'No, Mother, she is not. I have come direct from Birch Cottage to find her.'

'Eh? Not at home?' Sir Charles Hayter shook his son's hand. 'You are welcome, my dear boy. Is she at East Lane with the girls, I wonder?'

'I had better go there to East Lane Cottage at once,' said James. He was dusty and tired, and thirsty, but he wanted to find his wife, and could not be dissuaded. In darkness he left the hack to be rubbed down by the groom, Padding, and mounted a fresh horse from his father's stable. He rode to Melton Abbas, and East Lane Cottage, the home of his three female cousins. But Catherine was not at Melton Abbas either, and James was by now nearly distraught.

'What can have become of her, Fanny?' To his eldest cousin, the most sensible and practical-minded of the three young women. 'Can she have gone to her cousin at Warminster, d'y'think? Old Henry Armitage?'

'He died months since, James. She cannot have gone to Warminster. Why do not you sleep here tonight, and tomorr——'

'Then where? Where has she gone?' James shook his head in sighing despair, left his cousins and returned to Melton House, and went to bed, exhausted. On the morrow, early, he returned to Winterborne.

And there found Catherine, alive and well and just returned from Weymouth, where she had gone for a change of air—a day or two, at the inn—in their neighbour Mr Brimley's borrowed carriage, taking Tabitha and the infant boy with her, and leaving Jaunter in Mr Brimley's stable.

'How glad I am to see you, my darling, my darling.' James clasped her to him, tears starting in his eyes. 'I thought that you was lost to me.'

'Lost, James. Why should you have thought it? Did not you ask Mr Brimley where I had gone?'

'I did not, I confess. I was upset and distracted. I was quite certain, for the second time in a short while, that I should never see you again.' And he told her of his close escape from death and of his ordeal in the Grand Bagno at Tunis, and at the end tears had started in her eyes also, and she hugged her beloved husband to her, and murmured:

'All is safe, my darling. All is come right, at last.'

＊ ＝◆＝ ＊

'He suffered what?' Rennie looked very narrowly at Mr Soames, the Third Secretary.

'You heard me right, Captain Rennie. An attempt was made to kidnap Sir Robert.' Mr Soames lifted a white lace handkerchief from his black sleeve, and mopped at his forehead. The day was very close in London, and the air in Mr Soames's office at the Admiralty was stale and oppressive. Rennie had felt sticky and uncomfortable in his dress coat all the morning, but what Mr Soames had just told him made Rennie forget that discomfort. He leaned forward.

'The attempt was very violent and persistent, there was five or six men, at night, near Sir Robert's house at Kingshill. But the attempt was foiled.'

'That was good luck——'

'Nay, it was not luck. Sir Robert had requested a detachment of marines to be on hand at his gatehouse, and they heard the commotion—Sir Robert's shouts, and the coachman's—and straightway came down and drove off the assailants.'

'Good heaven. Was Sir Robert injured?'

'He was not, I am happy to say.'

'Was any of the assailants apprehended?'

'They was not.' Lifting the handkerchief again, and brushing away a bead of perspiration on his upper lip. 'One of the marines fired his musket, and bloodstains was later discovered on the cobblestones nearby, but no further trace.'

'I hope that Sir Robert has quite recovered from his ordeal?'

'He has recovered from the manhandling, aside from a bruise or two—but I fear he is very exercised about another matter . . .'

'The upheavals in France, I am in no doubt. It has been a profound shock to us all.'

'Indeed. Indeed, profound. But that is not the matter vexing Sir Robert.' He looked at Rennie.

'Ah. Ah.' Uncomfortably. 'Then, may I know the cause . . . ?'

'I fear his present mood is directly related—to the events at Rabhet, Captain Rennie.' A sad, restrained half-smile, and the odour of his cologne drifted from the lace handkerchief.

'Ah. Hm. I—I have sent my comprehensive account to their Lordships, in a long letter, that——'

'It has been received, Captain Rennie.' The same mournful little smile, and a slight inclination of his head to one side. 'Received—and read.'

'Yes? Has it? Very good, Soames. Hm.—Has—has Sir Robert read it, d'y'know?'

The creaking of the inner door as it swung open, and a deep voice answered:

'He has.'

Sir Robert Greer appeared, and came in. The silver top of his ebony cane, and the silver buckles of his shoes, gleamed faintly in the dull light of the office. His white stockings were in severe contrast to the black of his coat and breeches. Everything of his manner and appearance was designed to evoke his power. His tread, his deep and resonating voice, his dress, the square pallor of his face, his deep dark dispassionate gaze.

'He has indeed, Captain Rennie.'

'I—I had not known you was there, Sir Robert. I had thought you was elsewhere in Whitehall. Good morning.' A brief, disconcerted bow.

The black eyes briefly hidden by bloodless lids, the head briefly inclined. There was nothing of welcome, nothing of pleasant acknowledgement in that gesture. A dry gesture, one almost of distaste. Rennie saw this, and felt it; and felt a beginning dread.

'Will you tell me, Captain Rennie, the present whereabouts of Lieutenant Hayter?'

'He is in Dorset, Sir Robert.'

'Dorset?' Coldly.

'Aye, sir. At his family home there.'

'Why is not he here with you?' Sir Robert advanced to Soames's desk, and without even a glance at the Third Secretary—who had stood up—sat down in his chair and laid his cane on the desk-top. 'Well?'

'He has a wife and child. He has been long away, and wished to see them. I found no impediment to that wish. I had not thought that he would be required to come to London at all, Sir Robert, when it is I——'

'But he is required, Captain Rennie.' Over him. 'He will be required to answer for himself.'

'Answer?' Rennie felt a chill run down his spine.

Sir Robert regarded him, and regarded him, in stony quiet. At last:

'The King of France lives in fear. France has fallen to a very wretched, deleterious and foolish insurrection.'

'I know of it. Who does not?'

Another long, regarding silence, and:

'You have heard, perhaps, of an attempt upon my life?'

'Yes, just now. Mr Soames has told me——'

'Leave us, Soames, will you?' Sir Robert did not look at the Third Secretary, did not even glance in his direction, and Soames gave his sad little grimace, nodded in obedience, and withdrew. The click of the door behind him. Rennie waited, began to speak:

'Sir Robert, I do not understand——'

and was abruptly cut off:

'You will be made to understand, Captain Rennie, very soon.'

'May I sit down? I have had a long journey overnight from Portsmouth, and——'

'You may not. You will remain where you are, on your legs.'

'Sir Robert, I wish to——'

'*Wish*? You *wish*? Your *wish* does not signify, sir. Not here, nor there, nor anywhere in England, that you have betrayed.'

'That I have—betrayed?' Staring at him. The chill now becoming icy fear, that he hoped did not show in his face.

'You did not imagine, did you, Rennie, that I would not understand your scheme? Hey? The "loss at sea, to a superior force" of Rashid Bey's fortune? The abandonment of Rabhet, entire, following upon a mere show of defiance, a token of resistance? *Hey?*'

The voice now menacing, the eyes glimmering with the cold fire of accusation.

'I—I had no such scheme,' Rennie heard himself say, aware that his own voice sounded weak. 'Good God, d'y'think I am a man that would contrive anything so blackguardly as that?' Fear in his throat, and mounting anger, and the sense that he must at all cost keep his emotions reined tight.

'Not you alone, Rennie, in course. No. You are not a man of superior intellect nor education, are you?'

Rennie swallowed hard, swallowed down a furious response, and:

'I do not perfectly understand you, Sir Robert.'

'As you have already said, not above a minute or two ago. You do not understand.' Drily. 'Very well, I will lay all before you, for your . . . understanding. Lieutenant Hayter thought of it, in the first instance. 'Twas his scheme, his notion, his contrivance. However, he knew that he could not manage it alone. He required assistance, and he asked for that assistance. You gave it.'

'Gave it? Gave *what*? Sir Robert, I think you have gone mad.'

The stark hint of a smile in that chalky face. 'You think that, do you. Will I tell you what I think? I think that Lieutenant Hayter has got it. He has got all of it in his care. He has a brother, whose friends are Lambles' the bankers. A very old-established, discreet, careful firm in Lombard Street, that will do the bidding of just such families, whatsoever that bidding may be, without the blinking of an eye, as a matter in course. And no awkward, indiscreet, prying questions. The attempt on my life was arranged, arranged very precise, to remove me from the pursuit. It did not succeed.' The bloodless lids briefly covered the black eyes. 'I have an high regard for my own life, and there are others beside yourself and Mr Hayter that wish to see it ended. I had asked for a marine guard at my house, and so the attempt failed. As all such attempts will fail.'

'You have gone mad. How could all this have been arranged, when we was at sea?' Rennie felt the floorboards move beneath his feet, he saw the stuffy room begin to blur and turn. Felt his heart thudding in his chest under his heavy dress coat, and his bowels turning to water.

'Yes, you quail, sir.' Sir Robert. 'It is time for you to quail. No man that has stole a million of money, and has sent agents of murder against a servant of the King, should do anything else. In these perilous days, when all of Europe may descend into dark, forbidding tumult and wickedness, he *should* quail, the wretch!'

Rennie attempted to speak, lifted a protesting hand, and opened his mouth—but only hot, desperate breath was in his throat.

'Soames!' Sir Robert continued to fix Rennie with his black, unrelenting gaze. 'Soames! Y'may call the guard, if you please! It is time to place Captain Rennie under arrest!'

'Arrest!' At last Rennie had found his voice. 'On what charge?'

'Treason, Captain Rennie. It will be my signal pleasure to see you hang.'